June

Helen May Williams

LEAF BY LEAF

Published by Leaf by Leaf
an imprint of Cinnamon Press
Meirion House
Tanygrisiau
Blaenau Ffestiniog
Gwynedd, LL41 3SU
www.cinnamonpress.com

The right of Helen May Williams to be identified as author of this work has been asserted by her in accordance with the Copyright, Designs and Patent Act, 1988. Copyright © 2020 Helen May Williams. ISBN: 978-1-78864-909-4

Designed and typeset in Palatino by Cinnamon Press.

Cover design by Adam Craig © Adam Craig

Cinnamon Press is represented in the UK by Inpress Ltd and in Wales by the Books Council of Wales.

Acknowledgements

The sources for this novel are multiple and various. My mother told me stories of her early childhood and of her extended family all through my childhood and on into my adult life. Around 1980 I sat her in front of a tape recorder and tried to capture them for posterity. The results were disappointing: the enchantment didn't survive her self-consciousness. She gave me a litany of family history stripped of her storytelling magic. Around 2007, when she had already suffered heart failure and multiple strokes affected her memory, she wrote a handwritten memoir at the behest of my daughter, Georgie, in the sheltered accommodation flat she had moved to after my father's death. Her short-term memory was particularly affected and a few years later she started to write this over again in a Herefordshire care home. In 2011 she came to live with us. Caring for her was tiring and I was suffering from cancer at the time. However, I did my best to converse with her about her memories and ask for clarification on her written memoirs. Remembering how the tape recorder had inhibited her before, I didn't record these sessions and only made hurried notes after they had finished. After her death in 2014 I discovered further brief handwritten memoirs, one, dated from circa 1985, recalled details of life in Stranraer more vividly than the later works.

Other family sources include an undated, typed memoir of my great grandfather, the Reverend Wesley Allan Rodger, written by my mother's cousin Helen Annie Lurring (née Macpherson, 1910-2005) and sent to my mother shortly before her death, conversations with and email communications from Jonathan Hepburn, Andrew Bryson, Hilary Rumley (née Stewart), Marian Anderson (née Lurring) and Ann Baynes (née Rodger). My mother kept up a prolific correspondence during her lifetime to her extended family and to her school and university friend. On the occasion of her ninetieth birthday I invited everyone in her address book to send a brief greeting, starting with the phrase 'Do you remember when...' The response filled a large A4 folder and I am grateful to all those who responded. Other snippets of information came from telephone calls after her death including Jean Glasspool (née Kirkland), who remembered the curly hair on June's first day at Merchant Taylors' School for Girls.

My research in Stranraer was helped immensely by the Reverend Stephen Steele and Margaret Hastings of Stranraer Reformed Presbyterian Church, Dalrymple Street, the Librarians at Stranraer Public Library and Christine and Eric Wilson of the Stranraer and District Local History Trust. All of these people were unstinting in their generous assistance, sharing and seeking information for me. I also used many of the Stranraer and District Local History Trust's excellent publications.

My research in Blundellsands and Crosby was greatly facilitated by the Reverend Michael Marshall of Blundellsands Presbyterian Church and Church Hall shortly before its final closure and by Lynne Barker of The United Reformed Church Mersey Synod. I am also extremely grateful to Anita Barry, Merchant Taylors' School for Girls archivist, and Trevor Hildrey, Merchant Taylors' archivist. Both responded generously to my numerous requests for information and Anita gave up much of a Saturday morning in late June to talk to me and show me highlights from the archive.

Research for this novel has involved reading and consulting innumerable published works of history and social history, but it would not have been possible without the internet. Two sites stand out: Ancestry and Wikipedia. As little as a decade ago, it would have been impossible to double check and incorporate the detail I aspired to without a great deal of additional effort.

I have sought permission to reproduce an extract from *The Holy Bible containing the Old and New Testaments: Translated out of the original tongues: and with the former translations diligently compared and revised, by His Majesty's special command.* London: Cambridge

University Press, n.d. — but with an inscription in the fly leaf that dates it to September 1928. The inscription is in my maternal grandmother's hand is as follows: 'to June / from Mummie / Sept 1928.'

I thank all those mentioned above and anyone else I have unwittingly neglected to name.

Finally, my thanks go to my husband, Ian Williams, who has consistently supported me through the writing process. I couldn't have done it without him.

June

A hand that can be clasp'd no more—
Tennyson *In Memoriam*

For my grandchildren

God, let her live, please let her live.

Uncle Alf poured himself another whisky. It was three in the morning. This would warm him briefly. The baby was restless and gurning the whole time.

Poor wee mite, if I'm feeling it she must be starved with cold. Maybe a wee dram would do no harm. Thank the Lord she was born big and bonny; she'd never stand a chance now otherwise.

My Great Uncle Alf.

He leaned into the cot to feel her forehead, fearing that ghastly chill. But, after all those years in general practice he didn't need a thermometer to tell him the fever had flared again. He lifted her gently and loosened the blankets he'd wrapped round her earlier when her temperature had plummeted. His six-months-old niece looked like a tiny ghost; her face pallid, the skin near translucent and a sheen of perspiration glistening eerily in the candle light.

She'll be lucky if she outlives her father; I can see us burying them in the one grave at this rate. Poor May, I doubt she'll be able to cope with that.

He'd had his skirmishes with pneumonia before, especially down in Liverpool's Chinatown. But this was one patient he didn't intend to lose, even though the odds were stacked against him. This was his wife, Minnie's kid sister's only child; soon this tiny apparition would be all she had. He couldn't remember how many nights he'd sat up with her.

God, let her live, please let her live. I'm doing the best I can for her. You can have her father, but please let her pull through.

He thought about promising to give up the hard stuff, but wasn't sure he could keep such a promise. Instead, he reached for her tiny silver christening spoon and poured a wee dose of whisky. He poured himself another wee dram while the bottle was open, administering the whisky to the sweating infant. What more could he do? Wrap the blankets tighter, loosen the blankets, pace the room, trying to avoid that squeaky floorboard, gently holding and soothing her till dawn struck through the net curtains.

She didn't remember this. She couldn't have, she'd been too young. Mummie and Auntie Dolly must have told her later, sitting round the 19 London Road range, going over and over those disastrous weeks, telling the story, knowing that however they told it the outcome could never be changed. *Alex died. Baby June survived and now they all kept alive somehow on Grandma Rodger's 10 shillings a week pension, and the money from Fred Andrews' board and lodging. And Auntie Dolly's wages from the Town Hall. Telling the story one more time...*

What June thought she remembered, was the cold light of the candles and the rough warmth of Uncle Alf's knitted waistcoat as he held her pressed against his heart, pacing the back-bedroom floor, avoiding the creaking floorboard.

She remembered seeing Auntie Dolly dash off to attend advanced shorthand evening classes. Later, she heard people whisper that the Sheriff's Clerk was a friend of the family: *that's how Dolly had got the position.* But Auntie Dolly told the story differently, as she lifted her hands to the keyboard: 'I felt that, as a gifted piano player, I would have no problems tapping a typewriter, and I was right!'

They told her over and over how Fred Andrews came to be their boarder. An old friend of her favourite Uncle, Eddie, was looking for digs. A big man, a former rugby player, he had started going blind at eighteen. He had a private income and had been living with his sister Maggie and her banker husband, but they moved to Lundin Links in Fife and Fred didn't want to leave his friends and the familiar town.

'So Fred was hit by a calamity! But it turned out okay in the end, because he came to live with us.'

June had been next door, out of Mummie's and Auntie Dolly's hair. They'd be glad when she was old enough to go to school. She'd come back carrying next door's moggie's kitten. They turned their backs on her and carried on dusting and feather-dusting the parlour. June could hear her Mummie shoving the bottom frame up, shaking the doilies and antimacassars out the sash-window, slamming the bottom frame down again. The shove... shake... slam... receded till it could have been at the other end of Stranraer.

She was playing with the kitten, teasing it with a leaf of paper tied to a length of string. It was a butterfly, a mouse, a winged bird, it was the one that got away each time. The kitten was entranced, its eyes round as saucers as it tried to catch its paper prey. Its paws batted, faster than Auntie Dolly playing keyboards... tum-tum-tum, tum-ti-tum tee. And still June whisked the paper away just in time. It was a battle she was winning. Each time the kitten started to look away, she twitched the mauled piece of paper again and the kitten was drawn back.

The light shone through the glass pane above the front door, catching motes of dust in the hallway stirred up by their game. The floorboards creaked above her head. She froze. Fred descended the staircase. His heavy rugby-player feet in sturdy black boots, taking each step unerringly. She looked up from where she knelt, crouched over the kitten. Her voice deserted her; her limbs had turned to stone. Her forehead shone with sweat and she shivered.

'Will you look at that child! Mind out Fred's way, June! How's he supposed to know you're sat at the foot of the stairs playing. Take that wee moggie back where it belongs. Then come help lay the table!' June shuffled back, grabbed the poor kitten by the neck, got to her feet and sobbed her way silently to next door's.

Sally Adams looked up with a welcoming glance as June hesitated in the back doorway. 'So there you are then. We missed you for a while. Have you been playing with Chummy?'

'Is his name Chummy?'

'It is now!' She said with a smile as she gently lifted the exhausted kitten out of June's determined grasp and laid it back in the cardboard box in the corner of the kitchen beside the mummy cat.

'And,' gesturing towards the mummy cat laid out in a state of resignation, June enquired, 'Is her name Maggie?'

'Maggie it is, for sure.'

June loved Sally; because she was such a small woman June never felt threatened by her, she felt more like a playmate than a middle-aged adult.

'I'm just fixing potato soup for mother's lunch,' Sally said. 'Here, have a slice to nibble on. You must be hungry.' June took the slice of raw potato eagerly; her favourite treat, hers and Sally's secret. 'Why don't we go and say hello to Mother, before you go?' June took the proffered hand and followed Sally through the hallway into the dim sitting room. As always Mrs Adams was in her armchair. June couldn't remember ever finding the sitting room curtains fully open, nor seeing the oil-lamps burning. Her eyes adjusted to the different hues of black. The corners of the room were full of shadows. She tried to ignore them and looking straight ahead went to Mrs Adams to bid her 'Good Day.'

'Here's June again, Mother,' Sally said brightly.

Mrs Adams observed her through milky blue eyes and smiled slightly. Her black bombazine dress rustled and the pattern of its shadows shifted as she stretched her thick, gnarled hand to June. June shook it weakly and stood back fidgeting slightly.

Mrs Adams was so fat! She wanted to ask Mrs Adams what she thought about all day long as she sat in that darkened room, but didn't dare. She tried to keep her eyes on Mrs Adam's dress, tracing the pattern of lacework round her collar, wondering how she managed to do up those tiny hooks and eyes with her distorted old lady's hands, watching the vague play of shades of black each time she drew breath. But she couldn't help herself; she had to follow Mrs Adams' gaze and turn her head to gawk at Mr McKinstrey. It didn't matter how many times she looked at his portrait, each time she was terrified. He was all whiskers and beard. From under his dense eyebrows, sombre eyes glowered her around the room. She shifted awkwardly from foot to foot, feeling as if her bladder would burst. He was watching her, waiting to reprimand her. She made an effort not to look at his eyes and settled on his grim-bearded mouth instead. Any moment now his lips would part and that dismal mouth would utter dour sayings...

'Look, Mother! She's staring at Mr McK again,' offered Sally cheerily, breaking the clutch of fright. 'Hmm!' replied the old lady. 'Is my soup ready yet?'

'In just two ticks of a lamb's tail,' Sally replied and bustled June out of the room back to the relative light and air of the kitchen.

Through the back door, they could hear Auntie Dolly calling for June from their kitchen door. 'June! June! Come along now! Your soup's getting cold.'

'Mummie, am I a Hepburn or a Rodger?'
   'Both, my love.'
   'Which bit of me's a Hepburn?'
   'Your long face, your dark eyes and your dark, dark hair... and that serious, brooding look, as if you were just stepping back from another world.'
   'So which bit of me's a Rodger, then?'
   'All the rest of you from your squiggly wiggly toes to your funny yummy tummy button to your squidgy widgy nose!' And she tickled her far too precious only child, till muss-haired and nighties awry they collapsed, breathless and giggling on June's narrow bed.
'Mummie.'
   Dreamily: 'Yes, my pet?'
   'Where did Daddy go?'
   'He's in Heaven, pet.'
   'Mummie, why isn't he buried with Grandpa Wesley?'
   'Because Grandpa Rodger is buried here in Stranraer, dear.'
   'But why isn't Daddy here? Didn't he live here?'
   'Yes, dear. He lived here in this house. We were married in this house, in the parlour.'
   'Who by, Mummie?'
   'By Uncle Ernie.'
   'When were you married, Mummie?'
   'On December 21ˢᵗ 1920, six and a half years ago.'
   'And when was I born?'
   'Fifteen months after we were married. Remember you had your birthday at the start of March?'
   'And why am I called June when I was christened Valerie?'
   'You were christened Valerie June. I wanted you to be called Valerie, but your Daddy wanted you to be called June.'
   'Why, Mummie?'
   'Because he said he'd already got one month, May, and would have another one, June.'

And she gently tickled June's tummy button.

'Didn't he want me to be called Valerie?'

'Oh, yes, he agreed, but he said you should have two names because you came from both of us.'

'Why did you want me to be called Valerie, Mummie?'

'Because I named you after Lady Valerie in Galloway. She's always so beautifully dressed and I wanted you to be as fortunate as her.'

'Then why aren't I called Valerie now?'

'I don't know, pet. Somehow, your Daddy was right; you were June all along. He used to tease me and say if I'd known Latin, I would never have chosen that name for you. But he'd never say why.'

June knew there was no point asking Mummie what Latin was; she would have to save that up for when she started school.

'When I go to heaven, will I be Daddy's lamb?'

'Whatever gave you that idea? Because...' June sang back to Mummie the old lullaby Rodger women had sung to their children for longer than anyone could remember:

Bo-bye, Baby
Bo-bye, Lamb.
Mummy's pet
a-a-nd Daddy's lamb!

'Oh, pet, you can be Daddy's lamb all you want.' Mummie's voice was strange and strangled. She took a deep breath, then added, 'But first of all, you're going to be your own woman and get the education I never had.'

Auntie Dolly appeared in the doorway. June knew bedtime was over. She arranged herself carefully on her back and gave Mummie one last hug goodnight.

She watches through the open doorway: Mummie and Auntie Dolly side by side in front of the dressing-table mirror, unpinning their hair and letting it down. Auntie Dolly's jet-black and falling straight to her waist; Mummie's blonde in comparison, with gentle waves to below her shoulder blades. Then Mummie's shoulders shudder slightly. She sobs, gulps for air, sucks breaths between the next sob and the next.

'Oh, Dolly! Why me? I sometimes think I can't bear it

any longer.'

'There, there; you'll get over it. It'll get better, you'll see.'

Swivelling to face her little sister, 'How do you know? You've never been married. You can have no idea how I miss him, what it's like without him.'

'I miss the Athenaeum. I lost that you know. You can't know what that feels like sometimes. To have got through that audition, even though I played the piece by ear, when they wanted me to sight-read it. To feel I could be a proper musician, even a soloist one day. To have lost all that, because Daddy died and Mummie can't manage without us.'

Their eyes narrow, their nostrils flare, their shoulders rise. Then subside again. They hug. They whisper into one another's ear, murmur things about... June cannot quite hear. Something about Grandma Rodger and Grandpa... They caress one another's backs and arms and brush one another's hair till each strand catches the candlelight from the candelabras beside the mirror. Then they catch a glimpse of June, silent in the doorway, standing on one leg, the other twined around her ankle.

'Come here, June! Let's have a look at your hair!' Auntie Dolly reaches over and undoes her bow and starts to brush out the kinks and knots from the day's mussing. 'We're going to have to put papers in her hair when she's older,' muses Mummie. 'She's not got my curls, that's for sure.'

She didn't remember this, she couldn't have, she'd been too young.

Grandma Rodger, Mummie and Auntie Dolly sat huddled over the kitchen range, telling it over and over. How the Landlord had come, how he'd said he wanted to live in this house himself. Mummie cried into her hankie.

'There's no use blethering,' Grandma Rodger kept saying, holding her back even straighter than usual and her lips as tight as could be.

'We've no redress,' Auntie Dolly confirmed. 'I asked Douglas.'

'Who's Douglas?'

'He's the new lawyer, just down from Glasgow. No experience, but he knows his law books all right, better than most of them. I trust his advice. There's nothing we can do.'

Mummie wrung the damp hankie in her hands till it was a squidgy tight ball of crushed cotton and wept some more.

June slipped next door.

'Sally, what's *a dire calamity*?'

'Something bad, pet,' not looking up from peeling potatoes. 'Why do you ask?'

'Well one's hit my Mummie. How did it hit her? Does it have arms?'

'Calamities come in all shapes and sizes, pet. Some have arms, hands, feet and treacherous hearts. Some have bright eyes and good looks. There's no telling where or when a calamity will strike, until it's knocked you for six.'

'Is Mr McKinstrey a calamity, Sally?'

'Bless your heart, no, child! Whatever gave you that idea? Mr McKinstrey was the best thing that ever happened to mother and me. But it wasn't to be. Calamity struck him. No, *he* wasn't the calamity.'

She paused and absentmindedly passed June a slice of raw potato. June equally absentmindedly took it and put it in her mouth, mulling over this baffling new dimension to her world as she stared out the kitchen window at the drizzle falling on the little backyard.

June lay on her narrow bed, anxiously watching the flame from the nightlight flickering in the draught from the open top-window. She tossed and turned; one moment she felt too hot and threw the bedclothes from her, the next she felt shivery and curling into a tight ball, pulled the blankets up to her chin. She knew it was way past the usual time she fell asleep, but she didn't dare get up and go into Mummie's room and disturb her.

She heard Fred calling, summoning help. *Such a big strong chap, such a shame.* She listened, her ears just above the rasping bedclothes, as first Auntie Dolly then Mummie shuffled on dressing gowns and rushed to assist. She heard him retching and the sounds of the two sisters bustling downstairs for clean cloths, bowls of vinegar and tepid water, smelling salts, a glass of soda water. Clucking and cooing over his distress for an hour or more. Then Auntie

Dolly at the kitchen door, sloughing off her slippers and shoving her feet into the clogs that sat on the doormat, before tapping woodenly across to the privy.

June lay on her back and imagined the contents of the bucket clunking in Auntie's hand. She squeezed her eyes and ears and nose shut and tried hard not to... It was no good. Fear overwhelmed her: fear of the dark as the nightlight burnt lower, fear of the nausea rising in her stomach, fear of the landlord, who uncannily resembled Mr McKinstrey.

She let out a yelp. Then another and another, gulping snot and salt tears and the sick feeling in the back of her throat, retching uncontrollably into the dark.

And Mummie was here, smelling of lavender water and vinegar, holding the basin in one hand and June's sweaty forehead with the other. Clucking and cooing reassurance. And here was Auntie Dolly to clean the mess and change her sheets and bring soothing soda water, which she must slip very, very slowly.

'That's it, June! It's all over now.'

'Is Fred ill, Mummie?'

'No dear, Fred's just upset, that's all.'

Auntie Dolly bought her another nightlight and lit its wick from the dying flame of the old one. She told Mummie to go and get her beauty sleep, because she'd need it in the morning. June was puzzled. Auntie Dolly was the youngest of Grandma Rodger's nine children. Yet it was always Auntie Dolly, not Mummie, who knew what needed doing. And it was Auntie Dolly who had to get up in the morning and be at the Town Hall bright and early. She had her own keys to her office and she said those young lawyers from Glasgow were wet behind the ears, but she would sort them out. June wondered if she kept a cloth and a bottle of vinegar behind her desk for the purpose.

For now, Auntie Dolly carefully rearranged June's bedding and, as she did every night, placed June's head straight on her pillow, then placed her two arms on top of the folded, clean sheet, lifting first her left forearm to rest lightly on her right shoulder, then her right forearm to rest on her left shoulder.

'There now. Baby Jesus will keep you safe till morning

and the cross made by your arms will keep you from all harm. You lie here quietly and God will watch over you.'

Did God have a knitted waistcoat? June wondered, as she drifted into sleep.

Finally the house was still. In its darkened bedrooms three generations of Rodger women lay still on their stretched-straight backs, arms crossed on top of their neatly folded sheets, to ward off the Devil and the Devil's thoughts. While Fred Andrews dreamed fitfully of the longest try he'd ever run, ramming the oval ball down just beyond the touchline over and over again till dawn.

Grandma Rodger, Mummie and Auntie Dolly sat huddled over the kitchen range.

'We managed before; we'll manage again,' Grandma Rodger said.

'How did we manage before, Grandma?'

The three women turned their gaze from the range to look at June, their mouths open, not knowing what to say to her. Then all three turned back abruptly. But they relented. *Telling the story one more time...*

How, after Grandpa died and Grandma had to leave the Manse, they kept alive on Grandma Rodger's 10 shillings a week pension and the money from Fred Andrews for board and lodging. *And* Auntie Dolly's sheriff's clerk's wages from the Town Hall.

'We couldn't have managed without Dolly coming home,' Grandma conceded.

Why Auntie Dolly? What could she do Mummie couldn't?

And as if they'd heard her unspoken question, 'Your Auntie Dolly's a strong woman, June. She reckoned, if she could play the piano keys like she did, she could learn to hit the typewriter keys.'

'And I did!' Auntie Dolly exclaimed triumphantly. 'It didn't really take me that long; I can do anything with practice.'

'But she drove us half-crazy, practising every night for a month, without a break.'

'Except Sundays, of course,' Grandma added hastily, in case June got the wrong idea.

'You know, I reckon I could take on some of the cases

those young Glaswegian lawyers do. I do most of the hard grind for them as it is. I could sort out a simple probate as well as any of them. There's nothing to it really.'

'How would that help us, Auntie Dolly?'

'It would be a bit more pin money in my garter, chick! Wouldn't it now!'

How would that find them somewhere to live?

This time, no one answered her unspoken question, although all the women in the room had heard it.

Through the open doorway, Mummie and Auntie Dolly sit side by side in front of the dressing table mirror. Mummie gasps, sobs, gulps for air.

'Oh, Dolly! Why me? I nursed Father when he was dying. I'll nurse Fred till he dies.' Another violent gust of sobs. 'But she wouldn't let me near Alex to nurse him when he was dying, when he died. The one dying man I should have been beside. He was my husband. I should have lain in his bed by his side.'

'There, there, May. There, there. Gertie's a trained nurse. I'm sure she meant it for the best.'

'I hate that sister-in-law of mine. I hate her, Dolly.' Mummie's hand flies to her mouth to muffle the words she can't stop herself from saying, 'I'll never forgive her, never!'

'You'll get over it. It'll get better, you'll see.' Auntie Dolly caresses Mummie's shoulders, back and arms.

'Shush now, May! Shush! We don't want the whole house to hear.' She brushes her sister's hair till each fair strand gleams and catches the candlelight from the candelabras beside the mirror.

She didn't remember this, she couldn't have; she'd been too young.

'Please Sally, can I come and play with Maggie's Chummy. Mummie and Auntie Dolly are busy and Grandma Rodger told me off for getting under her feet. They've got to clean the parlour before the lawyer comes.'

'Is your grandma cleaning too? It must be serious!'

'It's very serious. It's momentous! It's the most important day in Mummie's life... after having me and getting married and meeting my Daddy on Liverpool station and him dying of T.B. and...' She took a big breath. *Had she forgotten anything?* 'Mummie's beating the carpets on the line and Auntie Dolly's doing the windows with vinegar and newspaper and Grandma's getting on with the dusting and they've got to polish the teaspoons and the little knives for afternoon tea.'

'You come and play with Maggie's moggies then, June; maybe stay for a bowl of soup with me. I'm sure they won't miss you.'

She knew that the serious business was somehow good luck. And she knew that Fred wasn't moving away after all. They would all live together happily ever after. She wasn't sure what this had to do with spring cleaning or getting under Grandma's feet. It was Fred's feet she was scared of, but apparently that was all wrong. Fred was their saviour. *Did Gentle Jesus wear sturdy black boots?*

Together she and Sally tied leaves of paper to pieces of string and soon they were down on their hands and knees teasing the wee moggies to distraction on the flagstone floor.

Later that afternoon, when she crept back into number 19, she could hear the lawyer's voice through the half-open parlour door.

'That's the recitals accounted for,' he was saying. 'And now to the serious business in hand. If you'll make your signature here, Mr Andrews?' She peeked as the lawyer guided Fred's hand on the legal document. '...and number 9 King Street will be yours.'

A pause, while she heard the rasp of the stylus on the thick legal parchment and the three women holding their breath. 'And Mrs Hepburn, if you will sign the document here, as discussed, to say that in return you will agree to care for Mr Andrews till his dying day.' And her mother politely murmuring beneath her breath as she scratched her signature on this solemn legal contract.

June didn't remember this. She'd been too young to remember the momentous event.

But she remembered arriving at 9 King Street, at the other end of the town of Stranraer and indeed much of the life they led there for the next ten years.

Did she spend the removal day in Sally Adam's kitchen, playing with the moggies to keep out of everyone's hair? Did she shake hands weakly with old Mrs Adams one last time and gaze goodbye at Mr McKinstrey's grim-mouthed beard and glowering eyes? Did Sally Adams let her gnaw on a raw slice of potato while she made her fried potato cakes for lunch? Did Sally skim the cream off the milk to save for the apple tart at teatime, then pour June a big glass of fresh milk to drink with her potato cakes? And did they let Chummy taste a wee drop of the cream on a small saucer?

And when it was getting dark, as if King Street were a million miles from London Road, did Sally say, bundling the kitten and the leaf of paper on a string into June's outstretched arms: 'Here, June; you take Maggie's Chummy with you to King Street, to remember us by. He's always happy when he sees you!'

And when they came to collect her to ride with the last load of furniture, did she scream and cry and cling onto that kitten, until Mummie relented and said, 'Well, if you really don't mind, Miss Adams, thank-you. I'm sure he'll make a good mouser, by and by.'

'Straight as a ramrod, Ma Rodger. Rules them like a rod of iron, too!'

'Not her last two, she doesn't!'

'Emily May was always flighty.'

'Stayed home and nursed her father in his extremity, mind.'

'I'll grant you that; but flighty, all the same.'

'Pretty, if you like them on the plump side.'

'Seems our dentist does.'

'Never!'

'Oh, yes. I heard she was round there after closing time again yesterday evening.'

'Pity his poor wife.'

'Can you blame him though; she may be rich, that woman, but she has a face like the backside of a cow.'

'You can't call Dolly flighty now.'

'I never did.'

'That girl rules the sheriff's clerk's office!'

'Sorts out those fresh-faced young lawyers come

straight down from Glasgow.'

'Takes them down a peg or two!'

'And they all adore her. Can't help themselves, poor boys!'

'They don't stand a chance; she's only got eyes for Barclay Charmers.'

'Running rings round him with those big black eyes of hers.'

'Way I heard it, he's been running rings around her.'

'It's a crying shame those two girls are so poor now, isn't it?'

'You wouldn't think it to look at them; always dressed neat and pretty, always with their hair just so.'

'And Ma Rodger's straight as a ramrod; you never see her falter.'

'Will of iron, that woman, will of iron.'

When I think of 9 King Street, I think of Lizzie Craig. She had just left school when we moved and seemed to arrive with the house.

They could afford a maid now they weren't paying that landlord his rent. Fred had bought the house, with the money from his rugby-playing days. Telling the story one more time, now watching the logs dry beside the King Street kitchen grate while Mummie stirred potato soup on the Valor stove, which stood in its badly-lit corner... *How Daddy died, baby June survived and they all kept alive and well on Grandma Rodger's 10 shillings a week pension and the money from Fred Andrews for his board and not forgetting Auntie Dolly's sheriff's clerk's wages from the Town Hall, with a bit beside to pay for Lizzie.*

Telling the story one more time...

'But we'll need to think about taking in boarders, now we've got one attic room to spare,' Grandma decided.

And so her mother spent her days looking after the boarders as well as Fred Andrews, and the drawing room was *their* sitting room, not *hers*.

Little Lizzie Craig arrived straight from school, aged thirteen, and no growth on her. She would arrive every morning about 8 a.m. having collected *The Bulletin* from the newsagent's in George Street and rolls from Gillespie's the baker's across the road.

She always brought a brown paper parcel tied up by string. She would very carefully pick out the knot and take out her pinafore. Before she went home at the end of the day she would reverse the procedure.

Lizzie was stood on an upturned box to reach the stone kitchen sink. I was standing beside her while she peeled potatoes. I was very fond of raw potato and from time to time Lizzie would hand me a piece.

The large white sink was situated under the window, which looked out onto the garden. Lizzie, only fourteen and no growth on her, was washing the dishes. She was stood on her box to get to the taps, singing 'Always' under her breath and smiling to herself. She handed June a slice of raw potato, saying, 'Funny your Mummy's name is "May" when there's May's the Grocers at the foot of the road.'

'But Mummie's "May" is a Christian name; Grandma told me so.'

'Yes, but it's a coincidence all the same,' she said, handing June another sliver of potato. 'His delivery boy's named Jimmy, you know.'

'There aren't any Jimmys in Mummie's family…'

'No, maybe not.'

'But there's Great Aunt Jemima. She's my Daddy's aunt.'

'Funny, all the same,' Lizzie continued as she carefully stepped down, carrying the peelings in a piece of yesterday's *Bulletin*, adding, 'He offered me a lift in his delivery van yesterday.'

'Great Aunt Jemima's very fond of me.'

Under her breath Lizzie tries out the phrase, 'very fond of me.'

Lizzie, only fourteen and no growth on her, all the kitchen chores done for now, in the calm of the afternoon, sat at the kitchen table and taught June to play Ludo. 'It's all about getting home before the other players. A lot of it's luck of course, unless you know how to throw the dice.'

That morning June woke early. Grandma was up and as

usual dressed impeccably, even before breakfast. Black bombazine all smoothed and not a grey hair out of place. Having donned her pinny, she was trimming the oil-lamps' wicks at the kitchen table and refilling their reservoirs, lips tight shut in concentration. June got her white pinny off the peg and pulled it over her head, struggling to tie its bow at the back of her waist. She picked up the big milk jug from beside the stone sink and looked to Grandma for permission to fetch the milk; the milk van was due any moment and she thought she heard its horse's hooves clopping at the top of the street.

Grandma hadn't finished and Lizzie wasn't here yet. 'I don't know what's got into that girl, mooning around May's delivery boy again, I'll warrant.'

She nodded to June, who trotted out the front door and into the waking street. The milkman filled her jug to the brim from his big urn. 'And, there's an extra drop of cream for your Chummy, now.'

Where was the extra drop in all that still-warm-from-the-cows' milk? She couldn't see it. Which drop was Chummy's?

June peered into the jug as she stepped back into the front hallway. Not looking where she put her feet, she tripped on the step and the jug of milk spilt down her clean white pinny.

She bit her lip then howled and howled. Her hanky was a frazzled mess of soggy cotton that rumpled and creased as she wrung it in her hands. At breakfast she sobbed and gulped over her thick porridge. By lunchtime she had the hiccups and no amount of holding her breath or drinking water from the other side of the glass would stop them. She swallowed her soup dutifully; it set off her hiccups all the more. Mummie kept saying, 'No use crying over spilt milk!' But that set her off again, as Grandma sniffed her disapproval.

'Well,' said Auntie Dolly, 'given that man owes his livelihood to Grandpa, I don't suppose he minded that much refilling your jug this once.'

Later that afternoon, Lizzie, all the kitchen chores done, said, 'I know, I'll show you how to play Snakes and Ladders.'

It was better than Ludo. It was a complete philosophy

of life in a board game. Whether you climbed the ladder or slithered back down the slimy snakes all depended on the throw of the dice.

Grandma Rodger did not agree; your life was God's will and your task was to know it and bend to it. *Thy will be done...*

Did Grandma's God have sturdy black boots and a woollen waistcoat? Was he always gazing at her wherever she might be, from above his whiskers like Mr McKinstrey, waiting to see if she bent to her destiny? And how did Baby Jesus meek and mild fit in? Why did he suffer the children? Were children a disease?

Grandma and Auntie Dolly both put her to bed that evening. Mummie was out on an errand to the Dentist's.

'Grandma, why does the milkman owe Grandpa his livelihood?'

'He was very warm-hearted, your Grandpa, and generous to the point of extravagance. Whenever he went out the front door, I made sure he didn't have more than sixpence in change in his pockets; whatever money he was carrying when he went out, he would have given it away to some needy parishioner by the time he came back home again, even if he only walked to Stair Park, across the road and back. He would have given the coat off his back if he could.

'You remember, Dolly? When he went away, he would arrive home with presents for every one of you. And when he left, I always made sure that he had a return ticket. Because sure as anything, there'd be no money in his pockets when he came home, just those presents.'

'But how does that affect the milkman, Grandma?'

'I'm getting to that... Grandpa was paid quarterly by the Church. Four times a year, he would walk down to the Church on the first day of the month and the Treasurer would hand over his stipend. On those days, I gave him strict instructions to come straight back home and talk to no one on the way. But...'

June leaned on her elbow and sat back up. This was a very grown-up story.

'On one occasion I had a rude shock. He came back home from his meeting with Mr Hastings, the Precentor, and he had to confess that, having just received his quarter's salary, he had given it *all* to the milkman.'

Propped against her pillow, gazing into Grandma's wrinkled face, June could see a faraway look of sadness and admiration. She wished she had known Grandpa Rodger.

Grandma continued, 'He said, otherwise the milkman would have had to sell his horse and cart and stock to pay some debts. That's why the milkman won't begrudge you that jug of spilt milk. He's never been able to repay the money Grandpa gave him and Grandpa wouldn't have expected him to. That was money freely given to someone who was in more desperate need than we were. But it was a difficult three months. I had to run up some hefty bills with Jack the butcher and with the grocer, the green-grocer, and Gillespie's too!'

'But they didn't mind, Mother; they all knew how generous he was. What would the whole of Stranraer have done without their morning milk deliveries? The whole town owed him a debt of gratitude for that.'

'True, Dolly, but that wasn't the way he saw it. He just responded to a man in need without thinking of the consequences.'

This last declaration carried a lot of weight.

'But from that day to this, the milkman has never asked me for as much as a penny for the milk he delivers to the Rodger family. He won't begrudge a little girl who tripped over the front doorstep one jug more.'

The following morning, Grandma looked up as she finished trimming the oil-lamps and said, 'Come with me, June, while I put this one back in the drawing room.' She carried the lamp with its green stained-glass base carefully up the stairs and placed it back in position to be lit again that evening. 'This is what I want to show you, June.'

And she lifted out of her cabinet the handsome ebony inkstand, with its various pen trays and compartments and its several ebony elephants. The elephants were exquisitely carved, with their tiny feet and diminutive eyes, their wrinkled skin and miniature tusks and trunks. June tried to imagine what it must have been like to take a piece of raw ivory and carefully carve it into these intricate, interlocking shapes. She would have been afraid to mess up the final elephant, having spent days carving the rest. But here, they all were perfect little replicas, without any sign of a hand slip.

'The Christmas after Grandpa gave him that money, the milkman gave us this present. He said it was just something he'd seen that he thought the whole family might be able to use and appreciate. But we all knew it was his way of saying thank-you to Grandpa. And that was when I knew that we'd never see that sum of money again.'

June wondered what it must have felt like to share this present with so many brothers and sisters. She sighed as she stroked the elephants' backs and tickled their tusks. She would never know what it was like to have a brother or sister.

'Grandma, how did you and Grandpa Wesley meet? Tell me again!'

'I was an Ormrod, child. I was christened, Emily Annie Ormrod. That's why your Mummie's christened, Emily May, after me.'

'Is that why she stayed at home to nurse him when Grandpa was dying, because she was called Emily?'

'In a manner of speaking, child, in a manner of speaking.'

'And what did your Daddy do, Grandma?'

'He was an ironmonger: Ormrod and sons, Ironmongers, Lytham St Anne's.'

'Where's that, Grandma?'

'In Lancashire. Far away south from here in England.'

'A fair distance from here?'

'Yes, June; a far distance from here—and from now.'

'Tell me again, how did you meet?'

Grandma's back unstiffened and her eyes glistened. 'I was skating, June. I was a wonderful skater, even though I say so myself. I could whizz round the ice on that rink. I loved to bend my body at the knees and set off in faster and faster circles, till my hair nearly flew away from me. The ice was uneven, but I never slipped or fell. I would feel breathless by the end, but so exhilarated. There's nothing like it, June, nothing like it.'

'Then what happened, Grandma?'

'He saw me there. One afternoon he saw me there. That's enough now. Time to say your prayers and go to sleep.'

'Yes, Grandma.'

'Grandma?'

'Yes, June.'

'Will you take me there, one day?'

'Yes, June. I'll take you there this summer, before you start at the Academy.'

As she drifted off to sleep, the bogeymen stayed away while Grandma Emily Annie Ormrod and Grandpa, the Reverend Wesley Allan Rodger, whizzed round and round the rink till their hair nearly flew away and then... they flew away.

When she woke she pattered bare foot downstairs. The kitchen had a stone floor. It felt cold beneath her feet. The iron grate with ovens on either side, used for drying wood to light the fires, wasn't lit yet. Soon she would start school but for a little longer June could watch Grandma trim and clean the oil-lamps each morning.

Grandma Rodger glanced up from filling the red glass based lamp that went in the dining room and reminded her, as she did every Wednesday, 'Mind you don't get yourself dirty this morning. You must look neat for visiting this afternoon!'

June went through the back door into the garden. It was surrounded by high walls: over one of them was the stone wall of the beautiful Presbyterian church next door. St Margaret's; Uncle Ernie's first church before she'd been born. Even though it was exquisite she found it slightly menacing. It wasn't their church; they still went to the Dalrymple Street *Reformed* Presbyterian Church. Each Sunday afternoon, June would sit in the Church Hall, gathered around the huge stove that sat in the middle of the room, staring at its chimney stretching up to the ceiling and disappearing through the roof, or looking through the pane-glass doors to the pews of worshippers. While Jessie Cochrane told them stories about Jesus, she would listen for the sermon that resonated from the wooden pulpit to end and for the sound of the tuning fork preluding the final metrical psalm.

June stepped over the cobblestones by the back door and mounted the three steps up onto the grass still wet with dew. The early morning air was laden with the scent of sweet peas that covered the trellis at the end of the patch of grass. *The fairies loved their perfume; it caressed and soothed them.* June began to reach up to pluck the just-open blooms to take inside. They would look pretty in a glass jar and Fred would smell them and say, 'Has someone been picking flowers, again, today?'

As usual that Wednesday, straight after lunch, Grandma gathered up her basket of provisions and patent medicines and grasping June's hand set off on her weekly visit to the poor people from Grandpa's congregation. On these afternoons it felt as if the backstreets of Stranraer were full of poor, sick people in dirty, smelly houses. Being a Reformed Presbyterian felt burdensome; she was sure not everyone her age got taken to visit the poor, the sick and the elderly every week.

Thursdays were worse, for then she was dragged round all the old ladies in Agnew Crescent. On Thursday afternoons it felt as if little old ladies populated the whole of Agnew Crescent.

That Wednesday, Grandma came home still grasping June's hand, marched in the front door and declared, 'It's no good, I can't take her anymore; she keeps butting into the conversation.'

Mummie looked up from *The Free Press*, sighed and murmured beneath her breath, 'It's not the first time I've heard you say that.'

'Little girls should be seen and not heard. Your duty is to serve the community!'

That evening, Mummie stayed home for her bedtime. Telling June the story one more time... 'When we lived in London Road, Grandma always took you in your pram on her visits to all the poor people from Grandpa's congregation, till one day she said—and here Mummie sat up very straight on the side of the bed with her chin tucked in and her lips pursed tight: "'It's no good, I can't take her anymore, she keeps butting into the conversation."' Then she laughed and tickled June's tummy, the way she used to do when June was a toddler and they still lived in London Road. As she got up and kissed June goodnight one last time, she added:

'She's a Reformed Presbyterian minister's wife, June, serving the community. You've got to learn, that's who she is—who we are.'

At breakfast the following morning, they found something else to tell her. When Auntie Dolly took her finals, they had to put her in the desk at the front on her own, because she talked so much all of the time. Maybe, it wasn't such a bad thing after all to be talkative, even as a little girl.

Mummie wasn't always there for her bedtime now. She often had to go out to run an errand. She always powdered her nose and did her lipstick, tucked in her stray hairs and dabbed a little *Shalimar* fragrance behind her ears, before she went.

Sometimes in the afternoons Grandma Rodger, Lizzie and June would sit in the kitchen; Grandma cutting up squares of *The Bulletin* meticulously and tying them together with a thin piece of string run through one corner to hang by the toilet. The outstanding piece of furniture was the large, bleached cupboard, stretched along the wall from the door to the green stove with its three burners and its paraffin reservoir at the right-hand end. This cupboard had known more spacious days before June was born, when it graced the kitchen in the Manse, where Mummie and Auntie Dolly and Uncle Eddie and Uncle Henry and Uncle Ernie and Uncle Johnny and Uncle Stanley and Auntie Kate and Auntie Minnie had been reared. The table too was over-large, but that was where Lizzie and she would spend hours with plasticine, wax crayons and colouring books. Sometimes in the afternoons Grandma Rodger or Lizzie would put aside their chores and read to June, carrying on till Lizzie got up to take off her pinny and wrap it neatly in its brown paper parcel tied with string and it got so dim that Grandma got to her feet with a half-suppressed sigh and began to light the oil-lamps. Then Mummie would lay the table for tea and Auntie Dolly would arrive with a brown-paper bag of scones from Gillespie's.

Lizzie, only fourteen and no growth on her, stood on an upturned box to reach the stone kitchen sink, singing *'al-al-al-alwaaays,'* under her breath, glancing out the window onto the back garden from time to time and smiling to herself. June was standing beside her while she peeled potatoes; from time to time Lizzie handing her a piece, saying, 'Me and Jimmy, we've got an *understanding.'*

June chewing her raw potato, digesting this news. *Did Lizzie need to stand on a box to reach their Under-Standing,* she wondered.

She could catch the faint smell of rhubarb jam and scone on Grandma's breath, she was so near as she folded down her sheet.

'Grandma, how did you and Grandpa Wesley meet? Tell me again!'

'Not now, June; it's time to say your prayers and go to sleep.'

Straight as an Ormrod, Grandma Rodger. So near and so distant... so fair and so far. Gentle Jesus, meek and mild, pity me a little child, round about my pillow keep... the bogeymen away while I sleep. So far away, spinning on the ice while the bogeymen gathered and murmured and conspired to cheat Grandma-Ormrod-and-Mummie-and-Auntie-Dolly-and-Lizzie-and-June of their slight chance of happiness.

The General Strike took place in the May of 1926, before June started school in the autumn. Labour organised monster demonstrations. Prime Minister Stanley Baldwin issued a message: 'The General Strike is a challenge to Parliament and is the road to anarchy and ruin.' There were idle pits everywhere. At the Gas Works black-coated workers struggled as stokers. Running battles broke out between police and miners in Fife. Newspapers printed pictures of up-turned trams on Glasgow streets. Nine days later, newspaper headlines proclaimed: 'No Strike Tonight', 'Strike Decision Official.' Did my great-grandma read about the Strike in *The Bulletin*? Did she recall her late husband sacrificing everything to support the ship workers in Southampton when they went on strike? Did she tell Lizzie about workers' rights and social justice on those becalmed late afternoons? After the strike, Outram

Press in Glasgow only employed non-union labour. The Scottish TUC Strike Committee called a boycott urging everybody 'not to purchase' any of its titles: *The Glasgow Herald, Evening Times, The Bulletin, Glasgow Weekly Herald* and the *Glasgow Evening Citizen*. Did my grandmother continue to read *The Bulletin* regardless?

When June discovered G. D. H. Cole's writings as a student, did she remember overhearing Grandma's muttered lectures to Lizzie? Did she learn her concern for social justice over crayons and colouring books?

At first it was Lizzie or Grandma who read to me, but when we went to school, words on paper were the first thing to be taught and books were the most wanted gifts.

She was a mixed infant now; finding friends amongst the other mixed infants.

Their teacher, Miss Lamb, was mild-natured as a lamb, like the Sunday School picture of Gentle Jesus. They filed in from the playground and were told to sit themselves at a desk. Each desk seated two pupils and each place had a hole for an inkwell in its top right-hand corner. But for now they would use chalk on slate. They shared their *First Readers* between two and sat staring at the ABCs, repeating them by rote all morning then starting to draw them scratchily. When Miss Lamb turned to the blackboard and showed them how to form the 'A' correctly—*three separate strokes for the capital 'A', mind, not a lazy curl at the top*—Alan McHaffie, who sat behind her, reached over his desk, sniggering under his breath, 'a lazy curl!' and pulled her long hair. *Horrid Alan McHaffie*. His father had a tobacconist's shop in the middle of the town and his mother was a great friend of Mummie's, so he and June had played together before going to school. She didn't like him; he was always teasing her, pulling out the curls Mummie had taken such pains to put in with strands of hair tied round knots of paper all over her head, or pinching her surreptitiously when his Mummy and hers were deep in whispered conversations.

Soon she made a special friend, Muriel Killops. Muriel didn't like Alan either; he was a bully, she said. He'd made her cry once, but never again; she wasn't going to give in to him, not anymore! So they asked Miss Lamb if they could sit together. And because they were good little girls and Miss Lamb didn't need to keep too much of any eye on them, she moved them to the back row together, where they shared the least battered desk in the class. Muriel's father was a detective and his job was to find people who had been bad and broken the law; he never found out about Alan McHaffie.

When Miss Lamb had had enough of teaching them to read and spell for one day, she would tell the girls to get out their knitting needles and wool, while she gave the boys extra words to copy silently, telling them strictly not to fidget while they improved their orthography. Muriel and June sat side by side, knitting needles in hand, tongues pushed out between their lips as they learnt to handle the strand of wool with their right forefingers and keep pushing the stitches along the needle to the tip with their left hands. They dropped a few stitches initially, but by the end of term they had knitted and sewn up a strange doll's 'frock' to give to their dollies on Christmas Day.

Soon June could read and spell with little difficulty. She would come home from school to Lizzie. All the kitchen chores done and in the calm of the mid-afternoon, they would sit at the dining room window to read her comics— *Rainbow*, *Tiger Tim*—and she wasn't sure who helped whom. Mummie and Auntie Dolly didn't read books, just *The Bulletin* and *The Daily Express*; Grandma Rodger mainly read *The Bible*, with its gossamer thin pages and tiny, cramped print, and her daily commentary on a Bible passage from *The Bible-Reading Society*, which she pondered religiously last thing at night as she went to bed and first thing each morning before getting out of bed. June hoped they would buy her a book for Christmas, rather than more doll's clothes.

Muriel's father was such a good detective he was moved to Belfast. Over there, there were more people who had been bad and broken the law than in Stranraer. June felt sad for a long while.

There was God's law that Grandma read from The Old

Testament and there was 'The Law.' Norah Grant told June her father was 'The Law.' Because Auntie Dolly worked with all the lawyers, June asked Auntie Dolly, what did that mean?

'Mr Grant is our local policeman,' Auntie Dolly explained. He lived at the back of the Sheriff's Court building, so he could be on hand whenever he was needed.

Norah Grant said he was 'the strong arm of the law' or was it 'the long arm?' She wasn't sure.

Norah's Mummy said, 'Don't be daft! It's the uniform that counts. Without that he'd be nothing,' as she ironed his shirts and pressed his jacket in their cluttered kitchen. Norah Grant was June's best friend now; she was allowed to go round there to play on her own. She would walk importantly past Auntie Dolly's office window on the ground floor on the left, through the Sheriff's Court's front door and on down the dingy green corridor to the Grants' flat at the back. She could have gone straight to their front door on the side of the building, but she adored the frisson of marching past the lawyers and their clients as they sat waiting to be called. Norah was Mrs Grant's youngest and they played at dressing up with all the discarded odds and ends of frippery and finery from Mrs Grant's youth that Norah's three elder sisters no longer wore.

When I think of 9 King Street, I think of little Lizzie Craig, with Jimmy's ring tied on a piece of string round her neck and concealed beneath her blouse all day.

Little Lizzie Craig was hit by a calamity. But that came later; first there was Fred Andrews's.

But to tell the story, I need to explain...

On one side of their double fronted house was St Margaret's Church and on the other a billiard hall; 'the sacred and the profane,' sniffed Grandma from time to time. Beyond their porch was a hall wide enough for a Victorian table to sit against the wall—it had a marquetry shell, which Mr McCluskie said was a sign of the Victorian era—and a very large picture of the Battle of Waterloo on the wall behind it. At the far end of the hall, the stairs swung round gracefully to a first-floor landing and the large window in their wall had lots of red and blue stained glass, as had the inner front door. In the porch there was eventually a gas meter that took penny coins. There were five other doors in the hall: first on the right was Mr Andrews's sitting room, then behind it the door to the kitchen; first on the left led into their dining room, which had to double up as their living room, and behind it was the door to the bathroom—a long narrow room with a window into the garden. Tucked under the curve of the stairs was the lavatory with a little cupboard off it. The lavatory seat was a large wooden box, which stretched right across the little room.

Upstairs there were two small back bedrooms; Grandma slept in one, which adjoined the wall of the billiard hall. Within, you could hear the noise of cue touching ball and Grandma was frequently pestered by their plentiful supply of mice. The billiard hall was a place of mystery where men went in and out all day, where schemes and intrigues were surely planned and deeds of darkness carried out. Mr Grant was called there from time to time, usually on a Friday or Saturday night; but to June's knowledge, he never managed to find the evidence to prosecute them. *Muriel's father, Mr Killops the detective, would have done if he'd not been moved to Belfast.* The only thing they ever proved against them was the plague of mice. Once it got so bad that they truly invaded Grandma's bedroom and Sammy, the local man-of-all-trades, had to remove the fireplace to clear their dead bodies. Grandma said that these things were sent to try us, but June hated the mice. She didn't know which she was more afraid of: them or the bogeymen. For weeks she went to bed and lay shuddering, viewing that scene over and over till the mice infested her dreams.

At the front of the house was the larger bedroom where she and Mummie slept in one bed and Auntie Dolly in the other, and next to it the largest room in the house with two windows overlooking the street. It was called the drawing room and in it was a three-piece settee covered in chintz, the piano and Grandma's 'chiffonier' that held china in the glass cabinet part. On the ledge underneath were Grandpa Wesley Allan Rodger's big books containing pictures and histories of *County Seats of the Noblemen & Gentlemen of Great Britain & Ireland* in four volumes. There was also a battered German helmet, which Uncle Ernie had brought home from the war as a doubtful souvenir. But what she loved most about that room were the shutters *inside* the windows, which could be drawn to keep out the cold in winter, and the iron shutters, which drew across the front of the grate and guaranteed a quick flame when the fire was first lit. In the other rooms, a page of the newspaper was held in front of the infant fire to encourage it to grow. More often than not the paper itself caught fire; it was a wonder that only once did a chimney catch fire and June had to dash across the road to fetch Mr Pat McKinlay, the vet, to come and put it out.

They seldom sat in the drawing room. They hadn't been long in the house before the boarders arrived and the drawing room was theirs. Mummie, Auntie Dolly, and, reluctantly, June used to trespass into it; they would play the piano and she would practise. They claimed it for special occasions. Once every few years she was allowed a party on a Saturday afternoon and the boarders were banished to their attic bedroom.

Over the years there were four boarders June remembered. There was Mr Stepps. Then there was a reporter who worked for their local paper, known to its readers as *The Free Press*. You paid for it. The 'free' denoted freedom of speech; its official name was *The Galloway Advertiser*. Most of the news concerned the reports of the prices raised at Friday's cattle market and other agricultural matters. But on a few occasions, when the reporter had some 'real reporting' to do, Mummie had to rise early to give him his breakfast before he caught the mail-boat that left the harbour at 6 a.m. to cross over to Larne. His name was McCluskie—she never knew his Christian name.

And then there were Guido Bonugli and Mr Hetherington, who shared one attic as a bedroom. When she decided she no longer wanted to share Mummie's bed, she moved into the other attic room. She thought, although this might have been her imagination, that she could catch a glimpse of Loch Ryan from her attic window. Mr Hetherington travelled for Fyffe's Bananas and played the flute. He didn't have a lot to say for himself and after some years got married. But Guido Bonugli was different. There were two ice cream parlours in Stranraer. The one at Port Rodie overlooking the Loch, situated where the buses came and went. Mr and Mrs Adami owned it—one of their daughters would be in the same Guide Pack as June—and there were little red tables to sit at and a big high counter. Mr Bonugli owned the other. It was situated opposite the Town Cross at the corner of the next street parallel to them. They lived in King Street and Mr Bonugli's shop was on the corner of Queen Street. By the time June was twelve or thirteen, it was a very smart establishment and June and her friends would patronise it.

Mr Bonugli's nephew, Guido, came over from Italy to work in Stranraer and lived with them. He was about twenty when he landed in Stranraer. He was dark, energetic and talked a lot, eventually in English, but always with a strong Italian accent. The house was so much livelier when he was there. When she had her parties, he would arrive with a huge tub of ice cream and tease all her playmates and generally cause excitement. Once there was so much horseplay the chandelier in the room below fell and nearly knocked out Mummie, who happened to be standing below it.

When June was sixty-five, her cousin, Mavis, phoned her on a Sunday in January to say Guido Bonugli—George Bonham, as he had become—had died before Christmas at the ripe old age of 88.

He loved tinkering with electronics. He had a special order at Penman's the Newsagent's for *Amateur Wireless and Electrics*, which he collected each Saturday morning. 'Marconi was the greatest Italian of all time,' he would exclaim, immersed in its explanations. He would take a radio apart and lay its components on his bed, then by nightfall, would have reassembled the whole thing and got it working better than ever. Eventually he left Stranraer for Plymouth to work for Uncle Johnny. By the time he was in his forties, he owned a chain of electrical goods shops in Devon and was the Mayor of Plymouth.

But I'm getting ahead of myself, jumbling the tale in the telling. Let's start over again.

Fred Andrews had the first-floor back bedroom, away from the mice and the noise of cue touching ball, and the downstairs sitting room. June and Chummy weren't afraid of him anymore, although they kept out of his way. He was big and blind; brooding and proud. Now and again Mummie or Auntie Dolly would remind her they owed their good fortune to his infirmity, so she must make allowances and be kind. His infirmity was his first calamity; he'd had a successful career as a rugby player before he started to go blind. His second calamity had been the saving of them, when he decided to buy this house rather than move away to live with his sister and her husband. But his third calamity was the one that broke his spirit.

Chummy the tabby cat was voiceless. He was often found sleeping on one side of the old-fashioned kitchen range and occasionally singed his tummy fur as he stepped across the coals to the other side for a change. June would put him in her doll's pram and wheel him round the streets of Stranraer, and he'd sit there, good as gold. Then he would return to sit and roast in front of the fire, but he would never ever say, 'Meow!'

One day, she had brought Chummy back into the house and was wheeling her doll's pram through the kitchen door to the large brick-floored outhouse, where all sorts of things were stored when not in use. Afterwards, though she swore blind she hadn't closed the kitchen door, Chummy was stranded in the hall. It was almost lunchtime and Fred was making his way downstairs, his heavy rugby-player feet in sturdy black boots, taking each step surely, unerringly as ever. He was middle-aged but too proud to use his stick in the house. Maybe Chummy heard the mice in Grandma's room, they'd never know, but that tabby cat was prowling silently upstairs intent on something other than Fred's big boots. Chummy never let out a 'Meow!' But Fred did.

After he broke his leg he had to have a bed in his sitting room and never went upstairs, or down, again.

Auntie Dolly got to have a bedroom of her own for a while, until the fourth boarder, Monsieur E. E. A. Debetaz, arrived.

That was the first calamity in King Street, unless you counted the plague of mice and the chimney fire. Whenever she walked past Fred Andrews's downstairs sitting room, the feeling of a life blighted hung in the air.

The next calamity was little Lizzie Craig's, sweet sixteen and still no growth on her, with Jimmy's ring tied on a piece of string round her neck and concealed beneath her blouse. She was waiting for Jimmy to name the day, perhaps next spring. For Christmas, she would ask her friends and family for whatever they could afford towards her trousseau, like she did last year. And by next spring she'd have enough to make do.

But first there was the October fair and she knew she'd spend a few pennies there. Well, it would be a shame not to. Especially with the toffee apples and roasted chestnuts in their twist of paper. She'd been looking forward to them all year.

The fair was held down on the breastwork by the sea front. As ever there was great excitement when the fairground-folk arrived. Lizzie was going with Jimmy on the Saturday night, but she promised she would take June on Friday after school. She stayed on late and had tea with them, before they sallied out into the damp autumn evening, June clutching her saved farthings and halfpennies in her gloved hand. They rode the carousel and the music played and played 'It all depends on you' and 'I'm Nobody's Baby' making June want to wave her hands and tap her feet to the infectious, ragtime rhythms. They tried their luck at the coconut shy, then went to buy toffee apples and a twist of hot roast chestnuts to share. It was blissful. Despite the dank night air June felt exultant. Her senses were teeming with the bright fairground lights, the hollers of the fairground folk, the thrilled yells of all of Stranraer's children, the sweet, earthy aroma of roasted chestnuts and the sound of the water lapping in the harbour beyond.

Lizzie let out a screech, a shriek so piercing June felt winded and breathless. The carousel kept on turning. 'I'm nobody's baby' kept on playing. The people kept on throwing coconuts at the coconut shy. But Lizzie's Jimmy was standing by the roast chestnut vendor, his left arm round the shoulders of the dairymaid from Leswalt. His right hand gently caressing her belly, huge with child, as she complacently peeled hot chestnuts placing first one in her mouth then one in his. They watched Jimmy remove a chestnut from his mouth, suck it and place it in hers, sealing it with a kiss. *He had deceived her with that country girl.*

Lizzie grabbed the first missiles to hand, an armful of coconuts, and shied them at the pregnant girl before flinging herself at Jimmy tearing at his mouth and eyes. She grabbed him round his lying throat screaming, 'You promised me! You promised me!' Or as Mr Grant put it when he escorted them back home: Lizzie accosted him on the fairground and became quite hysterical.

Late that evening she was still so agitated that Grandma administered a few drops of tincture of laudanum in a mug of warm milk. June slept with Auntie Dolly that night, while they put Lizzie to bed in June's attic room.

Little Lizzie Craig, sad sixteen and no growth on her and never likely to be now. She came back to work on the Monday morning bringing her brown paper parcel tied up by string. When she went home at the end of the day she couldn't sustain her patient way. She tore off her pinny, snatched her brown paper and length of string and crushed it all into a ball, clutching it to her tummy, then fell on the cold kitchen flag-stone floor and rolled around in sodden rage.

That was the second calamity in King Street. The plague of mice and the chimney fire didn't seem so dire as the irreversible demise of Lizzie's dreams. Although June still shuddered when she thought of all those mice tumbling out the fireplace in Grandma's room. Lying in her attic bedroom on the verge of uneasy sleep she thought she heard their squeaking. And she wasn't sure but the squealing mice got jumbled with Lizzie's shriek tumbling out and infesting the entire night-time sky.

Lizzie was diagnosed with hysteria; the doctor said she must have complete rest for six months. It was difficult without her. For a while, Mummie didn't have so many errands to run in the late afternoon and early evening. Staying home more didn't improve her temper. It was during these first couple of weeks without Lizzie that June learnt to swear, saying 'Bugger-it!' with a sharp intake of breath like Mummie did when some household task caused her annoyance. June's bedtimes weren't the pleasurable moments when stories were shared like hidden secrets anymore. She would climb the stairs and say her prayers, then wait for Mummie or Auntie Dolly or Grandma to come and see that she had her arms crossed dutifully on top of her neatly folded-down sheet. Sometimes none of them came. Only when they had gone back downstairs, or she had given up waiting, would she commence telling her dolly (but in truth herself) the Rodgers' women's stories, like treasures that had to be recounted or lost.

After a couple of weeks of this Grandma said enough was enough, she was going to find a replacement even if she were only temporary. One morning while waiting for the milkman's wagon to arrive she spoke to Mrs Murray's daughter. Annie Murray's sweetheart had gone to fight in the Great War and never returned. His name was carved on the plinth of the war memorial at the bottom of the street. *Was the soldier standing so upright, left hand poised above his heart, right hand holding his musket, 'for King and Country' her Donald?* So Annie helped her mother who fostered Catholic Orphans in the house across the road. Grandma approved of the good work despite their not being Presbyterians. It was a shame that Annie Murray had never married, but she could express her maternal instincts in caring for one orphan after another, as many as six at one time in the house, which was no bigger than theirs. June envied the Catholic Orphans because they always had one another as playmates. She determined that when she grew up and got married—*she would get married, there wouldn't be another war*—she would have six children. They would always have plenty of playmates and she wouldn't be restless and irritable like Mummie was with an only child to look after. The following day the Murrays' eldest Catholic Orphan, Margaret, arrived promptly on the doorstep at eight o'clock already wearing her pinny.

'I've come to help you,' she explained to June. 'You better show me where to make a start; I want to make a good impression.' Margaret was willing; this was her big step into the real, adult world. She was somebody now, not just another of Mrs Murray's orphan girls.

June was soon left with her in the evenings. Mummie's errands started again and later in the evening she might be playing badminton, which she was very good at. Auntie Dolly would be rehearsing for the annual operetta and Grandma, ill or indisposed, retired to her room and Bible soon after high tea. Margaret didn't sit and read with her and she didn't know how to make pretty patterns by cutting out a square of paper then adding a finishing touch of crayoning. She could be persuaded to do a simple jigsaw, but soon tired of it. But she'd entertain June in a different way. The winter was drawing in and on dark evenings the rain would be pelting outside, accompanied by a noisy wind. She'd tidy away the last of the tea things, lock the back door to shut out the *Bogeys*, and they'd huddle round the fire. June wasn't sure which of them was the most scared on these late evenings when Margaret wouldn't hurry her up the stairs until they heard Mummie or Auntie Dolly at the front door.

Sometimes Guido Bonugli came into the kitchen and would laugh and say, 'Time for little girls to say their prayers, no?' And he would carry her upstairs kicking and screaming with delight as he sang something bright and full of Italian sunshine to chase *gli stupidi Boghii* far away.

Margaret was fond of June's grandmother. She said she owed everything to her. 'Your Grandma is a real lady,' she would say. 'She's kind to everyone she meets. The whole of Stranraer knows that but she never boasts or makes you feel small. She's a gentlewoman, is Ma Rodger.'

June had never regarded the weekly drags round the poor, the sick and the elderly in this light. She'd learnt it was her duty and that if she failed in it she would find herself in God's bad graces. Now it seemed that her Grandma was an adorable gentlewoman, not an exacting, straight-laced figure, who disapproved of June several times each day. To Margaret, Grandma Rodger was her saviour; she would do anything to please her. Soon she was buying Grandma little presents and shyly presenting them to her before she left at the end of the afternoon.

This was rather a worry, especially when the laundryman said he hadn't been paid for weeks. There was an interrogation in the dining room. Margaret stood shamefacedly and shuffled her toes on the Persian carpet, before she admitted her sin—blurting it out like a grown baby. The laundry book was kept in the dining room cupboard. Each Friday after Fred gave Mummie his board for the week, she put by the weekly payment placing it inside the laundry book. Margaret had been trusted to pay the laundryman but it turned out that she had been taking the money to buy, among other things, presents for Grandma. After her childhood of penury the temptation had been too great for her.

Grandma said that she should talk to Jesus in her prayers and he would surely help her to know right from wrong; he would tell her how to be strong and to do right in future. Mummie pointed out that Margaret was a *Catholic* Orphan and hadn't learnt how to talk to Jesus properly, adding defiantly that maybe *that* was the problem all along. For once Grandma deferred to her flighty daughter and Mummie took Margaret to the priest and left her with him, saying he'd have to sort things out.

When June was about the same age Lizzie had been then and had moved away from Stranraer, she tried to write a story about Margaret: how she'd messed up her one chance to escape being just another of Mrs Murray's and Annie's Catholic Orphans. But she couldn't capture Margaret's eager bustle and desire to please, her superstitious mind and her giving in to greed. She could only write about her grief, weeping down by the shore on her own, as she'd seen her one day soon after she'd had to leave.

It's all jumbled in the telling and I've missed out what was happening at school. *Telling the story one more time...*

In the autumn of 1927 when June was five and a half, she went up into the first form. She was sad to leave Miss Lamb. They all were. She'd taught them their alphabets, to knit and, when they were tired, let them sew the wee cards with brightly coloured raffia. But now they had Miss McCaig and soon they loved her too and felt superior to the children in mixed infants.

When she was aged six and a half, June went into the second form. Their teacher was called Primrose Petit, a farmhand's daughter.

Primrose Petit loved axioms. 'Young ladies (and gentlemen) are attentive to their spelling and always cultivate good diction.' She would wince when her pupils spoke Galloway Irish, although she grew up in a family where only the dialect was spoken. 'Mind your Ps and Qs. We're living in the twentieth century, not the Dark Ages.' They quickly learnt to 'speak proper' when in class.

'Whatever your Mammies and Daddies do, you control your destiny. The sins of the fathers aren't necessarily visited on their children.' But Daddy hadn't sinned. He'd been too good for this world and God had called him young. Although Grandma, who knew God well, said *It was tinkering with his motorbike in that biting wind at the back end of summer that had killed him.*

No consonants could be swallowed in Miss Petit's class, especially the Ts in her name. 'Slovenly speech denotes slovenly manners and slovenly manners are a sign of slovenly morals.' June felt her hackles rise when Miss Petit said this, but appreciated some of her maxims and took them to heart.

'Neat handwriting is the sign of a cultivated mind.' June set to learning to write regular cursive script as if her life depended on it.

'Young *ladies* are fastidious regarding personal hygiene. Young *gentlemen* too. What is next to Godliness?'

'Cleanliness, Miss Petit.'

She was rumoured to wash all over every morning. June started to rise a few minutes early to wash every day. She prided herself on smelling of fresh soap and water, like Miss Petit.

One day June was sick in class; the boy who sat beside her had to clear it up. She felt dreadful about that, embarrassed and humiliated. Primrose Petit sent her home. She walked the length of Lewis Street alone. She passed the Sheriff's Court and thought of going in to Auntie Dolly. She didn't dare in case she was sick again. Past St Ninian's. God couldn't help her now. Past the Inn. She tried not to look at the men downing their lunchtime pints. Her thoughts strayed to the sound of burly men heaving their guts onto doorsteps each Friday and Saturday night. Once more she felt ill. Left past the Town Hall. Over its doorway, the three-masted ship bobbed at sea. Its motto: 'Tutissima Statio.' She knew this was Latin for the safest haven. She caught the sound of men's voices in rowdy debate in the upper room. Her head ached. She felt giddy. She steadied herself at the corner of King Street, straightened her shoulders, then walked the last few yards to her front door. And to Grandma's outstretched arms.

She was courageous. She'd learnt from Mummie and Auntie Dolly already. Women alone had to stand up for themselves. There was no one else to do it for them. As Grandma tucked her up in bed and held a cool flannel soaked in vinegar to her forehead, she remembered the previous week.

She and her friends built a den in the playground. For one glorious day it was their domain. Then the big girls tried to seize it. Her friends let them and slunk away.

Apart from June. She stood her ground. She battled to the last.

Christmas was coming. Barrels of apples arrived from Canada; one came from Fred Andrews' friend from his rugby playing days. He'd emigrated and now owned orchards and a successful fruit export business in Manitoba. The other was from Grandma Rodger's brother who was head municipal gardener in Winnipeg. Not Great Uncle John James, who'd emigrated with Aunt Emily and had six children, but Great Uncle Charles who lived with Auntie Louisa, a dressmaker who'd never needed a man to look after her.

June searched for these strange sounding place names on the World Atlas she'd been given for her birthday. Canada was pink, like a lot of the world, and its apples were 'Pink Ladies.' Fred said the Canadians had stolen the best English apples from Herefordshire over a century ago, but Mr McCluskie said that was 'all tosh.' Grandma raised her eyebrows disapprovingly. McCluskie ignored her and said he'd emigrate to Canada in a flash, if they'd have him in Vancouver. June loved the apples and ate half of one every morning at breakfast. That winter she learnt to peel and cut them into slices. When they were all gone spring was on its way and soon Grandpa Hepburn would be sending her the first apples of the autumn picked from her tree. He'd planted it in his Crosby garden the moment she was born.

She wished she could go and see him and Grandma Hepburn and the back garden where Daddy had sat in the revolving shed that Grandpa had built him. He made it so that it could be turned to face the sun to help keep Daddy's chest warm and him safe from harm. Except it hadn't kept him safe. But Grandpa Hepburn and Grandma Hepburn had done the best they could, until her Mummie had come along and spent the two happiest years of their life together. Mummie was plump, pretty and blonde. Grandma was sure she didn't know where Mummie got it from! But Mummie loved to laugh and have fun, despite all the hard work cleaning and cooking for Fred and the boarders, and looking after Grandma, who wasn't as young as she used to be.

Christmas was a magic time, with Mummie's open mincemeat tart, made in the big, china pie-dish with heaps of mincemeat and served with a dollop of cream. There were roast potatoes and stuffing and pigs in blankets and bread sauce to go with the goose. They tucked in heartily and in the afternoon little Lizzie Craig came to visit, bringing June a flimsy, clothbound copy of Lewis Carroll's *Alice in Wonderland*.

June hugged her and clung to her neck, exclaiming, 'Oh! Please get better and come back to us soon, Lizzie! We miss you so much!' But what she meant was that she really missed Lizzie and their times together, peeling potatoes, crayoning or reading comics in the dining room window seat. She hadn't known this till she said it so the thought made her burst into tears.

Grandma disapproved and told her to control herself.

Mummie smiled, put an arm round June while she stroked Lizzie's forearm with her spare hand and said, 'We all miss you, Lizzie. You know there's a place waiting for you here when you're ready. But take your time,' and, gulping back tears, 'but I know, if anyone in this house does, how hard it is to get over such things.'

Grandma looked upset and Mummie added (inadvisably but she'd had a whole glass of sweet sherry before Christmas dinner and, as she told Auntie Dolly later, it went to her head), 'We all know you're widowed, Mother! But you had Daddy for the best years of your life. You had enough children with him and you brought us all up *with him*, before he died. So don't expect me to wear widow's black bombazine for the rest of my life.'

Grandma held her hanky to her mouth and said stiffly that she was feeling rather faint after all that food and if they didn't mind she would retire to her room and sit quietly there for a while.

Lizzie helped her out then came back saying, 'Bless you, Mrs Hepburn, you've made me see I'm not alone. I reckon we've all got our crosses to bear in this life, haven't we?'

That we have, Lizzie; that we have.

When June was grown up and moved away, slightly older than Lizzie had been then, she tried to write a story to send to *G.U.M.*, the *Glasgow University Magazine*, all about the October fair and the carousel and coconut shy and that same bittersweet song playing over and over and Lizzie's grief and sodden rage. Her words could never capture that piercing cry on the sea breastwork, nor the mute anguish that surrounded Lizzie in all her patient doings once she'd recovered from the six months of hysteria and taken up her place in the King Street household again.

Spring came eventually, with her seventh birthday party. It was the time the chandelier nearly knocked Mummie unconscious. And then Easter arrived with the return of Lizzie. Everything was back to normal. Yet never quite the same. June was more grown-up and had more comics than ever to read each week or fortnight. She adored *Sexton Blake*.

Uncle Ernie, the Presbyterian minister, and Uncle Eddie, the borstal headmaster, visited more in the summer months. They always asked for them when they came to visit. The first thing they said to her was, 'Have you got any *Sexton Blake*, June?' Now she was seven, *The Schoolgirl* appeared, with Bessy Bunter, the fatty! It came out once a week, so she'd be straight down to Penman's Newsagents. She didn't throw the comics out and didn't let Grandma tear them up neatly for toilet paper. Instead, she kept a huge pile of them behind the curtains on the dining room window seat. She and Lizzie would read their favourite stories out loud to one another over and over, but now that June could read so well, they would entertain one another, putting on different voices for the characters, taking turns to play the goodies and the baddies—Pat the Pirate, Bimbo the Clown, Dr Grunter and his Scholars—transforming the comic strips and animating them into their private playhouse where they were simultaneously actors and spectators.

On 30ᵗʰ May 1929, the 'Flapper' Election took place. It was the first in which women between twenty-one and twenty-nine were allowed to vote. My great grandmother would have voted in the previous general election (and subsequent by-election) since she turned thirty in 1923. For my Auntie Dolly this would be the first time she was eligible. In 1924 the Liberal member of parliament Cecil Randolph Dudgeon lost. Following the death of his

Unionist successor he lost again at the by-election in 1925. In 1929 with the memory of the General Strike still raw in the constituency, he regained Galloway. The result was close; he won by one hundred and one votes. The likelihood is that my maternal ancestors voted Liberal.

Autumn came with the start of another school year. Now they had Miss Bryden, from a farm down Whithorn way. June would come home from school to peel off her wet woollen socks and put them to steam by the kitchen grate and maybe Lizzie, sad seventeen and still with no growth on her, would give June a scone or a girdle cake to tide her over till teatime. And in the calm of the mid-afternoon all the kitchen chores done for the day, they would sit at the dining room window to read her comics old and new—*Tiger Tim's Weekly, The Rainbow, The Girl's Own Paper, Sexton Blake, Bo-Peep and Little Boy Blue*. Sometimes, Lizzie would get up quietly, pick up *The Bulletin* or *The Daily Express* or *The Free Press* even, and slip into Fred Andrews' sitting room, leaving June who could read and spell very well on her own now, to the pleasures of the window seat and her well-thumbed copy of *Alice in Wonderland*, while the daylight fell. Eventually Grandma would rise to light first the oil lamp, then later the new gas lamps that hissed and bubbled the evening away.

June was often left on her own with Lizzie in the evenings. She usually stayed till late and sometimes slept in the spare bed in June's room rather than walk home at night. Mummie was prettier, plumper and gayer than ever. The happier she got the more the house sang and swayed, as if the hours danced themselves away each day. In contrast, Grandma seemed to diminish and recede. She wasn't really any smaller, but her domain was contracting and she spent more and more time sitting in her room studying her Bible and daily Bible reading commentaries. She had done all she could, she said, and it was in God's hands now. Mummie would laugh and say there was nothing sinful in a game of badminton. Auntie Dolly would go into the boarders' drawing room, sit at the piano and play. She would range up and down the keyboard, playing harmonic chord after harmonic chord, introducing a strong rhythmic element that reminded one of hearts on the point of breaking from excess of emotion. She could read music, but June didn't remember her ever doing so when she sat to play. She would ask what everyone wanted to hear and make it up as she went along. Her improvisations had something of Debussy and Ravel in them, with highlights from Italian opera for Mr Bonugli. Then she would finish by playing 'Dizzy Fingers' effortlessly at top speed. Mummie needed the sheet music—'Ain't we got fun?' and the piano music of Samuel Taylor Coleridge were her favourites—but Auntie Dolly had only to hear a tune and beneath her fingers it was transmuted into sumptuous sounds filling the drawing room and escaping through the doorway to reverberate around the hall and stairs.

That autumn they got their first dog. His name was Pickles. He was a mongrel terrier and had an awfully bad temper. He had to be put down in the end. It happened like this: Auntie Dolly bent and held out a bit of food to tempt him. She was holding it in front of her face and rather than take the morsel, he went for her eye and bit it. This happened soon after Lizzie had come back. Doctor Roberts said it could have been a calamity for Auntie Dolly, but she got off lightly. She had a black eye for a week or more, which turned purple, then green, then yellow, then she was all right. Auntie Dolly's calamity hit her several months later.

His name was Barclay Charmers. He was the next young lawyer newly qualified from Glasgow come to do his Articles. Mummie wondered with the name of Barclay whether he was a distant cousin on Grandpa Hepburn's side of the family. *His* name was John Barclay Hepburn after his grandfather, who had been John Barclay. Daddy's name was Alexander Hepburn and he was named after his grandfather who was also Alexander Hepburn. Great Grandpa Alexander Hepburn had married an Isabella Barclay who'd had lots of brothers and sisters; so Barclay Charmers might have been the son of one of her sisters. But they never found out. What they did discover was that like a lot of men he couldn't be trusted.

He lived up to his name. He mounted a charm offensive

on Auntie Dolly. And he won. She had been so proud and independent, running that Sheriff's office, *showing them all how it should be done*. Effortlessly touch-typing with the same grace and ease with which she played the piano. Playing badminton nearly as well as Mummie. Leading the Amateur Operatic Society every year. Singing with her beautiful voice in Church on Sundays. Always sure-footed and lively in the Scottish Country dancing, keeping the whole set on their toes and in time with the swirling, rushing music. Bright, sharp, quick-witted, an excellent cook and so beautiful with her jet-black eyes, long dark hair and the jet necklace and earrings. *Showing them all how it should be done*, as a young woman in a town like Stranraer with a widowed mother, a widowed sister, and limited means. So no one else had seen her weakness: her hunger for praise, love of their puppy-eyed idolatry. It was as if she'd run on a self-sustaining metronome, keeping time and playing the most wonderful melodies with her young woman's vitality, and he'd come along and quite casually, but brutally, stroked the metronome and ever so slightly changed its pace, just enough to leave no one in doubt that now he controlled her heartbeat, her every move, each moment of the day—and night. Soon she wore his engagement ring and June wondered if it ever so slightly tilted her balance as she tapped the typewriter keys all day. Or, coming home and going into the drawing room to play the piano keyboard, was the excess of emotion playing her rather than she playing it? Were her 'Dizzy Fingers' now dizzy in a slightly different way?

June didn't witness the moment calamity struck Auntie Dolly. She only heard them talking about it: Mummie, Auntie Dolly, Lizzie, Mummie's friend, Mrs McMaster and even Annie Murray. This was 9 King Street's third calamity after Fred's and Lizzie's. Auntie Dolly must have been in God's good grace because her anger was of moral outrage, not miserable, sodden and self-destructive. Auntie Dolly was engaged to Barclay Charmers. So, when she got wind of the fact that he'd made a baby with one of the farm girls she was furious. She found out on a Friday, the day of the cattle market. She saw him on Saturday and they went to the cinema together. She waited to see if he would say anything. How she got through that Sunday June would never know. On the Monday morning when he walked into the sheriff's clerk's office she threw the ring at him.

Then she had the presence of mind to retrieve it, saying haughtily, he could pay that price for having dared to deceive her; that farm-girl wasn't going to get to wear *her* ring. Straight away he was the one who was vanquished and humiliated. Not her. It was as if she'd suffered a fever. Now it had broken and she was fine again, she said. He hadn't finished his articles but hastily arranged a transfer and moved back to Glasgow. The farm girl was left to her own devices. They heard she went away for a while. Less than a year later Mrs Murray and her daughter Annie had the bonniest baby orphan to foster. Grandma commented that those orphans were only Catholic once they were born and the nuns got their hands on them. Auntie Dolly said at least they gave the poor wee things a home and some sort of family, which was more than their fathers did. Grandma thought that Auntie Dolly reminded her more and more of her sister, Auntie Louisa; the one who'd emigrated to Canada.

June wondered what God thought about all this. She tried to talk to him every night as Grandma Rodger taught her, but she couldn't be sure he heard her. It was difficult to know what to say. Sometimes she imagined that his whiskers got in the way. In Sunday School they were told that Jesus loved little children and always wanted to speak with them, but she wasn't certain she knew where or even who he was exactly. At different times of the year he seemed to be in different places and indeed to be a different god. She knew he was God-made-man: sometimes a baby, sometimes a lamb, sometimes a grown man. And from what Lizzie and Auntie Dolly said, it was looking as if you were a fool to trust any grown man farther than the eye could see.

When she'd grown up and moved away from Stranraer, June never tried to write down the story of Auntie Dolly and Barclay Charmers. The episode had been beyond her comprehension. She hadn't witnessed any of it, only heard them telling the story over and over. And with each telling, Auntie Dolly came out of it the triumphant heroine. Years later when she was pushing forty, Auntie Dolly met Birrell Bryson, married and moved to Dumfries. They were happy until the war with Hitler's Germany. So Barclay Charmers hadn't been a calamity after all. As Auntie Dolly put it when Lizzie said how she wished she'd had Miss Rodger's sang-froid when she'd suffered her calamity: Barclay Charmers was a calamity narrowly avoided. The calamity would have been if she'd not heard about the love child and gone ahead and married him.

Now that she was older, in the evenings she would go with Mummie to the Masonic Hall and play badminton until eventually, she revolted against the boredom of being with 'old people.' She much preferred to stay home and read a book.

More and more now she lived in her own world spending time with her friends from the mixed infants. They would be going up into the fourth form in the autumn. It was called: 'Lower IV' (with a Roman numeral), followed by 'Upper IV' and then 'Lower V', unless they had to sit the year again, like some of the farm boys did.

Autumn came and the start of another school year. Once again she would come home from school to peel off her wet woollen socks and put them to steam by the kitchen grate. Lizzie, an agreeable eighteen with an imagination that grew more vivid every day, would give June a scone to tide her over till teatime. Mummie cherished Lizzie for her long-suffering acquiescence and an ingenuity that nourished June's powers of invention, as much as for her proficiency in whipping up drop scones on the griddle to feed her famished child.

Often now June would arrive home too late for her scone and only just in time for high tea. For this was the year she would stay behind with Norah and their loyal initiates in the playground after everybody else had gone home. These were the times she enjoyed most; lingering as dusk fell, ignoring the gnawing hunger pangs, revelling in their illicit freedom at the end of the long school day. No question of there being any older girls loitering or waiting to bully them or to try to take over their den. Then back in their Camelot they would all be kings and queens and the large tin shed, where the school doctor, nurse and dentist used to see them periodically, became mysterious and romantic.

Christmas was coming again; the first Christmas of the Thirties. The barrels of apples arrived from Canada; one from Fred Andrews' friend from his rugby playing days, who owned apple orchards and a successful fruit export business in Manitoba and the other from Uncle Charles, head municipal gardener in Winnipeg.

Or is that jumbled in the telling? June never told it the same way twice. Were there really two barrels each year? Did Fred have a friend who had emigrated? Did Uncle Charles really send a whole barrel of apples each year to just this one sister with her two youngest daughters living in impoverished circumstances? Did Fred's friend who owned the fruit orchard and exporting business send the barrel on behalf of Uncle Charles? After all, they had both emigrated to Manitoba. There's no one alive to ask and no literary memoir to consult. Just unreliable memories told to me as half remembered bedtime stories. So, telling it over...

The October Fair came. June went with her friends now. While they revelled in the carousel, the coconut shy, the toffee apples and the twists of hot roast chestnuts, she thought of Lizzie. *It all depended on one throw of the dice.*

Then Christmas came and with it carol-singing and much standing around Auntie Dolly at the piano in the drawing room, the boarders sipping sherry and joining in with the latest songs. Every three years, Jack McMaster (Mummie's best friend's brother-in-law who was a rubber planter in the Philippines) used to come home to stay with the McMasters at Stoneykirk for Christmas and New Year. Every three years, Jack McMaster gave them a lovely big box of Terry's All Gold on Boxing Day. Every three years, he would propose to Mummie. Every three years, they would decide he wasn't quite what she wanted. This Christmas was one of those years. So, this Christmas, accompanied by an indefatigable Auntie Dolly who made the keyboard come alive under her electrifying fingers, Jack McMaster added his deep bass tones to Guido Bonugli's soaring tenor as they sang rousing carols. Then they switched to their favourite popular songs. They'd all seen *The Singing Fool* at least once and knew the lyrics to 'I'm sitting on top of the world' by heart. Each man did his best to mimic Al Jolson's exaggerated, melodramatic style till no one could keep a straight face. Then Auntie Dolly played tunes they'd heard on Guido's radio. Her improvised accompaniments emphasised the rhythms and caused June to dance around the room—*I'm sitting on top of the world... I've danced with a man, who's danced with a girl, who's danced with the Prince of Wales*—till she felt dizzy and collapsed *just like Humpty Dumpty*. She sprawled on the sofa. For once Grandma didn't tell her to sit up straight. She was sitting upright, silently registering disapproval. Now Mummie was playing from the sheet music she'd ordered from the newsagents. Jack McMaster looked meaningfully at Mummie as he belted out the words to 'If You Knew Susie.' Grandma sat with pursed lips but let them sing it. She put her foot down at the suggestion they might sing, 'I Belong to Glasgow.'

'The man comes from Dundee and I'll not have songs in praise of drink sung in this house, not while I'm alive.'

Then, one gloomy mid-January morning, Jack McMaster returned downhearted again to the Philippines, *quitting the blues of the world...*

On Boxing Day her two uncles who lived in Ayr descended on 9 King Street. They'd driven down in Uncle Henry's car. Uncle Henry had his own business manufacturing sheep-dyes and other farm products. Daddy had worked for him when he was alive: using the car, he'd acted as a Traveller selling Uncle Henry's chemicals and other products to the farmers in the area. Uncle Stanley was a mystery; he was the youngest boy born before Mummie and Auntie Dolly. About once a year he would turn up out of the blue on a motorbike to borrow money off

Grandma, then disappear again. He was on his best behaviour this Christmas and brought Grandma a present of three fine lace handkerchiefs. For the rest he brought a huge jigsaw with a thousand pieces. It took them till New Year's Day to complete: a huge picture of a Scottish rural landscape with farms and mountains and cattle in the fields. Working out which piece was part of a Beltie and which a bit of a farmhouse window was by no means as easy as it initially appeared. Nothing was said about the money he owed Grandma and nothing about the life he led. June had no clear idea what he did for a living. She thought it was something to do with the dentist's, though he wasn't a dentist. She had even less idea about his personal life; for all she knew he was married with a family of his own, but there was something about his manner that made her think he probably wasn't concealing a brood of unknown cousins.

What marked this Christmas as special was Aunt Jemima's gift that arrived in a big cardboard box carefully wrapped in heavy brown paper. It sat beneath the Christmas tree for a full fortnight before she was allowed to open the parcel on Christmas morning. As she carefully unpicked the knots in the string and folded back the brown paper, she could see it was a book, the biggest book that had ever belonged to her personally; she didn't count the *County Seats,* since they had been Grandpa's, were now Grandma's and not yet hers. It was the illustrated, Centennial Edition of Lewis Carroll's *Alice in Wonderland,* which had been published the year she was born. It didn't matter a jot that she had already read the story over and over in the old clothbound copy Lizzie had given her a few Christmases ago. In this edition, it was an entirely new book with layers of meaning she'd not caught a glimpse of in all those times she read and reread the story over the past two years.

It was such a big book. Not quite as tall and not quite as wide as Grandpa Rodger's *County Seats of the Noblemen & Gentlemen of Great Britain & Ireland,* but almost. And like *County Seats* it was bound in red with gold intaglio lettering. Her *Alice* had a wonderful golden intaglio on the front cover with the caterpillar on his mushroom, except that he looked for all the world like a snail with his house on his back. To the right of him the white rabbit turned his head to beckon Alice, while the dormouse scampered by her right foot. To the left of him the figure of the Knave crept away furtively, accompanied by an odd creature with whiskers. In silhouette it was impossible for June to puzzle out what this creature might be. A cat? A fox? A terrier? A hybrid? June opened the book and on the inside cover there were two black, white and orange woodcuts of the Mad Hatter and the White Rabbit. She turned the first page feeling the thickness of the paper between her thumb and finger. On the left-hand page the dedication block was waiting for her to write her name. She took her fountain pen with its finest nib and wrote her name very neatly in black ink, using her best Britannia looped cursive style that she had learned at the Academy.

There were more beautiful woodcuts at the start and end of each chapter, and the most amazing, elaborate initial capital letters. There were full-page coloured illustrations on glossy paper, each protected by fine Indian tissue paper that bore a short quotation and a small illustration. She lifted each of these in turn and gazed on the uncanny world of rational nonsense, weirdly alien yet instantly recognisable. The pictures fascinated, enticed, yet imparted an air of menace. Like the thrill of locking the doors to keep out the Bogeymen while still being able to gaze at them for hours on end. She adored the first picture of Alice and Dinah. Dinah reminded her of Chummy and Alice had a window seat just like hers with a curtain she could draw across to hide behind when she wanted to get lost and read her books.

Auntie Kate and Uncle Alec sent her a special book too: *My Own Fairy Book* by Andrew Lang. This was different from other books of fairy stories she'd read. The author had made the stories up altogether out of his own head. *So this was what happened if you read enough. Eventually you could start to write books too.*

Mummie didn't read books, just the newspapers. She read *The Bulletin*, a Scottish newspaper published in Glasgow, and *The Daily Express*. One time Mummie went to buy *The Bulletin* and came back horrified. In it there was a picture of a woman who lived nearby in Fisher Street. There was 9 King Street, then the Billiard Hall and the sweet shop and round the corner Fisher Street. It ran down to the castle at the end. It was one of the original old streets where fishermen had lived. It was not nice there. There was a picture of her with her twenty children; the woman was obviously a streetwalker. Mummie was so upset that people would see this and associate it with Stranraer. Grandma Rodger understood Mummie's outrage but commented that Mummie should not judge others lest she too be judged. 'Remember Emily May,' she added pointedly, 'there but for the Grace of God...' but as she went to light the gas-lamps in the upstairs drawing room she didn't quite complete her thought.

Mummie didn't read books and June didn't know there was a Public Library in Stranraer, so next summer she joined the local paper shop's library and read every thriller it had over the course of the school holidays. When she wasn't playing with Norah and their gang, or enjoying the unexpected visits from her uncles, she could read one in a day. *Mummie was so uneducated*, she thought. Mummie had left school at the age of twelve, but wanted June to get the education she'd never had. It would give her a better chance in life. Mummie had been unlucky with the throw of the dice, Lizzie said. *And so were you, Lizzie! And so were you.*

Uncle Eddie used to send Grandma Rodger books about the Highland Clans. She read those too. She was more interested in history than in nature. She didn't appreciate 'Nature.' In her mind it meant poverty—dirt, flies, spiders and mice; dim-lit rooms, which smelt of grubby clothes, squalid bodies and boiled cabbage; old men with hacking coughs and little old ladies with conditions that could only be whispered in Grandma's ear. 'Nature' eroded human dignity and reduced grown men and women to tears. 'Nature' meant a lack of education and farm girls that were put in the family way then disappeared to live with 'relatives' for the best part of a year. 'Nature' was what stopped Primrose Petit ever being more that the mixed infants' second form teacher, leaving her slightly more pinched every year. 'Nature' was what Mummie and Auntie Dolly battled with daily, rising above it with the weapons in their armoury, knowing that the fight ceased at night only to begin again the following day. 'Nature' was what slowly defeated Fred till he was the shadow of his former self, cut down in his prime. 'Nature' was what threatened to destroy Lizzie, but she got the better of it because she wasn't going to be cowed and admit defeat, although she had very nearly succumbed that one time. 'Nature' was those men from the billiard hall staggering home late on Friday and Saturday nights, pausing to splatter the pavement with their putrid vomit. 'Nature' was everything Grandma Rodger sought consolation from in *The Bible*. 'Nature' was pigeons spreading muck and disease on the pavements and house-fronts. 'Nature' was mice tumbling out the chimney breast into Grandma's immaculate bedroom, then scurrying around June's troubled dreams however hard she tried to look away. 'Nature' was Daddy succumbing to tuberculosis at the age of thirty-one. 'Nature' was the dentist (married to a rich but ugly wife) and the bank manager (still a bachelor but more than ready to settle) prowling round Mummie—for all the world like tomcats after a moggie in heat. 'Nature' was the stuff of nightmares. In small-town life, 'Nature' was a constant threat to respectability.

I forgot to say about the summer holidays; I need to wind back the clock a few years. Telling it over, all jumbled in the telling...

At the start of the summer holiday after her first year at school, Mummie lost patience with June's long, straight, straggly hair and the hopeless battle to make it curl. That first Monday of freedom from Miss Lamb, she marched her down to the Barber's in Queens Street and told Mr McGintie to chop it all off into an Eton crop. Grandma frowned over lunch but the deed was done. At least her hair wasn't a tangled mess that it hurt to brush out and comb at the end of every day. That was the summer Mummie and Auntie Dolly cut down Auntie Dolly's old, bright-red dress and made it into a lovely 'flapper' dress for her with two rows of gathers in the skirt and such a neat collar round her neck. It had three-quarter length sleeves so they wouldn't get in her way while she played. She felt grown up in it and wore it all summer long.

It was this first summer that a tradition started, which lasted until they left Stranraer. Cousin Margaret from Dublin came to stay for a week. She was about the same age as June. Auntie Kate thought she was too young to travel on the ferry by herself so Cousin Helen came too. Because Cousin Helen came Margaret shared June's bed. June realised that Margaret was the nearest she would ever have to a sister. They were almost the same height; Margaret was maybe half an inch taller when they stood straight back-to-back and Cousin Helen laid a ruler across the top of their heads. June's hair was dark and straight; Margaret's was a beautiful blonde and naturally curly. Margaret was a classically pretty little girl; she never got into trouble. She would just open her blue eyes wide and pout her lips so that no one believed she could be naughty. June had a squint and the visiting optician had tested her eyes as soon as she started school; she already wore steel-frame glasses. She didn't have dimples and her mouth didn't fall into a pouting smile. Instead, whenever she was accused of doing wrong, her lips would shut tight as if they were stopping the truth from exploding out her mouth. So Grandma always told June off instead of Margaret.

'It's not fair,' June exclaimed one morning while they lay on the beach letting the waves from Loch Ryan wash over their toes. 'Grandma's so strict with me. I don't deserve to be told off all the time.'

'Granny's getting old,' mused Cousin Helen. 'She used not to be so stern.'

'What was she like when she was young? Do you know?'

'Mummy tells me lots of stories about growing up with Granny and Grandpa,' said Helen, 'and some of them are quite funny.'

When Cousin Helen said 'Mummy' she meant Auntie Kate; Auntie Kate was Grandma's eldest child and much older than Mummie and Auntie Dolly. When Auntie Dolly was just a tiny baby, all the other children went down with scarlet fever apart from Auntie Kate and the newborn baby, Dolly. Auntie Kate looked after Auntie Dolly while Grandma and Grandpa nursed their siblings at the top of the house. Even when everyone had recovered Auntie Kate continued to look after Dolly.

'So,' continued Helen, 'Auntie Dolly still regards Mummy as her mother too. Mummy says that when she got married Auntie Dolly was really upset and said she had no right to get married and leave her.'

'How old was Auntie Dolly then?'

Helen paused for a moment and worked it out in her head. 'I think she was about nine years old.'

'What happened then?'

'Auntie Dolly did forgive her in the end, because she told me just the other day that when Mummy got married she found an old tin candlestick and polished it up to give her as a wedding present.'

They let the waves wash over their toes for a while longer. Then June asked, 'Did you ever see the Manse in London Road?'

'Oh yes,' said Helen, 'While we were still living in Renton I used to come for holidays to the Manse.'

Cousin Helen didn't say any more than that. There were so many questions June longed to ask her about those times, but didn't know where to begin.

After a while, Helen continued dreamily, 'Grandpa was a handsome, upright old gentleman in frock coat, clerical waistcoat and collar. He was a very forceful character, quick-tempered no doubt but full of charm and good humour. Somehow you always knew when he was in the house. Granny was a lovely person then, gentle and kind to us all but with plenty of quiet strength. They didn't exactly argue, but she had a way of standing her ground when she had to. I can remember one time they had words about something. Dolly said it was to do with money. Anyway he declared he was *head of the household* in such a loud voice everyone heard him all over the house. Auntie Dolly and I were stood in the hallway outside his study where they were arguing. I was only little and it scared me a bit. Then we heard Granny say—and she didn't raise her voice in the slightest, "Yes, but I am the *neck*, and the *head* can't turn without the *neck*."'

They all lay and watched the small fishing boats landing across the Loch, thinking about Grandma Rodger standing her ground with gentle, persuasive humour. Then and now, there was no gainsaying her. June thought that when she grew up it might be nice to be married to someone like Grandpa and quietly be the neck on which the head turned.

Cousin Helen was very grown-up and busied herself with looking after June and Margaret. As well as taking them down to the beach below Agnew Crescent, she took them for picnics round the 'Primrose Walk.' But mostly she let them play in the back garden while she gossiped with Lizzie. To June that patch of land contained the whole world. She and Margaret transformed it into any number of fairy-tale lands, metamorphosing the garden shed into a castle, or a cottage, or a gingerbread house and themselves into Lords and Ladies, King and Queen of the fairies and much else besides. The week flew; then at the end of it, Mummie told June she would be allowed to travel back on the ferry with Margaret and Helen, and stay for a whole week in Dublin with them. This was the pattern that continued for the next eight years, but in following years, Cousin Helen didn't come with Margaret. Having made the journey once with her, Margaret and June were trusted to be sensible on the ferry, each of them one way on their own and one way together. But unbeknown to Mummie and Auntie Dolly, even when Cousin Helen wasn't sleeping in the spare bed, each night after they'd said goodnight to them, Margaret would skip across to snuggle up with June in the one bed and they would fall asleep sharing secrets that softly slipped into drowsiness and entwined them together in their dreams. Then June was content: Margaret was indeed the nearest she would ever have to a sister of her own.

The following couple of summers, after she'd returned from Dublin, June used to pass the window of Auntie Dolly's office a lot, going backwards and forwards to play with Norah Grant. By now they played all sorts of imaginative games, pretending to be all kinds of characters; the long winter evenings of reading comics till she knew most of the stories by heart led to shared animations in Norah's backyard or June's back garden. And then there were the stories they'd read in class with Miss Lamb and Miss McCaig, which came to life on those endless summer afternoons. Half of the King Street garden was grass to play on; then a trellis of sweet peas separated it from the flower borders. Sweet peas and night-scented stock, nasturtiums and poppies: she would always associate these flowers and their scents with her mother and with her childhood games that entirely excluded her mother. In the middle of this proliferation of flighty blooms stood the magical garden shed. The foot of the garden adjoined another, which was always quiet. On the side away from the slightly menacing Church were the wash-house with its copper lit from underneath to heat the water, the cook-house and a large brick-floored house, which they used for storing unused possessions and, for a short time, as a home for two rabbits and their hutch. She got the rabbits one of those summers—in later years she couldn't be sure which. They hadn't survived long and Mummie had said, 'Good riddance. It was a silly idea in the first place.' Between the washhouse and the bathroom window, for their bathroom was a converted ground-floor room, was another small raised flower bed backed by the windowed wall of the billiard hall next door. Sometimes they borrowed Lizzie's box to stand on and peered inside to see what dark secrets the men were plotting.

One summer when they were eight years old, June and Norah started a secret society. They devised an initiation ceremony for their unsuspecting playmates; it always took place in the washhouse. It was dark there, even on the brightest summer day. They would take it in turns to be the one to usher the gullible recruit into its darkness. The other one would rise out of the boiler with a white sheet over her head making weird noises. Then each recruit was sworn to secrecy, but finally after they'd initiated Margaret Carnochan and she'd run all the way home blubbering to her Mummy, both June and Norah were scolded and sent to bed early one lovely August evening. After that they resorted to *The All Story Wonder Book*, which Mr Stepps gave June for the Christmas of 1929. There was one story they took from it that they never tired of playing. They'd enact the drama of the fairy of dreams. She was sad because she couldn't dance with the rest of the fairies each night. Her mother had gone down to the sea and married a merman; she'd never returned, but asked her fairy relatives to bring up the child. She didn't have a fish's tail instead of legs, but limped a little and couldn't dance. June would always play the fairy and make Norah be the Fairy Queen who gave her an ivory book of dreams that you could only see at night. Norah would wave her fairy wand to strengthen June's wings so that she could fly away to share her beautiful book with all the poor little children, who were lonely or having a bad time. Then Norah would play the little children who were in pain but still went to bed without making a fuss. And June would hold the magic crystal pages in front of her till they both entered them and enacted all the loveliest dreams they could imagine. This was a story they could play over and over, inventing new dreams of pixies, elfin pipers, fairy weddings, the old woman with the big basket whose contents made the unhappy queen smile again, the prince who would only marry the neglected Cinders whose foot would fit in the crystal shoe and the magic tree whose leaves could make your wishes come true.

The summer of '31, June and Norah started a lending library and charged the other girls a penny each to borrow a book. And Margaret didn't blubber to her Mummy about that, ever. When they had accumulated enough pennies, they would go to the local paper shop and choose another book, which each of them read before it was added to their lending library stock.

On her tenth birthday June wasn't allowed a party; she felt disappointed for days beforehand. But on the morning of

March 5ᵗʰ, she was overjoyed. Sitting in the hall when she came downstairs was a proper, grown-up bicycle, covered in ribbons and a little bag of Auntie Dolly's fudge with a card in its basket. Mummie and Auntie Dolly must have scrimped for months to buy it for her. And how had Auntie Dolly made the fudge without her noticing? It was wonderful with its shiny chrome handlebars, its basket and its leather seat. More wonderful still was the promise it bore: she was growing up and now she would have the freedom to explore the town. Tea that evening was extra special with all her favourite things: tattie scones, Scottish griddle cakes, lovely creamy butter and raspberry jam (and not the usual rhubarb jam Mummie always made too much of). Then there was her birthday cake Mummie had made while she was at school, with lots of hundreds and thousands and pink icing and more raspberry jam and whipped cream in the middle. After they had eaten more than they could manage and drunk lots of hot, milky, sweet tea to wash it down, Mummie and Auntie Dolly reminisced about the bicycles they'd ridden as children. *Telling the story one more time...*

The Rodger girls had been the first women to ride bicycles in Stranraer; it had caused quite a stir, especially as they were the daughters of the recently arrived Reformed Presbyterian minister.

'But remember,' said Grandma Rodger, 'We were *Reformed*, because Grandpa Rodger was so rebellious and independent minded: he wasn't going to kow-tow to anyone, however wealthy or powerful. He always stood by his principles and his principles were modern, forward-looking, liberal and egalitarian. He was really very radical in his way.'

'Yes,' said Mummie, 'and we've taken after him one way or another, flouting conventions, either by choice or necessity.'

June's ears pricked up; Mummie didn't usually speak like this.

'We've always challenged the small-town, narrow-minded busy-bodies, who think theirs is the only way to live,' reflected Dolly. 'Not that we set out to; it just happened like that.'

'*Reformed* Presbyterian means knowing your God and knowing your own mind and not kow-towing to anyone, just because they happen to have shoehorned themselves into authority over you. Always stand by your beliefs and principles, but always pray they are the right ones and seek to improve them every day of your life.' Grandma Rodger was a strange mixture; she was telling June to follow her own mind and be rebellious, to stand against convention. But the way she told it felt a bit oppressive to June.

'Do you remember when Minnie and Alf came to the Manse soon after they were married?' Mummie asked.

'Don't I just,' exclaimed Grandma. 'Minnie was always the most rebellious of the lot of you; she took after her father in that. She was still the dare-devil, even though she was a married woman now.'

'You remember she borrowed an old bicycle from the shed that no one was using any more and took us both for a ride without telling anyone where we were going?'

'I've never peddled so fast in my life,' replied Mummie. 'Rushing downhill with the wind in our hair. We must have looked an awful sight to those old gossips.'

'And then the look on her face when that old bike just broke in the middle as she was speeding down Station Hill!'

'Anyone else would have knocked their teeth out and broken their nose, but she managed to jump clear and carry on running and laughing to the bottom.'

'Then we snuck that broken bike back into the shed and you and Grandpa didn't even notice it was broken for months.'

June expected Grandma Rodger to express outrage, but instead she smiled and gazed into the fire as if she were seeing those old times when Grandpa was alive, handsome and vigorous, the house was full of laughter, singing and recitation, and any number of people coming and going. 'Yes, Minnie took after her father alright; always independent minded and defiant—standing up for anyone who was being unfairly treated.'

'And she plays the piano just like you, Dolly,' said Mummie, 'anything and everything straight off by ear.'

'That's how she got her first job as a nurse, of course,' mused Grandma. 'You know she went and got it without a by your leave from Grandpa or me; just upped and left the house at sixteen to work in that mental hospital.'

When June went to bed that night, she had a lot to reflect on; it wasn't just her over-full tummy that kept her awake until the early hours.

That bicycle transformed her life. After the conversation she'd been privy to over her birthday tea she didn't always bother to tell anyone just where she'd been or how far she was planning on going next time. So the summer of '32 was the fullest summer holiday she could yet remember. Not only was there the lending library to organise every day, she was now allowed to go swimming with her friends. On hot summer days they would strap bathing-costumes on the back of bikes and cycle along the Shore Road, strip and plunge into Loch Ryan. They used to swim around in the harbour by the Creamery diving board or beneath the jetty for hours until the ferry was due. There was no such thing as swimming lessons; they all just learnt, watching the older boys and gradually leaving doggy-paddle behind to pick up breast stroke, back stroke and in some cases even the crawl. Sometimes she would leave the bike behind and walk with Norah or another friend along Agnew Crescent until there were no more houses. Primroses grew all winter and spring on the grassy bank that ran down to the Loch's edge. If they picked the right moment—about midday—the ferry from Larne would send big waves as it arrived at the jetty and for the next half hour they would sit on the shingle and let the waves caress their toes. At those moments, Stranraer felt like the only place in the world to be. All the malicious gossip she caught about Mummie and Auntie Dolly faded, constraints disappeared and she felt poised on the verge of an exciting life. She would work hard and pass the qualy to High School when she was twelve. Mummie hadn't gone to the High School, but spent a final year at the Academy before leaving school. She'd only started at The Academy when she was eight; before that she'd gone across the road from The Manse to Ruddicot. June would get a better education than her. And then she would go to Glasgow University. Mummie was adamant on that. And then as the granddaughter and daughter of independent-minded women, she would go out into the world and stand up for her principles and be rebellious like Auntie Minnie. She wasn't going to be dull and homely like Auntie Kate. She'd be someone in the world.

At other times when she woke in the middle of the night, stood on her bed and tried to glimpse Lock Ryan by moonlight from her attic window, she wasn't so sure. Then the world conspired to keep women shut in the house, gradually renouncing their desires and dreams, as it had Lizzie. She'd asked and been told more of the story about Auntie Minnie. How Auntie Kate, the eldest of all her Aunts and Uncles, had wanted to be a nurse when she left school. But Grandpa Rodger had firmly told her that her place was in the home helping her mother. So when it came to Auntie Minnie's turn to leave school, she didn't ask. She just got a job as a nurse in a Mental Hospital and left home. When it came to it, would June have the courage to act like Minnie? How could she ever leave Mummie on her own when she needed her so much? Auntie Dolly would be leaving soon to marry Birrell Bryson and then it would be just her, Mummie and Grandma. And Grandma Rodger wasn't getting any younger, as she kept reminding them.

But for now there were the summer holidays. So she tried hard not to worry about this. Then Uncle Stanley turned up out of the blue on his motorbike again. The house changed gear when any of the uncles arrived. The rush of avuncular energy ran through the whole house leaving doors swinging open and bats and balls littered around the hallway for Fred to stumble over if he wasn't careful. The back garden reached out to drink in all this bursting vitality and the whole street could hear the raucous laughter as Uncle Stanley chased June and her friends round and round till they dropped down on the patch of lawn exhausted to stare at the high clouds racing past. When he left, Grandma's purse was lighter again, but somehow it seemed worth it.

Uncle Stanley was not the only uncle (or aunt) to visit that summer. Uncle Eddie came down from Mossbank Industrial School to stay briefly after the end of his school's term—'To get a break from those boys and breathe the sea air for a few days.' While he was there Uncle Ernie and

Auntie Annie came down on the Friday night and stayed overnight; they had to get back to Giffnock for the Sunday morning service, because Uncle Ernie was a Presbyterian minister just like his father. They bought cousin Pat, who was a year younger than June and had come to stay for a whole fortnight on her own. They would share June's bed and do all sorts of exciting things, but the most exciting was that Uncle Ernie bred pedigree Golden Labrador puppies in his back garden. A kind parishioner had given him a champion bitch not knowing what havoc they were unleashing. The puppies helped to supplement his rather meagre stipend. And besides, he adored them: their wild dogginess. Auntie Annie laughed till she cried telling the stories of him sitting in his study trying to write sermons and looking up out of the window to see that those puppies had escaped from their pen in the middle of the lawn yet again. Time and again he would start up, narrowly avoiding knocking the inkwell and rush outside to herd them all back into the pen and secure it once more. Then he would spend ages stroking them all tenderly when he should be reprimanding them or getting back to writing his sermon.

'But they are a living sermon in themselves,' he mused. 'Trying to contain all that vitality however strong we build the pen. Trying to keep the litter of puppies within the Pale, when they don't know any better than to run riot and spill out everywhere. I must see what I can do with that.'

'It might be a bit too close to the mark,' muttered Auntie Annie darkly.

Anyway, two of the current litter hadn't turned out true pedigrees in all respects; they had white patches. He didn't understand how it could have happened; he managed it all absolutely scientifically. Auntie Annie snorted into her teacup. The long and short of it was he'd brought his little sister May a puppy to make up for Dolly's leaving her soon.

Grandma Rodger smelt of vinegar and Eau de Cologne and increasingly of smelling salts. Auntie Annie smelt almost the same, but in different proportions—more Eau de Cologne, less vinegar and smelling salts. Mummie smelt of the bergamot, rose and jasmine in *Shalimar*, and Auntie

Dolly smelt of Attar of Roses. At first Cousin Pat smelt of pavements and dusty classrooms, but after she'd been there a day or so, like June she smelt of grass, sweet peas, sunshine and salt winds. When she left the Academy, June would have to start using talcum powder and Eau de Cologne. But not this summer; nor the next. She could wait another year before being a young lady. Now she savoured the freedom turning ten brought. Uncle Ernie smelt entirely different; when they sat side by side in the dining room window seat reading through her pile of comics—a thing he loved to do above all else whenever he visited—she could smell the heat radiate from his avuncular body. It bore strange messages of masculine energy and confidence, lacking from her life the rest of the time. (She'd never dare sit this close to the boarders; Mummie or Auntie Dolly would tell her not to bother them.) Somehow, Uncle Ernie smelt of sermons and champion golden Labradors all in one; a heady cocktail of the sacred and secular spilling out and running riot in the surrounding purlieu, reanimating all her favourite comic heroes and adding another dimension to their stories of daring do and thrilling rescue.

When Uncle Eddie arrived the previous day the first thing he'd said was, 'Where's your comics, June? Have you got some new ones since last I was here?' As usual he'd made a beeline for the window-seat. He smelt of blackboards and unruly schoolboys; he carried a lingering odour of Headmaster's addresses to school assemblies and Headmaster's admonishments in his study, mitigated with compassion and good humour. June loved to snuggle close to either one of these uncles; she felt safe and secure in their protective warmth.

This summer Uncle Eddie was excited about some new financial scheme that would safeguard his savings and make a huge profit besides. You had to be careful where you put your money after the Crash but this was a sure-fire winner with gold-plated protection, he'd been told. Uncle Ernie said he was sticking to breeding pedigree puppies even if now and again his method failed. He picked up the tiny golden puppy with its white splotches, gave it a stroke and a kiss on the nape of its teeny neck: 'This is all the gold I care about, Eddie.'

'All that glitters is not gold!' remarked Grandma Rodger with her habitual sniff.

Uncle Ernie handed the wriggling, golden bundle across to Mummie. 'You'll have to bottle-feed him for a while. Truth be told we came away a bit too soon and he's not really properly weaned yet.'

June and cousin Pat were sent to the outhouse to search for the old bottle they'd used to feed the rabbits for the short time they were alive. They almost got lost in all the piles of junk they found. They decided they would return on a rainy day and build themselves a proper den out of it and ask Lizzie for bacon sandwiches to eat there once it was made. By the time they'd found the bottle and brought it back triumphantly the tiny puppy was tucked down the front of Mummie's blouse nestling between her ample breasts. June was almost jealous, but her frown came and went so quickly none of the adults noticed.

Guido Bonugli arrived home soon after. He'd been told that cousin Pat was coming, so he'd left work early and carried a big tub of Neapolitan ice cream round to King Street for them to share in the back garden. They sat round on deckchairs and upturned crates, facing the billiard hall to catch the last bit of afternoon sun that just peeked over its insalubrious wall while they ate. It wasn't just Auntie Dolly who was leaving them soon; this was the summer it was arranged Guido Bonugli would go and work for Uncle Johnny in Plymouth.

'And what will ye call the wee doggie?' he asked Mummie.

Mummie thought for a moment then said, 'He shall be called Guido, after you. When you're gone, he'll be the one to cheer us all up when we're down in the dumps, just like you always do!' She laughed as she said this but in the sinking sunshine June felt a chill wave shudder through her body. *If Lytham St Annes was far away, Plymouth was twice as far again. She would never be allowed to visit cousin Mavis, Uncle Johnny and Auntie Emily. Who would protect her from gli stupidi Boghii when Guido left?*

That evening, they lay in bed, planning the next day and the day after and the day after that. When they had mapped the first week, they were too excited to fall asleep and lay talking. June got to thinking how lovely it had been to eat Mr Bonugli's ice cream and share her latest comics with Uncle Ernie and Uncle Eddie. She wished her Daddy was alive and thought he would have been a wonderful mixture of the three—plus a dollop of Hepburn for good measure; just like a Neapolitan ice cream with cream on top.

She mused to Pat, 'You're so lucky to have a Daddy. It must make you feel happy all the time. I wish I knew what it was like.'

Pat didn't say anything. June wondered if she were falling asleep. She tried one last time, 'I wish we were sisters and Uncle Ernie was my Daddy as well as yours; he's so big and warm and lovely!'

'He's not like that all the time,' Pat said in a small voice. 'Somehow, he's different at home. I can't explain it but often it feels as if both Mummy and Daddy aren't quite happy with one another. They are always nice to each other, but it can feel chilly in the house most days.'

'Is that why he visits us here in Stranraer so often?' June asked. As long as she could remember Uncle Ernie had popped down, visited for an afternoon, stayed for high tea and then been on his way.

'I think it's *because* he visits Stranraer so often,' said Pat. 'Mummy's always more upset when he's away in Stranraer overnight.'

It was on the tip of June's tongue to say, 'Oh, but he doesn't stay overnight; he just stays for the afternoon and catches the last train home again.' Although she didn't know why, she did know that she shouldn't mention this to Pat.

June liked to pretend she was Pat's big sister. Pat was a year and one month younger than June; she was born on April 4th 1923 and June on 5th March 1922. Nevertheless, Pat had been given a big bicycle for her birthday, just like June's—a whole year sooner. To June's mind this was further proof of the advantages of having a Daddy as well as a Mummy; she decided not to mention this to Pat either. They'd brought it with them on the train from Glasgow. It had ridden the whole way in the Guard's van; Pat had been allowed to go inside and talk to the Guard. He had shown her the strange-shaped packages he was standing guard over: odd spares for agricultural equipment that needed mending, new baking tins for Gillespie's and brand-new, shiny urns for the milkman.

Mummie was preoccupied with the golden Guido. She was in the kitchen, feeding him from the bottle and cooing. So they got their own breakfasts and as soon as Lizzie arrived, persuaded her to make a huge stack of sandwiches to last them till teatime. On their way out of town they bought a bottle of lemonade each from May's, the grocers.

'Now be sure to remember to bring those bottles back, lassies, won't you!' said Mrs May. 'They're worth their weight in gold those bottles and I can't afford to gi'e them awa'.' Jimmy was there, looking much older than when June had moved into King Street six years ago. (Lizzie had heard that he'd four children already and, according to her, could barely make ends meet.)

Each day, they ranged further on their bikes, all round Stranraer and out into the surrounding countryside. They took their swimming costumes strapped on the back of their bikes and their pop and sandwiches in June's front carrier. June showed Pat everything: the 'Primrose Walk' beyond Agnew Castle, the best place to dive into Loch Ryan under the jetty, the trick of letting the waves roll over your feet on the beach below Agnew Crescent when the ferry came in at midday. They rode out on the Leswalt Road and even visited the milkman. His wife gave them huge mugs of milk and showed them where she cleaned the urns at the end of each day, ready to collect the fresh milk the following morning. They didn't keep cows themselves, but when there was milk over at the end of the round she made butter and soft cheese. Her bonny face glowed as she showed them her dairy. June felt so proud that her Grandpa Rodger's generosity had made such a lasting difference to this woman's life. She knew better than to mention this, but she began to see Grandma Rodger's point of view. Perhaps it was better to give and not to count the cost after all.

That fortnight Mummie trained Guido to bond with her; she carried him nestled between her breasts all the time except when she bottle-fed him. She even knew when he was about to pee and run outside just in time, mostly. June thought she treated him like a baby, but Pat said that was what you had to do to train them. Otherwise they wouldn't obey you and they'd run riot. Guido had to learn to think of Mummie as his Mummy too. Now June felt distinctly jealous, yet was also beginning to adore him. He was so squirmy and cuddly; when he wagged his tail, his body wagged too. So she learnt to forget her pangs of jealously and help to look after him, when allowed.

Eight days had passed already when they decided on a further adventure. They would catch the train to Portpatrick and walk round the headland down to the next bay, up to the Dunskey Estate, catching the train back at the end of the day. The station wasn't far from where the driveway emerged from the estate grounds. The journey was a roller-coaster with steep climbs and sudden descents. The train rumbled over the viaduct at Piltanton Burn. When it got close to Portpatrick, they felt as if the engine was going to drag them headlong over the cliffs and into the sea. Just at the last moment it veered sharply to the right. They nearly fell off their seats as it swung into the deep cutting overlooking the cliffs where guillemots nested. The station was cut out of the cliff face above the port. There were six sidings, but not much activity. Portpatrick had been too blustery to survive as a major port when Stranraer could offer a calmer landing. They felt the wind as they walked the cliff path. The spray from the waves broke on the rocks beneath them. They could smell the salt tang of the Irish sea. And the sweet scent of gorse blooms.

When they got down to the sheltered cove where the glen joined the sea, they paused for June to catch her breath. Pat bubbled with excitement. Living in Glasgow, she was never allowed to wander far from home. She said she envied June her freedom to roam all day without anyone telling her off.

'I sometimes wonder if things would had been different if Myrette were still alive.'

June was about to ask why, but Pat grabbed her arm and pointed silently. Less than a hundred yards away a roe deer was grazing. The doe sauntered along the edge of the forest, pausing now and then to munch the lush grass then lift her nose and sniff the air. She seemed not to hear them nor catch their scent. They stood stock-still and held their breath. Eventually the roe turned her head. For an instance they gazed into her deep brown eyes. Then off she bounded displaying her pale rump as she disappeared beneath the dense foliage. They followed her beneath the canopy of alder, beech and chestnut into Dunskey Glen. Still awe-struck they tiptoed along the narrow path to the old stone bridge at the top of the glen. There they stood entranced by the bell-like tinkle of the burn falling away far beneath them.

'Let's play Granny's footsteps,' suggested June.

And so they did along the path that led towards the farm. Before they reached the farm, they were tempted by the sunshine to open the rambler gate into the field and lie in the long grass looking up at the clouds drifting across the blue sky. On the fence beside the gate were two rows of mole carcasses. A gamekeeper had hung them upside-down, their velvety coats and wee pointy noses in various stages of decay. Just over the ridge was the manor house, out of bounds.

'When I grow up, I'm never going to settle down!' Pat declared.

June thought for a while, realising there were advantages to living with Mummie, who was busy looking after the boarders and rushing out at night to see the dentist and play badminton. She could come and go as she pleased; she could explore her world. For all that, she knew that one day she would want to settle down with a lovely husband, whom she would care for and who would always protect her and keep her safe.

'I think I'd like to have a few adventures when I grow up,' she finally said, 'but I do want to settle down when I'm older; it's not much fun if you don't.'

Later that week they took the train again and spent a day at Castle Kennedy. Pat was more adventurous than June. She egged June on and they crept into the Stair Estate and spent hours exploring in the grounds, playing hide and seek in the vast shrubberies, clambering over the ruins of the castle, and performing Lords and Ladies. Then as they were hide and seeking one last time and June was racing breathless and panting to get back to base, she came face to face with an old gardener. She stopped in her tracks, trying to catch her breath and bit her lip. Pat charged up behind her and nearly knocked her over. The old gardener merely chuckled, then opening his dark eyes as wide and frowning slightly he stooped to whisper, 'Beware! The Kennedys used to be cannibals and, you never know, the ghosts of their victims might still be haunting that shrubbery, trying to reassemble their half-gnawed bones!' He pointed to the heart of the rhododendrons where they'd built themselves a secret den.

Whatever else happened during the summer holidays, there was excitement and busyness, especially when aunts, uncles and cousins descended to stay a few days. No sooner had Uncle Ernie come back to stay for a night and collect Pat, than the following midday Cousins Helen and Margaret arrived off the Dublin ferry. They didn't have bicycles, but emboldened by her expeditions with Pat June organised more trips on the train, taking them to Portpatrick and the Dunskey Estate, and then another day out to Castle Kennedy and Kennedy Cliff. This time, she could tell them all about the Kennedy clan being cannibals in the sixteenth century. And they spent lots of time on the beach and swimming in Loch Ryan.

It was a while since Cousin Helen had visited Stranraer and both Mummie and Auntie Dolly exclaimed over how grown-up she'd become. But perhaps they hadn't noticed June was getting more grown-up too. Now, lying in the twin beds in June's attic room, Helen in one and Margaret and June happily sharing the other, the three girls gossiped about their Aunts and Uncles. Helen was a mine of illicit information that Mummie and Auntie Dolly never divulged.

'Pat says Auntie Annie and Uncle Ernie aren't that happy together,' revealed June, hoping Helen might know why.

'Well…' said Helen, 'that's possible. I heard that…' She

paused to reflect, then decided telling the story properly required her to begin at the beginning. 'Mummy says he was a delicate child. When he was little, he would say to her, "Kate, the wind's blowing," and she would know to catch him as he fainted.'

June wondered what that had got to do with anything.

Helen continued, 'He grew up to go to Glasgow University and from the O.T.C. there he enlisted straight away as an officer in the Great War.'

'What's O.T.C. short for?' Margaret asked her sister.

'University Officers' Training Corps,' Helen explained. 'It's a bit like a university club, but it's run by the army. Anyway,' she resumed her story, 'even though he was a minister he refused to go as a chaplain. He said his duty was to fight alongside his men. He comes to Dublin every Armistice Day and takes the church services in Daddy's church; every year he gives a lecture about his war experiences. All the women in the congregation adore him; he's their hero. His lectures are most entertaining; I don't know how he does it, but he makes them very humorous.' Helen was sounding grown-up now. 'He often tells the story about when his superior officers were killed and he was left as a very junior officer to lead an attack. He makes us laugh describing how nervous and inadequate he felt and how he hid it from the men.' She paused. 'I can remember when we still lived in Renton during the war, the *Pathé Gazette News* showed this incident and we all went up from Renton to Glasgow to see it. I remember Uncle Ernie looming suddenly very large on the screen waving his men forward. I was very young at the time and it scared me a bit. It was all over quickly though. Auntie Annie went to see it every day while it was on and cried all through it every time.' Now Helen lowered her voice even more. 'He never loved her, you know. He only married her because when he got conscripted to fight in the war he didn't think he would survive. He decided to get married so that some woman could have his war pension when he died. That's why he married Auntie Annie. Then he was blown out of the trenches. Mummy says that he was delicate to start with, but that he's never been the same since then. She says it's his nerves as well now.'

This was a new idea. Uncle Ernie hadn't married for love. How different from Mummie and Daddy, who had fallen in love at first sight and married despite Grandma and Grandpa Hepburn's wishes. Daddy had died of T.B. but Uncle Ernie had survived childhood illness, only to be shot to pieces in the Great War. So his sense of humour and loving to read comics with her was a way of hiding his nerves and his sense of having made the wrong choice at the start of his life. Was that why his parishioner had given him that Champion Golden Labrador? Had they somehow known that he needed a hobby to soothe him?

Helen paused. *Should she tell them this?* Then: 'Lizzie says... When he comes to visit you he always stays the night with Auntie Dolly's friend, Moira. She says Auntie Dolly told her so. He'll never leave Auntie Annie because of Cousin Pat but it's Moira he really loves.'

Moira the music teacher; the daughter of the sheriff's clerk and Auntie Dolly's friend!

'When Grandpa Rodger collapsed, he already knew about it.'

'Oh no!' gasped Margaret and June in unison.

That night, June lay awake trying to digest all this and readjust her vision of the world from the childlike to that of the adults surrounding her. Growing up was far more complicated than she had imagined.

The rest of the week flew by, but the innocent world of the back garden had become a stage for darker dramas than June had previously played there with her cousins and friends. In a thoughtful mood, she took the ferry to Dublin with Helen and Margaret. When she came back a week later she was still brooding on the ways of men, especially since Cousin Allan Rodger MacPherson had been so annoying while she'd been staying with Auntie Kate and Uncle Alec.

When she got back from Dublin there was still at least a week of the holidays left. The first morning back she wondered what to do with herself after so much excitement for so many weeks, when Mummie announced that Cousins Eileen and Shelagh from Crosby were coming to stay. June was needed to help clean her room and prepare it for their arrival; Mummie had been too busy to do it all week and it was still a mess from when they'd left it to go to Dublin. Mummie loved housework: getting the carpets out on the line and beating the dust out of them, getting the feather duster into all the nooks and crevices and polishing the furniture. But today she needed June's help. So they set-to together and by lunchtime June had beaten her doldrums away with the dust.

They arrived late that afternoon, exhausted after the long train journey but so happy to be in Stranraer. They said they envied June her freedom, living where she did. And they envied the fact that she was still a mixed infant. They went to a girls' school and said the teachers were crabby and strict. They weren't allowed to go out at all on weeknights. If they met them on the street during the holidays, they would still reprimand them if they thought they weren't deporting themselves like young ladies. Shelagh said their problem was they were all spinsters and so mean they wanted all their girls to grow up to be spinsters too. June would remember these remarks during the next school year, when she felt that spinsters were *the bane of her life* as well.

On their first evening, Auntie Dolly invited them into the drawing room to sit and relax while she played the piano. During a break between pieces, they both said at once, 'Auntie Dolly, you play just like Mummy does!' June wished she could play effortlessly like Auntie Minnie and Auntie Dolly. *Why hadn't she been born gifted?* When they finally flopped into their newly made beds in June's room, they told her how Auntie Minnie had got her first job and left home. As soon as she'd left school she'd answered an advertisement in the local paper: 'Nurse required in mental hospital—experience not essential, but ability to play the piano an advantage.'

'Daddy always teases Mummy and laughs about it.' Uncle Alf had been working as a doctor in that mental hospital and that's how they'd met.

'I hope I meet the man I want to marry when I'm sixteen too,' said Shelagh with a sigh.

Auntie Minnie's playing was so joyous and lively that

soon many of the mental patients would dance and sing just at the sight of her. She became extremely popular with the patients. She hadn't been so popular with those in authority. She'd championed the cause of the poorly fed and underpaid nursing staff, raiding the larder for the benefit of the nurses' dining room. When she was finally summoned to appear before a board of governors, she stated clearly what she thought of the working conditions of the nurses, in particular of the way they were fed. She could afford to speak out, knowing that she could go back home, and managed to effect some slight reforms. Eileen and Shelagh were clearly proud of their Mummy.

'Anyway, Mummy and Daddy were married very soon, so she didn't need to worry about that anymore,' they concluded.

This complicated June's worldview even more; she thought of Grandma Rodger as someone with such a strict code of conduct it was unbearable at times. Yet she'd allowed Auntie Minnie to leave home at sixteen and supported her when she stood up to the hospital board of governors. In effect, she'd encouraged her to criticise and question authority, but maybe she'd been doing that subtly herself too. For example, when she told Grandpa *she* was the neck that allowed his head to function. Life was a jigsaw; when you were little, you thought it only had about half a dozen pieces and when you put them together they made a really simple picture. But when you got older you discovered there were a thousand pieces and when you'd assembled them you had an intricate panorama to contemplate instead!

Compared to Cousins Pat and Helen and Margaret, Cousins Eileen and Shelagh felt more like tearaways. Mummie and Auntie Dolly called them 'madcaps.' Although from what Mummie and Auntie Dolly said—and did—from time to time, June thought this could have been a case of *the kettle calling the saucepan black*. It was Eileen and Shelagh who first thought of going down to the Agnew Crescent beach just when the Larne ferry arrived at midday and lying at the water's edge to let the waves from the ferry wash up their bodies, not just their toes and ankles. She'd always been told to be careful to avoid the wash from the ferry, because it was dangerous and could drag a little girl out of her depths into its cold undercurrent. But they told her she was a Goody-Two-Shoes and a Scaredy-Cat to listen to what her Mummy said now that she was ten. So they went and did that every day, urging one another to lie deeper and deeper in the water, till the pull of the wash dragged them right under then up again for half an hour at a time. June didn't like the sensation; the beach was rough, grey gravel, not soft golden sands, and the stones hurt her back as she lay on them being pulled back and forth. But after a while she enjoyed the danger in giving herself to the elements. She decided that by her age she wasn't going to drown in the cold undertow after all, whatever Mummie and Grandma might say. Besides, Mummie was too busy getting lunch at midday and Grandma didn't come out much anymore, so the risk of their being found playing games of *daring do* with the waves was minimal. Still, she felt a residual guilt. Just as the wash from the ferry pulled her body back and forth, her Presbyterian conscience and newfound daring and adventure pulled her emotions back and forth too.

'Granny and Grandpa live just around the corner from us,' said Shelagh dreamily. 'It's so romantic how they met.' June wanted to hear more.

'You know she'd been living in the Poor House for a while. It was the only way they could get help. Then she got a job as a barmaid in the Liver Inn. She had to move out and get digs then.'

'They found her somewhere cheap. In Bootle. So she had to catch the tram to and from work every day.'

'Even then it was a tough place to live, with lots of dockers and their families in those grimy redbrick buildings.'

'Anyway,' Shelagh continued, 'Grandpa worked down at the docks...'

'He was a marine engineer, you know.'

'...and when he wasn't away at sea, he always caught the tram from Crosby to get to work.'

'And that's how they met.' Her cousins finished the story in unison.

The waves caressed their bodies, dragging their limbs over the abrasive stones some more.

'It was love at first sight,' murmured Shelagh.

Before she knew it, the summer holidays were over. It was the first day of the Autumn Term and she was going into the Lower V, with all the other big girls and boys. And some of the boys were almost twelve because they'd sat through Lower and Upper IV twice over. And when the school year was over they would go out into the world of work, while June and her friends would stay on another year to sit the qualy. Mummie was adamant; June must have the education she'd been deprived of. She'd left school at twelve to help her mother in the home and spent the next thirteen years drowning in domesticity, until grandfather Rodger died of bronchitis in the summer of 1918. Then she'd miraculously found happiness for a few brief years, before the course of her life had been set: she would earn a living doing the one thing she knew how, keeping house for grown men. No way was June going to follow in her footsteps. No, June must take her qualy and go on to Stranraer High School to get the education she'd never had. Then she would have a future, whatever ill fortune came her way.

She was starting to feel very grown-up indeed and very different from the innocent child who had finished Upper IV only six weeks before.

The Great Depression. The National Government of Ramsey MacDonald was failing to solve the problems of mass unemployment. There was little relief and no redress for chronic poverty. The National Unemployed Workers' Movement organised Hunger Marches. They were the only way to intervene in the national debate. On 26 September 1932 marchers left Glasgow. The marchers were greeted by a crowd of about 100,000 upon their arrival at Hyde Park on 27 October 1932.

'I don't think we achieved much out o' it. But we let the people in the whole o' the country know the conditions that were going on as far as we were concerned in Scotland [...]'

Did June overhear Grandma Rodger, Auntie Dolly, Mummie and Lizzie telling the story of the Hunger Marchers as they tramped southward, sometimes welcomed by reception committees that gave them food and shelter for the night, sometimes unwelcomed and lodged in the workhouse, fed on a spike diet of two slices of margarine and tea, and locked in for two days while they earned their keep? Telling the story over and over, feeling sorry for those poor men and their families, knowing the outcome was not in their hands and thanking God for small mercies.

About the time the Hunger Marchers left Glasgow Mummie decided June needed elocution lessons. She would have them from her music teacher, Moira. Now that she knew about Moira and Uncle Ernie, June was fascinated by her and happy to spend an extra hour a week after school there. So one afternoon a week she would go straight from school with her sheets of music and books of scales and arpeggios, another she would arrive with her reading books: the stories of Andrew Lang and the poems of Alfred Lord Tennyson. Both Mummie and Auntie Dolly had Scottish accents, but none of the other Aunts and Uncles did. June could sense that Mummie felt inferior to her siblings; she didn't want June to grow up with the disadvantages she'd had.

What Mummie didn't know was that after Christmas Moira suggested that June learn some of Robbie Burns' poetry in the run up to Burn's Night.

'He's from round here and he's our national poet after all,' opined Moira. 'It would be a shame if you didn't know at least some of his better-known poems by heart.'

Then after Easter, she introduced her to the work of Hugh MacDiarmid and at the tender age of ten June learnt to recite '*Au Clair de la Lune*' and 'In the Hedge-Back'—*It was a wild black nicht.…* . She didn't understand them entirely; they spoke of complicated adult thoughts and emotions. But despite their difficulty she grasped enough of the bittersweet feelings, the loss and fear but also the human determination to find beauty and endure in the face of those elements that wore lives down to nothingness. She couldn't have expressed her glimmering perceptions like that, but she caught enough of the Scot's melancholy and fortitude to give a startling rendition that left Moira suppressing a sob by the end of the month of January. So while the elocution lessons with Moira helped June grow in confidence and enjoy performing, reciting and playacting, and while they allowed her to spend more time with the woman Uncle Ernie really loved, they did little to alter her Galloway accent. If anything Moira taught her to be proud of it and deploy its modulations to the best possible effect. What June really learnt from Moira was that inferiority was in the ear of the listener. She learnt to feel pride in Scottish history and Galloway culture and couldn't understand why Mummie didn't too. Soon she was digging into Grandpa Rodger's complete set of the novels of Sir Walter Scott; that clinched it as far as she was concerned.

There were two cinemas in Stranraer. Mummie and June went out every Friday night to the Kinema; it was their end of week treat. The first three rows at the front were more expensive; Lord and Lady Stair, the local gentry, always sat in the two front seats in the middle. Mummie and June always had the two middle seats, seats 13 and 14, on the first row of the cheaper seats. Mummie preferred the silent movies; the Talkies disappointed her. But June thought they were more exciting and glamorous. She hoped to act in plays when older and this dream contributed to her enjoyment of the elocution lessons.

While afternoons with Moira were a pleasure, June's days in the Lower V felt blighted by their teacher, Miss Kirkpatrick. June was realising how many women of a marriageable age in Stranraer were spinsters. At least Mummie had had her brief happiness before Daddy died, and as she herself said to June, still had June to love and care for. The Great War hadn't only upset Uncle Ernie's and Auntie Annie's chance at true love and happiness; it seemed to have destroyed the hopes and dreams of most of their teachers too. Lots of them had lost boyfriends or fiancés during the War. There weren't enough men to go around afterwards. It didn't help that at least one of them, the bank manager, was besotted with Mummie, even though she didn't seem the least bit interested in him.

June didn't like Miss Kirkpatrick; she thought she was vindictive and unjust. She wouldn't have minded if she told people off when they needed telling off, but Miss Kirkpatrick told people off because she had a terrible temper and couldn't—or wouldn't—control it. Margaret Carnochan was still in June's class; she hadn't been kept down a year with the farm boys, even though she was a bit slow. Maybe this was because she was the niece of Mr Carnochan Esquire, who lived in Agnew Castle. One day, Margaret was being slow as usual. When Miss Kirkpatrick thought she had taken too long to answer she flew into a rage. Margaret was June's friend, so without thinking she stood up and said, 'But Miss Kirkpatrick, she got the answer right.' Miss Kirkpatrick had a ruler, which she always carried in her hand. For her pains she brought the ruler down, smack on the back of June's hand. This did nothing to stop June's deciding to stand up and be counted whenever she saw an injustice in the classroom; if anything, her resolve to stick to her principles and rebel in the cause of fairness was strengthened. She thought about Auntie Minnie standing up to the hospital board of governors when she thought they were unfair and decided that from now on someone should stand up to Miss Kirkpatrick. So, June's experience of the injustice of teachers started young; it would continue through her education. There would be further injustices to follow, but the telling of their story comes later.... For now, there was much excitement in Lower V.

Once a year, Lord and Lady Stair opened the grounds of their estate for the day; it was always on Empire Day, the anniversary of Queen Victoria's birthday. The whole town went to Lochinch Castle to celebrate the dead Queen's birthday. This year the King and Queen were coming and the Lower V had been chosen to dance for them. They practised their eight-some reels after school and lots more complicated country-dances. By the time Empire Day arrived they were step-perfect. On the day itself the women dressed in their finest clothes with their jewels and finery on display. They wanted to see the King—but truth be told, they were more interested in what the Queen would wear. The display was to take place on the Dancing Green, a natural flat area of greensward in a shallow amphitheatre fringed by a shrubbery, near to Castle Kennedy in the Estate grounds: the scene of June's recent encounter with the old gardener. The rhododendrons, the first brought to Europe in the middle of the previous century, were in full bloom. As the class waited in the wings, their nervous anticipation threatening to rise to an uncontrollable crescendo, the luscious, exotic flowers in pinks, reds and subtle creamy colours surrounded them.

He came to the Stair Estate, but his wife didn't come with him. June danced before the King and didn't put a foot wrong despite her nerves. He sat and watched them while they went through their repertoire, from the simplest eight-some reel to ones involving highly complex figures, and smiled and applauded enthusiastically over and over. Afterwards, Mummie and Auntie Dolly and Grandma talked more about the absent Queen than the King and how much he'd appreciated her dancing. According to Grandma, Auntie Dolly and Mummie, *she* was lazy and would get out of things if she could; she was not the gracious queen she was made out to be. But he'd come and sat and watched her. *She'd danced before the King.*

When she died, June's best friend, Betty Gibson, would be buried there at Inch, near Castle Kennedy. But first, we need to tell the story of Betty and June's friendship.

Betty hadn't always lived in Stranraer. Her family moved into a big house near June's end of town in the spring of the Lower V year. Betty had to move schools for four terms before they went on up to the High School. Miss Kirkpatrick thought she would be well behaved and not cause trouble in the classroom since she came from a good home. So she placed her in the spare seat at June's desk. She was petite, pretty and bubbled with vivacity. At breaktime she nearly exploded with laughter over Miss Kirkpatrick's face when she told them all off for being too noisy leaving the room. June warmed to her at once.

'Is she always like that?' Betty asked, still attempting to smother her laughter.

'This is mild,' replied June, 'often she's worse.'

'Well,' with a toss of curls, 'I think she's simply ridiculous.' And Betty stamped her foot for emphasis.

'Mummie says it's because her fiancé was killed in the war.'

'That's no excuse. I bet if he'd survived and they were married now she'd be chiding him for getting up from the breakfast table too noisily to go to work and she'd be frowning at him severely when he came home at the end of the day for not closing the front door quietly enough!'

June admitted she'd got a point; maybe her disappointment had exacerbated things. 'She must have had a vile temper to begin with,' she concurred, 'or else why doesn't every single spinster in Stranraer fly into rages the way she does all the time?'

'Precisely,' agreed Betty. 'I say, what are you doing on Saturday? Would you like to come up to my house after lunch? We could go for a walk with the dogs and then have some tea. I'll ask the kitchen maid to make some of her scones for us.'

The *kitchen* maid? Did Betty's family have more than one maid? Indeed they did, as June discovered that Saturday.

She arrived at the front gates to Encliffe with Guido rushing around everywhere, despite his leash. He immediately set off Bruce, a big black Labrador sitting near the front gates who wasn't on a leash. It could have been a nasty moment. But Betty's father came up and grabbed him by the collar and told him not to be so stupid and that was that. June later learned that Bruce went everywhere with his master and never left his side in the house; a bit like Guido with Mummie.

Betty's father was the road surveyor for Galloway and had a car. Very few people had cars in those days; only doctors, vets and farmers. Although her daddy had driven one when he worked for Uncle Henry, driving round all the farmers taking orders for sheep dip and various other smelly chemical concoctions. Betty's father had a shiny black Austin Rover. He had been out in his driveway polishing it with turtle wax, anyway, so she shouldn't feel embarrassed about Guido's high spirits. He could see he was still a puppy.

'So, you're taking my eldest daughter for a walk are you? I suppose you know all the prettiest places round here.'

June said she loved to walk. There was something about his face, so kind and concerned, that put her at her ease despite his lovely big house with its huge garden that surrounded it on all sides. It looked so well kept and she could see what had to be the gardener in one of the flower borders, on his hands and knees weeding between the peachy-pink camellias, creamy-yellow daffodils and petite, gilded flowers she didn't recognise. Then she noticed it had a tennis court. She should have felt overwhelmed, but somehow he was so open and natural, she found herself telling him how she loved the freedom of walking out of town alone, and now they had Guido, she didn't feel at all afraid even on the loneliest stretches of road. After the confines of the classroom all week, it felt wonderful to breathe the fresh air and see the gorse hedgerows dotted with shy primroses. She didn't tell him how even walking a short distance could leave her slightly breathless and that the school nurse had said she was anaemic and her mother should feed her more red meat. *As if they could afford to eat beef every week.*

Then Betty came running out to greet her. She looked so dainty in a pretty pink flowered dress with a matching mohair cardigan. Her blonde hair was neatly arranged in gorgeous curls and her rose-coloured mouth broke from a slight pout into a glorious smile as she gave June a hug and bent to pet Guido. He lay down with his legs in the air letting her rub his tummy in a way he never did for June. But June forgave her. She would forgive her anything.

They had three dogs: as well as Bruce there was Danny and Daisy, two little cocker spaniels. They put them on leashes and formally introduced them to Guido and set off for their walk. They walked all afternoon, but June didn't even feel breathless. Her heart didn't do that funny thing it sometimes did when she got over-tired or too excited. They walked through the fields and round the edge of the wood where they could see the shiny green leaves of the native bluebells emerging beneath the still bare branches of the trees. They had walked most of the way back to town before they realised how late it was. Then they decided to cut through the cemetery back to Betty's house for freshly baked scones, homemade strawberry jam and whipped cream. No, her heart didn't do that funny thing, but something else happened to June that afternoon: she lost her heart to Betty Gibson. She knew that her coming to live in Stranraer had changed everything. Her world would never be the same.

At the end of her life, June would reminisce.

Then at some point my dearest friend, Betty Gibson, came to live at our end of town. But it made a big difference to my life.

That was all she would say. But she could still remember that first afternoon and the sense that her joy would spill over when they stood on Gallows Hill above the town and Betty said, 'We must do this every Saturday. Agreed?' It was agreed.

A 'fairy' wood covered the hill behind the town; it became their magic place. As the spring edged towards summer one end was transformed by a mass of bluebells. They told one another stories of the little people, the fairies, living there and making themselves fairy gowns from the flowers. Even though they were grown-up enough to know that this was all make-believe. But it was shared make-believe; it was their secret world and glorious. Then later in the summer when all the bluebells faded and the leaves were full on the trees, there were wonderful toadstools. They told themselves these were the entranceways to the fairy kingdom.

'But it should be a *queendom,*' mused June one Saturday, 'because it's always ruled by the Fairy Queen.'

'I wonder what it's like to be ruled by a woman,' pondered Betty after a while.

June thought about this. 'Like living at my house with Grandma Rodger,' she decided eventually.

'How does that feel; a house full of three generations of women?'

'Well, there's Fred and the other boarders. But, somehow, they don't really count.'

'But it's Fred's house, isn't it?'

'No, it's Mummie's now. He says he didn't want to wait till he died and left it her in his will. He says he's glad it's all sorted already and that he doesn't have to worry about that. He says he doesn't want his mean sister and her banker husband laying their hands on it.'

'Why not?'

'Mummie does everything for him; I think he feels his sister betrayed him when she moved away.'

'What do you mean, betrayed?'

'I'm not sure. Maybe he resents her being married when he never did and now he can't because he's blind.'

'But it's natural to want to marry, isn't it? That's what women do. I mean if you get married before me, I won't feel you've betrayed me; it's the way it is.' But somehow Betty didn't sound totally convinced.

A pattern was established. Every Saturday whenever possible Betty and June would walk their dogs up the fields over Gallows Hill, through the wood to the other side, down to Agnew Park, then back to Encliffe. For some reason—if asked they couldn't have told you why—they always cut through Glebe Cemetery on the way back to Betty's for high tea. They always paused at Grandpa's grave.

In Loving Memory of Our Dear Father
WESLEY ALLAN RODGER
1847-1918

The headstone was eloquent in its simplicity. It sat upright on the grass in the shape of a scroll. There was a blank space below the inscription and a roll of stone at the bottom waiting to unfurl the names of future generations. *Was this all that remained?*

Betty would hold June's hand in hers for a moment or two, before they carried on up the hill.

In all her life, this was June's most important female friendship. Surprising really, given the disparity of class. It didn't matter; they became firm friends. Until her wedding day no one else held quite the same place in June's heart; possibly even after.

The summer term lasted half a lifetime, but now June had Betty she didn't mind. After the dead Queen's birthday it felt as if time had turned a corner. The potato harvest began: the first earlies, then the second earlies. The most important was the first earlies; all the farmers wanted to get their crop to market before the Ayrshire crops came in. The tattie howkers came over in big squads from Ireland and slept in the farmers' barns, women, children and all. But one local family always tattie howked at Challock Farm: Hamish McCutcheon and his squad of children. Earlier in the year they'd helped with the planting and on the days June woke early she'd catch a glimpse of them at the top of the road, trailing out of the town by the light of the false dawn. The harvest was an essential part of their income. If one or two of the younger children spent their time dragging their feet after the soil had been turned and the potatoes picked up—and just maybe finding enough potatoes between them for an evening meal for the whole family—none of the farmers seemed to notice. When June was little she'd heard Grandma Rodger say to one of them that God would reward them for turning a blind eye. She'd puzzled for days trying to work out whose eye was blind and how turning it would help. But now she knew that this was how the McCutcheon family survived and she began to appreciate that this was how communities survived as well. There were times, such as these depression years, when to turn a blind eye was the best way to leave a man a remnant of dignity.

The McCutcheons lived further back from the sea, in a pokey house at the end of the High Street. Once a year—*only the Lord knows why, it was always around the longest day when you'd think she'd be feeling a bit better in herself*—Mrs McCutcheon would walk down King Street past June's house to the harbour. By the time she was eleven June was half expecting to see her each day. She looked out for her soon after they'd danced before the King, but a month went by before, on cue, she appeared one morning before June left for school. No one saw her to begin with; it was so early the street was still deserted. It just so happened it was June who put her head outside the front door to see if the milkman's cart was up the street yet. Instead, she saw Mrs McCutcheon's back disappearing towards Agnew Crescent and the beach. She felt a frisson of excitement and then felt heartily ashamed. *The poor wee woman's about to kill herself and you're treating it like a Saturday matinee performance*, she heard a voice in her head say. *But who best to tell?* Mr Pat McKinlay, of course.

She dashed across the road to his house, dressed in nothing more than her nightie and dressing-gown, and knocked violently on his front door knocker, shouting, 'Mr McKinlay, come quickly. Oh, please come quickly, Mr McKinlay!' He came rushing to the door in response to her urgency. Lots of other front doors were opening to see what the kerfuffle was about. 'It's Mrs McCutcheon, Mr McKinlay: she's gone down to the Loch already!'

She didn't have to explain; everyone in the street who heard her understood the gravity of the situation. By now Mrs Murray and her daughter were on their front doorstep. The latter rushed inside shouting to her current eldest orphan, Angela, to run to the priest's house and *fetch him quick, girl,* before snatching a hat from the hat-stand by her front door and setting off to fetch the doctor herself. By now Mrs McCutcheon had descended the beach and was calmly walking into the Loch and out into the sea. This had to be her thirteenth attempt at least to commit suicide, seeing as she had tried regularly once a year since her first-born came along. But Mr Pat McKinlay was a strong swimmer and if he could grapple a cow or a horse he could certainly grapple the resisting body of this worn-out woman.

June stood at the top of the strand ignoring Grandma Rodger's insistent command to go back home and make herself decent first. She watched in fascination as the vet caught up the corpse-like, drowning woman, turned her onto her back, held her head above water and swam a vigorous backstroke back to land. He carried her briskly up the beach and laid her gently on the pebbly grey strand. Her face was the same colour as the sand. He set to work pumping her heart and giving her mouth-to-mouth. By the time Annie Murray arrived with the doctor and his doctor's bag and Annie's eldest, Angela, arrived with the priest and his little crucifix, Mrs Hamish McCutcheon was coughing, spluttering and crying her heart out. As soon as breakfast was done and she was respectably dressed in her black bombazine, Grandma would be round to spend the day supervising the women folk who would turn out to help her: to look after the hoard of children, clean the house from top to bottom, offer what pieces of comfort and advice they could and show her that they did care, even if they couldn't be in her shoes every day of the year. As June would say near the end of her life:

She never succeeded; someone always rescued her.

Wednesday evening, June had lingered too long in the playground again. Now she must hurry to finish her piano practice before the boarders came home and she got flustered by their theatrical creeping around on tiptoe. She was trying to learn the whole of Samuel Taylor Coleridge's 'To a Wild Rose' that Mummie could play so poignantly. Maybe that was where the misunderstanding arose. She hadn't quite finished when Mr Hetherington entered. She felt the muscles in her shoulder blades tighten, but carried on to the end and for once got through without faltering. She later thought he couldn't have been really listening; he must have half heard her and in his head heard it played the way Mummie did—perfectly.

Whatever the reason, the following morning at breakfast he said, 'Well June, it's about time you and I played a duet, isn't it?'

Her mouth was full of fresh bread roll, butter and rhubarb jam; she had an excuse not to reply straight away.

'What a good idea,' she heard Auntie Dolly say. 'What were you thinking of playing?'

There followed a long discussion on the relative merits of Bach, Debussy and Ravel when it came to flute and piano duets. Auntie Dolly dismissed them all as too demanding to begin with.

So Mr Hetherington racked his brains for a minute then suggested, 'Fauré,' while June hurriedly finished her roll and got up from the breakfast table to get ready for school.

'That's settled then,' she heard Mr Hetherington say to her retreating back. 'The Sicilienne it is. Shall we start this evening when I get in?'

This wasn't really a question, but a statement of fact. She mumbled a half-hearted reply and set off for school.

That evening she'd just finished her piano practice when Mr Hetherington appeared in the lounge, carrying sheets of music. She was seated on the piano stool. He leaned both arms around her to set the first one up on the piano stand. She could feel the heat emanating from his body and the deep musky smell from beneath his clothes. She felt flustered already.

He stepped back and said nonchalantly, 'You can sight-read, can't you June? But take a look at this piano part while I sort out my flute. I might need to warm it up a bit before it's properly in tune.'

Depending on what Moira gave her she *could* sight-read, but to be expected to sight-read and keep up with his flute was deeply unfair. *Why didn't she just say so? What kept her so mute?* She didn't know this piece by Fauré that he'd chosen. She wished she could at least hear how it ought to be played before putting her hands on the keyboard, with him watching them while he busied with his flute. She got halfway down the first page, hesitant and faltering, until she came to bar after bar of arpeggios and halted.

'Let me play you the flute part to warm up, if you don't mind,' he suggested.

He leaned into her to read the music over her shoulder, the end of his flute nearly brushing her hair. The music was wistful, evocative, sensuous and elusive. It conjured disturbing images of places she'd never been and scenarios she'd never seen. *How could she possibly do justice to this strange, grown-up music that spoke of things she wouldn't dare to even dream of?*

When Guido Bonugli entered the room he murmured, 'Perhaps it's a bit too soon for us to have an audience without even a run through. When you've left for Plymouth, Guido, we'll have plenty of time to practice together without being overheard.'

Guido looked troubled, but didn't say anything in front of June. Mr Hetherington proceeded to put his flute away in its case while they chatted about how Marconi had been made President of the Royal Academy in Italy and how he'd received the John Scott medal by wireless from Philadelphia. Guido voiced his concerns about Marconi's fascism. It troubled him. 'It's baloney what he says;' he spluttered, 'to join electric rays in a bundle, is nothing like what Mussolini's doing in Italy with his Black Shirts. He compares his discoveries with Mussolini's merging the country into a bundle for the greater greatness of Italy, but a lot of my family are getting squeezed in that bundle.' Guido looked even more troubled.

Maybe Mr Hetherington sensed her trouble and decided to desist, or maybe when they retired to their shared attic bedroom for the night Guido Bonugli said something to him. Either way, Mr Hetherington never did bring out the Fauré for June to accompany him again and never uttered a word more about his urge to have them play duets.

On Saturdays when it was not possible to go for a walk because the weather was just too poor to venture far, June and Betty went to the cinema. June always had enough money for a bar of chocolate; for tuppence she could have a Fry's Turkish Delight or a Cadbury's Dairy Milk Chocolate bar. It was usually the latter. Mummie was distressed that she and June stopped going together, but she didn't try to stop June from growing up. Besides she and Betty would start Girl Guides together at the end of the summer when they went up to High School; that was on a Friday night too. Gradually she drifted further and further away from Mummie. Betty was her best pal now.

One Saturday they'd been to watch *Little Women* with Katherine Hepburn as Jo.

'I don't care what anyone says,' stormed June, 'I think she's brilliant.'

'But you couldn't call her pretty like Amy.'

'I wonder if I'm related to her.'

'You don't look much like her.'

'Don't I just.'

They went into Mummie's room, sat down and stared at their reflections in the mirror. 'I think those fringes were silly. I'm never going to have a fringe again.'

Betty demurred. 'Joan Bennett looks more glamorous without a fringe, but she looked pretty with one.'

Once the issue of fringes was resolved they snuck into the boarders' lounge. June loved to hear Betty play the piano. Even at eleven she was an accomplished pianist in comparison with June. She sat down to her daily piano practice willingly and told June how good that time at the keyboard always felt; she said *it was like becoming a fairy and being able to fly for a while.* June didn't quite understand this about Betty; she dragged her feet reluctantly up to the boarders' lounge each afternoon after school hoping no one would be there to listen to her mistaken arpeggios and faltering chords. Now Betty played to her heart's content while June curled on the window seat, watched the rain trickle down the window panes and wondered if she could ask Uncle Eddie and Auntie Mary to give her *Little Women* for Christmas.

June didn't only spend time with Betty. Friends were important to her; sometimes when she was restless and couldn't settle to a comic or a book she would seek out other friends after school. She knew that Margaret was always happy to play; they would walk all along Agnew Crescent as far as the lovely houses beyond it. Margaret's uncle, Mr Carnochan Esquire, lived at the end of the crescent in Agnew Castle. It wasn't really a castle, not like Castle Kennedy or Lochnaw Castle out to the west where the Agnews lived, but it had tall chimneys that looked like turrets and a maze of corridors and rooms where Margaret and June were allowed to explore. Margaret's uncle knew the Agnews well. The previous baronet, Sir Andrew, had been an officer in the Territorial Army. Soon after he'd married he'd commissioned a famous American artist to paint a portrait of his wife, Gertrude. June was fascinated by this. Would she ever have a husband who lived in a castle and owned French eighteenth-century furniture and beautiful exotic furnishings? How lovely to possess the time to sit in your prettiest gown, converse with the artist and have your beautiful image preserved for posterity.

'She was a beauty, that's for sure,' Margaret's uncle pronounced when she questioned him about the painting. 'And quite a lively lass with it. You can see that in the painting. There's always something about her look. You feel as if she's gazing at you and appraising you. Although she never actually made any personal comments about anyone; it's not generally known but she was just recovering from the flu when she sat for her portrait. To my mind it makes her look slightly languid.'

'I wish I could be as elegant as she was,' sighed June.

'It's not so hard when you have no children to look after,' opined Margaret's aunt.

Later June asked Margaret, 'If Lady Agnew didn't have any children who's the Baronet now?'

As usual Margaret was vague on details. Her uncle overheard them and being in an extremely good mood that afternoon, told them all about the 10th Baronet Agnew.

'He's a totally different kettle of fish from his uncle. You know he ran away from school to join the army, when he was seventeen. Caused no end of problems for his father. And then, it must have been about the time you two were babies, he set off on an expedition to cross the Atlantic. If that wasn't enough, he jumped ship in San Francisco. He worked in Hollywood. You've probably seen him at the cinema, June, without realising. He was an extra in lots of movies. He drove a chariot in *Ben Hur*.'

June was amazed. The film had been spectacular. For once she had agreed with Mummie that silent films could be breath-taking. And this one had been in colour, which had transformed everything. Grandma had expressed doubts about her being allowed to see it because she thought it was blasphemous to depict Christ. But Mummie had insisted, saying that it was a very moral film. June wasn't so sure about that, but it had been thrilling.

'Yes, he's a different kettle of fish, alright. Different views on most things. He's tried his hand at farming, but he's a restless soul. Always travelling, always visiting new places. I'd say he's got a deep love of the earth.'

June wondered what he meant, but Margaret's uncle thought the conversation had ended and wandered off back to his library.

She mulled this over for days. Maybe 'nature' wasn't all disgust and filth. Nature was setting out early on holiday mornings, walking along Agnew Crescent and past Mr Carnochan Esquire's, till the grassy bank where primroses grew. Nature was swathes of snowdrops in early spring and later bluebell woods with their air of fairy magic. Nature was the brilliant yellow of gorse on the hillsides, their scent a rich, wild version of vanilla ice cream. Nature was the fresh, restorative fragrance of the lavender she gathered in her basket for Auntie Dolly to dry and sew into sachets to hang in the wardrobes. Nature was hot summer days when a gang of friends and cousins would strap bathing-costumes on the back of bikes and cycle along the Shore Road, strip and plunge into Loch Ryan.

Then the day came when she took off her white costume with a red stripe across the hips and found she had started her first period. With the early onset of her monthlies her dream world of elegant society women in white dresses with lilac sashes dreamily staring into the eyes of an exotic artist who had been born in Rome was turned upside down. Nature and human nature had just become a much more complex process than she had ever imagined.

Late summer 1933, Duff Cooper and his beautiful actress wife, Diana, who starred in *The Miracle*, went on a motoring tour through Germany. They noticed that everywhere all the men fit to bear arms were dressed in military uniform, as had been the case in Britain fifteen years before. They nearly had an interview with Herr Hitler, but he felt fatigued after writing his speech for the Nuremberg Rally and instead they were presented with tickets for the rally, which they attended the following day. They found Hitler's speech so tedious that they left before the end. *The Illustrated London News* and *The Scotsman* covered the rally. Rumours of war didn't form part of my mother's memories of this time. Her battles were fought closer to home.

When I got my beautiful book back, Margaret's little sister, Betty, had scribbled all over it in Biro. I think my teacher was motivated by spite. Her name was Agnes Smith. She was a spinster. Mummie was a beautiful widow with a few gentlemen friends. Auntie Dolly was a striking beauty and a gifted pianist. She could play 'Dizzy Fingers' perfectly by ear. We had a hard time in Stranraer.

Now they had a minister of their own again. His energy and enthusiasm was reinvigorating his congregation. He challenged everyone to do more; to search deep in themselves and discover what buried talents they could bring to the church community and to God. A fervour swept through the church like a south-westerly blowing across from Portpatrick. His inspiration even blew as far as Sunday School.

Sunday School was the domain of women. Its mainstay was Miss Smith. Her first name was Agnes, the same as Miss Lamb from the Academy. Miss Lamb was true to her appellation; she was mild, gentle, adorable. Miss Smith was bony angles and nervous energy. She was quick and undoubtedly clever with an imperious impatience. June never found out what had happened to Agnes Smith. Like Auntie Dolly she had gone up to Glasgow, although she hadn't studied at the Athenaeum. Like Auntie Dolly she had returned home to Stranraer. Having had that exciting glimpse of cosmopolitan culture—for Glasgow was a vortex of intellectual activity at the turn of the century—they both felt stifled by the small-town attitudes back at home with sharpened cognizance. That was where the resemblance ceased, as June found to her cost.

One Sunday not long after the start of term, Miss Smith announced that they would do *Alice in Wonderland* for their Christmas play. They were to perform the theatrical version by Henry Savile Clarke. During her Glasgow years Miss Smith had performed Alice in it. She had learnt all two hundred and fifteen speeches; never once in a week's run had she needed a prompt. She didn't expect them to manage as well as she had; they would just perform the first half, based loosely on the *Alice in Wonderland* book. It was more a pantomime than a play; there would be a lot of singing and dancing to be rehearsed as well as the dialogues. She had enlisted the assistance of Charlie, June's music teacher's brother. June and Betty were convinced she had a crush on Charlie and that was why she had decided to do a musical production. He turned out to be brilliant as a music coach but not the slightest bit interested in Miss Agnes Smith.

Auditions were held the following Sunday during Sunday School. A lot of the children were already filled with trepidation knowing they'd never match up to Miss Smith's brilliance. But there was excitement and anticipation. Who would get to play Alice? June wondered if she'd get the part and, if so, would Chummy play Dinah? She was a good actress and she knew the book better than Betty even. When they went to the sheriff's clerk's house for the first rehearsal June gallantly offered to bring both her copies of *Alice* for them to use: her beautiful, illustrated edition as well as her old, tatty copy from Lizzie.

The following Saturday afternoon Miss Smith held the first rehearsal at Moira's and Charlie's house. The way she behaved you'd have thought the house belonged to Miss Smith, not to the Stranraer Sheriff's Clerk. June felt at home at Moira's and always came away from there happier than when she'd arrived. But not that afternoon. It transpired June hadn't needed to bring her precious books:

110

Miss Smith had enough copies of the play to go around as long as some people shared. Margaret Carnochan and her little sister (another Betty) would share for instance. Miss Smith started by allotting the parts. June was the Mad Hatter. Betty was Alice. Margaret Carnochan would play Bill the Lizard. Margaret's little sister, Betty, was the Dormouse. *Of course, Betty was chosen to play Alice; who else in Stranraer was pretty enough.* June secretly agreed with Miss Smith's discerning taste, while hating that she'd cast her as the Mad Hatter. *Was it because of her prominent teeth?* She didn't look that much like the illustration in her book—'the March Hare and the Hatter were having tea'—did she? *And it was cruelty that Margaret Carnochan was the hapless Bill. The audience would laugh at Margaret, not at Bill the Lizard.* June felt full of moral outrage and indignation at the way they had all been type cast.

Miss Smith and Charlie needed a few moments to discuss how they would proceed. In the meantime, could June show everyone the illustrations in her book? So the children crowded round her and pored over the beautiful illustrations, as she carefully announced each quotation then lifted each sheet of fine Indian tissue paper in turn to show them all the curious characters in Alice's curious world. Then she put it to one side and joined enthusiastically as Charlie and Miss Smith rehearsed the opening scene, in which everyone except Betty would sing:

Sleep, maiden, sleep! as we circle around thee,
Lulled by the music of bird and of bee,
Safe in the forest since fairies have found thee
Here where we come to keep tryst by the tree.
Sleep, Alice sleep! these are magical numbers,
Songs that we learnt from the mount and the stream.
Ours be the task, to keep watch o'er thy slumbers,
Wake, Alice, wake to the Wonderland dream.

June couldn't help thinking that this was a travesty of the opening chapter, which was brilliant because you couldn't be sure whether Alice was asleep or wide awake when she followed the White Rabbit down the rabbit hole. But she had to admit she enjoyed singing and dancing. She started to plan what costume Auntie Dolly could make her for the part of a fairy. She could rely on Auntie Dolly to make the perfect Mad Hatter's costume as well. As the afternoon drew to a close Miss Smith exhorted them all to learn their parts carefully before next week.

'Mind, now! I expect you all to be word perfect so that we can concentrate on your performance and delivery. We've got plenty of time till Christmas, but this is a very demanding piece and we can't have any shilly-shallying around it.'

When it was time to leave Miss Smith gave June's illustrated, Centennial Edition to Margaret and her little sister to take home with them. 'I'm sure you can spare it for a week, June,' she said. 'It will help wee Betty no end to look at the pictures.'

June couldn't think of anything to say and returned to King Street with her old, frayed, clothbound edition.

Next Sunday they had Sunday School, as usual in the morning, then a rehearsal all afternoon. That would be the pattern throughout the autumn term. Mummie invited Betty to stay and share Sunday lunch with them. June was embarrassed that her mother served such tiny slivers of the roast to everyone. But she more than compensated with her Yorkshire pudding that always rose magnificently and with loads of roast tatties. When they got back to the Church Hall everyone had brought their copies with them. June was relieved to see that Margaret had bought her beautiful book back to return to her. She rushed over to her to retrieve it. Margaret held it out with her eyes averted. She mumbled something about little Betty being silly as usual and shuffled away.

Norah was playing the Duchess and Miss Smith decided to rehearse her part with her. June had time to sit and flip through her beautiful book while they watched. As she turned the pages her heart skipped its beat. Not once but repeatedly. Arrhythmia set in as her heart raced, staggered and tumbled. She felt dizzy and could hardly catch her breath. Her cheeks blanched and blushed, blushed and blanched. Her front teeth bit deep into her lower lip. *She was heartbroken. And it was all Agnes Smith's doing.* If she had felt moral outrage and indignation at Miss Smith's typecasting the previous weekend, there were no words left to express how devastated she felt now. The woman had torn her world apart, as surely as little Betty had torn 'Bill the Lizard,' 'The King and Queen of Hearts in dispute with The Executioner,' and 'The King and Queen of Hearts seated on their thrones.' Moreover, little Betty had utterly destroyed 'The White Rabbit splendidly dressed, came trotting along in a great hurry' and 'The Cook at once set to work throwing every thing within her reach at the Duchess and the Baby'. All that was left was shreds of tissue paper and tatters of the page on which the illustrations had been mounted. Miss Smith had snatched June's precious world of Alice and without lifting a finger, ravaged it.

When Betty's father came to collect her June was still pale, shaken and breathless. He saw at once something wasn't right and insisted he give her a lift home. Once inside the front door she finally broke down and sobbed her heart out. Grandma Rodger emerged from her room with alacrity and swept her into her arms. There wasn't a hint of reproach or disapproval.

'There, there, June. There, there. You're home now.'

She stroked her hair and caressed her back over and over. Mummie and Auntie Dolly came running from the kitchen and clustered round. Eventually her sobs subsided enough for her to breath properly. Grandma Rodger released her from her starched bombazine bosom and handed her to Mummie. She was hugged even tighter in her soft and ample bosom while Auntie Dolly was sent for a glass of water for her to sip, *ever so slowly*.

Later around the tea table over drop scones and griddle cakes with rhubarb jam, the Rodger's women mulled over and digested the implications of Miss Agnes Smith's spitefulness.

'Whatever she might say, she knew what she was doing all right, sending your precious *Alice* back with Margaret and Betty Carnochan.'

'She might be holier than thou, running the Sunday School single handed, but she's a spiteful, bitter old maid.'

'She wasn't always like that. Life's been cruel to her.'

'That's no reason for her to be cruel to June.'

113

'She's jealous, of course. She lost her one chance of happiness and she hates us for ours.'

'Happiness! Am I happy now?'

'You had Sandy; you've got your memories. She can't take those away from you. And you've got three men all head over heels in love with you.'

Here grandma couldn't quite repress her customary sniff of disapprobation.

'I'd swap them all to have Sandy back. My happiness is in the past, yours is in the future. That's another reason for her to be jealous. You're marrying Birrell next summer.'

'What bothers me is that she can get away with it. There's nothing we can do. The town would take her side if we made a big fuss about it.'

'I hate this town. Everyone's so petty-minded.'

'Don't worry; you'll be leaving to set up home in Dumfries. But we'll still be here pretending we don't hear the mean-mouthed gossips.' Then Mummie turned to June. 'There's nothing to be done, June. You must maintain your dignity and not let on she's hurt you.'

'Hurt me! She's destroyed my childhood!'

'We'll get out the Sellotape and patch up the pictures as best we can.'

'And Mr Hetherington will help; he's first-rate with those fiddly tasks.'

'As for the rest, you'll just have to hold onto them in your mind's eye.'

And that's what she did until the day she died.

Now come the difficult years, the stories of how her life was affected by boys and men, men and boys. The years between eleven and eighteen; the years that led to the Second World War.

Betty and June joined Girl Guides at the very moment The Girl Guides Association for Scotland was established with its own constitution. They were eleven and Girl Guides were just under a quarter of a century old. To be a Girl Guide was to be modern; the movement had been founded in 1910 after a group of young women had appeared at a

Boy Scouts Rally the previous year calling themselves Girl Scouts. This was about being taken seriously. It was about universal suffrage. It was about challenging the restrictions on women that had held back Mummie, even if they hadn't held back Auntie Minnie. It was about being part of an international movement, not just parochial. June soon realised it was about receiving a training in citizenship and preparing yourself to participate actively in political and social life. It was a modern approach to equipping yourself with the skills you would need to serve the community. As each successive Friday night came and went the 'community' expanded in your imagination to become international. These were heady times and Friday nights at Girl Guides conferred on you a sense of importance beyond the cosy companionship you'd shared with Mummie as you'd gone to the pictures together when you were still a child.

They learnt to say the promise every week and recite the law. June preferred some parts of the law to others. She felt proud that a guide's honour was to be trusted, a guide was loyal, a guide's duty was to be useful and help others, a guide was a friend to all and a sister to every other guide. She had no problem with 'a Guide is courteous' and 'a Guide is a friend to animals,' so long as that didn't include mice. But she found more problematic 'a Guide obeys orders,' if they came from someone you despised like Agnes Smith. And 'a Guide smiles and sings under all difficulties' smacked of making the best of a bad job, rather than striving to change things for the better. Mummie and Auntie Dolly were welcome to do that, but she believed society should be made fairer; a woman who was widowed through no fault of her own shouldn't have to live in penury and risk becoming a social outcast amongst the more respectable gentry class of her home town. She could see the point of 'a Guide is thrifty'—there was no point wasting your money whether you were rich or poor, but when she grew up and left home she hoped she'd earn enough to afford a few more luxuries than Mummie managed. And then there was that final law: 'a Guide is pure in thought, in word and in deed.' She wondered what 'pure' meant in that context. Was it another way of saying naïve and gullible rather than worldly wise? If so, she wasn't sure how 'modern' that law was. The Boy Scouts' version was similar, but somehow it suggested that boys were manly, whereas theirs implied that girls were weak. And she had no intention of remaining naïve nor gullible for very much longer.

Guides was held at St Ninian's church hall next door to the Sheriff's Court and not far from school. So that autumn Betty and June started a tradition. Every Friday night after Guides, Betty and June would walk back down to the town centre and get something to eat. In winter they would have a fourpenny fish supper from the fish shop in Queen Street. They were closer than ever now. Even when Betty admitted feeling slightly shocked by her outspokenness, June loved sharing the rebellious thoughts that played on her mind over the delicious battered cod and generous portion of freshly fried chips doused in salt and vinegar. She enjoyed thinking out loud in Betty's company. Betty was an attentive, appreciative listener. One theme June developed over that autumn and winter of 1933 to 1934 was: 'what do we mean by "Nature?"' It began because they were both in the Pigeon Patrol. She told Betty how she'd learnt to hate pigeons as a young child, how they were associated with dirt and disease in Grandma Rodger's mind and how she'd learnt to adopt this attitude unconsciously.

'In my mind they go with all those visits to Grandpa Rodger's poor parishioners. Their houses were always smelly and insalubrious.' She'd learnt this word quite recently and relished the opportunity to use it nonchalantly. 'And now,' she continued, 'we're sworn to be a friend to animals, including birds I suppose. Otherwise why would our patrol be called Pigeon Patrol? But they're still disease-bearing pests, aren't they? I wouldn't mind if we were in the Swallow Patrol or even in the Sparrows. Trust our luck to end up a Pigeon.'

Her dismay was mitigated somewhat the following year when she was made the Patrol Leader. She felt proud to be a leader and enjoyed telling the other patrol members what to do more than she dared admit even to herself, let alone to Betty. Besides, Grandma Rodger no longer seemed a formidable figure of authority commanding her respect.

She no longer rose at the crack of dawn and appeared fully clothed, laced and polished for the day at the breakfast table. Some days she even had a cup of tea and a piece of toast in bed before she finally got up. She didn't go out on her weekly rounds to Grandpa's poor parishioners anymore and there were times when no amount of Eau de Cologne could disguise the fact that she smelt positively musty. She was diminished in many ways; she had visibly shrunk and moved slowly and stiffly, even though it seemed just yesterday she had a back like a ramrod and her every movement was brisk and purposeful. At times June could barely contain her impatience at her dithering, although June berated herself afterwards for being so harsh to the Grandma who had loved and cared for her more consistently than Mummie through her childhood. So gradually the Pigeon Patrol changed from a source of annoyance into a badge of pride to be added to the material badges she was earning and sewing onto her uniform as the months passed by.

When spring turned to summer, they stopped going to the fish shop and patronised Mr Bonugli's ice cream parlour instead. After Guides June would lead those who could afford it along Fisher Street and into Bonugli's, where they would gather for ice cream sodas. They felt frightfully sophisticated and modern. June was still philosophising on the dual nature of Nature. She hadn't lost her fear and disgust at its messiness and how it could demean you, but in the aftermath of Jenny Paravensi's exhortations to appreciate the natural world and to allow your mind and body to develop in harmony with it, she would wax lyrical on the benefits of fresh air, hiking and swimming. Jenny Paravensi ran the Girl Guides. She lived with her mother. Her method of coping with spinsterhood was different and she was whole-heartedly energetic, determined to prove to the world—and possibly herself—how little a single woman needed a man. She was determined to acquire every survival skill, so she would never be beholden to a man. She was equally determined that her pack of Girl Guides would do the same and grow up self-reliant and to be relied upon in times of a crisis. One evening Jenny told them about how the Girl Guides had helped during the Great War. She herself had led patrols that collected sphagnum moss, which was used to cover and treat war wounds. And although it was top secret she could personally avouch for the fact that Girl Guides had been found to be more trustworthy than boys in delivering important messages for the Secret Service Bureau. 'Remember girls, above all "Be Prepared!" Who knows but the way things are going in Germany you too may be called upon to undertake top-secret military intelligence missions.'

Over a month of Friday night ice cream sodas June warmed to her theme. 'Be prepared' was the secular equivalent of Grandma Rodger's 'serving the community.' But they wouldn't just serve a parish; they would serve the Nation or maybe even the newly formed League of Nations. It had been born just before they were; they were the first generation to inhabit this brave new international world of peace. She would go so much further than her beloved grandmother. For as Grandma was getting visibly frail, June realised how much she owed to this indomitable old lady. Indeed, how much she adored her for all her pursed lips and stiff black bombazine. She ardently wished she would be as spirited as Grandma when she grew up and that eventually her future husband would fall head over heels in love with her—though maybe not while skating—but as romantically as Grandpa had fallen for Emily Annie Ormrod all those years ago. Maybe not when she was twenty; maybe after she'd first served King and country or the entire Free World for a few glorious years.

That summer they would go on their first Guides' camping holiday at Stair Haven on Luce Bay. Throughout the summer term Friday nights were dedicated to learning outdoor skills. They would have to dig latrines, build fires and cook all their meals on them. They learnt what types of wood they should collect and what to leave alone. They spent hours learning to identify edible plants and even more importantly those that were toxic. They were going to camp very near the shore; they would be able to bathe in the sea every day to keep clean. They would collect their drinking water from the well at the Fisherman's Cottage; Jenny had already arranged this with the fisherman's wife. They went over what kit they would need and what not to bring. And they spent hours not only at Guides' meeting, but in odd times during the rest of the week sewing and knitting as much of their kit as they could, for few of them had that much money to spare to buy it new.

Jenny Paravensi organised their palliasses; it was rumoured they were the same ones that the tattie howkers slept on at Whitecairn Farm. Wisely, perhaps, Jenny Paravensi wouldn't confirm or deny it. She also arranged their transport, inveigling the dairyman to transport the girls and their kit from the Church Hall to Luce Bay after he'd finished his morning round. It took him most of the morning, since he had to make four trips there and back before he was finally done.

It was the start of the summer holidays; they would spend two weeks at Luce Bay living in the open air and fending for themselves. June was in charge of her patrol and was to keep a sharp eye on the younger ones. She was amongst the first dray-load to be transported.

'Mind now, sit very still and don't any of ye girls be peering over the edge as you go, in case a sudden jolt throws you into the track!' warned Jenny as they set off up King Street.

And they minded her. The first day was spent setting up camp: digging the latrines, putting up the canvas shelter around them, putting up their patrol tents, which slept six and were also made of waxed canvas, organising their palliasses, erecting trestle tables for their food preparation, heaving great bucket-loads of water from the well and peeling a sack-load of tatties. They would be peeling many more before the first week was out. Their diet consisted mainly of lumpy porridge—it was impossible to get it thick, creamy and smooth the way Grandma and Auntie Dolly made it, loads of oat cakes—because they kept better than fresh bread and heaps of boiled tatties. In addition Jenny had arranged for them to go and collect as many eggs as her hens would lay from the farmer's wife who lived at the top of the track above the haven. They had various other root vegetables in big nets but very little in the way of fruit. However Jenny had instructed everyone to bring a pot of homemade jam. June was glad she had; she craved its sweetness by the time they settled to their early tea.

Although she wouldn't have whispered this to anyone, not even Betty, she felt a bit homesick by the end of the first day. It rained softly in the night. There was a strange rustling around their tent. As she listened to the waves lapping on the shoreline she wasn't sure if they were lulling her to sleep or inviting her into a realm of nightmares.

The drizzle cleared early the following morning. As she sipped sweet tea from her enamel cup, June felt braver. The sun rose higher in the east and warmed her chill bones. That first Sunday morning they dressed in their parade uniform and marched in formation up to Luce Valley Church. The pastor knew they were coming and had prepared his sermon accordingly.

'I take as my text,' he pronounced, 'Matthew Chapter 6: verses 25 to 30. *Therefore I say unto you, Take no thought for your life, what ye shall eat, or what ye shall drink; nor yet for your body, what ye shall put on. Is not the life more than meat, and the body than raiment? Behold the fowls of the air: for they sow not, neither do they reap, nor gather into barns; yet your heavenly Father feedeth them. Are ye not much better than they? Which of you by taking thought can add one cubit unto his stature? And why take ye thought for raiment? Consider the lilies of the field, how they grow; they toil not, neither do they spin: And yet I say unto you, that even Solomon in all his glory was not arrayed like one of these. Wherefore, if God so clothe the grass of the field, which today is, and tomorrow is cast into the oven, shall he not much more clothe you, O ye of little faith?'*

June listened intently, but found his argument troubling. Was he saying they should be like Hamish McCutcheon and his family? Or like the tramps that came and went in the town and around Challock Farm? Margaret MacCaig said they had regulars and you could pretty much tell the time of year, nay even the time of day, by when each of them reappeared—feckless and scrounging off others who worked hard to make an honest living. Surely, even Grandpa Rodger, who had been bankrupt once, always found a way to support his wife and family and not rely on the charity of others? The Rodgers and the Hepburns worked hard to keep themselves respectable, decent and able to serve others in the community who were less fortunate than them. This was morally right and it proved that they were the beneficiaries of God's Grace. She couldn't accept that God bestowed his grace on common tramps and ne'er-do-wells like Hamish McC., although she'd make an exception for his long-suffering wife who had taken her annual suicidal dip in Loch Ryan only a fortnight ago.

'And I say unto ye,' the minister was nearing the end of his peroration, 'as Jesus said on the side of the Lake of Galilee nineteen centuries ago, *Take therefore no thought for the morrow: for the morrow shall take thought for the things of itself. Sufficient unto the day is the evil thereof.*' But the day didn't feel evil. It was as if the pastor had jaundiced-tinted glasses.

Little did that pastor know what harm he'd wreaked that Sunday morning in early July 1934. His sermon, so at odds with the lessons she'd imbibed all her childhood at the Reformed Presbyterian Church in Dalrymple Street, sowed the first seeds of religious doubt. How could the Christian faith be true if it were capable of such contradictory interpretations? How could you take the word of God and insist it meant what you wanted it to mean and still claim that God's divine word was absolute? This pastor was more like Humpty Dumpty; Christ's Gospel meant what he said it meant because he said it meant it. June was lost in reverie as they stood to sing the final metrical psalm, the first part of Psalm 119: *Blessed are they that undefiled, / and straight are in the way; / Who in the Lord's most holy law / do walk, and do not stray.* As she sang the words of the final verse—*That I will keep thy statutes all / firmly resolved have I: / O do not then, most gracious God, / forsake me utterly*—her mind wandered back to Humpty Dumpty saying: *When I use a word, it means just what I choose it to mean—neither more nor less.* She imagined herself as Alice confronting the pastor afterward and saying: *The question is, whether you can make words mean so many different things.* Especially the word of God.

The following day no longer in their parade uniforms but dressed in homemade camping uniforms, which were not *that* uniform despite Jenny Paravensi's best efforts, they walked up to Ghaist Hall where the Glenluce Devil had terrorised the Campbells. They searched for the Devil's Well, into which the Devil had lured Janet Campbell to throw herself; they imagined the execution of the famous beggar and atheist, Jock of Broad, picturing him swinging

121

from a lone tree whose skeleton still stood by the derelict hall. Another day they would walk all the way up to Carscreugh Castle, the first home of the Stairs. It felt strange to view its ruined towers and think that this was where the present Lord Stair's ancestors began. They must have been rough and wild compared to the elegant Lord and Lady who graced the Stranraer cinema every Friday night.

In a few short days, despite the privations of diet and toilet facilities, the Pack's collective imagination was nourished and its mind expanded beyond anything previously dreamt. Many of them had been fed tall tales and folk legends throughout their childhoods. This led them to experience a heightened, feverish and fanciful awakening. No wonder they all experienced vivid dreams, even if they slept soundly after long days of activity in the open air. One member of June's patrol slept more soundly than the rest—and dreamed more intensely too.

This was Jennie Adami, the daughter of the Port Rodie Ice Cream parlour Adami and Jose Adami's little sister. She was the youngest member of June's patrol. June had strict instructions to keep a careful eye on her. She was bold and reckless, no doubt made more so by having a brother five years older than her. She would throw herself down the sandhills, run the fastest and swim the furthest out to sea each day when they bathed and washed. June soon decided that she didn't need much watching; she could fend for herself if any of them could. What she didn't know was that Jennie could get the night terrors and would sleepwalk while she had them. At home it was Jose's task in the middle of the night to gently whisper in her ear and lead her back to her bed without waking her. It wasn't clear if her parents knew how regular an occurrence it could be, especially when she got over-excited. And like all of them she was increasingly over-excited as the week progressed.

It happened on the Wednesday night, around midnight. Jennie disturbed June, sleeping fitfully that night, by crawling over her to leave the tent. June tried to turn over and get back to sleep but her palliasse, stuffed with coarse straw, was lumpy and uncomfortable. Jennie seemed to be gone a long while; it wasn't that far to the latrines.

Eventually, June roused herself and thought she better go and see if Jennie was alright. She pulled her knitted cardy round her shoulders and staggered out into the night air. It was a full moon. There were wispy clouds in the sky; still the camp was bathed in moonlight. June went across to the latrines and in a loud whisper called Jennie's name. There was no reply, so she went in to look. She wasn't there. June felt annoyed; that girl was thoughtless going off in the middle of the night on some madcap adventure. She wasn't sure what to do but decided to walk around the campsite in ever increasing circles till she found her. It didn't occur to her that she should wake Jenny Paravensi and tell her what had happened; that could wait till the morning. Right now, she just wanted to get back into their tent and curl up on her palliasse, which wasn't that uncomfortable compared to stumbling around the uneven ground by the light of the moon. She tiptoed as best she could in and out the tents describing ever increasing circles until her feet touched the soft sand that indicated the start of the beach.

She would never know what prompted her to do this but instead of circling back round again, she decided to strike out and go down to the shoreline. There was something magical about the sea seen from the shore by full moonlight; its pull was irresistible.

And then it was that she descried a lone figure wading out to sea. Thigh high in Luce Bay. Waist high in Luce Bay. Breast high in Luce Bay. *Aiming for the Great Scare.* June was transfixed for what felt an eternity. Then she shrieked at the top of her voice, 'Jenni!' And she wasn't sure whether she was calling Jennie Adami to turn around and wade back to the shore or if she were screaming to Jenny Paravensi to come and rescue her before she drowned. In any case her scream was effective. Jennie froze, the chill waves lapping round her shoulders, and Jenny came rushing down to the beach, tearing her clothes off, and dived into the sea. She was a strong swimmer and was already halfway towards Jennie by the time the whole pack had assembled, bleary-eyed and shivering, at the water's edge. Jenny came alongside the girl and they watched as she trod water beside her for a while before expertly lifting her into floating position, cupping her head in her left arm and swimming, more slowly now, back to shore with her.

'Pigeon Patrol, you stay with me! The rest of ye, get back into your tents and under your blankets now; get some sleep! There's nothing more to see here.' And they all obeyed her mutely and instantly. 'Now June, will you organise a good fire for us. We need to get her warm again and maybe all have a cup of cocoa.'

And so it was. In the early hours of the morning Pigeon Patrol sat huddled in their blankets around a blazing fire, sipping sweet cocoa from their enamel cups, while Jennie told them her dream.

'I dreamt I was Jennet Campbell and heard the Devil whistling to me, whispering to me, drawing me on towards a deep well. It was like a long tunnel leading to a whole world under ground. I knew there was water there, but it was more like the pool of tears in the rabbit-hole than a proper well, or the sea. Just like the picture in your beautiful book, June. I wasn't at all scared. I felt more curious than ever before in my life. I was on the verge of discovering a vast world we didn't know existed until now. And then, and then...'

She faltered. It was as if words could never do justice to this world she'd dipped her toes into. Although it wasn't just her toes; she'd been immersed to her neck. She could have drowned and it would have been June's fault. June brushed away the tears gathering at the corner of her eyes; she was determined not to cry in front of her patrol. Jennie resumed her story.

'Then I heard your voice calling me, June. Just like Alice heard her big sister telling her to wake up at the end of her long sleep. And then Jenny was calling me back to safety.'

The Adami knew the Paravensi well, so Jenny didn't reprimand her for calling her by her Christian name rather than Brown Owl. As the sea lapped the shingle and something rustled in the nearby grass, June realised all of them thought of her as Jenny and often forgot to call her Brown Owl. She never minded; she seemed to encourage them to be more grown up than other adults did. Maybe that was why she was so special and such a darling friend to them all.

'And yet,' Jennie was still telling her story, 'and yet, I

almost wish I'd gone on. Now I'll never know what else is down there, is out there. I won't get a second chance.'

Here she broke down sobbing and Jenny wrapped her competent arms around her and comforted her.

'He won't call me again,' she wailed. 'That's my chance over and done with.'

And then she burst into even more hysterical tears.

'There, there,' soothed Jenny. '*You'll* get a second chance. Don't you worry your wee head no more.'

And June registered that Jenny must also be feeling unsettled by Jennie's distress, for just like Alice, *she was so surprised that she quite forgot how to speak good English.*

The following day, Thursday, was a mild, soft day. Pigeon Patrol felt lazy that day. They bathed in the sea and lay on their backs watching the cirrus, cumulus and strata clouds drift up from the south-west. They played a guessing game of where each cloud came from: Bangor? Blackpool? Dublin? Liverpool? Ramsey? Whitehaven? The rules kept shifting; at first, whatever place you named you had to name one person who came from there. June loved this: Dublin—Helen and Margaret. Liverpool—Eileen and Shelagh, or her Daddy. Lytham St Annes—Grandma Rodger. Then, what did your cloud resemble and what had it looked like when it left Bangor? Ramsey? Whitehaven? Blackpool? This was more taxing; how could you know how much it had shape-shifted in its journey across the Irish Sea? And finally, you had to make up a story about your cloud, incorporating your person, your place, the object it resembled when it set out and the object it looked like when it arrived overhead.

My Daddy used to sit in a special summerhouse on wheels in the back garden in Moor Lane, Crosby. Grandpa Hepburn would come out every so often and move it around so that he was always facing the sun. He could watch the clouds all day long. One day he spied a cloud shaped like a rose. He made a wish that this rose-cloud would float in the sky above the Irish Sea until one day it spied his daughter lying on this beach and bore a message from him that he would love her always.

She couldn't tell that story. So she made up another about Eileen and Shelagh lying on the beach at Crosby watching a bottle-shaped cloud dozing in the sky above them, shouting loudly to wake it up and send it all the way across the sea to pass on their message. But when the cloud reached Luce Bay, it had changed shape so much it looked like a drop scone and had forgotten what it was supposed to say. So, it merely waved 'hello' then disappeared.

'Just like the Devil,' Jennie mused. 'He waved hello then disappeared from my sight.'

'It's just as well he did,' admonished June, remembering her responsibilities as Sixer. 'Come on now girls, it's our turn to peel the tatties for everyone this evening. Let's go and get started while they're still away, then we can join in with everything round the camp fire when they get back.'

And so the six stood at the trestle tables, washing, peeling and chopping into small chunks tatties, carrots, onions and swede. They fetched more firewood and got all the patrols' campfires lit. When the rest of the pack returned from their afternoon's ramble, each had a pot of water coming to the boil on it. 'Brilliant, Pigeon Patrol!' said Jenny.

'And as a special treat, we've been given some bacon from the farmer's wife at Sinniness to add to our stew pots this evening.'

Bliss!

It was a magical evening, sitting dreamily around the main campfire at the end of a lazy day, hearing what the rest of the pack had been doing and retelling their cloud stories. Then they sat and sang songs: 'The Bonnie Banks o' Loch Lomond,' 'I'm sitting on top of the world,' and 'The Bluebells of Scotland': 'O where and O where does your highland laddie dwell; / He dwells in merry Scotland where the bluebells sweetly smell, / and all in my heart I love my laddie well.' They divided into two groups to sing this, one group the questioner, the second the responder. When they first learnt this song with Jenny, June had loved it because of the bluebells, which reminded her of Saturday afternoon walks with Betty. But that evening it was the last song and she climbed into the tent feeling deeply affected by the final verse:

Suppose and suppose that your Highland lad should die.
The bagpipes shall play over him and I'd sit me
   down to cry.
And it's oh in my heart I wish he may not die.

She supposed it was because the clouds had made her think about her Daddy growing up in Crosby and falling ill even before he met Mummie. She was under-slept from the night before like the rest of Pigeon Patrol. If she'd been at home, she might have cried a little into her pillow, but she couldn't do that here in the tent with her patrol. Besides there wasn't a proper pillow, just her clothes bundled beneath her palliasse to lift her head. She was so tired she fell asleep while she was still thinking she might give way to tears... only to be woken some time later by a strange scratching below her ear. It felt as if her palliasse was budging. And it was! Something inside was shifting and shoving against her cheek. Her eyes were wide open and her ears. *What could it be?* Then she realised: there was a mouse in her palliasse. *A mouse!* June shrieked. She couldn't help herself. If there was one thing she hated more than any other it was mice. She leapt out the tent and stood in the cold moonlight, trembling and sobbing. *She couldn't bear this, she couldn't bear this any longer.*

Brown Owl was by her side in a jiffy. She put her arms round her and held her close, warming her against her comforting body. 'There, there, June. There, there.' And her words were as consoling as Grandma Rodger's, Mummie's or Auntie Dolly's. 'Whisht, now. Don't you worry! I'll get rid of him for you.'

June didn't look and didn't ask how she did it, but a quarter of an hour later she was back asleep, reassured that there'd be no more mice in her palliasse, at least for one night. The following night she found it more difficult to sleep soundly, uncertain whether the mouse might have crept back, finding it the cosiest place in the whole of Luce Bay. She kept waking and surreptitiously feeling up and down her mattress to check for a rodent invasion, then dozing fitfully before waking herself to conduct another check. By breakfast time she felt worn out and for the first time that week was tense and breathless. She sensed her heart beating erratically and this made her feel all the more exhausted and panic-stricken. She didn't dare say anything to anyone: Pigeon Patrol had caused more than its fair share of drama that week already. She carried on as if she were perfectly normal, helping with the morning chores.

This was an important day because parents were invited to visit and to share a cup of tea with them that afternoon. They were to make drop scones over their campfires to offer with the tea; this open-air baking preoccupied them up until it was time for a hasty lunch of bread and bacon.

When Mummie arrived, June smiled bravely. Mummie could tell instantly that all was not well. She only had to say, 'What is it, June? What's the matter?' and she dissolved into tears.

'Take me home, Mammy! Please take me home with you!' And she did.

After that, June was warier of Nature in the form of pigeons and mice than ever before. She didn't abandon her secret dream to serve her nation or even the League of Nations, but it wouldn't be through healthy outdoor pursuits that she would achieve this. She would follow a different path from now on. In the meantime there would be boys. If she'd felt exulted and free on Friday nights in the company of her fellow guides, now she pondered more the perplexing ways of boys and men.

The Rodgers men, the dark ones that is, were all over-sexed. Not Uncle Eddie, who was fair. But Cousin Teddy, Uncle Eddie's son, was a menace when we were young.

After the debacle of Guide Camp June was glad to look forward to a summer of visits and visiting. As soon as they got back home that Saturday evening, Mummie was on the phone to Uncle Ernie. 'Hallo, operator,' she shouted into the mouthpiece, 'Can you put me through to Giffnock 442, please?' A long pause intruded as everyone held their breath. 'Annie!' Everyone's heart sank. 'How are you keeping?... Can't complain... yes, yes. Well what a coincidence; that's the very reason I'm ringing. Oh! We'd love that... no, no problem at all. It's just what June needs; she's had a difficult time at the Guides camp. One of her Six nearly drowned in the sea. No... no not her fault... the wean was sleep-walking can you believe. That Adami girl... Ernie should know who I mean. Is Ernie there? Can I have a word?.... Oh, all right then. But he'll bring Pat with him when he comes? Tuesday? Oh... that's even better. Tuesday afternoon it is then... Yes and to you... and June sends her love, she can't wait till she sees Pat again.'

Which was true; after the trials and tribulations of the past week, the thought of ten days with Pat was just the fillip she needed. Mummie wasn't quite so happy. 'That woman!' she muttered as she placed the earpiece carefully back into its cradle, 'Why she couldn't let me speak to my own brother, I don't know.'

'Envy, I should think,' murmured Auntie Dolly, too quietly for Grandma to hear. 'Just like she always copies the clothes you wear, May, even though they look ridiculous on her figure.'

'That woman's got no taste of her own, that's true enough. If she'd only ask me I give her my best advice. But oh no! she's far too uppity for that.'

'Yes, but you have to feel sorry for her, what with Moira and everything.'

'Do I, Dolly? Do I?'

And for reply Auntie Dolly gave the slightest of moues, before they changed the subject and spoke loud enough for

Grandma to hear every bland word they uttered.

The telephone was busier than usual during the summer holidays. The following evening it was Uncle Eddie ringing them. Auntie Dollie got to it first. 'Hello!' she said excitedly. *Who did she think it might be,* June wondered, *it wasn't long to the wedding now.* 'Oh! Eddie! What a coincidence!... Yes, of course. No, no problem at all. He can share with Mr Hetherington. No, we haven't found a replacement for Guido Bonugli yet. No, the bed's spare, really. That will be such fun for them all. Yes... why don't you give Ernie a ring? Then he could come down with Pat on Tuesday? Yes, she's coming to stay for ten days till Ernie comes back a week Thursday as usual. Well, we can pop him on the train on Saturday if you like. No, I'm sure that'll be fine. We'll expect him on Tuesday then unless we hear otherwise. Bye now... bye!'

So June and Pat had to put up with cousin Teddy for the best part of a week. It wasn't so bad during the daytime, especially since there was a flurry of preparations for the wedding, which they were pressganged into helping with. But at night it could get difficult. On Tuesday night Pat and Teddy were tired from their train journey. But on Wednesday night June and Pat lay awake for ages.

Pat wasn't happy. As they lay in bed in the attic room next to where cousin Teddy and Mr Hetherington were sleeping, she confided in June. 'It's as if I can do nothing right anymore. Whatever I do nowadays, Mummy criticises me and says Myrette was so much better at it than I am when she was my age. Don't get me wrong, I loved my sister and it was awful when she died like that, but sometimes it feels as if she's blighted my life. Mummy seems to blame Daddy and me for her death. It wasn't our fault the anaesthetic killed her. I sometimes think she'll never love me again, ever. It's as if she resents the fact I'm still alive while Myrette's gone.'

How awful: June didn't know what to say. Whenever Mummie and Auntie Dolly spoke about Aunt Annie it seemed they'd had enough of her ways. She had a habit of copying their outfits, which they found intensely annoying. They'd carefully plan their dresses and choose the fabrics, going back and forth between The Glasgow House and

John Findlay's, spending hours poring over bolts of cloth, matching braiding and buttons, before making their purchases. Although they were short of money they'd buy *Vogue* twice a year to be sure to follow the latest fashion trends. Then Auntie Annie would make a mental note of their new outfits and get her little dressmaker to replicate them.

June was lying there turning over in her mind what was worse, to lose your husband to tuberculosis or your eldest child on the operating table, wondering if perhaps Mummie and Auntie Dolly were being a bit harsh on Auntie Annie considering. She heard the slight rasp of the rusty hinge on the bedroom door, then a furtive creak of the loose floorboard. She groaned inwardly; each muscle, which a moment before had been drifting into sleep, tensed as she held her breath and waited for the inevitable lifting of her bedclothes. He was in her bed, pressed up beside her.

'Pat! Pat! Wake up! It's Teddy!'

His hands were caressing her thighs. His lips were slobbering over her breasts. Once more, she cursed the fact she'd developed such big breasts so soon. Again, more urgently: 'Pat!'

Pat woke this time. She was out of bed and across the small room in an instant, beating Teddy's head with one of her shoes. June managed to extricate her legs and started kicking his shins and further up too. With their combined onslaught he admitted defeat and withdrew.

They usually laughed about it afterwards; they could always beat him off between them. But this night they were both too upset to joke about it. Pat still felt raw with the sense of not meriting her mother's love and June still felt disturbed by the thought that Auntie Annie had lost a child and wasn't really loved by Uncle Ernie. Life felt complicated for both of them; the carefree sense of childhood stretching on for years to come had disappeared and in its place was the prospect of unhappy women's lives whose conditions couldn't be altered and amatory men who preyed on girls with not a thought to how they might feel. *Were all men predators and all women born to suffer?* June hoped not; she earnestly prayed that night that Auntie

Dolly would be happy with Birrell Bryson, before adding a little prayer that perhaps she and Pat might be happy in love and marriage too when the time came. In the meantime, *would He please prick Teddy's conscience and help him reform his ways?*

Teddy wasn't all bad; during the day he could be fun. In daylight hours he would treat Pat and June the way he always had; ostensibly teasing them for being tomboys while forever urging them to cycle further round the Loch, swim further out of their depth, climb higher and explore dangerous places they usually avoided. He had an unerring knack of discovering the highest trees and slipperiest ruins. On Thursday morning they paid their 9d each to catch the bus to Portpatrick. Mid-morning, they were starving; they bought a twist of chips each, with lashings of salt and vinegar, which they ate down by the harbour. Then they climbed up the steep coast path towards the next bay, so they could come back round through the Dunskey Estate.

'I'm so thirsty,' said Pat and June in unison. 'So am I,' said Teddy, 'but we've run out of money. I know, let's go and ask at The Portpatrick Hotel; I'm sure they'll let us have something to quench our thirst.'

'We can't do that,' said June appalled.

'Why not?' asked Teddy. He marched through the main doors and marshalled them down a dark corridor away from the airy lounge with sea views, before any of the guests had noticed. 'Come on!' he chided, walking into the huge, noisy kitchen as bold as brass.

One of the cooks was taking a short break, wiping her moist forehead on a dishcloth as she surveyed the familiar scene of organised chaos. It was like a demented ballet; everyone chopping, beating, whisking, stirring huge basins and pots, darting back and forth for some forgotten ingredient and turning pirouettes as they hurled themselves from work surfaces to ovens and back again. Through this manic choreography, waiters threaded their way with impervious, precarious plates balanced along their arms, or trays held high above their heads on the palm of one hand. June gasped and held her breath, incredulous that the whole culinary dance didn't end in smashed plates, shattered glasses, scalded kitchen porters and angry voices.

Teddy strode confidently up to the resting cook, looked her in the eye and said, 'I'm so sorry to bother you, Mam, but my sisters and I were so long on the tennis courts we ended up missing lunch and our parents are punishing us by refusing to ring room service and order something for us. I don't suppose...' Here he paused and gave her his most winsome smile. 'It's bad enough at boarding school where there's never enough food to feed a growing boy, without having to starve in the holidays too!'

June couldn't believe his nerve, but tried to smile sweetly at the cook when she glanced her way.

'And do these two go to boarding school to?'

'Oh, yes,' he replied. 'We only get to see one another in the holidays...' He faltered as if he might utter an unmanly sob if he tried to carry on talking.

The cook executed a *chassé en tournant* followed by a *jetée*, leaping across a temporarily clear patch of tiles, grabbed a tray on which were piled ends of roast meats, wedges of cheese and quarters of apple. With her other hand she plucked three bottles of lemonade from the open door of a pantry cupboard and performed a *glissade précipitée* back to their side.

'Now then, you just take this picnic out the kitchen door there and find yourselves some shelter over by the boiler house. No one will catch you there. Just remember to leave the bottles and tray on the kitchen step when you've finished; no one will be any the wiser.' And that is precisely what they did.

By the time they returned to the cliff path the sun was past its zenith. June could sense the sunrays caress her left shoulder then stroke the fields stretching away to her right. Teddy strode confidently ahead towards Maidenhead Bay. Pat and June followed, elated by their adventure with the cook. For once June wasn't breathless; she breathed deep gulps of sea air and felt light footed. She skipped down the slippery path to Port Mora to join Teddy who was lolling by the nearest of the twin hexagonal pavilions, built a lifetime ago to house the telephone cables that connected Scotland with Ireland.

Teddy was having none of it. 'A telephone exchange here in this cove; that's ridiculous! These are smugglers' huts; everyone knows that.'

June felt a wave of annoyance break across her enjoyment of the afternoon. Her brow ruffled, eyes narrowed and jaw tightened. Pat caught her attention and rolled her eyes melodramatically. It was no good; they both dissolved in uncontrollable laughter. They rolled around on Mora's sand to the extreme embarrassment of Teddy.

When the laughing fit was over, June and Pat lay on the finger of gritty sand listening to the waves and letting the last of the sun's rays stroke their faces. Teddy forgot about his embarrassment and let himself sink into the sand beside them. For once there was no tension between them; they just *were*.

'I wonder what "Mora" means.'

'Daddy says it means tiny.'

'My Daddy says it's to do with Scottish law.'

'Hindoo says it's short for moratorium.'

'Mmm! That makes sense. This beach feels like a moratorium.'

As soon as Teddy said this, the spell began to be broken. All three became self-conscious again. And with the return of adolescent consciousness, June and Pat thought about what they'd done at lunchtime. Their recent elation turned to fretting.

'Do you think what we did was wicked?'

'Well it wasn't sinful, but...'

'It was wrong what we did, wasn't it?' And they uttered that final question in unison.

'Perhaps,' admitted Teddy. 'But,' he added triumphantly, 'we got away with it, didn't we?'

The sun was sinking lower over the waves at the mouth of the bay and catching the crumbling walls of the ruined castle, looming above the rocks on the next promontory. They stood up, brushed the sand off their shorts and scrambled over the promontory towards Laird's Bay.

As they turned to take the path up through the pine woods June wondered if the Hairy Apparition of Dunskey was watching from its shattered battlements. *Did a ghost haunt you if you did wrong?* They all fell silent as they entered the woods. They could still hear the waves breaking on the pebbly beach. Then the sound of the sea was supplanted by the trickle of the waterfall as the burn flowed down to the cove. Its subdued murmur only emphasised a strange stillness among the trees. At their feet was a carpet of tall fescue, fleshy-leaved despite the gloom. Their moment of goat-footed lightness was overtaken by the dark shadow of past misdeeds and a fear of moral recklessness. June could feel her breath shorten and her heart flutter.

'It *was* wrong, what we did!' she declared.

Pat reached out and grasped her hand. Teddy assumed his insouciant look and tried to stare them down. His two cousins fixed their gaze in unison and returned his stare.

'It's not wrong what we did. It was a bit of harmless fun. That food would have been fed to the pigs otherwise.'

'But what about the lemonade?'

'They won't notice it's gone.' He shrugged.

Two faces spoke of shared incomprehension.

He became surly. 'The boys in Dad's school all did much worse than that. If you want to know what "wrong" looks like, come and stay for a while!'

'But,' replied Pat, 'they're not all wrong. My Daddy says your Daddy helps them to mend their ways.'

'Yea,' was all he said. And he kicked a stone off the path into the silence beneath the branches' sharp canopy.

June let go of Pat's hand and asked, 'What's it like, living in a Borstal?'

She watched Teddy's shoulders square up, as if he was trying hard to be manly. 'Well,' he joked, 'it's not exactly a bed of roses.' He paused. 'I sometimes think Daddy cares for his boys more than he does for me.'

June couldn't look him in the eye. His chin quivered. 'Why?' she whispered.

'He's so patient with them. Don't get me wrong. He's really tough on them. But somehow, they know he's kind. However firm he is they all still love him.' He paused again. 'I guess that's what they all need. No one's loved them, ever. When they come to Mossbank they feel cared for. Did you know two of his boys from the early days come back every Christmas? They bring presents for all of the boys and they put on a bit of a show. One of them has a beautiful tenor voice. The other one, Harry, he's a comedian. He does a brilliant pantomime dame.' Teddy chuckled to himself.

'Some of the jokes he tells, I don't know how he gets away with it. But Daddy never seems to mind; he just roars with laughter along with the boys.'

Teddy's shoulders seem to relax. They all fell silent for a while, pondering that fine line between morality and immorality. *Life was so messy and complicated. If only everything really was just light and dark, black and white.*

It was Pat who spoke first. 'So why do you think we got away with it?'

Teddy thought he knew the answer. 'If that cook knew we're all the grandchildren of the Reverend Rodger, she would have clipped our ears and sent us packing. But she thought we were the children of people rich enough to stay at the hotel and send their three children to boarding school. It was her job to serve us.' He looked puzzled. 'If we were who we said we were, we were spoilt little brats who were disobeying our parents. So,' he flushed with triumph, 'she wasn't very moral either, was she!'

Just here, their path brushed up against the hedge that formed the boundary around Dunskey House gardens. They were walking on the estate, but beyond the hedge were the private gardens that the public weren't allowed in, except on special occasions. Teddy dared them to sneak into the private gardens.

'I bet you two wouldn't dare creep through this hedge and get into the maze!'

Afterwards June would wonder why they'd agreed and Pat would remember this moment all her life. When she grew up and had a family of her own, she would tell her daughter, Ann, about that summer's afternoon when she and her cousins played on the Dunskey Estate. Though she would keep some of the details a secret and take them to her grave.

They knew that the hedge wasn't just a hedge; it marked the boundary line between where they were allowed to roam and the private gardens that were out of bounds. As she scrambled through the hedge June felt as if she'd crossed a line. She felt a surge of defiance: *why shouldn't they wander in the gardens, get lost in the maze and play in the fairy glen? Weren't Rogers and Hepburns as good as Orrs and Ewings? After all she had a right to wear the Barclay Clan tartan, a right passed down from her paternal ancestors. She was as good as them, even if her mother was a poor widow who took in boarders to make ends meet.*

'Come on, girls,' shouted Teddy. 'Let's find the maze!'

They wandered through carefully tended gardens, past an ornamental lake and skirted round the back of the huge Victorian greenhouses.

'This must cost a pretty penny in gardeners' wages,' mused Teddy.

The thought was strangely sobering. They entered the maze as curls of cloud clustered and fringed the sinking sun. June felt the late afternoon air cool on her back. They each took a different path through the maze in a race to find the centre, but their hearts weren't in it anymore. When Teddy reached the centre first June and Pat were quietly relieved; now they could catch the last bus back to Stranraer and the reassurance of scones and rhubarb jam for tea. Teddy found his way to the entrance and stage-whispered them to hurry up and join him. A few minutes passed; he called again. He couldn't quite conceal the anxiety in his voice. The sound was contagious; June caught it. She felt flustered. She worried she'd forgotten which way she'd entered the maze and began to backtrack.

Then from over the other side she could hear Pat suppress a sob.

'Are you all right, Pat?' she hissed. 'Are you lost?'

This was too much for Pat and she burst into voluminous tears. *Oh no! What'll we do now? We're going to get caught? And we're going to miss the last bus home.* June also began to cry.

At the entrance to the maze Teddy was getting distinctly uneasy. Even he was beginning to have regrets. At that moment the least observant onlooker would have seen he was feeling dejected and suffering remorse. June and Pat couldn't see him; they were getting more and more lost in the maze as they both panicked. But someone could.

That someone was the Head Gardener. He was just doing his final check of his glasshouses and preparing to secure them for the night, when he heard Pat's plaintive sobs and June's answering wail. *Like two wee chicks who've wandered too far from their Ma.* He clamped his lips, assumed his most ferocious stare and strode across his immaculate lawns to the maze entrance.

Teddy heard his footsteps, froze and tried to look brazen. Then fear got the better of him and he broke into a run. *Two lost chicks and a frightened kit!* mused the Gardener as he grabbed Teddy by his right ear.

'What have we here?' he asked in his fiercest voice.

Stuck in the dusky maze June and Pat felt mortified and hiccupped sobs in counterpoint. The next words they heard stopped them and their sobs dead in their dusty tracks.

'I suppose you're the brave ring-leader, are you now, Master Rodger?' Teddy was unmanned; he almost wet himself. *What would happen to them all?*

What actually happened was even more of a shock. The Head Gardener's pursed lips started to quiver, his eyes screwed up, his nose snorted and he burst into uncontrollable laughter.

'Come on, now, Master Teddy. We better rescue your two young cousins before their Ma sends Mr Grant out to search for them!'

It took him less than a minute to guide June and Pat back to the entrance to the maze. He turned to June.

'And quite how do you intend to get your cousins back to King Street, young lady?' he asked.

June didn't know. *What would happen now? Would he leave them here overnight? Would her mother have to ring Betty's Da and ask him to fetch them?* Relief turned back to panic.

'Don't worry, my wee chick. You can hitch a ride with the Missus and me.'

He fetched his horse from the stable and fixed it to his cart.

'I've got some spare chrysanthemums for planting on the back,' he said. 'You'd better take a few for your Ma, hadn't you?'

Chrysanthemums! Mummie would be so pleased; she would forget how late they were.

'Molly will be wondering what's keeping me,' he continued. 'Jump in! We'll meet her at the gate.'

With that, he lifted June and then Pat onto the cart, leaving Teddy to tumble onto the back as best he could.

And sure enough Molly was there at the Dunskey

House gates, standing just beneath the big bell. She smiled to her husband when she saw them.

'Well if it isn't those three Rodger cousins again.'

He looked quizzically at her.

'They were in my kitchen at lunchtime, playing *Let's Pretend*... let's pretend we're rich!'

Grandma Rodger was insistent. Dolly *would* have a sprig of white heather in her wedding bouquet. *For luck*. Kate, Mary, Minnie had, Annie, Emily, May had: she counted them off on the fingers of her hands, all her daughters and daughters in law. *Tena* wasn't going to change tradition now. You knew Grandma was very cross when she called Auntie Dolly 'Tena'.

Mummie took Auntie Dolly into the back garden to see how the sweet peas were progressing. *Would they be ready in time for the wedding?* They planned to decorate the wedding breakfast with their fairy colours and sweet, balsamic scents.

'We could add some sprigs of white heather to the arrangements,' suggested May. 'Mild, yielding sweet peas and resilient, upright heather that can stand a battering without breaking...'

She left the idea lingering in the air, mingling with the subdued floral fragrance. Dolly sobbed, hiccupped, sniffed and in sniffing inhaled their delicate scent. Her shoulders relaxed. She became lost in thought.

'They're like hyacinth, orange blossom water and wild hedge roses, rolled into one. But we can't put them anywhere folks will brush against them; the perfume changes once you touch them. Have you notice that, June?'

June hadn't known they were aware she'd followed them out.

'I think I have.' Her mind went back to early childhood, picking them and placing them in a jar for Fred to smell at breakfast. *Was it that faint trace of stress the blooms gave off when she'd picked them that he'd been alert to every time?* 'Lavender might be nice with them,' she volunteered. The two sisters gave this careful consideration; she suddenly felt grown up in this conversation.

'That's a nice idea, June, but I'm not so sure; there's

something about lavender that suggests sick rooms and aging. I want my bouquet to emanate sensuality, love and life.'

'Like a magic potion?'

'Yes, exactly. Like a good fairy's spell.'

All three tried not to think about the bad fairies that had lurked at some family weddings recently. Mummie picked the first sweet peas for the house and June brushed her hands against the lavender bushes, trying to decide what she thought they smelt of: youth or old age.

Auntie Dolly was still pondering. 'I think roses might work: la Reine Victoria or Comte de Chambord or Bourbon Queen.'

June was amazed. *Where had Auntie Dolly learnt so much about roses?*

'I remember them from the Botanic Gardens at Kelvingrove.' It was as if she'd heard June's question, 'The Suffragettes planted an oak tree there when women got the vote. Some women, that is. I would go to watch it grow. That's when I discovered the rose beds. They're like taffeta drenched in French perfume. I went back when I felt lonely and drowned in their scent. Those were the ones I liked best; I didn't even know I'd memorised their names until now. I must have one of those: Bourbon Queen. It's got to be Bourbon Queen.'

And it was. Birrell loved this about his bride. She was dark, vivacious and headstrong. They were well matched. Grandma got her one sprig of white heather in a bridal bouquet of pink bourbon roses and more stiff white heather to set off the alluring honey of the sweet pea profusions, tactfully placed on windowsills beyond the reach of careless hands.

Auntie Dolly's decision regarding flowers determined the wedding dress, its material, its texture, its colour and its design.

'It has to be a tabby. I'm only getting married once in my lifetime; it's got to be the best.'

From the hallway, June could hear Birrell clear his throat as if he might try to dissuade his strong-minded fiancée. A long pause. She could just imagine Auntie Dolly's eyes sparkling jet-black, daring him to disagree. Then Birrell succumbed, as she'd known he would. *But why a tabby? What had Chummy got to do with Auntie Dolly's wedding dress?*

When he'd gone, she couldn't stop herself asking, 'What's a tabby?'

She thought Auntie Dolly might be furious with her for eavesdropping, but she was only too happy to explain.

'A "Tabby" is a very special dress made from taffeta; it's rich and luxurious. It has a special texture. I'm going to order waved silk taffeta. And,' she hesitated, 'it will be ivory. It will be difficult to work with but I know I can do it.'

'What will our dresses be made of?'

'I don't think there's time to make another three dresses in silk taffeta; my bridesmaids will have rayon taffeta. It's easier to sew.'

'Will our dresses be ivory as well?'

'Yes, June, they will. White's too cold a colour; it reminds me of Jack's the butcher's. It drains all the colour from your cheeks.'

'What will we wear with it?'

'May, can you knit three boleros in time for the wedding day? I think they should be in soft rose pink to match the Bourbon Queens.'

'Of course I can. Should I do a lace pattern, do you think?'

'That would be lovely.'

'And pink silk sashes, Auntie Dolly?'

'Yes, you can have pink silk sashes.'

Grandma Rodger sat more upright than ever in her chair and made a sharp intake of breath. But even she didn't dare contradict her youngest child. Auntie Dolly would have her Wedding Day.

They chose Paton's Beehive Fingering 3 ply for Mummie to knit a pattern described as *an enchanting little bolero in a fascinating lacy stitch, with a round ribbed yoke*. It was an eight-row pattern; Mummie was thankful they were only boleros, not jackets. June learnt not to chatter around her, but she didn't mind if she turned on the radio. When the three boleros where finished, lightly pressed and their seams neatly sewn, Mummie decided that her little sister needed a surprise present from her. Looking back June couldn't understand how she'd managed it. But she had. She'd lighted on the pattern in *Woman's Own*.

'It's worth 2d a week every week just for this,' she exclaimed. 'Who needs to buy *Modern Marriage*!'

Grandma Rodger said nothing.

Meanwhile, Auntie Dolly worked away at her treadle sewing machine in the first-floor bedroom. She moved it to be as close to the window as possible to get the best light. She would wake at dawn and start sewing while Mummie mumbled, turned over and pulled the bedclothes up over her face. When she'd brought the material home she'd taken it straight upstairs, but June had seen how it shimmered in the light of the hallway. It was a light silk taffeta and she'd chosen a Simplicity pattern; she didn't dare cut such expensive material without one. A true bias cut, the dress would hug her figure, gently accentuating her curves. The waistband would rise from her natural waist to a rounded arch that snuggled under her bosom. This would carry the eye of the beholder upward and then down to follow the softly flowing, slim swirl of the skirt and the discreet train that flowed beyond her modest ankles. On the day just the toe of her soft satin-heeled shoes would peep out. She would look as beautiful and fascinating as Claudette Colbert. Under her translucent veil her jet-black hair would be caught in an elaborate bun. *For Birrell to undo on their wedding night.*

She had never taken such care over sewing, adjusting the tension and setting the stitch length as long as possible to prevent any puckering. She worked the treadle more slowly than usual, holding the material taut, the tip of her tongue licking the left edge of her lips. When it came to pressing, everyone had to leave the kitchen; there could be no distractions. The pressing cloth had to be washed and hung to dry before she would use it. The iron had to be just so: warm not hot. She agonised the first time she placed it on the pressing cloth and lifted it off almost at once. It had worked: the seam was perfectly flat. The material was still pristine. Then she hand-finished each seam with bias binding. She'd considered French seams, but her nerve failed her. When the garment was finished it was the one thing she regretted. It left her time to embroider her dress;

this was nerve-wracking enough. *What if she ruined it at the last minute?* But she did it anyway. Bourbon-pink satin stitch roses. Emerald-green satin stitch stems and leaves. Then her *pièce de résistance*: bourdon stitch for the tight buds that clustered round her ruched neck line and trailed from those rose sprays down the swirl of her skirt to waft with each step. On her wedding day no one would notice at first and then they would catch a glimpse of tight pink buds promising to blossom like their sisters.

May continued to crochet the lace bolero for Dolly. Not pink like the bridesmaids', but in ivory silk yarn. Very delicate. Very fine. So luxurious that Birrell would hardly dare touch it for fear he might spoil it. She would give it to Dolly on her Wedding Day for her to wear after the ceremony, at the Wedding Breakfast, and when she went away to Dumfries at the end of the afternoon. It would be the perfect gift. She had to let June in on the secret because June would be her lookout, warning her each time Dolly was near. She knew they'd had their moments, but she loved her younger sister dearly. She wanted her to look as glamorous as the movie stars, even if it were just for one day. Birrell had been tasked to buy Dolly's gloves—he'd been given a snatch of material to compare and strict instructions that the match must be exact.

'It feels like the last challenge the prince is set, before he can claim the king's daughter for his bride,' he joked.

But it was no laughing matter. He was so anxious, he waited for a Saturday afternoon when he could take Betty, June and Pat to Glasgow House. He made them responsible for getting it right. Then to their utter delight he bought three pairs of three-quarter length gloves, the same design as Dolly's but in the most perfect rose pink to match their boleros. And then he bought the 2-inch-wide ribbon for their rose-pink sashes. Walking back to King Street, the girls practised their deportment, pointing their toes forward and holding their backs as if they carried a volume each of Grandpa Rodger's *County Seats* on their heads.

'You look like Princess Mary posing for the photographers,' Birrell quipped.

Auntie Dolly used the same pattern for the bridesmaid's dresses. She started with her largest bridesmaid's dress material, carefully measuring June before making changes to the paper pattern.

'With your bust, June, it's just as well I'm starting from a larger size!'

Then she measured Pat, trimming further excess off the paper pattern. Then finally petite Betty.

'Thank Heavens you're so slim. The paper's all tatters round the edges from these dratted pins; I daren't pin it to the fabric anywhere it will show.'

They were her sharpest, best pins. Her temper was fraying round the edges. The material was a perfect match for the bourbon roses. But it wasn't silk. It looked wonderful: rich and luxurious. The inside had a smooth sheen; they felt like starlets when they stepped into the finished dresses. The outside was nubbly; there was no other way to describe it. Cut on the bias, first the warp would catch the light, slantwise round their torsos and thighs; then the eye would be caught by the uneven weft, back and forth, back and forth. They felt as if they shimmered as they walked. The fact that they felt sweaty and clammy within a few minutes of putting them on was a minor sacrifice for a day of film-star glamour. This was what Betty and Pat would remember most. Although, even this memory would fade and, for Pat, only the day on the Dunskey Estate endure. For Betty, it would be the day she and June bought talcum powder for the first time. And for June, the talc and the perfume. But all that was yet to come at the end of the summer holidays. First there was the wedding day.

The ceremony took place at St Ninian's, 'the handsomest ecclesiastical structure in the town'. Built in 1884, it had a rosace window and a spiral staircase to the gallery. The north and south aisles were flanked by columns of axed, silver-grey granite, each with a band of polished red granite. Their bases and capitals were finely carved, as was the interior masonry of red Annan freestone. The sidewalls above the pillars were pierced by a row of clerestory windows. At the west end stood an organ in its alcove, surmounted by a round, stained-glass window. To the south side of the organ alcove stood a finely carved and inscribed pulpit, with steps at the rear leading to the vestry, where the marriage was registered after the ceremony:

> E. *Ormrod Rodger Minister of Giffnock South*
> *Parish, officiating minister.*
> Andw. *Carson, Woodlea, Stranraer, Witness.*
> Agnes F. *Smith, Melbourne Villa, Stranraer, Witness.*

So different from the austerity of Dalrymple Street Chapel, with its unaccompanied singing and the sounding board above the pulpit.

June remembered nothing of this.

The thing June did remember from the wedding day was the babble of accents around the wedding breakfast: Mummie's and Auntie Dolly's uneducated Lallans Scots, Uncle Eddie's and Uncle Ernie's educated Scots—they'd picked this up at Glasgow University; Uncle Johnny, Aunt Emilie, Mavis and Kenneth all spoke with a rich Devonian burr; Auntie Kate, was somehow nondescript, bland and dull, although Allan, Margaret and Mary had pronounced Dublin lilts already; Auntie Minnie sounded English because of the school she'd been to; Eileen and Shelagh had a nasal twang Mummie said reminded her of Daddy. Uncle Henry and Uncle Stanley were more like Mummie and Auntie Dolly but not so broad; they'd spent the first few years of their lives in the vicarage at Southampton. They were the only ones to motor down on the day of the wedding; they'd set off at the crack of dawn. Then there were her Great Uncle Alf, a confirmed bachelor, Great Uncle George and Great Aunt Ethel; they spoke warm, broad Lancashire, like their wives. Cousin Catherine, their spinster daughter, came too. June remembered the time Grandma had taken her to stay at Lytham St Annes, when she was still a little girl. She couldn't remember exactly when, but she could remember being allowed to play at the back of the ironmonger's shop, till she tripped over something sharp and was roundly told off.

June liked Great Uncle Alf; he was well rounded, cheery and comforting. He'd been a refuge for her to retreat to in Grandma's Lytham family. And when she'd felt close to tears from the unexpected sharp words he'd quickly consoled her, taking her to look at the coloured pharmacist's jars in the adjacent shop window, with their bulbous bases and tall elegant necks.

'At night, when everyone's fast asleep in their beds, they unleash those stoppers to release the Rainbow-fairies who fly away to little girls' bedrooms, where they watch over them sleeping till the crack of dawn.'

'Do they really, Uncle Alf?' June had been old enough to remain incredulous. 'Well not every night, June,' he'd admitted, 'only when the moon is full!'

Great uncle Alf liked a joke; everyone said so. Still, she'd slept better in the bed she'd had to share with cousin Catherine after he'd told her that story. Now it was as if he'd read her thoughts.

'Well June,' approaching her glass in hand, 'the Rainbow fairies will be delighted when they see you bridesmaids in those pretty dresses. You look like their first cousins, the Rosebud fairies, today!'

June smiled. It wasn't so much what he said, it was the gentleness with which he said it.

'I reckon you three pretty maids will drive the bad fairies far away from this marriage ceremony.' He glanced across the room at his big sister, Emily Annie Ormrod, as he still liked to teasingly call her. 'I surmise your Grandma must be feeling relieved on this day to witness her youngest child married so well. There's no bad fairies in the neighbourhood anyways.' And he chucked her under the chin before moving on through the room.

Grandma Rodger felt old. She hadn't cried at Kate's wedding, nor at Minnie's, although she'd shed a surreptitious tear at May's. It had taken her back to when she was a bride. Then she'd remembered she was already a respectable widow, who'd had to move out of the Manse, her last family home and in many ways her happiest. Now she felt like crying her eyes out; the tears welled, her breath shortened. She desperately needed to sob and wail. She held her breath for as long as she could until a tiny strangled sound transpired.

It was odd. Who or what had emitted this noise? It couldn't have been her. It was indecorous. Animal-like. Uncontrolled. Untamed. Raw. But here was another and another. Wild. Savage. A roaring in her ears. A flash of blinding light. Was Wesley here beside her? Where was she? Had she gone to Heaven already?

Her head rolled on her neck. Spittle was dribbling down her cheek. She felt queasy. She regained consciousness and looked blankly at Stanley.

'I think I need to lie down,' she managed to whisper.

He was all gentleness, this wayward son of hers whom she barely understood. *Why had he never married? Never had girlfriends even when he was young? Why was he so loving in his way? He was a dental nurse of course. That would explain it.* But even in the aftermath of this little stroke, she knew it didn't entirely. *Death had stroked her. Beckoned her, on this her youngest daughter's wedding day. And soon she would be reunited with her splendid bridegroom. Soon. Not yet.*

Stanley was helping her to her feet. So solicitous. So tactful. No one even noticed, as he put his arm around her, supported her discreetly under her right arm and held his left arm out for her to lean on as they moved slowly through the room. So many times she tucked him in as a child. Now he was tucking her in, fetching her a glass of water. *In her heart he'd always been her favourite.* Stroking her brow, smoothing the wisps of hair that had escaped so that they wouldn't bother her as she lay resting.

As the summer of 1934 drew to a close in Nuremberg the National Socialist Government held its sixth congress, the Rally of Will. Leni Riefenstahl filmed there and created her *Triumph of Will*, hailed as the purest, most powerful propaganda film, where Hitler emerged as the metonym for a Germany that would last a thousand years. June had other matters on her mind.

One Saturday afternoon it was too wet for walking and after they'd been to the cinema, Betty and June scurried across to the Chemist's.

'There'll be a raking shower soon, lassies. You'll see,' shouted Jimmy as they ran past May's the grocers.

'He's sounding more like a farmer than ever now,' commented June bitterly.

Her annoyance with Jimmy soon dissipated because they had some important things to decide that afternoon. They would be going up to the High School in less than a week and they needed to settle what talcum powder and perfume they would wear from now on. They had already agreed that they would each need to choose different ones so that they didn't smell the same. Mummie wore a heady, exotic one named *Shalimar*. Grandma Rodger had told June in no uncertain terms over breakfast that she was not allowed to wear that scent until she was a grown woman with a ring on the fourth finger of her left hand. Mummie had made a little moue, but hadn't said anything.

It was quite easy for June to decide on her perfume; it had to be the one called *June*.

'That will suit you perfectly,' said the Chemist's wife, who had come out from the maze of corridors in the back of the shop to help them choose. 'It has a lovely fresh bouquet; just right for a young lady your age.'

Betty took a bit longer to decide, but eventually plumped for Yardley's Old English Lavender, both for her scent and for her talcum powder. June didn't know what to do about talc; she couldn't have the same as Betty and there wasn't a *June* talc. Mrs McKay opened box after box for her and dusted a tiny sprinkling of powder on the opposite wrist to the one they'd tested the perfume on.

'The important thing is that it has to complement the scent of the perfume, she said. 'It mustn't contradict it in any way.' She frowned over the array of opened powder boxes and their upturned powder puffs. 'None of these are quite right, are they?' she mused. 'Let me sniff your wrist again and see how the perfume is developing on your skin.'

She held June's right arm up and slowly lowered her face till her nose almost caressed June's wrist. She breathed in deeply and held the breath for a long time as if she were swimming under water in the Loch. Finally, she lifted her head and drew a fresh breath, for all the world as if she were coming up for air after diving right to the bottom. She stared into the middle distance. The two girls watched her in awed silence. They felt as if they were initiates in a

149

female ritual that was far more profound than they'd imagined as they'd run laughing into the shop shaking off the rain drops half an hour earlier. Mrs McKay seemed like a hierophant amongst the Chemist's huge glass vials with their fat round bases and long curvaceous necks, aligned according to their intense hues, which mirrored in their proper order all the colours of the rainbow. Finally, she made a pronouncement.

'There's only one possibility. It has to be Eau de Cologne talcum powder. I'm sorry June, but I really couldn't let you wear anything else. It wouldn't be right.'

June saw that it was far more expensive than the others they'd tested; she only had just enough money saved for the ordinary talcum powders. Crestfallen, she tried to hide her embarrassment while she thought what she could say to excuse herself from buying it that day.

'Of course, you realise that whatever you get, this is a gift from Mr McKay and I, don't you?'

June looked up and frowned. *Was she the object of the Chemist's charity now?*

'When your Grandfather Wesley Rodger—God rest his soul—went to his grave, I promised the Dear Lord I would find a way to repay his kindness to us one day. And when Mr McKay came and told me I was needed in the shop because a certain young lady had come to make a very important first purchase of perfume and talcum powder, I knew straight away that this was the Lord giving me the chance I'd been waiting for. God bless you, child, and God bless your dear departed grandpa. He was a very special man was the Reverend Rodger.' She leaned down and gave June a brief hug, then turned briskly and busied herself wrapping their purchases and finding the right change for Betty.

June never knew precisely what Grandpa had done for the Chemist and Mrs McKay, and Grandma was vague when she asked her the following day. She imagined it must have been some small kindness that had touched Mrs McKay's heart at a difficult time. It clearly hadn't made too great a dent in the Manse's household budget or Grandma would have remembered, however uncertain her memory was becoming. But Mrs McKay was true to her word. From that day until she left Stranraer June never had to pay for her perfume and talc. Mrs McKay seemed so attuned to June and her scents that she would know when June needed new supplies without June ever having to ask.

Did they run back to 9 King Street to wait for the rain to blow over, giggling and laughing at the thought that they had just been initiated into the realm of women's rituals? Did they exhale their slight bewilderment at Mrs McKay's intensity through high spirits? Did they tumble up the stairs into her mother's and Auntie Dolly's bedroom, roll on the bed, holding their sides to ease the stitches occasioned by the running and try to control the bursts of painful laughter? Did they sit side by side at her mother's dressing table on the upholstered stool and, staring at the mirror and its wing mirrors, consider in all due seriousness now, for this was a very important matter, how they would wear their hair in High School? June's Eton crop had grown out to become a shoulder-length pageboy and Betty's naturally curly fair hair surrounded her pretty face and head like an ornate golden, baroque halo.

'I think I will put papers in my hair each night; it will be worth it,' mused June. Not saying what they both understood. She would thus look more like Betty: one with fair curly hair, one with dark curly hair, similar yet dissimilar, the perfect pair.

Did they contemplate their two images, reflected not once, not twice, but thrice and then multiplying in each wing mirror to infinity? Did Betty pick up Mummie's pink-backed hand-mirror, inlaid with its symmetrical design, and hold it up for June to see how her hair fell beneath the nape of her neck now? Did June reciprocate for Betty, showing her the exquisite point at the top of her dainty spine, where the curls sat in a neat line just hovering above the braiding on her collar? Did June say, *How I wish I had a father like yours, who smoked a pipe and had a faithful black dog and an Austin Rover.* Or did she just think it? Did Betty say, *How I wish I lived in your house, with no one watching your every move and no maids waiting for you to misbehave and get told off.* Or did she just think it?

And maybe, just maybe, there had been a bad luck fairy waiting in the wings that summer. And maybe all the silk taffeta in the world, all the Bourbon roses, talc, perfume and the insouciant bravado of youth couldn't finally banish her. A decade later, on 24th February 1944, Thomas Birrell Bryson was lost at sea. He died when the HMS Manistee was attacked and sunk by German U-boat, U-107. Grand Admiral Karl Dönitz's son captained this particular U-Boat in law. Grand Admiral Karl Dönitz, who later wrote the history of the U-Boats for the Americans.

Mummie's friend was married to a village schoolmaster. They lived near where Betty was buried, just outside Stranraer. She used to come into Stranraer to market on a Friday morning. I remember one morning she came into the house and she was terribly upset. It turned out her husband had been interfering with one of the boys. There was a bit of a scandal about his being a paedophile. It all seemed a bit strange to me; although I know I had trouble with my headmaster.

Her periods could be erratic. Anaemic before they started, now there were days each month when she felt wiped out. With the anaemia the breathlessness was worse than ever. Then there were times in between she felt as if her body couldn't contain the restless energy. At those times, Grandma Rodger would look apprehensive over the breakfast table and June would rush her food to escape her censorious gaze.

Her first day at Stranraer High School was such a morning. June had excuse enough to bolt her breakfast and dash out the house. It promised to be a perfect autumn day. The slight sea mist that rolled up King Street was dissipating; the sun was breaking through. June was bubbling with anticipation. *This is what joy felt like.* She was walking down Lewis Street not just to her new school, but to a world of knowledge beyond the confines of 9 King Street. She would get the education her mother missed; she would be so much wiser.

There were a hundred children in her year and twenty-five in her class—'D'. The girls outnumbered the boys, just. However theirs was only one of four classes in that year and in other classes there were far more boys. Not all parents believed education was the best route for a girl. Most of her girl classmates from the Academy would stay there for an extra year in the Advanced Division, because they'd not passed the Control—what they all called the qualy. Then they would return to help their mothers at home until they in turn became mothers. Just like *Little Women.* June knew she would meet the man of her dreams and get married one day, but not yet. First she would explore the world of ideas—and the world. She wanted to know everything and see everything before she settled down.

The girls tended to stick together. There was Betty, of course, then Margot McMaster. She was Jack McMaster's niece. Sometimes June and Margot would fantasize about Mummie marrying him the next time he came home for Christmas and proposed. Then they'd be cousins. Perhaps they would move into the spare cottage on the farm. *But then what would become of Fred?* Norah was there too. She had just scrapped through the qualy. Like June she wanted to have some fun before she got married; she'd seen her sisters grow up and marry young and she wasn't going to end up looking like an old wreck in her early thirties. Then there were new friends to make; those who'd made it through the Control, but lived out in the countryside had to journey into Stranraer each day, leaving before dawn and returning after dusk as the autumn stretched into winter. Jean Hunter from Whiteleys Farm, whose older brother Stephen had left school already. Margaret MacCaig, who had a twin brother, Stewart. They lived a few miles away at Leswalt. Margaret and Jean were used to living with brothers and treated them with the contempt they deserved. However, as the year progressed they were invaluable intermediaries between the separate spheres of male and female domains.

There were far more male teachers to deal with. There was the Headmaster, Mr John A. MacDonald, and the Science teacher, Mr Hendry. Then there was Dr Hill, who taught History, Mr Sutherland, Maths, and the Geography teacher, Mr Graham, whose first name they discovered was Herbert. There was the school music master, Frank Lewis, who came from Lancashire, just as Grandma Rodger did all those years ago.

Here's where it gets tricky. Telling the story one more time... remembering those instances one more time... burying them one more time. Hints would escape. As decades passed... as inhibitions faded... glimpses would emerge from the leaden box she'd entombed them in.

One Friday morning Margot and her mother arrived in time to share a cup of tea over the breakfast table, as they often did on Market Day. Mrs McMaster seemed upset. When they were out the front door and striding briskly towards the school gates, June asked Margot what the matter was. Margot brushed it off; she couldn't tell. And soon the conversation changed to whether they could remember the intricate new step they'd learnt at Scottish Country Dancing last week. They would find out this afternoon in the final period. While the rest of the class did gym, they would rehearse these steps until they were perfect. For they were both in the country-dancing team.

Half term came. The McMasters booked a holiday cottage at Cairnryan for the week. Margot overheard her parents talking, saying it would be a new start.

Her father said, 'Not much of a second honeymoon though, with three children in tow.'

Mrs McMaster invited June to go with them and help Margot look after her younger sisters, Fiona and Morag. Mrs McMaster told them that her husband had some important matters to think over and she would value their help with the little ones. So June and Margot were in charge of bedtime. The McMasters slept in one room and the four girls shared the double bed in the other. It was a tight squeeze in bed. They put the little ones head to toe in the middle. June and Margot would slip in head to toe on either side later. Fiona had got a thorn in her finger trying to pick late blackberries as they'd gone for a ramble that afternoon. June found a sewing needle, lit a match to sterilise it and teased the thorn out of her hand.

'There now. I'll kiss it better, shall I?' She felt very grown up being nurse.

Morag complained she had the tummy ache, but they told her it would teach her not to be so greedy blackberrying.

'That's not fair,' said Fiona. 'She's hardly ate anything all day.'

Margot shrugged. Morag was like that, scoffing one day, being picky the next.

'You'll be fine, Morag,' she cajoled. 'Don't bother Mummy now. You have a good night's sleep and you'll be right as rain in the morning.'

They went back down to sit up a while longer. The room felt heavy with unspoken thoughts. So as the evening drew in the two friends decided they might as well go up to bed and leave the adults downstairs. They could carry on talking in bed if they spoke softly. They crept in between the sheets. Both Margot's sisters had fallen asleep.

'What did I say?' whispered Margot. 'She's always complaining about her tummy and it's always fine.'

With that, she turned over and fell asleep at once. June lay awake. It was difficult to settle. She wasn't used to sharing a bed with *three* other girls. Finally she drifted off...

'Margot! Margot! I feel sick.'

Morag was crying and sitting up in bed holding her tummy. This woke her sisters as well as June. Margot was asking her what was the matter, when she vomited over the bedclothes. June rolled over to avoid the splatter and fell onto the floorboards.

Margot was flustered. 'I need a basin. Where's a basin?'

June got up feeling her bruises and tried to remember where she'd seen one. Too late. Morag was sick again.

'I need a poo,' she wailed.

June gathered her wits and found the potty from under the bed and handed it to Margot. Then she clattered down the stairs to find another basin. She would need a mop and bucket. And they would need to strip the bed. She got the basin from the kitchen sink and took it back up. Margot was in tears. She was afraid to wake her parents.

Morag wailed louder than ever. 'My tummy really hurts. Where's Mummy?'

'I think you better fetch your mother,' June said. This was beyond what they could cope with.

Margot left the room, leaving June to stroke Morag's brow and hold back her hair as she vomited into the basin. It was disgusting. Yet while she comforted the suffering child she felt a surge of affection. How often had Mummie and Auntie Dolly held and soothed her when she was ill in the night? Now it was her turn to care. She applied the lessons she had learnt unconsciously from them. It felt good.

It turned out she had appendicitis: very unfortunate!

Morag's appendicitis was the least of the McMaster's misfortunes. The story got out. When they started back after half term the boys in their class were talking about it.

'He did it to my brother, Jimmy.'

'And to our Bobby.'

'And my brother Bill too. He's only seven.'

It was disgusting. Even though June didn't fully understand, she knew it was sickening. She felt more nausea thinking about what Margot's Daddy had done to those little boys than remembering that night in bed with Morag. Morag would be fine once she'd recovered from her operation. *Would Jimmy, Bobby and Bill ever recover?*

When she told me that story, this story always came next. Her memories weren't organised according to chronology, but followed a different principle. The holiday cottages made an obvious association but I wonder if the unspoken connection was the ways of boys and men.

One friend of mine was a farmer's daughter. Her name was Jean. They had a cottage in Glenluce, called The Briars. I went to stay with her there and her older brother, Stephen, came along. I remember listening to the wireless, late at night; it was a commentary on a live boxing match.

The Hunter farm was called Whiteleys. From the front it was a traditional stone-built farm cottage, like a child's drawing of a house. Around the side and back, outhouses and barns proliferated. The Hunters kept these building whitewashed; every spring a new coat was applied. As June rode her bicycle out of town she would peer ahead to spot the gleaming walls. In spring sunshine they dazzled passers-by. The Hunters were horsey. They bred pedigrees for huntsmen. It was a lucrative business. The family owned a cottage near Glenluce, situated in a lonely spot called The Bents. On warm summer days Jean and June would cycle there from Whiteleys. Once they were allowed to spend the night there; Jean, her younger sister Nancy and June.

The cottage was called The Briars. Two rambling roses were planted either side its front door; in summer they covered the front brickwork entirely. The flowers bloomed in late spring. They were almost as pink as Auntie Dolly's Bourbon Queens, but they had fierce thorns that discouraged anyone from picking them. That didn't stop Nancy though. The first thing she did when they arrived was to march outside and gather an armful. She didn't seem bothered by the scratches up and down her forearms as she plonked them in an array of empty milk bottles. They smelt heavenly.

They took their sandwiches and rode out under the viaduct all the way to The Abbey. It was a gentle ride to an idyllic ruin. However hard they tried they couldn't conjure any unhappy ghosts in this dingle. Jean and June got supper that evening and let Nancy sit up past her bedtime. There was a big wireless in the living room Guido had made for the Hunters before he left for Plymouth. June wondered how many more homemade wireless sets Guido had left behind in Stranraer. Nancy fiddled with the dial and tuned into a live commentary broadcast from Maddison Square Garden Bowl. It was just beginning.

Through the static they could hear gales of laughter from the crowd. *What was going on?* The commentator said something about Greta Garbo they couldn't quite catch. Jean jumped up and fiddled with the dials until she found a clear signal. The commentator was describing Max Baer's antics and comparing him to a circus clown as he walked up to the ring.

'He has this huge crowd in the palm of his hand.' More gales of laughter. 'Braddock enters the ring looking very serious in his blue bathrobe. He's trained hard for this prize fight, but this kid from Hell's Kitchen's in for a *hell-uv-a* shock. Just before the match he was telling us he's ready to fight all the way. He even compared his opponent to a house pet. Well, despite Baer's clowning outside the ring, I think Braddock will find Baer's more tiger than pussycat once the fight begins. And now he's slipping off his robe and showing his pink back to the crowd as he struts around the ring raising both fists in the air.'

They sat listening to the commentary as the evening

light faded. Neither Jean nor June thought to get up and light the lamps.

'Now Baer's entering the ring, he's climbing between the ropes backwards. What a clown.' The commentator barely suppressed a chortle. 'Now he's pretending to waltz Braddock... but Braddock's having none of it. Braddock may be on his high horse now, but by the end of the evening he'll be turned back into "Cinders." Let's hope he can get home before his carriage turns back into a pumpkin!'

None of them were interested in boxing, but the novelty was captivating. Surrounded by Nancy's bunches of sweet-scented roses they sat glued to the wireless. In the mind's eye the three girls watched the faraway scene, as the older boxer, dogged and deadly serious, took heavy punches but kept on coming back. Nothing would stop him. This wasn't a clowning contest or a dance competition; this was a fight for survival and dignity. The commentator had alluded to the story of Cinderella before the fight; now it didn't seem so farfetched. Baer wasn't looking so smart now; he was perplexed that his opponent kept on getting back up off the floor. And Braddock was technically brilliant. The older man was giving the younger champion a lesson he'd not bargained for.

'He's coming at him again. Will nothing daunt him? He's starting to wear Max down.'

Darkness had fallen outside the open windows, but now the moon was high in the night sky. It was nearly full and its light illumined the room. There was the sound of a car engine and a brief glare of lights before someone switched off the engine. Jean's big brother, Stephen, had motored over to see if they were all right. He entered the room on tiptoes, not breaking the spell and crouched by the wireless set, transfixed by the commentary.

They stayed up half the night, caught up in the drama as across the world two men battled for the championship. With the prize title came fame and—more important in these Depression years—fortune. Men could box their way from rags to riches in one night if they had the determination, discipline and guts to risk all. *It was all very well the commentator comparing Braddock to Cinderella, but it was*

160

different for boys and men. They didn't have to sit around in their rags waiting until the prince came and found you.

There was a third memory about staying at a holiday house. It involved men too. Or rather one man. Her uncle. This one was harder to resurrect. We'll leave that one buried a while longer.

These years would get jumbled in the telling, as if she didn't want to admit too much about teenage June. What was clear was that there were men she was supposed to respect, who interfered with little boys or molested her, and there were boys her age who lusted after her. She remained resolutely silent on her feelings about all this.

The previous Christmas Uncle Eddie had given her a splendid book: *The Louisa M Alcott Girls' Book.* It wasn't as exquisite as her *Alice* before it got spoilt. There were only four illustrations, but they were enough to suggest how women had dressed and looked seventy years ago. It contained two complete stories, *Little Women* and *Good Wives.* It caused her to think about Grandma from a different perspective. It made her ponder what would happen when she grew up. It seemed a woman's role was to be the moral centre of gravity: she had to learn to curb her unruly passions, think of others and never be selfish. And yet it didn't seem such a bad thing to be boyish and headstrong like Jo March—and Katharine Hepburn— either. It was a balancing act and a woman must never be distracted or else she would fall. A woman was supposed to distinguish between honourable men and fast men, to gravitate towards the former and avoid the latter at all costs. The March girls had their Marmee to guide them on their journey to adulthood. But Mummie wasn't a bit like Marmee. She seemed more in need of a Marmee than June. Grandma Rodger no longer ruled the household; she had reached the decline of her life. Auntie Dolly had moved to Dumfries with Uncle Birrell and Mummie lost her anchor. The March girls played at being Pilgrims and progressing towards perfect womanhood, with Marmee for their guide. But June had no firm guide; she knew she'd have to find the path to happiness on her own.

She met Alastair Baird through Jean Hunter. Jean had known him since they were little because they'd played together whenever the family stayed in the Glenluce cottage. He was a couple of years older than them. Jean Hunter held a Christmas party to celebrate the end of their first term at Stranraer High School. She invited Alastair, even though he went to school in Newton Stewart.

'He'll help to even out the numbers,' she told June during lunch break. She and June both stayed for school dinner every day. Their mothers had insisted on that and they were glad. The girls who went home for dinner seemed fagged out in the afternoon. June loved the hot dinners and the steamed puddings for afters. And she had more time to spend with her friends.

'What's Alastair like?' June asked.

Jean thought for a moment as she finished a mouthful of chicken pie. 'He's got blue eyes and sandy coloured hair. He bikes a lot and he's slim and fit. We've played together since we were wee bairns and he's always gentle. Not like other boys.'

'Why do you think that is?'

'His Dad's the doctor in Glenluce. And he's our doctor too. He's always so kind when I'm ill. Alastair's just like him.'

'Will he follow his Daddy?'

'His older brother, Hugh, will get the practice. But he wants to be a doctor anyway. He told me he couldn't imagine any other life.' She toyed with her peas. 'Isn't it funny. When I grow up I can't imagine doing anything other than looking after the farm and the horses.'

'I don't know what I want to be when I grow up. I don't want to be like Mummie. And I'm not sure I want to be like Auntie Dolly, alone in her house while Uncle Birrell's away at sea.' June pushed her peas around her plate before shovelling them into her mouth. 'Maybe it would be different if I were a doctor's wife.' The both laughed and spluttered their peas, till the new science teacher, Mr Miller, came and told them off.

At the party, Jean made sure Alastair was introduced to

June. Auntie Dolly had made her a new skirt for Christmas and Mummie let her wear it to the party. It was burnt orange, of soft wool weave cut on the bias. It was fashionably calf-length and flowed and swirled as she walked into the room. She'd a new cream silk blouse Mummie had made her, because she was growing so fast and the buttons on her old best blouse kept coming undone. Over it she wore the lacey rose-pink bolero Mummie had crocketed for Auntie Dolly's wedding. She'd washed her hair the night before and slept with it pinned in rags, so that it fell in waves. And she'd parted it just like Katharine Hepburn in a low side-parting to accentuate the waves above her forehead. She was tall for her age and to Alastair seemed the most grown-up girl in the room. He worried she would think him too timid and shy, but he discovered she was not ebullient and boisterous the way Jean could be. At the end of the evening he asked her if she would like to go to the cinema with him in the holidays. And she agreed.

It was awkward. Betty didn't have a steady boyfriend. In fact none of the girls in her class did. Then Alastair had to study hard most weekends, because he was determined to go to Medical School and become a doctor.

'You have to get really good marks to get in,' he told June on their first date, 'and it would break Daddy's heart if I didn't.'

'But what about you?' she asked. 'What do you want to do?'

He took her question seriously and stared up Loch Ryan, as if the answer hovered on the horizon somewhere out at sea.

'I want to be a doctor more than anything else in the world,' he told her solemnly.

They decided they would meet once a month and go to the cinema together. That way he could swot the other weekends and she wouldn't neglect Betty. And that's what they did for the best part of a year. It took Alastair an hour to cycle over to King Street. He would arrive in time to take her to the Saturday matinee. There they would sit in the stalls—the same seats as she and Mummie had always sat in—and hold hands. Afterwards they would go for an ice

163

cream soda at Bonugli's ice cream bar and Mrs Bonugli would tell her news of Guido. Sometimes Giuseppe, who was in her class, would come and talk to them, but he would soon get bored and wander behind the counter into the back room. If it was a nice evening they would stroll to the Loch and saunter round Agnew Park. Then they would make their way back to 9 King Street. Alastair would say goodbye and give her a peck on her cheek. And that would be that until the next month.

Soon after the night of the boxing match June went to stay the night with Jean at the farm. The following morning Alastair came cycling with Jean and June. His Daddy had told him he needed to stop studying so much and get out in the fresh air. He'd be no good as a doctor if he neglected his own health. So the three of them rode all the way from Whiteleys to Port William. They showed him where they'd camped at Stair Haven and laughed about the mouse in June's palliasse. She felt that he understood in a way Jean never did. Nothing seemed to frighten her. June had to admit she was getting fond of Alastair, with his serious look and gentle, timid ways. It was six months since they'd first met and they got along fine. *But would she be happy spending the rest of her days in Glenluce?* She couldn't decide.

There were two other farms I used to stay at. Margaret MacCaig and her twin brother, Stewart, lived at Challock a few miles away at Leswalt; she was one of five children. John, the eldest, was to take over the farm; by the time I left Scotland he had become very fond of me. The other girls whose farm I stayed at once or twice were the daughters of a friend of my mother's called Mrs McMaster. Her brother-in-law, Jack, who was a rubber planter in the Philippines, used to come home every three years and propose to my mother—he always brought a lovely big box of Terry's All Gold. We decided he wasn't quite what she wanted.

The McMasters were plagued by scandal. Not only was Margot's father abusing wee boys, but also his sister-in-law was brought before the Sheriff's Court for torturing her maid. June wished that Auntie Dolly were still working there, so that she could tell them the gossip. She gleaned what she could from the *Free Press* when Grandma wasn't looking. She'd tied the maid to the bed and whipped her till the poor girl was terrified for her life. Then she'd left her tied up, turned the key on the door and walked away. Somehow, the maid had managed to struggle free of her bonds, escaped through the window and run half-naked to the nearest cottage to raise the alarm.

'But why would she do such a thing?' June asked Margot one dinnertime.

'Jealousy,' murmured Margot as her cheeks turned pink.

June persisted. 'What was she jealous of?'

'My uncle got her pregnant.' Margot's eyes were directed at her plate of beef stew. She concentrated on finding the last bit of red meat from amongst the tatties and carrots.

June chewed on a bit of gristle, extracting the flavour, then spat it out. She went quiet as she digested this confidence.

That March, June turned thirteen. Easter was late that year but the April weather was still disappointing. Then on Maundy Thursday the skies cleared and it felt pleasantly warm. Mrs MacCaig rang Mummie and asked if June would like to go and stay for the Easter weekend. The daffodils were in full bloom and her cherry tree was a delight to behold. June jumped at the chance. Margaret was always fun to be with and Stewart never bothered her.

It took June about twenty minutes to cycle to Challock. Margaret was one of five children. June envied her. *She would have at least five children when she grew up.* The farmhouse was set back from the road. At the entrance were two stone pillars. She dismounted her bike and pushed it up the drive to the farmhouse, which was surrounded by beech trees. In the front garden the first thing she saw was the cherry tree. She didn't know if it had been trained or just grew like that, but its canopy spread out flat to offer shelter from the sun—or even light rain, as she discovered when she and Margaret sat there sipping lemonade and eating Mrs MacCaig's delicious sultana scones. It was a busy dairy farm and milking was in full swing when they finished their afternoon tea. Margaret took her over to the cowsheds to watch.

John, the eldest, was in charge. He would take over the farm when his father retired. Already he had lots of responsibility; he patiently showed June how they milked the cows and explained what would happen to the milk. There were two dairies in Stranraer. His father had always used the same one, down near the Loch, but he'd started playing them off one against the other for the best price. If you stayed with just the one all the time they would take you for granted and pay less, he'd discovered. He was proud of his enterprise and looked even prouder when June expressed her admiration of the ploy. He offered June a ladle of fresh milk to sip.

'Taste it,' he coaxed. 'It's so much sweeter straight from the cow's udder.'

She took a tentative sup. It was warm, frothy and so creamy. *Heaven.* Mrs MacCaig kept a churn back now and again to make soft cheese. It was delicious: rich, velvety and with a distinct tang that excited June's taste buds. She couldn't have told you why, but it felt naughty to be eating something so luscious and earthy. They ate it for supper with a fresh, homemade cob and Mrs McCaig's cherry jam.

'Now, you'll tell me if you don't like it, June,' she fussed. 'I won't be offended. It's not to everyone's taste.' She glanced at Stewart as she spoke.

It was a new taste for June: slightly tart and sour but mingled with the sweetness of the preserving sugar, it felt heady and exciting. She liked it and said so.

'I like the combination of the cheese and the jam, Mrs McCaig. We don't eat them together at our house,' she added, 'but they go really well together.'

'You've said the right thing there, lass,' said her husband.

'She'll be inviting you back now, that's for sure,' muttered John. A shy smile lit up his ruddy face.

John spent much of the weekend showing her round the farm. He was a few years older—he'd left school already, but treated her as an equal. It was flattering. Margaret didn't notice how much attention he was paying to her. She took her eldest brother for granted along with her other brothers, but she enjoyed his explanations as much as June.

'He's never told me half as much since he left school as he's told you this weekend,' she commented.

June felt a glow of satisfaction.

Monday afternoon came too quickly. It was time to leave. She wondered whether she would see John to say goodbye, but he was busy in the milking parlour. Or so she thought. She'd just got to the pillars at the bottom of the drive and was about to mount her bike, when he came sprinting down the drive.

'Here. Take this cheese home with you since it pleases you so much.' He handed her a packet of his mother's soft cheese, carefully wrapped in waxed paper. While she found a safe place to stow it in her full bicycle basket, he shuffled from foot to foot.

'I'm sorry, I'm keeping you from the milking.' She looked him in the eye.

He returned her gaze. 'Not at all,' was all he said.

'Well goodbye then,' and she held out her hand. 'And thank-you so much for showing me round the farm. I've really enjoyed it.'

He took her hand in his larger one and held it just a second too long.

'June…'

'Yes.'

He hesitated. 'Would you like to go to the cinema next Saturday? There's a film on I'd like to see, *David Copperfield.*'

She wasn't sure. He was so much older. Grandma might not approve.

He saw her qualms. 'I'll ask Margaret and Stewart to come as well, if you'll go.'

'In that case, I'd love to,' she replied.

Margaret and Stewart accompanied them that first afternoon. Still it felt like a date. John sat next to her, with Margaret on the other side. When Mr Mudstone thrashed David, she winced. John took her hand and held it for the rest of the picture.

And so a pattern developed that continued for the next couple of years. One Saturday a month she went to the pictures with Alastair and held hands. One Saturday a month she went to the pictures with John and held hands.

The intervening weeks she went with Betty. Each matinee was special and she would have hated to have to choose between her companions.

By the time I left Scotland he had become very fond of me. Sadly he died soon after of T.B. When I married thirteen years later I was pleasantly surprised to receive two fine linen pillowcases from his mother whom I had never seen in all that time. I felt that there was something symbolic about that present.

When I look back I realise this was a pattern which continued when she was a teenager in Crosby and later with Denny in Southport and the other suitor in London. Was his name Patrick? I tried to suppress her telling me this after Denny died. It was too painful to hear.

June was happy at the High School and did well there. After long hours of solitude spent with Grandpa Rodger's edition of *The Waverley Novels* and his *County Seats*, she loved English and History. Miss Graham taught both subjects. There was an undercurrent of romance about Miss Graham. Word quickly spread that Mr Sutherland was soft on her. He would connive to share dinner duty with her and on those days they knew that they could linger, chattering over their pudding and delay going out into the *dreich fret* for their dinner-break 'breath of fresh air.'

Many of her friends from The Academy were in her class and she made new friends easily. Being chosen for the Scottish Country Dance team helped. She hated gym lessons; they left her dispirited and breathless. But she never tired of learning new dance figures. Maybe it was because she spent too much time on her own as an only child, but she loved the connection with others as they moved together to perfect ever more intricate patterns. Then there was singing together in the choir. She couldn't find the words to describe the pleasure of combining her voice with three-dozen others. She didn't know that Dr Richard had a quiet word with Frank Lewis one morning after Church, saying that singing would benefit her breathing and reduce the breathlessness. Mr Lewis said he would be happy to encourage her singing voice. He would have accepted her anyway; hers was a promising voice, not naturally strong, but sweet. And he was short of mezzos.

He almost regretted his decision when he took the choir to the Newton Stewart Festival at the end of her first year. They had to arrive early at school that morning to catch the charabanc to Newton Stewart. It took the best part of two hours to make the journey. As they entered Newton Stewart he looked dismayed. The driver missed the turning up to the school.

'Archie,' he exclaimed, 'You should have turned left back there.'

Archie seemed unconcerned. He drove deliberately over the old Cree bridge. When he reached the other side he stopped and parked the charabanc.

'Now what's he up to?' Mr Lewis ran his fingers through his hair till it stood on end.

'These lads and lasses aren't going to sing well on rumbling tummies,' was all Archie said. He got down beside The Toll Bar. Once it had been The Toll House and the Toll Keeper collected a penny from everyone crossing it, but now it was a wee shop.

'Now what's he doing?' Mr Lewis fretted. 'We'll be late at this rate.'

Archie stepped to the tiny window on the side of the Toll House and knocked on the shutters. Mrs McAllister opened them. He beckoned to his passengers and they tumbled out. They all liked their music master. He never used the strap and never made them feel stupid. He had a warm singing voice. When she sang for him June experienced a heartfelt thrill. Usually he remained calm in the face of inevitable annoyances, so that everyone stopped being naughty out of a desire to please him and make him smile. But this morning June led the way and everyone followed. They disobeyed his frantic pleadings for them to get back on the bus. Mrs McAllister's salmon sandwiches were legendary. Coming from Lancashire, Mr Lewis hadn't heard about them until that summer morning. Everyone had bought their tuppence ha'penny with them. You didn't visit Newton Stewart without getting a fresh salmon sandwich.

Melt in the mouth flakes of salmon, bread still warm from the oven and Mrs McAllister never stinted the creamy butter. As they ate they wandered across the bridge to watch the river tumbling topsy-turvy in its course. Then they crossed to the other side and looked downstream. Here the river widened and the water ran smoothly. Sunbeams caught the gentle ripples on the surface, broken by reflections of the whitewashed cottages and trees on the riverbank. Thirty-six choristers stood watching the river change from shaggy to smooth while they wolfed down these delicacies. Frank Lewis nearly tore his hair out rushing around trying to prevent them eating before they sang.

What was he afraid of? Being late? Crumbs stuck in throats? His failure to maintain discipline? He needn't have worried. They loved him all the more for this singular lapse in masterly authority. When they got on stage they sang as one, drawn together by that delicious interlude on the old bridge that no other master would have sanctioned. He was their conductor and they thanked him by singing their hearts out for him.

Alastair was in the audience listening intently, his blue eyes fixed on her face. Her body vibrated with the melody. All year Mr Lewis had drilled technique into them. She enunciated clearly, kept time punctiliously and concentrated extra hard on maintaining the pitch. All those evenings of choir practice came together and something else happened. They became the music: it flowed through them and they flowed through it. No wonder Alastair stared so. He'd never seen her look so ecstatic.

Afterwards she felt guilty. The previous weekend, she'd given John MacCaig the photo of herself he'd asked for and he'd told her he would carry it in his breast pocket till the day he died.

After Daddy died, Auntie Dolly told me he had a photograph of me in his pocket.

In autumn 1940, Alastair turned up at the Men's Union Freshers' Dance. He was in his third year. He walked her

170

home and with a chaste kiss left her on the doorstep.

I had the first two years at Stranraer High School before we moved to Crosby. I remember that I was looking forward to going into the third year, because then I could drop Science.

Not all the masters were as benign as Frank Lewis. June's grasp of maths and science wasn't as good as her skill in singing and spelling. Mr Miller, who taught them science for a while, could easily be brought to a pitch of exasperation over her ignorance of the periodic table and her bungling over Bunsen burners. She tried but it didn't make any sense to her and her experiments never turned out the way the textbook said they should. In fact, the more she tried the worse it got, until she'd find herself forgetting how to spell correctly as she tried to write up her failed experiments. One afternoon she was feeling particularly stupid. She had cramps in her tummy and was praying the bleeding wouldn't start till she'd got safely home. Usually she had a couple of hours grace when all that appeared was a slight rusty-brown stain. But the pain was getting insistent and she felt slightly sick. She glanced at the clock on the wall above Mr Miller's head. Only half an hour to go.

He saw her look at the clock. 'June Hepburn.'

'Yes, Mr Miller.'

'Would you be so good as to tell the class the names of the Noble Gases?'

All she could think of was *Ivanhoe*. 'Wi...' she began— the name, Wilfred, was on the tip of her tongue—then halted as her cheeks turned from ghastly white to bright red. She tried again.

'Fluorine, chlorine, iodine and... and gromine,' that wasn't right, 'and bromine, Sir.' *Phew, that was a narrow escape. Maybe now he would leave her alone for the rest of the lesson.*

But, 'No, No, No!' he shouted. He walked over to the high desk where she was sitting behind a Bunsen burner, reached over and picked up her textbook. He opened it at the periodic table and pointed at it.

'Is it so hard to din this into yerself?' he screamed.

'Heaven knows, yer've had enough weeks to learn it.' He paced back the length of the lab, then noticed he was still clutching her textbook.

He turned around, bent back his right arm and threw it at her with all his might. It bounced off the side of her face and fell to the floor. She got down from her stool, retrieved it and put it in her satchel. Then she gathered up her pencil, rubber and pen. She placed them deliberately into her pencil-case and put it in her satchel. Finally, she picked up her exercise book, folded it shut and, when she'd put it in her satchel too, turned her stiff back on him and walked out of the science lab.

Hindoo found her sitting on the floor in the corridor, clutching her stomach and trying not to cry. She didn't ask any questions. Instead, she helped her to her feet and took her to the empty staff room. Here she administered a cup of hot, sweet tea and a compress soaked in cold water. She even lent her a sanitary belt and gave her a sanitary pad, so that she could get home safely.

Hindoo to us because she was so dark-skinned.

Her name was Miss Henderson and she taught science. June wished she still had her instead of Mr Miller. Stewart had heard that he was an 'interim,' while Mr Hendry was away at Glasgow studying. She wondered if Mr Hendry would have thrown a book at her in front of the whole class. Hindoo would never do that. This wasn't to be the last time Hindoo would come to her rescue.

She loved acting. All those evenings sat with Lizzie, pretending to be characters from her comics, had enhanced her talent for playing different roles. She got leading roles when she auditioned for the end of term plays. This prompted her to audition for the role of Margot in the annual operetta. Mr Lewis said her voice technique had improved greatly over the year. Her breath control was much better and her voice had a richness to it that was unusual for someone her age. This encouraged her, since he would be in charge of auditions with Hindoo as his assistant.

They realised that the operetta was an important moment in the school calendar when the Headmaster got involved. He left the singing and acting to Frank Lewis and Miss Henderson, busying himself over the 'elements of spectacle.'

'The visual aspect is as important as the words and music in a production such as this,' he pontificated. 'The audience must be conveyed to Morocco for the entire evening.'

The story was quite risqué, but none of the teachers seemed concerned. If it had been set in Wigtownshire it would have been a different matter. But with its exotic setting it was just harmless make-believe. The Headmaster was adamant that the scenery and costumes must suggest 'the Orient'; he was a stickler for detail. He was particularly concerned that the lead female characters, Azuri and Margot, look the part. On the first night he fussed around Pearl and June, tugging here and tucking there. Finally he was satisfied with Pearl's appearance. June hoped he'd let them both go and take their places in the wings. She was starting to feel slight stage fright. Her whole family would be watching: Mummie and Grandma of course. Uncle Eddie and Uncle Ernie had travelled down on the Glasgow train together and Auntie Dolly had joined them at Dumfries. She wanted to show them what a good actress she'd become and, truth be told, show off in her glamorous costume.

'Hmm,' he muttered, holding June at arms' length, 'that's still not quite right.' Another tweak and he was done at last. Until the interval.

For the next scene June was to wear a headband holding a scarf that was supposed to flow down her back. As she emerged from the dressing room, he looked at her and tut-tutted.

'Come into my study a moment. The light's better in there.'

She had no choice but to follow him and stand still while he adjusted her headband. He was taking an age, caressing the folds of the headscarf, rearranging her bodice, moving her head in every direction 'to get a better view.' She was glad when Hindoo opened the door and pretended surprise to find them there.

'Excuse me, headmaster,' she said. 'I was looking for Azuri's basket.' She paused, then added. 'I think June looks perfect now, don't you?'

He had no choice but to let June go, grumbling that Pearl should be more careful with her props.

It was only later I realised that the fumbling by the headmaster back stage might have had something to do with my prize for 'all-round improvement.'

Grandma Rodger was very strict; her whole code of behaviour was so strict.

'Operator! Oh! Is it you yourself, Jeannie?... Yes, it's May here... Yes, I am a bit. It's Ma! She's had a funny turn. Yes, I need to fetch Dr Richard right away. Can you put me through to him, please? Oh, and Jeannie, after that can you put me through to my brother Ernie?... Yes, that's the one in Giffnock... You know his number better than me... Oh! Would you? Say she's taken a turn for the worse and I think he better come down today.'

She waited for Dr Richard to pick up his receiver. It was a matter of seconds but it seemed an age to her.

Then back to her ailing mother, who, having woken feeling faint, had decided to have a long lie-in that morning. May was used to nursing her parents; she'd left school to nurse her father in the last two years of his life. She had a naturally gentle, sickbed manner; her affection poured into attentive caring. She fetched the china potty and helped her mother sit up in bed to relieve herself. She never thought to fetch Dolly from the town hall. And June had got up bright and early to go for a long bicycle ride in the country with Jean from Whiteleys and Margaret from Challock. Anyways, she was used to coping on her own in the sick room. Even though her mother was experiencing shortness of breath and dizziness, and even though she'd summoned the doctor and her big brother, Ernie, she couldn't fully accept her intuition that her mother might be approaching her last breath; she was too focussed on making her comfortable.

Dr James Richard M.B. Ch.B. arrived post haste. He knew Ma Rodger well and felt a strong respect for this indomitable old lady. Like May his mind didn't want to accept the evidence of his eyes. He took his patient's pulse, got out his stethoscope and placed it on her chest above her heart. He bent over solicitously and listened intently. He maintained a professional demeanour but by the faint furrowing of his brows May could tell he was concerned by what he heard.

'Ha' ye experienced any pains, Mrs Rodger?' he asked as he straightened himself.

'Well, yes, Doctor. I keep getting this sharp pain in my neck... then sometimes it shoots down my back.'

'Do ye get it in your arm as well?'

She looked as if she were reluctant to admit this was the case. 'Yes, doctor,' was all she said.

Then turning to May, 'How's your mother been these past few days, Mrs Hepburn? Have you noticed anything different?'

'Well, Doctor, she's been complaining of feeling tired of late. That's all, really. You know Ma, she's got a will of iron. But she's been spending more and more time in bed.'

'How long's this been going on?'

'Oh, I'd say since the start of the Easter holidays. You remember, Ma, you had such a lie-in that first morning of the school holiday, we joked about it... said now June's becoming a teenager she's more tiring than ever?'

Ma Rodger nodded weakly and Dr Richard decided he might stay a bit longer, accepting Mrs Hepburn's offer of a bowl of homemade cock-a-leekie soup and a generous slice of white bread and butter. Ma Rodger's agreed to try a little mouthful to keep her strength up, but only managed a few spoonfuls of the broth, spitting the leeks back out into her bowl. She slept fitfully about half an hour then woke complaining that her neck and jaw were paining her. She tossed fitfully, unable to get comfy and finally declared she wanted to get dressed before June got home. Dr Roberts reluctantly allowed her to; he knew she'd do it anyway if she'd a mind to. He packed up his leather bag and said he'd let himself out, but that he might pop by later when he'd finished the rest of his afternoon rounds. *Just to check once more.* May helped her mother wash with a flannel in a basin and get dressed. It took a long time; May was so patient and tender towards her, it made the old lady shed a tear. She lifted her head and grasped May's hand to her cheek.

'Thank-you, May. Thank-you so much for all you've done... all you do for me. I know it's not been easy for you, but I want you to know... I want you to know... that I...that I... I appreciate it... very... much... indeed...'

She reached for the arm of her chair and lowered herself gingerly into her seat, when she bent over double onto her left side. May watched aghast as the sweat beads gathered on her mother's forehead, then all over her face and neck. She gasped for breath and her face contorted in agony.

'I think I better lie down again,' she rasped in a breathless whisper.

When June finally arrived back to King Street, a glow on her cheeks and a sparkle in her eyes, the blinds were drawn.

Dr James Richard M.B Ch.B. filled out the death certificate at four o'clock on the afternoon of the 12th April 1935. As cause of death he stated: 'Coronary Thrombosis—1 day, Arterio-Sclerosis and Senility.' The following day Uncle Ernie registered the death and the death certificate was signed by J. Bradford, Registrar. The funeral took place on the 15th April.

Like her husband before her, Grandma Rodger had always been a strong advocate of Temperance. Uncle Alf, who had caught the train with his wife and family, to attend the service, was heard to murmur at the wake: 'Now who's to say whether a wee dram taken once a day might not have prevented that thrombosis?' A slight frown furrowed Auntie Minnie's brow, but she chose to pretend she'd not heard his remark and turned to talk to Auntie Annie, who was piling her plate high with cake, as usual.

Once all the family had gone back home, Emily May Hepburn and Valerie June Hepburn were more than ever on their own.

By the time she wrote her memories they were jumbled. And the two years between starting Stranraer High and moving to Crosby were the most fragmented. As if some things were best forgotten.

Grandpa Hepburn was a minister. Cousin Margaret's father was the minister at the Abbey Church in Dublin. Auntie Kate married her father's best friend's son, Alec McPherson, and he went to the Presbyterian Theological College in Cambridge. I went to stay with them every summer while we lived in Stranraer. I would catch the ferry to Dublin and be met when I got there. I remember we used to catch the tram to Phoenix Park, where there was an elephant you could ride on. One time the tram pole fell through the roof of the tram. I remember the River Liffey: Margaret and I would walk down to the shore. We went down steps to a sweet shop; there was a woman there who made homemade toffee. Margaret McPherson was the nearest thing to a sister to me.

Then there was Cousin Allan in the Gorbals. Years later, after you'd been born, Cousin Margaret rang to say that Allan was dying and he wanted me to know. Whenever I was going to Dublin from Stranraer to stay for the summer holidays, I was put on the boat at Stranraer and the Captain kept an eye on me. Usually Helen or Mary came to collect me at Dublin, but one time, Allan came to collect me instead. On the bus back home, he fell on my shoulder all the way to Dublin. I was upset it wasn't Helen or Mary who had come. Years later, he eloped with a young woman from his congregation.

Cousin Helen had got married and didn't live at the Manse anymore. Both Mary and Margaret were busy recording one of the entertainments they regularly wrote and performed for the radio. So Cousin Allan was sent to fetch her. He was sixteen years older than she was. As the only son he had been destined for the Church. He was twenty-nine years old and not yet married. He was tall, lean and dark like his father. This summer he sported a moustache, which accentuated his sensuous lips. June felt his deep-set, intense gaze before she picked him out in the crowd standing waiting on the quayside. He rushed forward to greet her warmly, grabbed her suitcase, grasped her hand in his and led her pell-mell through the crowd to the tram. The driver was starting to leave, but Allan hailed him and pulling June along with him, sprinted the last few yards and dragged her onto the tram.

They collapsed in the first available seats, he laughing, she panting to catch her breath. She felt ruffled and bothered by his highhanded manner.

'Phew,' he gasped. 'That was a close shave. If we'd not caught this one we'd have had a half-hour wait.' He laughed and with mock-exhaustion laid his head on her shoulder. Where it stayed for the entire journey into Dublin.

Dublin was exciting and disturbing. When she looked past his head out the tram window, the streets and houses unsettled her. She reminded herself she always felt this at first. She was in another country now, where people did things differently. She stopped trying to count the motorcars. They were everywhere. She couldn't see how they didn't collide with one another, nor with the horse-and-carts and pony-traps that trotted briskly alongside and occasionally darted across their path. Then there were the bicycles, often two or three abreast, weaving intrepid through the congested traffic. And the jay-walkers, stepping jauntily off the curb-side and striding through the lanes of traffic. The only person controlling this pandemonium was the traffic policeman, stopping and directing traffic with his white-gloved hands. Even the implacable trams stopped and queued in obedience to his dextrous commands. The trams were so tall, they loomed over the rest of the traffic, with their advertising slogans: BOVRIL, Millar & Beatty, O'Hara's, Players, Denny's Bacon, Heaton's Coal, Wallace's Coal, Sutton's Coal, Tyler's Boots, Royal Baking Powder, CLERY'S. She felt her foreignness when she didn't know what these names referred to. And there were more slogans on the roadside: Hospital Sweep Derby 1935 in foot-high lettering; Vote Sinn Féin, an old election poster, weathered but triumphant. And the people, crowding the pavements, crossing the roads, looking full of purpose, though occasionally a man would loiter, staring at the city bustle before he dove back into it.

It was almost twenty years since the Uprising. Yet she tasted the lingering fear and excitement of it as she wet her lips and swallowed nervously. (Allan was still resting his head on her shoulder and she didn't know how to budge him without seeming rude.) How did a people do that? Take up arms and be prepared to lose their lives just to seize a bakery, a post office and a public park? Two brothers fighting on opposite sides? The rebels getting their arms from the Germans, while mother's sons were away in Flanders dying in the Great War? She sensed it in the atmosphere, even on this tram: the mix of English and Gaelic reaching her ears, the dogged determination in some men's eyes and the dreamy look of others. While her father had been dying of T.B., Irishmen had fought for Independence and given their lives to the cause. She wondered if she would ever feel strong enough to risk her life for an idea.

The initial sense of Dublin's foreignness didn't wear off on this visit. Grandma's death that spring, quickly followed by Fred's, had altered her. She'd grown up in a household that lived under the shadow of death, her Daddy's. But he'd always been dead to her. This was different. Her world had undergone irreversible change. Death was a reality now, whether from sniper fire, the firing squad or the body wearing out with chronic disease and age. What you thought was permanent—the way things were—could be transformed in a day. Just as Auntie Dolly could make over her best red dress into a summer dress for her four-year old niece, or as MacDonagh and MacBride and Connolly and Pearse could change Ireland utterly.

Volumes of Yeats's poetry were strewn about the Manse. Yeats' poetry was an inspiration to the whole family. They enjoyed declaiming it and each year June was commandeered as a new audience member. Uncle Alec read 'Easter 1916' with passion.

'Yeats is a visionary,' he said. 'His vision is for a Protestant, liberal nation. A United Ireland where Protestants and Catholics can coexist without conflict. Our church,' he meant *his* church, 'is at the heart of Dublin right where the rebellion began. It would be wrong to ignore this fact. These were ardent men who believed in their dream. I have to offer my congregation hope and faith that supports them.' He paused to reflect. 'Our role is to be true guides, who put folk in touch both with their Irish culture and the living God—not with a collection of reliquaries.' He looked at Allan as he said this. He was preparing to pass the mantle on to his son.

'The priests have a lot to answer for,' mused Allan. 'They either make folk into revolutionaries or sheep.' This was a side of Allan she'd not seen before. 'People have to be free to discover God for themselves, to think for themselves and to build a future as an independent, modern nation.'

Mary loved to learn new poems by heart and recite them to everyone after tea. One evening she recited 'A Prayer for My Daughter.' She was word perfect and had the right accent for it too: the family called it Anglo-Irish, like Yeats himself. June thought this was a bit pretentious, but maybe Mary and Margaret had developed a way of speaking that blended the bland Englishness of Auntie Kate with the native Dublin of Uncle Alec. June didn't understand the poem, but she loved the sound of it as Mary rolled it round her tongue. One line stood out: 'May she become a flourishing hidden tree.' *Was that what a woman was destined to be? Was that what Helen would be now she was married to Bob?*

The poem seemed to remind Uncle Alec of his eldest daughter too.

'Do you find things have changed here at The Manse with Helen gone?'

'The linnet has flown the nest,' muttered Allan, his unruly side peeking through.

'Well,' Auntie Kate sighed, 'it's a shame you couldn't get to the wedding. But Helen understood, of course. Such a shame about Fred. How will May get on without him, do you think?'

June couldn't have said what it was about Auntie Kate's voice that irritated her so much. But it did. Perhaps it was the lack of a Galloway Irish accent with its inherent warmth. Just to listen to Mummie and Auntie Dolly was comforting—a cradle of words to keep you safe. Auntie

Kate always sounded so proper, as if she lacked sympathy.

'I'm sure she'll be just fine, Auntie Kate,' she answered haughtily. 'You know he signed the house over to her a while back now and he left her his shares in his will.'

'Did he now? Well it's no more than she deserves. She's sacrificed a lot to care for him all these years.'

June hadn't thought of it like that before. She couldn't imagine how her life would have been up until now without Fred always there.

'Anyway, you deserve a break from all that. The weather's set fair. Perhaps you could take the girls to Phoenix Park tomorrow, Allan.' This wasn't a suggestion, but an imperative.

June had trouble getting to sleep that night, dreading what he might get up to at the Zoo. However, Allan behaved impeccably. She hardly recognised the unruly cousin of her arrival at Dublin in this upright, God-fearing, trainee minister. Phoenix Park was about four miles away, so they hopped on a tram. June was hesitant to climb the narrow winding stairs to the open-air top deck, but Mary and Margaret surged up and she had no choice but to follow. Besides, she feared that Allan might take advantage of her hesitation to offer her an affectionate hand-up from behind. Once safely sat in the front seat between Mary and Margaret, she breathed more easily. Soon she felt the exhilaration rise as she gazed at the busy streets and pavements. She started to see details she'd missed yesterday: how stylish the women looked in the latest spring fashions. She wondered how many of them made their own clothes. *Could all these pedestrians afford to buy a new outfit in Delaney's twice a year?* She tried to imagine how it would feel living in a big foreign city, earning a sufficient living to always dress smart and stay fashionable.

Where in Scotland could you see African lions? As she gazed at the male pacing in his enclosure, Margaret told her that this was the lion that roared at the start of every Metro-Goldwyn-Mayer movie.

'You're kidding me!'

'No I'm not,' Margaret replied indignant.

'Actually,' intervened Allan, 'you're both right. Slats was born here in Dublin Zoo but he's retired. He was on all the silent movies they made. His son took over for the talkies; he's called Leo the Lucky.'

'Why Lucky?'

'He survived a plane crash in the Arizona desert.'

'What happened?'

'The plane crashed miles from anywhere and the pilot left him in his cage while he went to get help. He walked for four days before he found the nearest telephone. When the rescue party finally reached the plane Leo was fine; he'd survived on milk and water.'

'Do you believe in luck, Allan?'

'Now June, that's a serious theological question you're asking there. You know we believe in God's Grace, not in the operations of the Goddess Fortuna.'

'Yes, but what about the animals? Does God look after them as well?'

'We discussed this at Theological College. There are different points of view on the subject. St Francis of Assisi says we are all God's creatures. Others believe that Nature was made to serve mankind; like the ass that Jesus rode upon. But then again, Jesus says: *Behold the fowls of the air: for they sow not, neither do they reap, nor gather into barns; yet your heavenly Father feedeth them. Are ye not much better than they?*'

'I've never understood that verse. Is Jesus saying we should be idle all our lives and not strive to work hard and to improve ourselves and the world?'

'That's a good point, June. Martin Luther hit the nail on the head about that. He said that God provides food for the birds but does not drop it in their beaks. God provides us with his beneficent world, but it's up to us to act as worthy stewards and husbandmen, not idle loiterers.'

By now they were by the monkey enclosure. June was fascinated by their antics; they seemed so sociable. They weren't that much different from human beings. She was fascinated but slightly disturbed that she enjoyed gazing at the mothers nursing their babies and pairs of grown adults contentedly picking fleas from one another's coats.

'Can we have a ride on the elephant, Allan?' asked Margaret.

'Yes, please Allan,' added Mary. 'I'm sure June would like that.'

June put her disquiet to one side; there was nothing she would like more than to ride on the elephant. *How often would she get such an opportunity? Allan was in a good mood after their theological discussion.* She put on her most winning smile and added her pleas to those of her cousins. Allan couldn't resist.

June and her cousins rode on the elephant. All day there was an on-shore breeze, a blue sky, what the Catholics called Mary's colour, and light feathers of cloud high in the atmosphere. Swaying lazily in the howdah, drifting beneath her floppy sunhat, June daydreamed she was in another country far from home. She decided she would travel and see exotic places before she died.

By the end of the afternoon the wind was blowing more strongly. The three girls felt thirsty and fatigued by the heat. As they boarded the tram Allan grabbed June's arm and steered her to the seats at the back.

'Aww! Can't we go up on the top deck?' Mary complained.

'No,' was all he said.

'Why not?'

'You three have had far too much sun already today. I'm supposed to be looking after you. Mummy will be cross when she sees how hot and bothered you all are.'

Margaret and Mary walked reluctantly after him until a large buxom lady, with perspiration shining on her brow, told them to get a move on; she didn't have all day and she needed to sit.

All the seats were soon taken; passengers stood in the aisles and clung to whatever they could find to steady themselves. Everyone was at the same pitch of exasperation as the buxom lady, who squeezed at the end of their bench seat wiping her face with a none too clean handkerchief. There was none of the good-humoured banter that usually eddied up and down the aisle. Even the tram-driver seemed impatient. He nearly clipped a horse and cart carrying a tinker family that darted across his path. June wondered whether he should be driving so fast. As he turned to cross Island Bridge the tram swayed. Allan put his arm out to steady her and she was almost grateful for his attention. The buxom lady tut-tutted her disapproval.

Although June wasn't sure if it was of the tram-driver or Allan, whose arm lingered a little too long around her waist.

'You know that was renamed after the Rebellion,' he remarked, as if he were unaware of where his hand was. 'But it's wishful thinking. They'll never persuade the Orangemen to leave Great Britain.'

'Nor should they,' added Mary.

The buxom lady blew loudly into her handkerchief with which she had been wiping her sweaty palms.

There was a general lack of conversation for a while. People were either too dozy with the heat or concentrating on keeping their balance. They got to Queen Maeve's Bridge.

'What a terrible name for a bridge,' Allan was saying, when there was the most awful clang and clatter. 'What was that?' he shouted. 'A thunder bolt?'

'Gunfire most likely,' retorted the buxom lady, with grim satisfaction.

The girls screamed with terror. Drowning the dreadful screaming on the top deck.

The tram screeched to a halt. Passers-by were glued to the pavements, gesticulating and pointing.

'It can't be gunshot,' Allan said stiffly. 'Those people wouldn't be standing and staring like that if it were. They would have run for cover by now.'

The buxom lady chose to ignore him and sat rigid, peering ahead to see what the driver would do next.

June could still hear the screams above their heads.

The tram driver mounted the stairs to inspect the damage. When he came back down his ruddy visage had turned pale. He alighted the tram and went across the road into the nearest shop, a tobacconist's.

'He'll have gone to phone for the Garda,' Allan surmised.

Then a young woman came down the stairs and shouted, 'Will no one fetch an ambulance? We need a doctor quick.'

People looked shocked, but no one moved. Allan got up from his seat and gently spoke to the man standing in the aisle. He spoke to the person in front of him and a Chinese whisper flowed to the front of the bus. In an orderly fashion the man at the front got off and everyone who'd been standing followed. Allan by now was at the front of the bus, calmly ushering the other passengers onto the roadside and directing them to gather further off, out of harm's way. Mary, Margaret and June were the last to alight.

They joined the rest of the passengers and turned to look. The tram pole had detached itself from the overhead wire and smashed into the top deck. It had cut through the deck at the front and was jammed. Allan was up on top now, dispensing solace, while they waited for the first ambulance to arrive. He ministered to everyone and they were grateful for his comforting words. This was a side of her cousin June had never witnessed. She shivered as the wounded were carried down the narrow metal stairs. There but for the grace of God...

My mother warned me about Uncle Ernie.

'How was everyone?'

'Fine.' She reached for another roll, still warm from Gillespie's oven, and took a huge dollop of rhubarb jam.

'Auntie Kate?'

'Same as ever.'

'She'll be missing Helen now.'

'Yes.'

'Mary and Margaret?'

'They're fine.'

'They'll be grown girls by now.'

'Yes. They both wear bras.'

'We must get you fitted for one. You're starting to fill out like me. I should have thought about that sooner.' June wished she had. 'But I've had a lot on my mind...'

'Of course, Mummie. It doesn't matter.'

Had she really not noticed before? A lot of her friends were still flat-chested, but she'd been struggling to fit into her vests for over a year.

'But it does. We must get you down to John Findlay's this week. We don't want the men bothering you.'

'No, Mummie.'

'How was Allan?'

'He was fine. He was quite the hero when the pole smashed through the tram.'

'Yes, but I mean...'

June looked up and waited for her to finish the thought.

'I mean, did he bother you at all?'

'No not really. He was fine, honestly, Mummie.'

Another awkward pause, while Mummie replenished her cup of tea.

'I've been meaning to say... Maybe now's as good a time as ever...' June held her breath. 'You need to watch out for some of the men in our family. The dark ones especially. They can act a bit funny at times and you're fast becoming a woman now. They'll notice. It's up to you to make sure they respect you. Don't do anything to lead them on.'

June bit her lip. She wanted to say something droll to break the tension, but she couldn't think of anything. She swallowed a mouthful of tea and waited. Mummie hadn't finished.

'Your Uncle Ernie… He's had a difficult life. He can seem so suave and amusing, especially when he gives his talk about his war experience—the time he won the medal for heroism. He charms everyone. And those children's tracts he writes.'

June had tried to read them when she was younger. They were full of moral precepts.

'But the war changed him and then the death of Myrette. He's never been the same since. He blames himself for allowing them to operate. He adored her. You know he's got a scrapbook with everything she wrote or painted neatly assembled in it. Her first bits of handwriting. All the cards she wrote him when she was little. Her school reports and certificates. He's got it all. He keeps it in his study. Aunt Annie says he hardly ever lets her see it. But she thinks he often pores over it when he says he's writing his sermons.'

For once, Mummie seemed to sympathise with Aunt Annie. Grief had softened her maybe. *But what had this to do with her?*

'The thing is, June, sometimes he acts in ways he shouldn't. I'm not trying to excuse him, but we should remember what he's had to suffer in his life.'

Hadn't Mummie suffered too?

'He didn't think he'd survive the war. It left him damaged. Not just the head wound. There are other wounds we can't see. We don't usually talk about them, but you need to know. And be on your guard.'

Lizzie came bustling in. 'Do you want me to fetch some peas when I go to May's, Mrs Hepburn? They're cheap and plentiful right now.'

'Yes please, Lizzie. Just put it on my bill. And tell them I'll be in at the end of the week to settle up.'

They never spoke of this again. June thought about it though. *What had Mummie meant?* She remembered the headmaster's back-stage fumbling and *the penny dropped.*

She first told me about Great Uncle Ernie when I'd turned thirty.

Uncle Ernie wrote sermons for children. When I was fourteen he tried to rape me.

The family holiday was always an exchange with a fellow minister. This was something his father had done before him. The Reverend Wesley Allan Rodger would take the job of locum in Helen's grandfather's, the Reverend Alexander Scott MacPherson's church in London during the summer holiday month. My great grandfather, the Reverend Rodger, had shown his older children London that way. Great Auntie Kate's childhood had been considerably different from that of her younger sisters, May and Dolly. At the end of her life, my mother's Cousin Helen wrote a memoir about their grandfather.

In it she reminisced: 'Later, when he was minister at Giffnock, Uncle Ernie came to Dublin to take anniversary services in my father's church and also give a lecture on his war experiences. His lecture was most entertaining, definitely very humorous, and altogether in a lighter vein.'

My second cousin Ann told me that her grandfather, my great uncle Ernie, exchanged with a minister in Portpatrick for the summer holidays. I don't know. Did the sexual assault happen at The Manse, Greenhill Avenue, Giffnock?

She'd visited Giffnock. She recalled him in his study, writing his tracts for children on Presbyterian morality, all the while, keeping an eye on the pedigree Labrador puppies he was rearing to make ends meet. Carefully, he constructed a pen of wire netting to keep them in. Occasionally they'd escape, then he'd jump up from his moral tracts and rush swearing down the garden path and beat the little beasts back within the Pale. He believed in covenant theology and 'total depravity.' In sepia tints he stands, still smiling—tall, bronzed, blond and 'very attractive to women,' as she put it.

Or did it take place seven miles from home at the Portpatrick Manse? Churches there had merged a few years earlier. In 1929, the Portpatrick Free Church united with the Church of Scotland to form the Portpatrick Trinity United Free Church. In 1930 the congregation of Portpatrick Parish Church united with that of Portpatrick Trinity United Free Church. In the nineteenth century, at

The Disruption, there had been a bitter falling out between the laird of Dunskey Estate and the Reverend Andrew Urquhart. By the early Thirties, it had all blown over—'it was a' southered up' as Andrew Campbell put it in 1933. But was the Free Church spirit one ingredient in the mix that formed the Portpatrick Parish Church congregation? When my Great Uncle Ernie stood in front of his summer holiday congregation delivering a sermon he'd delivered earlier that year in Giffnock, what did he see: unity or disruption? When he got down on his knees and prayed, interrogating his inner self, what did he see: unity or disruption?

Or at Southend-on-Sea, a long day's train journey from Stranraer: as she told me soon before she died, after the strokes and heart failure had rendered her memories unreliable.

For his holidays, he used to do an exchange with another minister. He would go and stay in their manse and preach to their congregation and vice versa. One holiday, he spent in Southend on a preaching exchange and I went to stay there with Pat. At night he came into my bedroom and I had a very unpleasant half hour. Years later he apologised. 'Think how much worse I'd be, June, if I weren't a minister, in the bosom of the family.' He interfered with Mavis as well.

I thought I could write about the experience. How hard could it be? But I can't.

I thought I could tie up a narrative loose end. Jack McMaster would come back one final, urgent time. Now that Grandma Rodger had died, would May take his proposal seriously? This would be the final time of asking. Neither of them was getting any younger. When Emily May rejected him yet again, I would find him a substitute bride. Auntie Dolly's friend, Moira, perhaps. Tired of being Uncle Ernie's bit on the side all those years. Realising at last that he would never leave the wife he didn't love. He had too much to lose. But that would be a romantic fiction. And this is my mother's life story, fragmented, incomplete and garbled in the telling.

I thought I could tie up another loose end. When Emily May rejected the bachelor bank manager again, he would determine to find a wife who would offer the comforts of married life he craved. He would choose Lizzie, who would accept him gratefully. They would live a perfectly happy life thereafter. But that would be a lie. Lizzie went on to have six children; one night the boys, three in a bed, were reading their comic by candlelight and set the house on fire. But the villagers where she lived helped and gave her enough to move back into the wee end house. And no one remembers who the father was of all those weans.

Mummie had a suitor, the Clydesdale Bank manager.

She was late home from school. With the new term came renewed activities. Her place in the choir was assured and this afternoon she had been auditioning for the Christmas Operetta. This year Mr Lewis had decided on *A Greek Slave*. It was quite old, but it would continue the exotic theme of last year's production and it was a playful, romantic comedy. He was sure it would be a grand hit. After her success last year she hoped to get the role of Maia. She had rehearsed '*Twas a pretty little maiden / In a garden grey and old*,' and felt she'd given a good rendition. The part was well within her vocal range. She would look suitably statuesque in flowing classical dress. *Who else could they possibly give it to?* Now she was tired and starving. She dropped her satchel, buckles downward, onto the hall table's marquetry surface and was about to make for the kitchen, to see what Lizzie had baked for tea. She paused and frowned. As always red and blue light flooded through the stained-glass windows. As always the Battle of Waterloo raged on. But something was different. A male voice sounded from Fred's old room. For a weird moment she wondered if his ghost had decided to return.

Then she heard Mummie speaking to it. What was going on? She knocked on the door and entered. Mummie and the bank manager, Mr McCash, were sitting close together on Fred's bed. Mr McCash looked up annoyed. Mummie blushed, stood and smoothed her skirt over her hips and thighs.

'June.' She sounded startled.

'Good afternoon, Miss Hepburn. May I call you June?' She didn't bother to reply. 'I've been advising your mother on the best way to reinvest the shares she's inherited from Mr Andrews.' He turned and smiled at Mummie. 'Some years ago, Mr Andrews had good advice from his brother-in-law, but markets change, times change. I believe I've found a very safe home for her money.' Turning again to Mummie. 'You should have a small but secure income, whatever events the world throws at us.' He patted her hand. 'And now all you need is someone to take care of you and cherish you.'

June's eyes narrowed. She stared hard at Mummie, then turned and stomped upstairs to her room. She hated his smarmy ways and the insinuating tones of his posh Edinburgh accent. She'd lost her appetite. She clambered onto her bed and stared out towards the end of Loch Ryan. She was so miserable she wished she could go and live with Auntie Kate till Christmas—and bugger *A Greek Slave*.

After Grandma Rodger died, Mummie was kept going by the local dentist. He was a very kind man, married to a rich, ugly wife. He had a son and tried to introduce him to me. The son had a sports car, but he was ugly too.

She got the part and rehearsals began. Mr Lewis decided they would spend the first half of term concentrating on the music; there were twenty-eight numbers to learn; she had three solos and three duets, including the penultimate 'Forgive' with Diomed (James McKinstry). She was late home from school most nights.

She wandered through the front door, rapt harmonies of *Ah! Forgive and let her happy be!* with *Ah! Forgive and spare my love to me!* floating through her mind. A package, long and wide, but no more than a few inches deep, lay on the hall table. *What was in it?* It was addressed to Mummie, but she hadn't opened it.

'What's this parcel, Mummie?' she shouted up the stairs.

Her mother appeared on the landing and hurried down, the soft light catching her errant hairs.

'I'm not sure. I thought I'd wait till you got home to open it. Maybe it's something from Auntie Dolly.'

Mummie carried it into the drawing room and laid it on the table. She untied the string and rolled it into a skein. She removed the brown paper, folded it into a square and put it to one side. Then she opened the cardboard box. There was a wee note inside. She lifted it out, read it and put her hand to her lips.

'It's from Mr MacCracken.'

'Not Auntie Dolly then.'

'No, Not Auntie Dolly.'

It was a light wool, turquoise gown, cut in the latest fashion.

'It's from Paisley's.'

'Will you keep it?'

Mummie and June looked at one another, weighing options.

'Try it on.'

'Should I?'

'Why not? There's no harm done to see if it fits, is there?'

They took it up to the bedroom. June sat on a bed while Mummie put it on. It fitted perfectly. It flattered her. It was her favourite colour. Mummie loved to wear pretty clothes. Auntie Dolly hadn't sent her anything this autumn; she was busy homemaking at 'Morroch' in Annan Road, Dumfries. So, Mummie continued to wear her summer dress and shivered, even with a warm cardy flung over her shoulders.

'He's got perfect taste,' she murmured, turning in front of the dressing-table mirrors.

'You look lovely in it.' *Ah! Forgive…*

Mummie smiled. 'There's a package for you too.'

That clinched it.

He was a very kind man, married to a rich, ugly wife. He had a son and tried to introduce him to me. The son had a sports-car, but he was ugly too. (At the same time as Denny, I had another boyfriend, a Doctor's son).

196

June told me this a year before she died. (I didn't recall her mentioning the doctor's son before; that would have been Alastair Baird.) A startling non sequitur, it made perfect sense to her. She had followed her mother's pattern of having more than one suitor at a time.

Once June came home from school and Mr MacCracken, the town dentist, was sitting in the kitchen, quite at ease, joking with Lizzie, his hand resting fondly on Mummie's knee.

Once she came home from school wet through, stripped off her stockings in the porch and carried them through to dry by the kitchen range. Mr McCash was sat there inveigling himself with Lizzie, while Mummie finished playing the piano upstairs. June ignored him and stripped off her wet coat, placing it over the back of a chair to drip onto newspaper.

Another time it was Mr MacCracken, warming his hand in front of the range, who helped her out of her soggy coat solicitously. He was a kind man. June warmed to him.

'You must meet my son, Kenneth. He's back home from Argyle.'

'That would be nice for you, June,' Mummie agreed.

Kenneth was named after his father, but in looks he took after his mother. After their first outing, she decided no one could make her go out with a boy with a sports car when his face resembled its rear end.

'He's offered to buy us one of those new bungalows they're building on the edge of the town.'

'Whereabouts?'

'Black Park View, off the Stoneykirk Road.'

'What will you do?'

'He'd support us. I wouldn't need to take in boarders anymore.'

'Mmm… pass the butter, will you.'

'And the jam?'

'Yes please.'

Once, she came home from school to find them standing

on the doorstep. Two suitors; neither prepared to back down.

'Will you come in? She asked politely and opened the door. As they entered the hallway she sensed Grandma Rodger's presence. It wasn't her ghost. Merely a reminder in the red and blue light that played on the stairs of that small but capable old lady, sure of the beliefs and behaviour she stood for. While she was alive she had been their anchor. Now she was no more the house had lost its moorings. June had lost her mainstay and Mummie her chaperone.

Christmas was coming again. June was a triumph in *A Greek Slave*. This year, she made sure Mr Hendy didn't lure her into his study to readjust her headband and girdle. Everyone came to watch her in the lead role of Maia: Uncle Ernie, Uncle Eddie, Auntie Dolly, Uncle Henry, even Uncle Stanley. Jack McMaster was there too.

'What's your uncle doing here?' June asked Margot during the interval, 'I thought he wasn't due till next Christmas.'

Margot shrugged. 'Mummy told him about your Grandma. He wants to offer his condolences in person.'

'How odd.'

That night, June lay in bed, too excited to fall asleep straight away. She thought about Jack McMaster. There was something truly romantic about his devotion to her mother despite umpteen rejections. She wondered if she would find a love that romantic; like Maia and Diomed... Suddenly her thoughts turned to Grandma and Grandpa Rodger. She didn't need to look to ancient Rome for romance. All she need do was remember Grandma Rodger telling her about meeting Grandpa skating on the ice. She wished she could meet a man like Grandpa Rodger when she was eighteen. A husband who would cherish and protect her, who would be respected and adored by his parishioners... but did she want to marry a minister? Would Mummie finally agree to marry Jack McMaster? If she did, would they have to move to the Philippines?

Christmas wasn't such a magic time this year. Auntie Dolly went to her new in-laws on Christmas Day. Grandma Rodger wasn't sitting in her chair, slightly censorious at the tipsy goings-on. Mr MacCracken was spending Christmas with his wife and Kenneth, of course. Strange: she realised she was warming to the town dentist. He was always kind towards her and she never felt threatened by him. Mummie could do worse than take up his offer and become a 'kept woman' on the edge of town.

Mr McCash was invited. He arrived with three bunches of hothouse flowers: one for Mummie, one for June and one for Lizzie. Lizzie blushed pink as the camellias, purple as the orchids, abandoned to June the stirring of the bread sauce and busied herself finding vases and arranging the sumptuous blooms to her satisfaction. Mr McCash helped her. He was very attentive and solicitous. June felt relieved. She had never liked him. But he would make Lizzie a dependable husband. She would want for nothing.

Mr Hetherington was there, playing his flute and singing twice as loud to make up for absent friends. But Mummie's playing didn't send anyone into raptures the way Auntie Dolly's did. On Boxing Day Uncle Henry and Uncle Stanley motored down as usual, and later in the week, Uncle Ernie, Auntie Annie, Pat, Uncle Eddie, Auntie Mary and Teddy visited them. Everyone felt subdued. They mainly reminisced about Grandma and even Auntie Annie got tearful.

Everyone had finally gone back home at the end of Boxing Day. There was just the two of them to clear the dishes and put the remains of the mincemeat tart and Christmas Cake back in their tins.

'When's Uncle Jack coming to pop the question?' June asked, nibbling a piece of pastry that had broken off.

'Tomorrow morning,' Mummie sighed.

'Will you marry him now?'

'No, I don't think I will.'

And she continued to dry the dishes.

The primroses were in flower. After school Betty and June had gone for a long ramble: down Agnew Crescent, past

Agnew Castle, along their primrose walk, up and over Gallows Hill, to arrive at Glebe Cemetery. June stood by the grave and said hello to Grandpa and Grandma. Betty held her hand a while. Then they parted for the day and went their separate ways home.

Mummie was waiting in the kitchen. She had placed the atlas on the kitchen table, opened at the map of England and Scotland. She sat looking at it. Beside her was Grandma's sewing box. *June had always loved that box: dark, inlaid, walnut, with a plush, padded, blue lining. As a child she'd loved to play with it. She'd fetch the key from Grandma's bedside, open it and gaze at the array of ivory-handled lace hooks and gleaming crochet hooks. She'd inspect the carefully wound reels of cotton and silk, the handsewn pin cushion and the packet of needles, all lined straight on their thin dark wafer. She'd reach to the little button under the lid at the back; when you pressed it the bottom drawer shot out to reveal tiny compartments, each with their wee blue silk lids and tiny handles to lift them by. When Grandma had been angry with her she would hide the key a while.* The sewing box was open. Mummie didn't say anything when June entered the room. She picked up the pincushion, pulled out a long pin and presented it to June.

'Close your eyes and stick it in.'

June closed her eyes and stuck the pin in the map.

If it came near Glasgow we would go to live near her brothers; if it were nearer Liverpool we would go to Crosby near her sister, Minnie and my father's family. To think that my whole future life depended on that pin.

She was very excited about her decision to move and poured it all out to him on the journey.

Easter Sunday, 1936. A month after her fourteenth birthday. They caught the excursion train on its way back from Portpatrick and alighted at Dumfries. Birrell met them at the station among the crowd of happy families back from their day out by the sea. It took half an hour for them to walk out to Morroch. Mummie stayed the night; they shared the bed in the spare bedroom. The following morning Auntie Dolly put her sister on the train to Liverpool. June stayed at Morroch all week. She spent her time indoors reading, moping and occasionally doing her piano practice, while Auntie Dolly weeded her garden, tended her Bourbon Queen roses, dusted, mopped and polished her house. Each afternoon she made another tray of Helensburgh toffee.

Erwin Ernest Aloys Debetaz was tall, dark, handsome and spoke English with a delectable French accent. He had eyes so dark they seemed jet-black in the railway-carriage light. He had a manly jaw and a charming smile.

I am not making this up, gentle reader. He could have stepped out of the pages of a Mills and Boon: *Arrows from The Dark*, *Secret Joy*, *In the Name of Love*. Had she brought one to read on the long journey? Not normally a reader, these romantic novels, which Gerald Rusgrove Mills and Charles Boon marketed in the nineteen thirties, might have appealed to my grandmother. In her late thirties, fleeing the entanglements of small-town romance that was only bringing her shame and confusion, to escape to a world where romance triumphed every time, might have been consoling. She didn't need to pick up the book, instead she found herself in a carriage with a dark, handsome stranger.

Erwin Ernest Aloys Debetaz was from Lausanne. His older brother, Jean, still lived there, torn between a barren wife, Agnes, whom he adored, and a mistress who might give him the children he craved. His other brother, Charles, had been tutor to King Fuad of Egypt's children. When the monarchy was compelled to restore powers to the parliament in 1935, Charles decided to return to Europe. He returned via Marseille and settled near Lyon where he made goats' cheese. His sister, Marie, fled Egypt with her husband at the same time. The way she told it, the monarchy had been overthrown, rather than have to bow to political pressure and restore the parliamentary powers that King Fuad had abrogated five years earlier. Tante Marie and her husband settled in Marseille, where he was the civil engineer, responsible for the city's sewage system. She remained a royalist all her life. 'Je suis royaliste, moi!' she would tell me. And: 'Il a été le responsable du tout-à-l'égout de Marseille.' She believed in taking a siesta every afternoon and the benefits of boiled rice for a delicate digestive system. Her speciality was a fresh pear cake, which she baked every Sunday when her half-sisters, the Barseminides, daughters of her father's Greek mistress, visited. They were the reason they had chosen to flee to Marseille.

Erwin Ernest Aloys Debetaz had initially been in banking. He had worked in the London branch of a Swiss bank. Ironic, when you consider how terrible he was at managing money. Then he had met a very elegant older woman. She had set up Lady in Black. The firm manufactured and sold sexy 'French' women's lingerie. Gentle reader, I am not making this up either. They married briefly. For appearance sake officially her sons ran the business, but she owned and controlled it. The marriage didn't last. But Ernest Debetaz remained in this country and continued to work as a Lady in Black travelling salesman. The same job as Grandpa Rodger's father, Edward; although he worked for very respectable Scottish Drapers, not for a firm that sold provocative female undergarments.

Auntie Dolly put her on the train and noticed 'a very

charming foreign gentleman in the compartment,' as she told June when she got back home.

She hadn't meant to enter a compartment that just held a tall, dark and handsome stranger. But the other compartments were full. It never crossed her mind to look in third class. He was very polite. He stood up immediately, lifted her suitcase onto the luggage rack and offered her the window seat facing forward. She hesitated. In a suave French accent he insisted. He couldn't dream of taking the best seat when there was a lady fellow traveller. She accepted. He sat opposite her and offered a cigarette. He smoked Black Cat.

'I collect the coupons,' he admitted with a disarming smile. 'This shirt is a Black Cat shirt. Feel how soft the cotton is.'

She didn't know how to say 'no.' She stretched out her arm and stroked the proffered sleeve.

'I smoke Du Maurier.'

'Ah! Because of Gerald Du Maurier, I presume.' He pronounced his name as if it were French.

'I first saw him in *Unmarried*. He reminded me of my father I think. I still prefer the silent pictures.'

'But you are not "unmarried?"'

Little did Erwin Ernest Aloys Debetaz know, when he asked that question, how pertinent it was. To answer it she had to retrace the last fifteen years of her life. By Carlisle, she had got as far as the move to 9 King Street, when he suggested he buy her lunch in the dining car. He was charm personified, subtly seductive and gently encouraging. She found herself telling this total stranger all about her difficulties with Jack McMasters, Kenneth MacCracken and Archibald McCash. She told him about her financial situation. She had the house and the shares from Fred; she had enough to support herself and her teenage daughter. She told him about her decision to move to be near her sister Minnie and her late husband's family.

By Kendal, she admitted, 'You remind me of my husband.'

By Wigan, she had given him her telephone number, Stranraer 262, and he'd arranged to visit her the next time he was in the area.

By Liverpool Lime Street, she had told him how she first fell in love with Sandy when he was sent to meet her off the train.

'This same train,' she sighed.

Erwin Ernest Aloys Debetaz smiled. 'Perhaps you have found the love of your life all over again on this felicitous train.'

She didn't contradict him.

A few weeks later he visited. He stayed for a few nights, sharing the attic bedroom with Mr Hetherington.

'I seem to have formed the habit of sharing the compartments of trains with single ladies from Stranraer,' he joked at breakfast.

Mummie had gone especially to Latta's to buy freshly-ground coffee, which he sipped nonchalantly. June watched her suppress a pang of jealousy.

'Really?' was all she said.

'Yes,' he continued, 'I travelled all the way from Euston with a Mrs Beatty Gibson.'

'Auntie Beatty?'

'You know her June?'

'Yes, she's my best friend's auntie.'

'She's a very interesting woman I think.'

Mummie looked rattled. Auntie Beatty was a wealthy widow. She owned a Bluebird. She was older than her but she would be a catch for a bachelor in search of a fortune. Ernest smiled at her across the kitchen table. She realised he was teasing her.

She didn't consider the consequences of this shared journey until a few days later after he'd gone. The whole town knew that May Hepburn had added another suitor to her lengthening list of eligible men and that this one had stayed the night.

Soon afterwards Mr Hetherington left to get married and settle down in a tiny house of his own. There was just the three of them left in the house. Lizzie was much preoccupied with renovating her trousseau for her forthcoming nuptials.

Erwin Ernest Aloys Debetaz continued to visit regularly that summer. He and Mummie abandoned all pretence that he was sleeping in the attic bedroom. Even June felt it was time to leave Stranraer.

Summer dragged on while Mummie sold the house and finalised all the arrangements. Auntie Dolly came to stay and helped her pack up the last fifteen years of her life. They needed June out of the house; she was getting under their feet while they sorted everything out. Uncle Ernie had been to theological college with a minister from Southend-on-Sea. They had kept in touch all those years. This summer they finally arranged a fortnight's preaching exchange.

'It will be a superb holiday for you,' Debby said. She couldn't quite remember when she'd started calling him Debby, but it seemed an elegant solution.

So, June went to stay in Southend with Pat. At night Uncle Ernie came into her bedroom and she passed a very unpleasant half hour.

She never told Mummie.

When I was two, Duff Cooper published his autobiography, *Old Men Forget*. In it he states, 'In the summer of 1936 I was sure that war was approaching. I believed that there was only one way of preventing it, and that was to convince the Germans that if they fought they would be beaten. I did not then know that the German Generals were convinced at that time that they would be beaten, and remained so for two more years.' A lifelong Liberal, I doubt my mother would have read it; although if it had turned up in our local lending library she might have taken it out, given her interest in history and politics that continued until her dying day. She read the paper until the day she died. She always did the crossword. That final day she almost completed it and amongst other clues got 'At Loggerheads.'

June has just turned eighty-seven. She has finished writing her handwritten memoirs at the behest of her granddaughter. After a severe stroke in January, the consultant told her daughter that she cannot continue to live independently in her one-bedroom flat. No more than a few blocks from this flat are the three Birkdale houses she lived in during her married life. Until she slipped on the ice last winter, on a good day she could still walk past them. She is being driven through Crosby to a care home near Hereford. It is early morning. She has a bottle of water, which she sips regularly, to avoid bladder infection. She hasn't driven so far for two decades. They are heading for the M53. The last time she drove on it she suffered a transient ischaemic attack. Denny couldn't drive anymore because of his stroke. She carried on driving through Liverpool, seeing stars floating in front of her eyes the whole way back home to Birkdale. We drive down Moor Lane and pass the end of Beech Avenue on the right. June remembers her mother's dog, the golden Labrador bred by her Uncle Ernie. The dog travelled first class with my grandmother. My fourteen-year-old mother travelled third class on her own all the way from Stranraer to Liverpool.

The furniture van was waiting for them outside 10 Beech Avenue when they arrived. Mummie had the key to the front door and opened it. The men began to unload.

'I'm sorry, Mrs Hepburn,' the carrier said, 'your furniture's too large.'

'What do you mean, too large?'

'It won't fit through the front door.'

'What, none of it?'

'Well, those bedside cabinets will, and the occasional table.'

'Is that it?'

They stood in the hallway and stared at the over-sized furniture strewn from the van, across the pavement, up the front drive and piled up either side the front door.

'I never thought to measure it.'

'It was *big enough* crammed into King Street,' June said. And immediately regretted it. Mummie seemed distraught.

Guido, who had been cooped up on a train all the long day, took the opportunity to slip out the open doorway. He inspected his new surroundings, marking his territory profusely. He sniffed around the side passage and the back garden. So many new smells. He lifted his nose. He sensed even more scent trails the other side of the fence. He found a gap at one end and wriggled through. Ah! A wonderful green field stretched for as far as the eye could see. Canine paradise.

June was sent to fetch him and spent a breathless half hour racing around the playing fields that backed onto their property. By the time she'd retrieved him, Mummie had sent the contents of the removal van to the local auctioneers. There was no way they could stay there the night. Or even the next few weeks. She decided to take the opportunity to thoroughly clean and decorate the house before they moved in. The builders had left a trail of saw-wood, plaster-powder, dusty footprints and dirty fingerprint smudges. Besides, she didn't want to replace the furniture until she'd got her cheque from the Auctioneers.

Mummie went to stay at her sister Minnie's. Guido went with her. She was given the little back bedroom where Uncle Alf had tended baby June while her daddy was dying.

'I remember it like yesterday,' he said, sipping a cup of black coffee. 'I must have covered miles pacing up and down, night after night. And every time there was that blessed floorboard that squeaked when I stood on it.'

June stared round the room, trying to summon some memory of her infant self. *How odd that they had ended back here, fourteen years later.*

It was arranged that I should stay at 'School House.' There were only two or three other girls; two were a little older than I was—the other was younger. We were supervised by the History teacher, Miss Ward, and the French teacher's sister, Miss Elsie Martin. It was not an auspicious beginning. About the first thing Miss Ward warned me against was having much to do with my cousins, Eileen and Shelagh, who had been pupils years before. I didn't understand at first, but soon realised the position. Auntie Minnie's husband, though a wonderful doctor, had been an alcoholic. Auntie and Eileen had only recently come back from London to live with him at Crown Buildings. He had cancer, had become Tee Total and replaced whisky with black coffee. It seemed Shelagh had left school pregnant—or been expelled—and although she was married (and remained so for over sixty years) it wasn't the sort of marriage approved of by Miss Fordham and her cronies. I never found out what they had against Eileen.

Miss Ward and the Misses Martin were members of 'The Big Four'—the coterie steered by the Headmistress, Miss Fordham. They effectively ran the school and set the standards of discipline for teachers and pupils alike. Miss Martin was a particularly stern disciplinarian. No wonder School House did not suit June. Every evening on the dot of eight they were told to stop what they were doing and sent to bed. After the first week June was allocated the attic room because she was taking so long to wash in the mornings. She had the attic bathroom to herself, but there was only cold water up there. Every night she would rinse out her underwear and leave it dripping on the side of the bath. She had strict views on personal hygiene and liked a clean pair of panties every day. Each morning she would wash all over, even when she had goose bumps because of the cold.

By half term she was fed up. She had been told off yet again about her long, curled hair.

After she died, I spoke to Audrey on the phone: 'She arrived with the rest of us and as we were standing outside the school front door waiting to be admitted. I looked at her hair with all those curls in it. I thought then, you're going to get into a lot of trouble! Long curly hair was strictly forbidden. June looked like a rebel right from the start.'

'But everyone knows that you don't turn up for school with curled hair worn loose down your back, especially if it's long,' Audrey told her when they finally became friends.

'Well I didn't then. I do now. *Rule 7: The hair must be plaited. Combs, slides and jewellery may not be worn.* Even so, I don't see why I should have to wear it in plaits all day long,' June retorted.

She hated the feeling of hair scrapped tight, pulling on her scalp. On that first day of school, Miss Fordham had grabbed her hair and muttered that she looked no better than a street girl as she passed through the imposing double doorway.

On the Friday afternoon at the end of the first half term, she let her hair down and let the breeze play with it as she walked back to School House. *A whole week when she could do as she pleased, as long as she were indoors by six o'clock each day.*

'*Nice* young ladies,' the way Miss Ward pronounced the word it sounded as if she were neighing. '*Nice* young ladies don't parade the streets with their curls flowing freely down their backs. Only loose women venture out in public flaunting themselves like that.'

June stormed back out of School House and went round to visit Grandma Hepburn. She was fuming. *Those bitches disapproved of everything. It was impossible to gain their approbation. And there was no point trying to talk to Mummie about it; she was far too preoccupied.*

The first time I went to see her at 'The Grange' she was sitting in the porch watching the world go by. Tears came to her eyes as the word 'Alex' came out of her mouth.

'*Prynhawn Dda! Sut wyt ti?*' Grandma was short, dark and broad in the hips. She'd had a hard upbringing, even spending some time in the workhouse when she was eighteen. It had been the only way to get any Poor Relief. Then she'd met Grandpa. They'd married and lived happily ever after despite the disparity of class.

'*Ofnadwy,*' June had learnt to say. But she had never meant it as much as she did today. It all came pouring out.

Grandma offered her a handkerchief, a glass of milk, and a Nice biscuit. She rocked back and forth in her rocking chair and pondered the situation. Then she heaved herself up, went inside to talk to Grandpa and made a few phone calls. Grandpa didn't come downstairs, but he shouted to June to come to the bottom of the stairs. When she got there, he sent a ten-shilling note fluttering over the bannisters. *Too shy to put it in her hand.*

'It's half term week and...' As usual, he didn't complete

the sentence, retreating into the upstairs parlour.

'Thank-you, Grandpa,' she shouted to his receding back.

Grandma came off the phone. 'Well, that's all arranged then.'

June looked quizzical.

'You'll come and stay at The Grange until your mother's got some furniture into Beech Avenue. Go and pack up all your things. You're to have your tea at School House and then Miss Ward will drive you round before bed time.'

What could she say? She didn't know whether to laugh or cry and ended up doing both. She hugged Grandma till she was gasping for breath and telling her, '*Paid!* Stop it now!' She even ran up the stairs, gave Grandpa a kiss on his cheek and ran down again before he had a chance to respond.

One of my first vivid memories of Crosby: sitting in Miss Ward's little Austin 7 with all my belongings in the back, wearing the over-large uniform with its ridiculous pudding-basin hat. We were held up at the traffic lights at the foot of Moor Lane, where for some reason I saw how ridiculous a situation I was in and dissolved into hysterical laughter. From then on, my time at Merchant Taylors Girls' School was doomed and there would be worse to come.

Actually it was a navy-blue, bull-nosed Morris. The Misses Ward, Jackson and M. O. Martin clubbed together to buy it. The Merchant Taylors' Archive contains many such facts: 'Hepburn, Alexander. Born August 1891. Attended Merchant Taylors' School 1900 - 1906. Son of John B. Hepburn.' The Archivist, Merchant Taylors' School, personal communication, November 27th, 2019. It also contains lacunae: 'Gertie and Jessie started together in January 1900 aged six and ten. Unfortunately there is a gap in the leaving register so we do not know when they left. Molly falls into this period of between 1912 and 1917 where we have no records; I cannot verify that she attended here.' The Archivist, Merchant Taylors' School for Girls, personal communication, July 9th, 2019.

These were times she didn't care to remember. Mummie floundered in this alien place. Everything was different and strange. She had a shock when she found she'd have to pay for June's education: £14 a term. This was the same school that all June's Hepburn aunts had attended; Gertie, Jessie and Molly. It was familiar to them. Daddy had attended the Boy's School down the road. He had been good at languages and so was she. She should have felt glad she was following in his footsteps. But she wished they'd stayed in Stranraer. There were advantages to being known in a town. Mummie had felt the disadvantages keenly after Grandma died. *But despite being left penniless when Grandpa Rodger died, Mummie and Auntie Dolly managed to be respected members of Stranraer society.* Now these teachers looked at Mummie and judged her as poor, uneducated and disreputable. It had been embarrassing explaining to her that she owed them the first term's school fee. 'And when she opened her mouth, did you hear the way she spoke?'

They assumed June was equally ignorant and stupid. 'She didn't start High School until she was twelve!' 'She knows next to nothing about English history.' So, they started her off in Lower IV. By the end of the second week, they conceded they'd made a mistake. The work was too easy for her; she put her hand up to answer every question and made the other girls feel foolish. So, they moved her to Upper IV. They kept her there until half term. When they sat down for the staff meeting that week and looked at her run of marks, they realised she was quite bright and could cope with the work *English* girls of her age dealt with. So, she ended up in Lower V^A. By now her novelty had worn off; making new friends wasn't easy.

When I moved to Merchant Taylors' I had to be called 'Valerie' because there were two Junes in the class already. […] I won the Latin prize at Merchants, because Mamie Niven would din it into us at Stranraer High School. […] The headmistress, Miss Fordham, was really bad. […] They wouldn't let me act in the school plays. […] I would have got a better education if I'd stayed in Stranraer. The teachers at Merchant Taylors' School for Girls were bitches.

It's ironic: at Stranraer High School her English teacher was Miss Ann Graham. She went on to marry Mr Herbert Sutherland, the Science teacher. At Merchant Taylors' her English teacher was Miss Graham. I can't discover her Christian name.

Miss Graham was charismatic. She had a magnetic presence and a very fine reading voice. It was beautiful. She instilled a love of literature into many of her girls. It was rumoured several fell in love not with the literature but the teacher. Crushes were strictly forbidden. If you were suspected of having one, Miss Fordham would give you a pep talk in the Headmistress's study. If you were suspected of talking to boys, the talking to was even worse.

The time had arrived; it was the annual audition for the School Play.

They knew what they were doing.

'Say "khaki pyjamas," Valerie!' Pronounced with a long English **ā** sound.

'Khaki pyjamas, Miss Graham!' Pronounced with a short Galloway Irish **ă** sound.

'I don't think we'll find a place for you in the school play, this year, Valerie!'

'No, Miss Fordham.'

Mummie always bought lovely clothes, even though we never had any money. Before we left Stranraer, she bought me two dresses from the dress shop round the corner. One was green velvet. When I outgrew it, I cut it off under the arms and fitted a waistband to make it into a skirt. Then I bought green wool and knitted myself a cardy to go with it. Another time, I bought a load of material and made myself a dress. The collar was a bit wonky; so I got a lace collar and put it on to disguise it. I remember the skeins of wool drying on the clothesline; especially in war time. Each year, we unravelled the jumpers we had knitted the previous year and reknitted them in a different style.

June also reminisced about a yellow cardigan she knitted that was particularly successful and flattering. It's possible they also dyed the wool a different colour each time.

For the first year I was very unsettled. Debby, my not-yet-stepfather, would come and stay with us for a few nights at a time when he had business in the area. He helped me sometimes with my French homework.

Finally, they moved into Beech Avenue. Strange. Just the two of them. Now that Mummie didn't keep boarders there'd never be another 'Lizzie.' These were times she didn't care to remember. Debby kept visiting. He continued to work as a travelling salesman and came to stay the night whenever he could. When he stayed he helped June with her French homework.

Miss M. O. Martin, the French teacher, lived across the road from Grandpa and Grandma Hepburn.

'Good afternoon, June.'

'Good afternoon, Miss Martin.' June closed the gate to 41 Moor Lane behind her.

'I wonder, do you have a moment? There's rather a delicate matter I need to discuss with you.'

June hesitated. *Why couldn't she leave her alone after school?*

'I'd rather discuss this outside of school hours, for your sake.'

Really?

'Yes, Miss Martin,' and she followed her into the house she shared with her brother the dentist.

'I've noticed that your French homework is outstandingly good... '

This wasn't so bad after all. Some praise at last.

'Sometimes.' A pregnant pause ensued. June didn't know what to say, so said nothing and stared at her fingernails. 'I wonder, would you like to offer any explanation? At times it's perfectly fluent. At other times it's good, but... how shall I put it? At other times, it's the sort of work I'd expect from a fourteen-year-old girl who's *quite* good at languages.' Still June stayed silent. 'How do you explain the disparity? I've racked my brains to think if

214

you've found a crib for some for the work I set you. But to my knowledge there are no such cribs. Last night's homework, for instance; *il est impeccable.*'

June couldn't help noticing that her French accent was tainted by very English diphthongs. 'I do it all myself, Miss Martin,' she began and blushed. She was a hopeless liar. There was nothing for it but to confess. 'Except that…'

'Yes?'

'Except that Mummie has a Swiss friend.'

'Ah!'

'He helps me, when he comes to stay over.'

'*He* stays overnight?'

'Yes, Miss Martin.'

After that the all-female staff watched her all the more closely.

June hated their scrutiny. It made her realise how irregular their situation was. *If anyone wants to marry me, he'll have to keep Mummie as well.* She didn't share this thought with anyone, not even Grandma Hepburn. She resented her mother. When you went through the marriage ceremony that was supposed to register that you were leaving your parents. She'd never be able to leave Mummie.

His frequent visits, first to Stranraer and then to Crosby, didn't simplify my life—long before the Sixties. I used to be asked some funny questions.

The boy next door joined the RAF. He was sent for armaments training at West Freugh. Over the garden fence it was decided June would travel up to Stranraer with the neighbours, when they went to visit him that summer.

At last, she was on the Glasgow train, travelling with the neighbours in a first-class compartment. She didn't know them well and felt a bit awkward. She was so excited to be going back to Stranraer. It was a whole year since she'd left. She would stay with Betty for the summer holidays. They'd kept in touch by letter, but so much had happened that she'd not felt able to write about. It would be easier face-to-face. *Betty would understand.*

At the end of August, she took the train from Stranraer to Dumfries, stayed overnight with Auntie Dolly, then Birrell put her on the train back to Liverpool Lime Street. This time she travelled on her own in third class. She stared out the window, glimpsing the last Beltie she would see in a long time and mused over her summer. Crosby felt strange, but it had felt strange going back to Stranraer too. Everything was the same, except that she no longer lived there. And that made all the difference. She had lost her niche in Stranraer society. People were kind to her, but they treated her politely, the way they would treat a stranger. She didn't belong anywhere anymore.

She caught the tram out of Liverpool and arrived back at Beech Avenue. Mummie and Debby had finished supper. Mummie had kept a plate back for her. June was famished. She'd not had any money to buy food on the train. Mummie placed the plate on the table in front of her. Her hand lingered before she took it away. Long enough for June to notice she wasn't wearing the same ring.

'What happened to your wedding ring?'

'Ernest, come here a moment.'

Debby sauntered into the kitchen and smiled at Mummie.

'June, meet your new stepfather.'

June's fork paused midway to her mouth. Her mouth stayed open a fraction too long.

'Stepfather?'

'I thought it was time to make an 'onest woman of your mother.'

'We got married while you were away.'

It was a bit easier when they were married in summer 1937. They got married while I was away, when I stayed with Betty in Stranraer. One part of me was pleased she'd married. I felt I couldn't leave her if she didn't, but I would have preferred somebody with a larger income. She could have married someone with a decent income, and she had to go and fall in love with Debby. I'm ashamed to say, I resented her and Debby.

The Marriage Certificate reads: *'Erwin Ernest Aloys DEBETAZ, 52 years, formerly the husband of Charlotte Debetaz formerly Boothier spinster, from whom he obtained a divorce, Manufacturer's Agent, 10 Beech Avenue, Great Crosby / Emily May HEPBURN, 44 years, Widow,——, 10 Beech Avenue, Great Crosby.'*

Was he still married when he met my grandmother? Was she cited as co-respondent in the divorce? Did they conceal this from June? Or did she know and conceal it from me? There's no telling. In the 1939 census, they had moved to Alderley, 70 The Serpentine, and he described himself as 'Clothing Manufacturer and Company Director.' After the divorce, did Charlotte get her revenge by ceasing to employ him?

Another school year passed. These were times she didn't care to remember. Eventually the school holidays came around again. June was waiting for her school certificate results. From a very early age, Mummie had told her that she must go to University and have a career so that she was never left a penniless widow like herself. She assumed all this education would be free. June wondered what would happen when she discovered it had to be paid for. She decided not to say anything in case Mummie changed her mind about her staying on to do Highers.

The boy next door had finished his training. The neighbours were travelling back up to Stranraer to witness his passing out ceremony. It was a big moment for them. They were very proud and talked about him and his achievements all the way to Glasgow. June felt tired and demoralised by the time they reached Stranraer Station. But her spirits were lifted by the sight of Betty standing there with Loch Ryan behind her, looking prettier than ever. This was just the tonic she needed.

They visited their old haunts: Agnew Park, Gallows Hill, The Glebe Cemetery. They cycled out to Challock and Whiteleys. One day, they went to Glenluce and walked to the Abbey. Another time they went to Portpatrick. The entire third-class journey home to Crosby, Robbie Burns' lyrics rang round and round her mind. 'For auld lang syne, my dear, For auld lang syne.' Stranraer was another country now.

It was odd, too, because there were no boys in my class and I'd been a mixed infant from the day I started school. And for as long as I could remember, on the lookout for a permanent male figure in my life to love, who would love me. It was to be eleven long years before I found what I wanted and needed. And fifty-nine years before I lost him and my heart broke.

These were times she didn't care to remember. She had been a mixed infant among all the other mixed infants. She had come from Class D, where the girls outnumbered the boys—in a year group where boys far outnumbered girls. She'd gone to the pictures and held hands with Alistair Baird one Saturday a month, gone to the pictures and held hands with John McCaig one Saturday a month and felt glad she didn't have to choose between them yet. She had been nearly raped by Cousin Teddy and Uncle Ernie. And now she was forbidden to talk to boys. June scoured the School Rules. Nowhere did it state: 'Girls must not talk to boys at any time.' It was the unwritten, sixteenth school rule.

'But why?'

'Because Miss Fordham says so,' was the only answer she got.

Later Audrey Sharples explained: 'She gave us a pep talk when we first started in Third Form. She made it very clear.'

'What if you've got a brother?'

'It's best not to be seen walking and talking with him on the streets.'

By now, June knew that Miss Fordham patrolled the streets of Crosby in a taxi every weekday evening to make sure none of her girls were out and about. That was another of her unwritten rules everyone knew, in June's case through bitter experience.

This wasn't going to stop her. Miss Fordham might rule her life between 9.00 a.m. and 4.00 p.m. but as long as she got her homework done, she saw no reason to be confined in that house that was beginning to feel too small for three people. Mummie tried to keep the peace. June could see she was torn in two: she adored Debby but was unhappy when he was so severe towards June. June had managed perfectly well without a father figure for the first fourteen years of her life and she resented the imposition of one now. He was always criticising her.

She found refuge in the church. Mummie was delighted to discover that Blundellsands Presbyterian Church boasted a new Church Hall; it had been built five years ago. Here badminton was played twice a week. June was equally delighted to discover that the church had a tennis club with two hard courts behind the church buildings. Across the road in the park, there was the very snooty Blundellsands Lawn Tennis Club, established 1880. It was a private club where wealthy, influential men fraternised at weekends, before going back into Liverpool and Manchester to do deals on Monday mornings. She was more than content with the Church club and went regularly, even on school nights. She often played tennis with Lily Fernie. Her father was the Session Clerk. And then there was Michael Howson, whose father was an Elder. Occasionally he would bring another friend from Merchant's and they would play mixed doubles. Gradually she and Michael invited more friends from the boys' and girls' schools. It was an oasis of normality.

Winter arrived. Mummie persuaded her to try badminton. She preferred to play with Mummie than sit in uneasy silence with Debby. It was Michael who thought up the idea of a discussion group. They'd all got used to meeting regularly to play tennis and sit around talking between matches. These were interesting times; there was much to discuss. They would call it 'The Curious Society.' He persuaded his father and, more importantly, Lily persuaded hers. Since the Session Clerk approved, the minister didn't veto the idea. They decided to meet every Sunday evening. *Miss Fordham wouldn't stop her meeting boys at the weekend, whatever she might say.* They couldn't use the Church Hall; the Bible Study group met there after the evening service. Then came the stroke of genius. They hired a room over Frank's Café in Waterloo. Of course, there would have to be an Elder present. Lily's father insisted. He was happy to take on the role.

Mr Fernie would only allow them to talk about religious

matters. This wasn't what they'd envisioned; they wanted to continue the conversations they'd had all summer, sat round in their tennis whites, drinking lemonade from the bottles: poverty, the class system, the economy, politics, how to make the world a better place, modern music, poetry, fashion. *Why shouldn't they talk about these things? They were going to make a better go at things than their parents had.* Mr Fernie tried, but he found it exasperating. One moment they were discussing the Parable of the Sower, the next educating slum dwellers. One moment they were discussing the Good Samaritan, the next Chamberlain's Housing Act. One moment the Lilies of the Field, the next Fred Astaire and Ginger Rogers in *Swing Time.* They became adept at pushing their conversations *beyond the pale.* Mr Fernie found it increasingly difficult to see where to draw the line. One evening he laid down the law. To his astonishment, they openly rebelled. He was an Elder of the Church, yet a dozen fifteen and sixteen-year-olds, including his own daughter, were telling him they refused to obey his strictures any more. That evening finished late. They dragged their heels through school the following day.

It was an uncertain week. Had they gone too far? Would Mr Fernie shut them down for good? Lilly was brilliant. She never explained exactly how she'd managed it. Instead she just smiled and said, 'I can get Daddy to agree to anything, if I put my mind to it.'

The little assistant minister was allocated the job of watching over us.

And then another crisis arose: whether I should stay on to do Highers or not.

August 1938. The next time June visited Stranraer, she would be twenty years older. On the last leg of the journey home she didn't know this. She took the train to Liverpool Lime Street, crossed the city by foot because she wasn't sure which tram to take and caught the electric train to Hall Road. She got off, not knowing where home was. Mummie had rung her while she was staying with Betty to give her directions.

'You can't go wrong. Just walk straight out the station onto Serpentine North. It's only five minutes away.'

She didn't understand why Mummie had sold their neat, semi-detached house in Crosby and moved to this large, imposing, old house in Blundellsands. It had a garden on three sides and a balcony running along one side. It was old and decrepit; it would be a nightmare to clean. It was called Alderley. *What did that mean?*

Mummie was watching for her and came to the door, waving an official looking letter. She handed it to June. It had been neatly opened with a paper-knife already. June felt disappointed with her mother. *It was addressed to her, not Mummie. Why couldn't she have waited till she'd got back from Stranraer?* At that moment she hated her mother. She put down her suitcase and took the letter. Mummie was smiling and nearly dancing on the spot. She had done well in her School Certificate.

'Just think, June. You'll get the education I never had.' She hugged her daughter.

'I've already got more education that you ever had.'

'That's true. Oh my! That's very true.'

June felt miserable. Mummie had spoilt this moment. And now she'd gone and spoilt it for Mummie. She asked to see her room and went upstairs to unpack. At least she would catch up with everyone at the Curious Society tomorrow. Find out who had done well. See if everyone was planning to go on into the sixth form. She only had twelve hours to get through till then.

She left the house as soon as Sunday tea was over and walked the whole way. She needed to get out. Michael, George, Richard and Alec were early. They were glad to see her and eager to hear how she'd done. She showed them the letter.

'Well done, June.' Michael gave her a hug.

'Yes,' said Richard and hugged her too.

'That's excellent, June. No more than I expected, mind you.' Alec gave her a shy hug. The smile shone through his pallid eyes and warmed her heart.

I mustn't cry. I mustn't cry.

It felt so good to have the approval of these clever boys, all about to enter the Upper Sixth. They were certain she must go on to do her Highers. And she must go to university. They were convinced she was brighter than the swots who didn't dare join in their discussions, because tomorrow was a school day and Miss Fordham forbade them to be out on a Sunday evening.

Mr MacDonald had written a pamphlet on 'The Church's responsibility for International Peace'. Fred— they had started calling the assistant minister 'Fred' rather than Reverend Bennett—said he could get copies for everyone and drop them off during the week. Could they all get it read for next Sunday? Of course they could. This was more like it. This was the issue that could affect their futures. June looked forward to debating: what was the difference between appeasement and peace? Was standing up for peace cowardly or brave? Was there such a thing as a just war? Under what circumstances would they be prepared to fight in one? What was worth fighting for?

Alec walked her home that evening. They held hands. She shared how her mother had annoyed her by opening her results letter. And how strange it had been to be rung at Betty's and told to return to a different home.

'Why do you think she did it?'

'I don't know,' she paused. 'Debby, probably.'

'Debby?'

'He probably said our house was too small. He wanted to live somewhere bigger.' She paused. Alec kept quiet. 'I wish she'd never married him.'

'Why's that?'

'It was bad enough when he came to stay but now he lives with us all the time. I don't really understand but his contract with Lady in Black has changed. He just supplies the big stores locally. Anywhere he can get to by train in a day. He says he's made a good bargain with them and is in charge of the North-West.'

'But it doesn't feel like a good bargain?'

'No, I'm sure money's tighter than ever.'

'Ah!'

'In fact, come to think of it: he's not made a good bargain with Lady in Black, but he's made a good bargain marrying Mummie.'

'I see.'

'It's Mummie that's made a very bad bargain. And I'm the one who suffers for it.'

Here, she couldn't stop the tears that had been welling up all evening. She broke down on Alec's shoulder. Anyone else and she would have been mortified. But Alec understood. He had his own problems, which he never complained about. He was albino. It left him by turns more pensive and more acerbic than the rest of them. Already he found relief from his sensitivities in writing poetry. It kept him sane, he told June, once her sobs had subsided. Would she mind if he showed her some of it sometime? Of course she wouldn't mind. She felt flattered he would trust her with something so personal.

They exchanged a chaste kiss on their lips before Alec turned to walk back home. That night they both went to bed consoled by their late evening's conversation.

June slept in on Monday morning. Long after the breakfast dishes had been cleared she emerged from her new bedroom yawning. As a special treat Mummie prepared a cup of Camp coffee for her. She breathed in its aroma and sipped it with pleasure, while they planned their day.

'You've grown out of your gymslip and your blouses. We'll have to buy you new ones.'

'Mmmm.' June was still concentrating on her coffee. 'Can we afford it?'

'Money will be tight for a while, but I'll manage. Can you keep the same winter coat until the New Year?'

'I'll manage.' She hated that navy-blue coat anyway.

'As long as you don't need any new badges, we should be all right.'

'Not much chance I'll get chosen as form captain is there?' They laughed at the notion—in June's case bitterly.

Immediately after a lunch of bread and tomato soup they went round to the Schools Outfitters. Monday afternoon was a quiet time and they had the shop to themselves. June tried on blouses and gymslips. The owner tutted, tugged and pulled at material, stepping back to consider, then darting in to make another adjustment, until she was satisfied they'd got the right fit. June wasn't happy; because she was so 'well-developed,' as Mrs Rawcliffe put it, she was obliged to wear a size too large. The navy serge gymslip felt voluminous around her hips.

'And might you need new stockings and knickers?'

June's heart sank; she hated those black lisle stocking and thick navy knickers. So different from the silk and lace confections that Debby dealt in. She glimpsed an anxious expression on Mummie's face.

'Thank-you Mrs Rawcliffe. I believe I'm fine for stockings and knickers. Maybe after half term I'll need new ones.'

Mummie relaxed into a polite smile. As she carefully folded the items, wrapped them in brown paper and neatly tied the parcels with string, Mrs Rawcliffe made conversation. She prided herself on establishing a personal relationship with her customers.

'So, Valerie, which subjects will you be studying for your Highers?'

'History, English and French.'

'She's always had her nose in a book, since she was a wean.'

Mrs Rawcliffe looked perplexed. 'Who's your favourite author, Valerie?'

She decided to say, 'Sir Walter Scott,' emphasising his surname a little too much.

'Of course, my husband's a native French speaker.'

'I didn't know your father was French, Valerie.'

'He's not…'

Mummie cut her off with alacrity, 'He's not actually French. He comes from Lausanne in Switzerland.'

'Ah! So, did you meet in Lausanne?'

'No.' Mummie looked flustered.

'Debby's worked in this country for ages. He was a travelling salesman when they met. He sells the most *exquisite* lingerie,' she said pointedly.

Mummie looked grateful.

'You called your father "Debby?"'

'That's Swiss French for Daddy.'

They contained their laughter until they'd left the shop and turned the corner.

'Nosey old cow.'

'Mummie!'

'Well she is. And I spend enough for her to treat me with a bit of respect. What does she want prying into my private life?'

June didn't answer that. *When would Mummie realise that no one around here respected a Galloway accent, no matter how excellent the dress sense of the woman who uttered it.*

Tuesday was spent going through the rest of her uniform, sewing missing hooks and eyes onto her bodices, darning the heels and toes of her black lisle stockings, replacing the elastic in her heavy woollen navy-blue knickers, brushing down last year's navy wool coat and her ridiculous, pudding-basin hat. In the afternoon she went to the hairdressers. She had it cut to just below her ears, slightly longer than was allowed, but not long enough to be restrained by a ribbon. She went to bed with papers in her hair. *At least she could wear her hair curled for a few more days without the risk of its being tugged straight as she passed by Miss Fordham.*

She woke early on Wednesday morning, having finally caught up with her sleep.

'Good morning, June.'

'Morning.'

'Alors, qu'est-ce qu'on va faire aujourd'hui?'

'Je n'sais pas.' She concentrated on browning her toast.

'Peut-être que tu voudrais venir à Bold Street avec moi?' It wasn't a question.

Valerie pouted.

'Wear your best clothes. I want to show you off in Bold Street.'

Since she had nothing better to do, she went and got changed.

She wore her green skirt, her yellow cardigan and a pale cream silk blouse. She put on her silk stockings, craning her neck in front of the mirror to make sure the seams were straight. She borrowed Mummie's lipstick; while she was at Mummie's dressing table, she dabbed *Shalimar* behind her ears and on her wrists. She felt sophisticated. With her well-developed figure she was sure she could pass for at least eighteen, maybe twenty.

Debby approved. As they sat opposite one another on the train into Exchange Station, he complimented her on her appearance.

'Tu as plutôt l'air d'un mannequin.'

She was flattered. He could be so suave. Especially on trains.

Bold Street was where the posh gown shops were. Debby dealt with two of the swankiest. He supplied them with his expensive Swiss underwear. This morning he was taking samples of the new autumn collection to show them. The lingerie was intimate and suggestive, as was Debby's tone with the buyers. He knew how to turn on the charm. These were hard-headed business women, yet June felt an illicit frisson as they bargained over terms and prices. She watched him fascinated. This was the first time she'd seen him at work. His smile was courteous, his manner was… *How to describe it? Yes. It was seductive. It was as if he were trying to seduce these women.* On a dull Liverpudlian morning, he brought a trace of exoticism and sheer sensuality to this business transaction.

When business was concluded to his satisfaction, he turned their attention to June.

'I don't believe you've met my stepdaughter, Valerie June, have you?'

Shakes of the head.

'She is a very bright girl. She 'as just passed her School Certificate. She is looking for an opening.'

First she'd heard of it.

'I wonder, might you have a vacancy…' He paused, waiting for them to supply a position that Valerie June would suit.

Twice he used the same allurement in his bargaining. Twice he lingered suggestively over the word 'vacancy' as these powerful women narrowed their eyes and assessed her qualities from well-brushed, curled hair to well-polished court shoes. Twice she was offered a job as trainee buyer cum model. Now she wished she didn't look so like a *mannequin*.

After the second offer, Debby said he would need time

to reflect. He took them to the Kardomah for a coffee.

'*Alors ? Lequel tu préfères?*'

She didn't want either. Somehow it appeared that wasn't an option. She shrugged her shoulders, took another spoonful of sugar and stirred her coffee.

'*Moi, je crois que Cripps soit le plus avantageux,*' he opined forcefully.

'You can't stop me getting an education,' she slammed the front door shut behind her.

Mummie emerged from the kitchen to see what the fuss was about.

June brushed past her and stomped upstairs.

She sat on her bed and pounded her pillow with her closed fist. Then she picked up her beautiful hairbrush with mother of pearl inlay and threw it across the room.

She stayed seething in her room until hunger drove her to join them for supper.

She ate sulkily. Not speaking. Not meeting their eyes.

'Debby's right,' her mother said. 'I don't know what I was thinking. We just can't afford it. That's all there is to it.' A pause. Still June refused to speak. 'I'll take the new uniform back tomorrow and say you've been offered this wonderful opportunity and it's what you'd like to do.'

Valerie glared at her mother. Finally, she spoke. 'You can't stop me getting an education.'

'*Sois raisonnable, ma petite. Il nous manque les sous.*'

'*Mais, comme même, je poursuis mes études,*' then turning to Mummie: 'If I can't study at Merchants, I'll go to evening classes after work in Liverpool instead.'

She shoved her plate away, pushed back her chair, scrapping the parquet floor and went upstairs to bed.

She wrote a formal letter to Miss Fordham stating she would not be returning to Merchant Taylors' School for Girls at the start of the autumn term, since she had secured a position in a high-class Ladies Outfitters, where she would train as a buyer. This was an opportunity too good to miss. She spent the week enquiring about and enrolling on evening classes and seeing how many of the books she would need to study were in the local library.

Late afternoon, the Wednesday following the

momentous trip to Bold Street, she came home having spent the day in the library. As she staggered through the front door, balancing a precarious pile of books about Medieval History, she noticed that Mummie had carefully rewrapped Mrs Rawcliffe's parcel and left it on the hall table ready to return in the morning. Seeing that parcel made the decision final somehow. She passed the evening in her room, ostensibly reading *A Guide to the Study of Medieval History*, but actually engrossed in *The Tainted Relic: A Historical Mystery*.

The following morning when I came down early I found my mother on her knees cleaning the grate, obviously very upset. She said I must go back to school and that she would find a way of paying the fees. I persuaded Miss Fordham, our very nasty headmistress, to let me come back in September 1938 and take my Higher School Certificate. The woman was a suspicious, narrow-minded tyrant as I had always suspected.

I'm a bit confused about the reason we moved.

Did this confusion come with old age and infirmity? Or was she confused even then, because they concealed much about their financial affairs? Did Debby decide they should move nearer to the train station, because it would be more convenient for his work—*après tout, elle ne voudrais qu'il soit en retard les soirs*. Did he find subtle ways of silencing my grandmother? Did she go out into her garden and worry about money as she dug her vegetable patch? Did June know that when she set about polishing the grate it was a sign she was really upset?

At the last Old Girls' Luncheon, Jean Glasspool, née Kirkland, said I would have had much better Highers results if I hadn't had so many boyfriends. But it was their conversation I enjoyed so much—most of them went on to Oxford. Had I still been at Stranraer High School it would have been so much more natural without a lot of old maids breathing down our necks!

Manor Road, Crosby

June—I've put a whole year into the wonder of you—and now it's all gone. Perhaps if I christened you anew with Valerie I put into a new Surname that new dream. But there are no words for what we had tonight—the fierce joy of an immortal hour. You were so lovely and I was afraid to tell you for fear you know too well. Your hair framed in the soft light a face with eyes more fine than any woman's I have known. Fierce and young, I hold myself close to you of course I wanted so to be with you—This must finish because I have so far to go tomorrow but you must have something waiting for you in the evening. I shall dream, I think, tonight, of heaven, which we took between our hands half-wondering, half-aware. You will never be sad I came, and I am so very glad. Take care of yourself and I shall write tomorrow,

Your Richard (R.E. Morgan)

Oct 23rd

[…] Now I find that you are with me more vividly than ever before. […]

So you see you remain my blessed lady and seem likely to do so. I would not have it otherwise.

Yours as ever,
Alec

These were affairs she didn't care to tell me about. She kept their letters in her bedside cabinet throughout her married life. She kept her virginity until after the war when she was P.A. to the Director of ECITO in London. She lost it in Hyde Park to an American G.I. called Jack, who was editor of *The Stars and Stripes*. On the night he announced he was going back to the States the next morning, he told her about his wife back home.

She loved the bright, intelligent Merchant's boys. Avatars of the deceased father she had known briefly in this place, but whom she couldn't remember at all, and whom Debby tried to supplant insisting he was her 'father.' She mustn't call 'im 'stepfather'—*jamais*. She loved to be adored by the cleverest Merchants boys. Their conversation was exciting, brilliant and full of new ideas. Miss Fordham wasn't going to stop her talking to boys, whatever her unwritten rules. And Debby had no right to tell her how to behave. He was a lousy father, sponging off Mummie. There was no love lost between them. She would find a better father figure than him. Someone who could look after her and Mummie. She threw her mother-of-pearl-inlaid hairbrush across her bedroom more than once that autumn and winter.

Sunday March 5th, 1939. Her seventeenth birthday. She walked along the beach from Crosby to Hightown and back, not once but twice that day. In the morning with Michael and in the afternoon with Alec.

And then the second bombshell occurred! It was decided I would be sent to stay with Debby's brother Jean in Lausanne and go to the girls' school there. I would enter the department for foreign students to learn French and after two years receive a Certificate for Teaching French. I don't like to remember the occasion when I once more bearded Miss Fordham with my news!

I remember coming downstairs in the morning and Mummie was cleaning the hearth vigorously. She was obviously upset that Debby was sending me away, but she didn't stop him.

This time Mummie didn't contradict Debby.

Mummie had developed a nasty skin complaint. Uncle Alf had been treating it as best he could and it had died down during the winter. When spring arrived it came back all over her face and was most unsightly. She preferred to say goodbye to June at home and let Debby accompany her on the first stage of her journey. So, on Monday 1st May, Debby and June caught the train for London. Michael came to see her off at Hall Road station.

They stayed overnight with Debby's ex-wife, Charlotte. June hadn't realised before she was Swiss. Only French was spoken, a harbinger of her next few months. They caught the train for Dover and stayed one night there, before she caught the early morning boat to Boulogne-Sur-Mer. From there she caught the train to Paris and then the overnight sleeper to Lausanne. The Orient Express. Uncle Jean, whom she had never met before, was waiting for her at the station.

Just before embarking at Dover she ran to a telephone booth, rang Alec's number and put her loose change in the box. There was just time to say a tearful goodbye and hear his gentle voice. He promised he would write.

Friday 5ᵗʰ May, 1939

Dear Alec:

   I thought you might like these for your stamp collection. I arrived here safely after two days and nights in sleeping cars—watching the stars at night and waking to watch the dawn across France. Missing the Curious Society intensely—especially your brilliant conversation, but I sometimes worry that we all gossip too much.

   Love from your, June x

Mr Alec Reid,
8 Park View,
Waterloo,
Liverpool 22,
L'Angleterre

Mr H. M. K. Howson,
22, College Road North,
Blundellsands,
Liverpool 23.

Monday 8ᵗʰ May

Dear Michael:

I had to write and thank you for coming to see me off last Monday morning. That doesn't sound warm enough; words can't convey how much it meant to me that you rose early and came to say goodbye on that windy Hall Road platform. Despite the chill, I felt a burning heat as you held me close and gave me a last hug farewell.

The journey was arduous but deeply fascinating, seeing so many new places and watching the French countryside and small towns as we whizzed past them. I won't bore you with too many details; suffice it to say, I arrived safely in Lausanne. Instead, I'll tell you about where I'll be living for the next couple of years.

Uncle Jean lives with his second wife, Tante Clara. She has two daughters, Denise and May. Denise has something the matter with her feet and walks as little as possible. "Mai Mai"—who's much livelier than Denise, is a lot younger. They live in a flat; just about every room has wood panelling. I don't think they've heard of wallpaper! The flat is on the road that runs down to the lake—Lac Leman. I can see I'll be spending long hours on my own here; so beware, I shall fill them with writing heaps of letters to you! My first morning, I ventured out and explored the adjacent streets. I found a Newsagents (I shall call it "un Tabac" from now on) and bought a stash of postcards, blank airmail letter forms—like the one I'm writing on now—and stamps. So you see, I shall keep my homesickness at bay by corresponding with all the members of The Curious Society—"C. S." for short. I have an admission to make: just before I embarked on the ferry, I rang Alec from the port at Dover. I think it was because he'd not been at the station to see me off like you'd been; you are the two most important people in my life, and I couldn't say a last goodbye to one of you and not the other.

I started my new school this morning. School starts very early, but it's all over by midday. I've made a vow to avoid all English speakers and to speak only French. I mean to improve my French as much as possible and show Debbie. I know it will make me feel homesick, but I'm determined. I'm not like you—I can't get things perfectly right, but I shall make a stab at it all the same. After lunch, I went out for a long walk on my own. I think this worried "Tante et Oncle" but they didn't tell me not to do it again. As I slipped out the flat—Tante Clara and Denise were both resting, and Mai Mai had been told to read a book quietly for half an hour—I heard the most exquisite piano playing through an open window. It came from across the road, from a house with a gate into it and metalwork fencing and a sort of patio in front. I heard the strains of music from across the road. It could have been Debussy or Satie. And my mind drifted back to my Auntie Dolly—you remember, I told you about how she helped bring me up as a little girl. I don't think I've heard such playing since she married Birrell. It made me feel doubly homesick. Anyway, I found I can easily walk down to Lac Leman and around the edge of the lake. I think I shall try to do this every day. And Tante Clara can't stop me!

On the way back, I went back to the "Tabac" and bought a beautiful lined notebook. I've decided I shall keep a diary while I'm here, and perhaps when I finally get back home to the C. S., I shall give you a reading of my impressionistic travel writing!

Please write soon. I miss you already. The memory of you holding me last Monday is all I have to keep my spirits up till I hear from you again.

Your loving,

June x

8 Park View
Weds

Preface

Dear June,

I wrote the letter on Monday but there are two more points I have remembered & wish to add:

I. Mike has not told me much about Monday. He has told me that there was a Monday & even mentioned an electric fire but that is all. I mention this lest You should think that Mike had spoilt it.

II. I fancy Lionel would like some communication from you. He also is a stamp collector.

You may now read the letter—if you can.—

8 Park View
Waterloo
L'pool 22

Monday May 8th

Dear June,

Thank you very much for the post card whose arrival was surprising and whose contents were gratifying. You will probably find that I write much as I talk, vaguely and chaotically. I just wander till I have no more to say or till I develop Scrivener's Palsy. You have been warned.

Secondingly I'm not sure whether you wanted me to write. Foreign correspondence is no joke if you have any amount of it at all. However, if you don't find this too much (my letters are overpowering) please write back. Irrespective of what you may say—and remember you have only to say "Shut up, Reid" and my pen will be stilled—I shall be pleased to hear from you. I collect stamps.

So much for the Preface. I shall now get to the main business of the evening. I have regained my own Faith in Life. I had lost it for a time. It seemed to me that I was wasting my youth, letting myself be hedged in by a mesh of orthodox outlook and I was very bored. I told you that my ideal was Beauty or Ecstasy and that the penalty was disillusion. For the last month I have had disillusion without Ecstasy. I was doubting if ~I~ it were worth it all and I was thinking strongly of being nothing but a bitter cynic sneering at Beauty and pretending that there was no such thing as Ideals. That Sunday at the Curious Society wracked me for I loved the music and hated the discussion. That night after I had been so rude to you, I got a nasty shock, which convinced me that there could never be a faith for me.

When Mike told me on Tuesday that he had found Ecstasy I was at once jealous, slanderous and pessimistic. However, my Byronic mood has passed. By telling me, Mike has ennobled me. Since I know now I am as great as either of you for I also have my magic. After seeing and hearing Mike I know that there is only one course for me: to seek true Beauty; never to doubt the faith, and to lay aside much of my shallow cynicism. I must be fair to myself, keep Faith with myself and with you two and lay aside all my policy of battening upon garbage, which only cheapens me in my own eyes. You see I am one of a Trinity, probably the cheapest and vilest member, but a member for all that—Mike has been above the Common Things of life for a week and I hope that you are too. If you feel as I do or look ~at the thing~ on Monday in any idealist light you are almost among the immortals. If you don't you won't understand a word of this. However I have my Faith. <u>You</u> "brought me for my dearth, Holiness

238

lacked so long / And Love and Pain."

How do you like Switzerland? I am told the hills are terribly depressing if you live under them. Have you found this out yet or are you too thoughtful of England and home to notice such vague impressions? I envy you very much. You are travelling just when you can best appreciate it.

I went to Formby with Mike last night. It was a glorious evening and we heard a cuckoo. The queer thing was that I enjoyed the woods far more that he did. For him they acted as a kind of mental goad, reminding him of somewhere else. But for me they were very Heaven.

I continue to read poetry. An Oxford Book of English Verse is my constant companion and I have flavoured this with Rupert Brooke and Dante. I can't quite make my mind up about our good Rupert. Firstly I can't decide whether he was a bit of a prig—it's a horrid thought I know, but did you read the Memoir!—and I'm sure he didn't know what he was talking about. Again, did he believe in God? One thing I do know, it was the best thing possible for himself and everyone else that he died young. Had he lived, the Armistice and our generation would have soured him.

If you have anything to say on the subject say it or rather write it. Forget that inferiority complex which said of the grandest thing imaginable "the subject is not of sufficient interest." Shame on you. By the way, don't think this patronising. I only began to live last January. I wonder if you understand. I hope you do for you'll have missed something grand otherwise—by that I don't mean my scribblings but rather the Ecstasy of which I speak. Tell me please if you think you understand what I mean. I can't do better than close with a quotation. Do you remember it?

> Though I may never see your face
> And never shake you by the hand,
> I send my soul through Time and Space
> To greet you. You will understand.

J. E. Flecker.

That sums it up. If I am right and you understand I have gained another friend. But whether I am right or not I can truly sign myself, by virtue of what you have done for me,

Your gracious ladyship's most humble and devoted servant.

F. Alec Reid

P.S. Quotation from Hamlet "This above all to thine own self be true, and it must follow as the night the day, thou cannot then be false to any man." F.A.R.

Mr Alec Reid,
8 Park View,
Waterloo,
Liverpool 22,
L'Angleterre

Thursday 5ᵗʰ May,

Dear Alec:

I received your letter; & think I understand. I'm very flattered you think me a worthwhile cause. However, I'm not sure that Rupert Brooke is a prig. Does that make me your intellectual equal?

Very exciting news—I'm to have piano lessons every day! There's the most accomplished pianist who lives just across the road, who will teach me simply for the love of it. Speaking of Love—

I'll write soon,

Your ever-loving June x

Mr H. M. K. Howson,
22, College Road North.
Blundellsands.
Liverpool. 23.

25, av. d'Ouchy 25,
Lausanne,
Monday 15th May

Dear Michael,

I have so much to say and so much news to tell you, I hardly know where to begin.

First things first: I still dream of our Monday morning moment. I don't think I shall forget it for as long as I live. That and the Thursday night last Easter, when we upset Lionel because we were both so distracted. I think it's important that we try not to hurt anyone's feelings again. Alec wrote to me and I got the impression you might have told him about us. He said you went on a walk to Formby together and that your mind seemed to be elsewhere. I love you both, and I wouldn't hurt Alec's feeling for the world, so please try to be gentle with him. I do hope this doesn't harm your feelings, but it's the truth.

Talking of walks—I've got into the habit of going for long walks on my own most afternoons. "Tante et Oncle" haven't actually said I'm forbidden, so I shall continue to do so. And here's my first piece of exciting news. The day after I arrived here, I went out exploring and I heard the strains of music in the distance. Someone was playing the piano. Immediately, my mind drifted back to the upstairs drawing room at Stranraer—remember I told you about it when we went for a walk to Hightown. I've not heard playing like it since my Auntie Dolly got married. (She's a terribly talented pianist.) Anyway, to cut a long story short, I'm having daily lessons from "Tante Léonie." I used to dread piano practice, but now I love these hours we spend together—I can't practice at home, since there isn't a piano in the flat. She finds me the most glorious, dreamy music to play. She doesn't charge me anything for it. I think she enjoys the company and I get the impression that Oncle Jean did her some big favour in the past and that this is her way of paying him back.

So now, I'm not so lonely and I'm starting to make friends at school. I've got a best friend already. Her name is Hannah and she's German Swiss. Her father owns a hotel. He's sent her to Lausanne to learn French. There are lots of German Swiss girls at the school, all there for similar reasons. Hannah won't mix with them, because then she wouldn't get to practice her French enough. We've got that in common—we both want to perfect our language—or at least try as hard as we can.

Obviously, I'll never be "word perfect"—I'm not a perfectionist after all. Mummy's favourite saying is, "If a thing's worth doing, it's worth doing badly." I think there's a lot of truth in that.

Anyway, you should hear us jabbering away in French together:—

"Il dit que je dois parler français couramment. Il est absolument nécessaire pour les hôteliers en Suisse. Mais je ne sais pas encore si je veux devenir hôtelière."

"Mon père a décidé que je dois enseigner le français. Il dit que ce sera un bon métier pour une jeune fille comme moi, puisque je ne voudrais pas devenir mannequin dans une boutique."

"Moi je voudrais bien être mannequin. Ça doit être chouette."

"Peut-être. Mais je veux aller à l'université. Je veux suivre une éducation plutôt académique."

We've lots in common. We're both homesick. We're both here in Lausanne because our fathers insisted. It's strangely pleasurable—sharing our feelings in the only available language.

I've decided I shall make the most of these two years. Who knows what doors it might open for me when I leave home? But in a way, I've left home already. By the time I return to Crosby, I'll be nineteen. I'm not going back to Alderley, at least not for long. I'll find a job teaching French somewhere. Then I'll do my Highers in evening classes. Perhaps I can move to Oxford, to be near you two brainboxes. Then you can help me with my Highers. Maybe, I'll get into a women's college. St Hilda's perhaps? Alec says I must overcome my inferiority complex. And that's true. I think it's because Mummy left school at the age of twelve and is so uneducated. It makes me doubt my own ability to get on. That and those awful teachers at Merchants. I would have got a better education, if we'd stayed in Stranraer. Maybe Debbie did me a favour after all, sending me away like this.

I must stop now. It's time for the evening meal, "le souper." I must tell you about Tante Clara's soups some time; they're delicious.

I know you must be very busy studying and preparing for your exams, but please write soon.

All my love,

June x

[Postmark Blundellsands Liverpool 9.10 AM 20 May 39
Miss V. J. Hepburn
25, av. d'Ouchy 25,
Lausanne,
Switzerland

22, COLLEGE ROAD NORTH.
BLUNDELLSANDS.
LIVERPOOL. 23.
18th May, 1939

Dear June,

Today is Ascension Day, a day of joy, for on it, long ago, the fire of faith in the hearts of the Apostles that despair had almost quenched blazed up again brighter than before. And to me now it is a day of joy. But do not think that the man of God (Lodge) has caused me to repent, return to the Christian fold and start preaching sermons. I would readily worship the Celtic god Bile, for the First of May is his sacred day of Beltane. On that day you kindled a fire in me. It was hard to believe that within you there burned another fire from which you kindled mine. I wrote to you and waited. That is why I have been so slow to write again. Your letter has answered me. I do not know what may come hereafter, save this, that if it lie with me, you shall not regret, nor shall I forget. You must not let yourself be troubled for me. Do always what your heart bids. Then you cannot fail to do what is best.

Sometimes I am glad that you went to Switzerland. For you might have grown tired of me: it is not at all difficult. But your letters have brought me pleasure, even that which you feared to be so harmful. I enjoyed reading of your journey and imagining you in the train. Do you not find trains fascinating? Cars, through long familiarity perhaps, "leave me cold." But trains have a magic all their own.

It seems surprising that the girls in your school are German Swiss. Which reminds me that you have not told me when you are to return to England and when you have to go back to Lausanne.

Let me be clear about us. Perhaps you feel as I do that to make our love known is to defile and cheapen it, to violate a shrine. No-Body really knows except Alec, and he understands much less than he thinks.

I think I can understand your feelings about Lausanne. But soon, surely, when you come to know the country better and go among the mountains, they will grip your heart so that it will be pain to leave them. Woods and meadows are very pleasant, the sea in all its moods is exhilarating, the dreary marsh and the wild heath have their beauty; I know them all. But mountains can uplift the soul as nothing else can save music and poetry and love.

As I write I wish that I were there with you, that I could see the "high peaks hoar" and "the torrent at the door," and hear, as I have heard,

"No sound
But the boom
Of the far waterfall like Doom."

Here in England it has been raining. It is good, for rain cools the mind; and even Lancashire seems less suburban when the woods and fields and the sea are seen but dimly through a swaying curtain of rain. It is a pleasant time in England; the thrushes sing, the lilac blooms, the laburnum trees are yellow cascades, the may is beginning to flower. But the land is too "green and pleasant" for me. Full of the spring feeling, the lawn strives to become greener and pleasanter every minute, so that everything in the garden is lovely, until you have to mow the grass. I suppose they have lawns in Switzerland too, though you will scarcely be expected to indulge in graminiculture. I expect they don't use mowers there, but flatten the grass with Swiss Roll, or get a flock of chamois to graze it, or spread cream cheese on it, or yodel at it—but enough. To talk nonsense is the privilege of politicians. But on second thoughts I suppose that this nonsense is too honest for the Champions of Democracy now so busily engaged in trying to get something for nothing from the Russians.

I believe Alec is going to advise you about religion. I should be wary of his philosophy, as you would of a dog of friendly but uncertain temper—George, for instance, in his tennisballivorous moods. Alec is at present urging that one should adopt some creed and stick to it; but he will probably prove his own disbelief in this theory by changing his mind before he writes to you.

But here I must break off for a while.

*

19th May, 1939

I have just heard some very sad news. You remember John McCulloch. He was one of my most valued friends, one of those very few like Alec, who understand and cared to talk to me of those things which mean most to me. To-night I read in the paper that he has been missing from H.M.S. "Repulse" in Portsmouth since May 7th. I remember the last time I was with him; we were returning through the darkness from a walk to Hightown, one of many he made pleasant for me; we talked of the future.

Ora pro nobis,

Michael.

P. S. Please excuse the ink—it has no strength of character.

[Postmark Waterloo Liverpool 9 A M [indecipherable] 1939]
Mlle. V. J. Hepburn
25, Av. D'ouchy 25
Lausanne
Switzerland

8 Park View
Sunday May 21

Dear J,

I have pondered over the enclosed for a week. It'll do. I fancy that Lionel has written to you. He did this without consulting me. If you decide to write to him don't go out of your way to hurt him.

Forgive the paper and the scrawl but Time waits for no man.

By the way, thanks for the warning on disillusion. I know how true it is. Sometimes I lose faith in myself and am then just a universal menace.

But more anon.

It was good to hear from you yesterday evening and as a sign of my appreciation I'll see what I can do about my writing. I'm afraid however that no amount of copper-plate authography will make this letter pleasant. I want to work off some depression without making you feel sick, or sorry or angry. You'll see what I mean in a minute.

On the first Tuesday I rang you up to suggest you should take me for a walk, I complained that I was bored. If you thought about it at all you probably considered it as mere cheap excuse only differing from the rest because of my passion for being different. You didn't take it seriously but it was quite true. Now what I meant was that life had become monotonous and I wanted a change. I knew that you wouldn't snub me and so I rang up. But that meant I was sick of my own company. And when that happens I feel very sad. It means that I can't amuse myself—that I am dependant on someone else. Now there is nothing in which I believe except myself and when that goes there is nothing left and I go through a Hell of depression. These depressed moods can last from half an hour to three months. Life ceases to be worth living when they come. Everything seems hollow worthless deceitful and everyone becomes a menace—to be hated and avoided. The Sunday evening before you went to Switzerland I cried myself to sleep because everything was so monotonous and uninteresting.

At present I can see no reason for keeping alive. That I am alive is not my fault—I had no say in the matter. But I do know that for the past ten months I have suffered the depths of despair, have been robbed of my ideas and left with a terrible sense of isolation. Why do I go on? Partly I suppose because I fear the unknown, but mainly because I'm used to it. After living nearly eighteen years it is difficult to imagine any other state. I have passed this week through the stages of despair and melancholy and have reached

245

Apathy. There is nothing to live for but equally there is nothing that justifies me killing myself and there is certainly no cause worth dying for.

Although I haven't let on so far it started being Monday at the bottom of the last page. Now let me define a twerp. "A twerp noun mas or fem— an upstart—a sneaking petty knave—a hound." Does that help? If not you must add the words hypocrite and deceiver. You will probably find samples of twerpishness (or is twerperie better?) as you read on.

I feel my isolation acutely. There are only two or three people here whom I trust and who can help me at all. Mike is the chief soul-saver and is worth nearly all the rest put together, He annoys me though because his very existence makes it impossible to be a complete cynic. The other people with whom I associate are fools or knaves but mostly fools. They fail to interest me.

At this stage I propose to reason with you about human nature. I personally am a swine. There can be no doubt of that. Now compared to my fellow human beings I am relatively decent. For all that I and they are swine and perhaps my biggest crime is that while I piously believe that I am a swine I am well content to stay one. Since I am not prepared to cure myself, I don't want to help others in any disinterested way.

I am convinced that it is the big things that matter. Until you grasp a big principle you can't appreciate the small things. I fancy that only after you had found and realised the principle of Beauty did you begin to appreciate these little things. I'll admit that at the moment you are making a much better job of your life than I am of mine, but for all that I adhere to my original contentions. One day you may come to hate people as I hate them. When you reach this stage you will feel very bitter and angry with yourself for ever having thought that your fellow-beings were good. At present as the French say "vous vous trompez." If you can keep it up till you die you will be very happy.

You used two words that have no meaning for me—worthwhile & Love. Nothing is worthwhile and if you mean by Love becoming passionately fond of anyone and thinking of them before you think of yourself, I can only call it criminal lunacy. As a means of forgetting this hum-drum existence it has got, I suppose, some considerable value but then since it involves the human element it is rather more unsatisfactory as a sedative than say music or poetry. How many people are in love with Love? Many who died in the war were in love with Death. This reminds me of Wilfred Owen. I bought his poems and a selection of Flecker recently and therein I found much to interest me. Thank you for mentioning Villon. I have read the Oxford Book of French Verse just because I wanted to read some of the good Francois and of course our old pal Ronsard. Yeats does <u>not</u> rhyme with Keats but with hates. Being Irish I feel strongly on the point.

I am feeling much better now which is perhaps as well for I have to talk French to some damned examiner on Friday. You know I've got to get a State Scholarship from this H.S.C. exam. This means at least one and perhaps two distinctions—in my case History and English. Gawd 'elp us. It looks as if I must go back to School for another year. I'll spend the winter hunting Scholarships at Oxford. I feel that an Oxford accent and a Balliol blazer are all I need to get the girls askipping.

I haven't time now to give you my ideas of the foundations of morality. La Rochefoucauld sums it up for me by saying "L'amour de la justice ce n'est que la crainte de l'injustice." You take my advice and keep in safe and shallow waters. You can't wallow there as I have done in my Slough of Despond for the last week. The early part of this letter is perfectly sincere and in no way a pose. I'm sorry for you in that you had to read it but I felt much better having got it off my chest. I hope you don't resent being used as a spiritual tin-can. For all the hard things I write to you I do appreciate your letters.

I thought very lovingly indeed of you last Saturday. In Lord Street Southport I found a Milk Bar called "June." Now a Milk Bar is just your vocation. You could treat your customers with that haughty disdain proper to a member of an exiled Royalty. You could convey admirably that subtle impression of contempt and disdain that at present is only to be met with in "Teashops kept by Gentlewomen." To be serious again. I suspect nostalgia—it's a disease from which I am singularly immune. I have never had a conventional "home".

Don't write unless you really feel you can't better employ your time. I am vain enough to suspect that you like writing me when the mood is on you. If you only write from a sense of duty your letters will not please, thrill, surprise me as your first two have done.

I must tear myself away and deal with Bacon, George 3rd and sundry other Rounds.

> Yours ever,
> Alec

P.S. I knew I had forgotten something. Flecker wrote it. Does it remind you of anything?

> And life stood still a moment, suddenly we passed
> The boundaries of joy: our hearts were ringing
> True to the trembling world: we stood at last
> Beyond the golden gate
> And knew the tune that sun and stars were singing.

M. H. M. K. Howson,
22, College Road North.
Blundellsands.
Liverpool. 23.

25, Av. d'Ouchy 25
Thursday 25th May

Dear Michael,

I simply have to write and tell you about the most wonderful school trip we went on yesterday. It was just for some of us foreigners. Not everyone was allowed to go; just the group who are making good progress. I suppose they thought we deserved a reward and would appreciate it. I wasn't sure I wanted to go; we had to be at school by half past six in the morning! But it was worth setting the alarm so early.

We crossed Lac Leman and went to Geneva. It's a beautiful city—in an austere kind of way. Everywhere you walk there are reminders of its protestant history: especially of John Calvin, who, whatever you say, was an incredibly important figure in the Reformation. And still is. Just think what religion would be like if he hadn't existed!

So it's funny really that we went to Geneva to see Spanish painting that is usually kept in Madrid, at the Prado. They were sent to Geneva for safekeeping at the start of the Spanish Civil War. Apparently, they're about to be returned, which is why we got a whole morning off school. It was quite wonderful. I mean, they came out of Catholicism; they should be anathema to me, but I can't get those dark, brooding crucifixions and those strange, magical landscapes out of my mind. Two artists stood out for me: El Greco and Velasquez. You must go to the library and see if you can find any reproductions of them. They're not like anything you or I have ever come across up until now.

Don't get me wrong. I love our church. It's architecture, the stained-glass windows, all that carved wood—you've no idea how bowled over I was by it the first time we went. There was a church a bit like it in Stranraer—my Auntie Dolly was married in it because Birrell's Church of Scotland—she loved the rose-coloured stone of its interior so she was happy to get married there. But I grew up worshipping in a very strict chapel. Blundellsands was quite a shock! But seeing these paintings—especially housed in Protestant Genève—was "bouleversant".

There's a strange power to their depictions of Christ's passion. As you stand there looking at them, you can feel his agony, as if your own limbs are being stretched to breaking point. And then there's El Greco. All his paintings seem otherworldly; he has these elongated figures. They're quite unnatural, and yet they seem right somehow. I don't know how to explain this to you, without your standing beside me, looking at a painting together. Please try and find a reproduction of *The Holy Trinity*. It's utterly different from anything you've seen before. God the father is more like a mother; he's so gentle and caring, cradling the dead Christ as if he were a baby. I can't explain it. And I'm still not sure why they had such a powerful effect on me. But it was worth coming to Switzerland just to see those paintings.

Then, there were wonderful portraits of the Spanish Hapsburgs by Velasquez. El Greco's figures are all strangely elongated and unearthly, but Velasquez's Hapsburgs looked pretty strange too! They all have long faces and jutting out lips! The oddest of all is a sort of group portrait. I stood in front of it for ages, quite bewildered. I'm still not quite sure what was going on in it; I think there was a little princess surrounded by her ladies in waiting—one of them looked like a dwarf. But then there was a portrait on the wall behind them of two old people who looked most austere, as if they were Calvinists! And there was a painter with a paintbrush and artist's palette in his hands, but he was looking at <u>me</u>—not at the little princess. And there was another man standing in a doorway at the back of the room; I couldn't work out what he was doing, but somehow, I don't think he was up to any good!

As you can imagine, after a whole day of looking at painting like this, my imagination was running riot. As we came back on the boat across Lac Leman, the lightning started. There we were in the middle of the lake, surrounded by water, and it was as if the landscape had stepped off an El Greco canvas, slipped out the museum and followed us! Really! We were <u>in</u> an El Greco painting, not just looking at it anymore. There was another painting I saw of Charon's Bark, by some earlier artist, I think, & at any moment I thought Charon would paddle towards us and bear us all off to some counter-reformation Hell! I finished the excursion in abject terror.

I hardly slept last night. Somehow, writing this letter has helped. I think I'll sleep soundly tonight.

I've just read this through and realised the whole letter is about <u>me</u>— and now I'm running out of space. I'm so sorry, but it's such a relief to pour my heart out to you and know you'll read and understand. However much Hannah and I get along, I couldn't tell her the half of this—and she was there! And Denise isn't much better; ~~she doesn't have an imaginative bone in her body~~ she's just not imaginative at all.

I must stop now. While there's still time to say I miss you very much and often think about you,

Yours,

June x

Mr H. M. K. Howson,
22, College Road North.
Blundellsands.
Liverpool. 23.

25, av. d'Ouchy 25,
Friday 26ᵗʰ May 1939

Dear Michael,

Today I got your letter written on Ascension Day. It was waiting on the hallway table when I got back from school. It was wonderful to read. I simply have to write to you—even though I've only just posted off my last letter.

I do see the mountains. Every weekend, we go up on the "funiculaire" for a picnic. The whole family goes, even Denise. Did I tell you she has something the matter with her foot? She and Tante Clara stay sat by the picnic things, while Uncle Jean, Mai Mai and I take long alpine walks. Uncle Jean owns a wool business. He says that in winter he skis up to the mountain villages where the women spin the wool. But now it's summertime; the cattle have gone up to the high pasture and the edelweiss are growing in the most inhospitable places amongst the rocky outcrops. Oncle Jean always carries a rucksack full of provisions. He's tall and agile—Tante says he comes from Alpine stock—he marches Mai Mai and me on long expeditions. Fortunately Mai Mai's younger and after a while she complains that she's tired and hungry. (I don't dare say anything—he's terribly intolerant!) But when Mai Mai asks, he stops immediately and finds us somewhere to sit and admire the view. Then we all tuck into fresh baguette and cheese, followed by lots of fruit. Sometimes, Oncle Jean gives us a sip of wine to fortify us. He adds it to our water and says, "Voilà, ce que coupera le soif!"

While we're walking, he tells me much about himself. It's so strange; during the week he's aloof and taciturn. It's almost as though he forgets whom he's talking to once we're high up in the mountains together. Apparently, he owns the business jointly with his first wife, Agnes. I suspect she's still his real love. They were unable to have children and he's keen for the Debetaz name to continue; I think he feels that Debbie hadn't done his duty in that respect—as in so many others. So, he's divorced Agnes and married Tante Clara, who's widowed. Because she's got two daughters already he hopes she'll prove more fertile. So far, nothing doing!

Last Saturday evening, when we'd got back, drunk on pure mountain air and a wee drop of red wine, my neck and shoulders were flushed from the fierce sun, I was feeling a bit miserable, because they were really burning, and I didn't think I would get much sleep. Oncle Jean must have noticed. He offered me the chance of ringing home. I'd been thinking of you the whole time we were walking. I dreamed we might come back here one day and walk the Alpine paths together. So I jumped at the chance of ringing you. It was so odd—a bit like when I rang from Dover. When I picked up the receiver and spoke to the operator, I didn't ask for your number. I rang Alec instead. Why was that? I'm not entirely certain, but I think it's because he's a kind of father figure to me. For all his posturing, he's always kind. And of course, he suffers so—with his eyesight and everything, and never complains. Besides, I wasn't sure what I would say to you; whatever it was, it wouldn't match our Monday moment. And I feared to lose the intensity of that in polite small talk. Anyway, I thought I better tell you, in case Alec mentions it. Please don't be upset. I wish I could see you in person soon. Might you come to Lausanne this summer? Would that be so impossible?

I love you,

June x

Stranraer,
Monday May 15th

Mlle. J. Hepburn
25 Av. D'Ouchy 25
Lausanne
La Suisse

My dear June,
I wish you were here!
(Believe me, this is no joke.)

Your best friend,
 Betty xxx

Dear Betty,

Thank-you for the postcard! I loved it. I was walking beside Lac Leman this afternoon, thinking about our walks around Loch Ryan. How long ago and far away that seems now. Do you still walk the dogs there on Saturday afternoons? I wish I were there with you now—or even better, that you were here with me and we could walk here together. You know the Stranraer town motto of course. Lately, I've found myself thinking about it a lot: "Tutissima Statio." Our "safe haven" used to be those walks by Loch Ryan. Then when I moved to Crosby, Stranraer and our friendship was my "safer haven" when I felt miserable. But now, I'm beginning to think that living in Switzerland would be the safest haven of all—at least for a while longer. I'm intrigued by what you wrote about Wig Bay; have you heard any more rumours lately? But perhaps you shouldn't write much about it, in case your letter goes astray.

As well as while walking by the water, I think of you every afternoon when I go for my piano lesson. Can you believe it? Me enjoying my piano lessons every single day! Tante Léonie plays the piano a bit like you used to. Once I've finished practising, she sits and plays to me before I go. I sit there dreamily listening and thinking of Auntie Dolly and of you. Her playing evokes a delicious feeling of nostalgia—not a painful, horrid sense of being homesick that I get at times.

Although, I've been much better recently. I'm getting quite used to living in Lausanne. So, on a brighter note, I'll tell you about Tante Clara's soups. We eat them every night, because you know the Swiss eat their main meal at midday. She makes a fresh one every evening. They're always thick, rich, broths full of whatever she decided was the best bargain at the butcher's and the greengrocer's that morning. And they're always accompanied by baguettes—I adore them! Eaten with lashings of butter. Oncle Jean says that's not the French way, but here in Lausanne that's how we do things. & chocolate—there's always delicious chocolate to round off the meal. It reminds me of our Saturday afternoons at the cinema. Except it tastes quite different from Cadbury's Dairy Milk.

On weeknights we eat Lindt, Swiss Milk Chocolate. It's so smooth and creamy. Then once a week, Oncle buys a box of Chocolats Halba. Bliss! I look forward to the weekends just for another taste of those chocolates! I'm convinced they're good for me. That and the long walks I'm taking every afternoon. And the weekly mountain walks with Oncle Jean. Anna, the Swiss-Romansh maid at the flat, worked in German Switzerland, near the factory where they're made on Lake Zurich. She told me she needs three languages to be a waitress. So she's working in all three parts of Switzerland before she applies for a job in Geneva. Anyway, she worked at the home of one of Chocolats Halba's employees. And they told her the company's been going through hard times because of the worldwide recession. So they're concentrating on the Swiss market now. But whatever happens, they'll never drop their standards. Quality's too important to compromise. And guess who gets the benefit!

You know, it makes me think of Mummy and her pet saying: "if a thing's worth doing, it's worth doing badly." I've been thinking about that a lot recently. I understand what she means: it's better to have a stab at something than not even try. But that saying is Mummy through & through: she's never had any ambition, nor any sense of standards. I'd only say this to you, Betty, but Mummy's ignorant about so many things that seem really important to me. Sometimes it's difficult to know what to talk to her about—apart from dresses and rig-outs.

So, you see, I'm growing to like Switzerland, despite the odd bout of homesickness. But I could never live here forever. All the women have pronounced goitres. Tante Clara says it's the lack of iodine in the water. And the other awful thing: the women here only wash their hair once a month! Can you imagine what I look like after four weeks! It's dreadful! Lank greasy locks. Tante says you shouldn't deplete the natural oils too often, but then, her hair's dry and frizzy. Not like mine My friend Michael is coming to visit me in August, and I've been looking anxiously at the calendar, trying to work out if I can wash my hair just before he's due to arrive. Thank Heavens, I think it should be Okay.

Talking of soups, Mai Mai's just come and told me that supper's ready, so I suppose I better finish this and pop out and put it in the post box this evening. I don't know when we'll meet again. Maybe you could come and stay here at the flat in the holidays. Should I ask Oncle Jean if that's Okay? Would your parents allow you to? Can you ask them and let me know?

I do hope they all say yes.

   Yours as ever,

      June xxx

Dear Lionel,

Thank-you for your letter, which arrived in the post at lunchtime today, and for your hilarious account of the last C. S. meeting. Poor Fred! It sounds as if you've all been quite cruel to him since I've been away. Have you heard of Moral Re-Armament? I recommend you go to the library and look it up. There's a book about it that came out last year; I've not read it, but Tante Clara's told me all about it. Apparently, it's sold loads of copies. If you want to rib the Reverend Fred Bennett, without behaving like total idiots, why don't you suggest that the C. S. discusses moral rearmament and see how he responds? It could be interesting!

What's been happening between you and Alec? He keeps writing enigmatic things about you. Have you been annoying him again—winding him up deliberately? You know that's not fair. I wish you two would get along better. You ought to try and see his good side. Granted, he doesn't spend much time thinking about the growing economic and political tensions in Europe. Alec can appear totally self-preoccupied at times. But there's more to him than that. I do wish you'd try harder to appreciate him. You know he's in awe of your table-tennis skills!

Have you been following the news lately? Michael sounds as if he reads the newspaper every day. I wondered if you all are at present. Did you hear about John McCulloch? It's so sad. Does anyone know how it happened? Has anyone else decided to join the R.N.V.R.? I suppose if Moral Re-Armament doesn't strike you as a solution that's the other way to respond to the mounting Nazi threat. I wondered if Michael might decide to volunteer or even sign up to the Navy at some stage.

I suppose you can tell from the above that I value getting letters from Crosby. I'm not sure how I'd survive here, if you all didn't keep in touch. I'm so grateful for the letters everyone keeps sending me. Mummy doesn't write letters. She prefers to give me a ring on the telephone. You should hear her: "I like to talk to you, June, not scrawl on paper. There's no feeling in that now is there?" That's all very well, but it means I only speak to her when she remembers to ring. When she does remember, it's always on a weekend evening that she rings, because it's cheaper then. So, it's usually when the family has just sat down to "le souper." To be honest with you, these are never satisfactory conversations; I feel awkward and stilted with Oncle Jean and Tante Clara listening. I can't express myself freely; I'd much prefer the privacy of paper. I can't say the slightest thing that might suggest I'm homesick, for fear Oncle and Tante think I'm criticising them and the way they're treating me here.

Perhaps it's just as well. Mummy agreed to my going; she'd feel badly if she knew how lonely and miserable I get sometimes. Besides, Mummy's got her own problems. She's not well. I'm pretty certain she's been feeling poorly for quite some time, and it sounds as if it's not getting any better. I suspect her symptoms are getting worse, although she won't admit that she's ill. You know what she's like. She says, "I'm fine, June" in such a way as to mean the exact opposite! So each time she rings, it ends up with me consoling her for ailments she won't discuss, but which she manages to let me understand she's suffering from anyway.

If you bump into her at tennis or badminton, could you ask after her please? And try to get beyond her stock phrase that she's "bearing up." I'm sure you'll know how to charm her and get her to let down her guard. After all, you managed it with me, her daughter, and I'm much more savvy than she is!

Please write again soon and tell me all the gossip. What films have come out since April? What's your favourite popular song at the moment? It's difficult to hear any decent songs here; the Swiss don't listen to anything from America if they can help it.

Lots of love,

June x

M. F. Alec Reid
8 Park View,
Liverpool 22
L'Angleterre

                                        Mardi, le 6 juin

My Dearest Alec,

You can't know how much your letters sustain me—even when you're feeling down, I feel honoured you should write to me with such honesty. I value our friendship so much. I'm glad writing to me helped you to rise above your depression. I don't mind how many times you call me "shallow" or use me as "a spiritual tin-can"; far better that than not hear from you at all. And I'd forgive you anything for that postscript! It's true. We shared this together that Wednesday evening. Do you remember—standing on the Serpentine looking out to sea?

You didn't say you'd cried yourself to sleep the night before I set out for Switzerland. Why didn't you tell me when I rang? Michael tries hard to be solicitous, to raise my spirits when I write and tell him how low and homesick I feel, but I'm not sure he really understands. I feel that only you think me worthy of your total trust. You've bared your soul to me, and to none other. Too often, Michael hides behind silly jokes, or self-conscious poses. Don't get me wrong. I miss you both. I love you both.

I went on a school trip to Geneva the other week to see the Prado's collection of Spanish paintings being held there for safekeeping. All their early depictions of the crucifixion and El Greco's amazing religious pictures have stayed with me and haunted my dreams for days now. (I wrote to Michael about them; ask him to tell you what I said, if you need more details. I would so like to be back at the C. S. and give you all a talk about them. There should be some reproductions in the library—please go and look at them!) Anyway, they were so powerful they got me thinking about religion. So much so that I really don't know what I believe anymore. You might say I'm in a bit of a spiritual turmoil. I was brought up quite strict Presbyterian, as you know, and by rights I should disapprove heartily of those Catholic images. But they conjured up such strength of feeling that I'm quite swayed by them.

Did I tell you about Tante Clara's newfound enthusiasm? She's got caught up with a group of people in Lausanne who follow the Oxford Group's Moral Re-Armament movement. I hadn't realised that its influence had spread to the continent so fast. She says it retains the moral essence of Christianity and brings it up to date with current affairs. (I hope that's a good enough translation of what she's told me.) She says a lot of Christianity is outmoded superstition, but that there's no need to throw the baby out with the bath water. Incidentally, did you know that this was a

German saying originally—that's what Hannah told me the other day: "Das schüttet das Kind mit dem Bade aus."

So here I am. On the one hand close to believing in the power of Catholic imagery and ritual, and on the other hand, about to abandon my Protestant faith in God for a modern, secular version of Christianity that might just help us combat the Nazis. At least that's better than Oncle Jean and Debbie—they don't believe in anything much, apart from woollen goods, silk lingerie and selling their latest lines. I'm not sure I could become an out and out atheist; that would be to betray my Grandma Rodger. But, neither am I sure who or what God is anymore. Back in Stranraer, he seemed to hover in the clear austerity of my grandfather's chapel, summoned by the tuning fork and those awful sermons that resounded all around the building and lingered near the ceiling. Then when we moved to Blundellsands, I was bowled over by those stained-glass windows, especially the huge one above the choirstalls: "The Lord of Hosts is with us"—in his rich, bloodred garments, surrounded by saints in blue and purple. How can the soul not be swayed by these images? I used to stare at them all through the sermons, until my thoughts drifted away utterly. Then I would find myself standing on the hill above Stranraer looking over Loch Ryan and thinking, "if God is anywhere, he's there!" But then I'd remember standing on Formby beach staring at the sun sinking on the horizon and turning the sky rose-coloured. Or even—and please don't laugh at me— seeing a vapour trail of an aircraft high up amongst the clouds gives me an indiscernible, ineffable feeling. And I wonder if that's what people mean when they talk of believing in God. Oh! I don't know!

And then there's everything Grandma taught me. However much I railed against her sometimes, I have to acknowledge she gave me a firm grounding in Christian ethics. I have to thank her for that. If I were to become an atheist, it would be a total rejection of everything she tried to din into me. I just have to work out what my true self is and not be swayed by other people. I think that is the most important thing and that I should concentrate on this over the next few weeks. You know me well; what do you think my true self is in all of this?

At your behest, I've been reading Rupert Brooke: "Heaven" and "Failure" for example. Does he believe in religion or not? For all his poetic obfuscation, does he really answer satisfactorily the question he puts: "But is there anything Beyond?" I'm not entirely sure. I'm not certain that you'll agree with me, but my attitude towards reading poetry is this. It's important we know something about the poet—his beliefs and his life. Or we might misunderstand him. But I think that everyone reads a poem differently, and we have to listen to what our inner voice says. You've read so much more than me—both poetry and people's ideas about poetry. So you'll probably think I don't know what I'm talking about. All the same, I think we have to inform ourselves first and foremost, but that we must also let the poetry speak to us as individuals. In fact, come to think of it, isn't poetry one individual trying to speak to another individual—to reveal their true self in the hope that their reader will respond from their true self?

Oh dear! I've rambled on far too long and I can hear Oncle and Tante going to bed now. I must finish this in haste. Please write again soon! I'd love to hear what you think about my struggles with religion and poetry!

Your ever-loving,

June x

[*Postmark Waterloo Liverpool 11.30 A M 13 June 1939*]
Mlle. J. Hepburn
25 Av. D'Ouchy 25
Lausanne
Suisse

8 *Park View*
Waterloo
Tuesday

Dear June,

Thanking you ever so for yours of yesterday and hoping this finds you as it leaves all us at present well. Seriously though, I was glad of that letter and I'll deal with it in a minute, but just let me explain why I am able to write back so soon. As they say in Belfast, I'm on the byru (i.e. not at my fixed employment). This is due to an epidemic of Scarlet Fever which has broken out. I am unscathed, but the Doctor advises me to stay off School and this suits me. I am not in quarantine or anything crude like that so I spend most of my days on the shore. Whenever I see a refuse cart I follow it crying, "Bring out your dead." I read morbid works such as Defoe's "Journal of the Plague" & learn cheerful ditties like Thomas Nashe's "In Time of Pestilence" of which the burden is "I am sick, I must die, Lord have mercy on us." It has also enabled me to get my ideas for this letter clarified. So here goes.

Let us get Lionel out of the way first. In advocating a clean break I was striving for his self-esteem. This is no longer endangered. Half Europe is a clean break enough for practical purposes. The policy was urged for Lionel's good, not yours, and as you admitted yourself his interests wanted watching. However, since Monday I hardly think that you will want to play the musical comedy heroine again.

Secondly, I feel a letter from you would cheer Lionel immensely without rekindling any untoward emotions towards yourself. That boy is no fool. He spotted your preoccupation in the earlier stages of Monday evening. He mistook it for calculated coldness. Why hurt the lad needlessly?

Thirdly, he is going to be immunised from Scarlet Fever. This is a highly dangerous and uncomfortable business in time of epidemics. My doc forbade me to have it & poor old Lionel has been bullied into it by Mr Wright & his people who don't seem to have had the view of any competent doctor on the subject.

Fourthly, a clean break in view of, and caused by, Monday will put me in a bad spot. Surely you see this. I am a pal of Lionel's, but I doubt I'll remain one if I make him lose a friend (or at any rate acquaintance) not for his good, but merely as a result of my somewhat doubtful machinations.

Lastly, he knows nothing and never need know about Monday. What harm can a conventional letter from you do? It will certainly cheer him up and God knows he needs it. I don't propose to say more on the subject. It's up to you. I hope I haven't hurt you in any way or annoyed you by this attempt to dictate to whom you shall write. If I patronise please forgive me. Well that's fixed Lionel.

We'll talk about you for a moment now. Firstly, about your religious beliefs; I fancy I can help there. Personally I'm an atheist. But it makes no difference at all to the main point at issue. I have one or two friends who are _convinced_ Christians and they get just as much if not more out of life as I do. It doesn't matter a damn what you believe, but what matters is the way in which you believe it. You must not waver. If you feel that a God will help you, that there is a God and that you can bring yourself to believe in him—go to it. If you can't fix the doubts you must bring yourself to be an atheist but on no account be an agnostic. Whichever you feel to be best believe in it with all your heart. Examine your doubts and where reason fails you _vanquish_ them by Faith. Conviction is all that matters. I feel that this is the best advice I can give you.

Now about "your True Self." You can't find it because it doesn't exist yet. You are shaping it now I believe. There are still at least 5 Alec Reids and I know of 3 Mike Howsons. I hadn't realised this about you before you went away and that's why you puzzled me. Now if you're about to form your True Self what is it to be? I say "nothing." _Your self_ is _yours_ determined by _your_ mind, _your_ tastes, _your_ people, _your_ education, _your_ prejudices, _your_ ideals—in fact by _You_. You are what you make yourself. I must not, cannot attempt to form you. I am no Pygmalion. Again I'm having ample bother with My Self. The most I can do is to show you possibilities and difficulties. That is all.

I have been working on my self these last six months or so. I had to decide if I believed in a God—I decided that I did not. I had to decide what my aim in life was—I decided Beauty. Then I had to sit down and see what this involved. I had further to decide how far Women were creatures of the Devil, how far they were the be-all and end-all of existence. After this I had to try to analyse my strengths and weaknesses. The result was that I had to get from somewhere a terrific unwavering idea of my own importance and qualities and also an ability to convince myself of almost anything. The result is that I am something of a mental thug—tough, almost slave-driving.

I convinced myself I am self-sufficient unto myself—I convinced myself as to where I am going. I believe that I can do anything if I want to. I also brought myself to be a cynic because it helped me to be more self-sufficient. I am an incorrigible Romantic at heart, but it is a weak thing to be. I have convinced myself too that I am a coward mentally and then reassured myself. These convictions however are to meet my own needs. I have to be tough because owing to my eyesight I shall have to fight like Hell all along the line. I have had to like my own company because when I was younger I was a confirmed invalid. Your needs are different; you must work it out for yourself.

What do you want? Do you want a God, do you want a steady mental life, or one of violent joltings? Do you want Mike's policy of Drift or mine of intensive analysis, do you want a small life like Lionel's? You must decide for yourself. Remember that once you decide you must stick to it. I couldn't go on without my power of convincing myself. I had to acquire it. It's your problem however and you must decide. I know three Junes, you probably know a few more. You must decide which you want to be and you must go for it.

Remember that an idealist is not an ideal. I, though a high idealist, am an out and out swine. You once felt that you wanted to batter my head in with a tennis-racket. The instinct was probably a sound one. I am a hypocrite (self-conviction makes me that). I am a coward (self-assumed cynicism and my intensive analytical habits). I am an utter twerp (think of what I said about you & what I said to you). I have a strong streak of cruelty (I love playing cat & mouse with Lionel). Again I'm just as petty as the rest of them—jealous, sneering, selfish, ambitious, factious. An idealist is just as clay-footed as anyone else. So for Goodness sake don't start idealising me. Frankly I don't like being one of the two most important people in your life. You see it tempts me. Again it means that you know very few people worth knowing. Besides you are more important to yourself than any one else is. Write to me, talk to me, think of me but for God's sake remember that I am a twerp. Distance lends enchantment and if you lived in the same house as I do for a month I think you would see me in a truer light. By idealising anyone you necessarily sacrifice your self, which is the most important thing in your life. When you die existence dies with you. I can't make a world for you—no one can. So always exalt yourself above all others, No idealisation of people at any cost. We are all muddy-metalled rascals.

Let's get down almost to Earth again. I'm all in favour of analysing poetry for myself. Anything that can stand thought is the better for it. Do you remember Mike said that Music conveys a Mental Impression? So does Brooke's "Failure"—exactly that conveyed by Keats "La Grande Dame Sans Merci"—it does to me anyway. The Modern Poets like W. H. Auden and T. S. Eliot have the same theory of poetry that it should describe impression rather than object. Auden would describe this letter as a jungle because that is the effect it produces on him. Can you follow this?

Your theory of poetry's appeal to the individual has its points. I'm far from convinced, but I'll give you another point. Auden says that Poetry is "memorable speech," that its value lies in its applicability i.e. how often you want to quote it.

Let me quote for you from W B. Yeats.

When you are old and grey and full of sleep
And nodding by the fire take down this book
And slowly read and dream of the soft look
Your eyes had once and of their shadows deep;

...

And bending down beside the glowing bars
Murmur a little sadly how Love fled
And paced upon the mountains overhead
And hid his face amid a crowd of stars.

I know why I love this so much. What do you think? If you apologise to me again, I'll scream. You are probably quite right in associating poet & poem. Whether you are or not you have no right to beg tolerance. Are you being ironical?

I shall never find Beauty & keep it. You see Time snatches it away. I have a memory & a future. Beauty is not like a pound of butter. It is unlimited; there is always some to be sought. You see I believe I'll find the Real Thing, but I won't keep it because I can't. I shall always have a quest. Do you see this? I can never write this letter again. There can never be another Monday. You may find that happiness again, but it cannot be the same because Time has been moving. Monday cannot have been Beauty, but only an expression of it. Don't idealise it too much, it can't happen again. Distance lends enchantment... Well that's all. God knows when I'll write again. I'd like you to write Lionel.

Don't forget my opinion of myself and don't idealise me.

I remain

As big a twerp as ever
Alec

M. H. Michael K. Howson,
22, College Road North.
Blundellsands.
Liverpool. 23.

Monday 12th June, 1939

Dear Michael,

Forgive me for writing to you yet again, but I have a big favour to ask of you. I hope you won't mind.

Mummy rang me last night. As usual, it was just as we were all sitting down to eat. It's difficult for me to remember whom I've told what to—obviously I don't keep copies of the letters I send to everyone, so I may be wrong, but I think I've already told you that she's not been very well, since I've been away. Each time I hear her voice at the end of the phone I feel anxious about her. She's been sounding dull and blue for a few weeks now. Up until now, she's not actually admitted that she's ill, but last night was different. She said she was feeling "worse than ever."

I think she's really ill and has been all summer, but didn't want to worry me about it. It's no good my asking Debbie to tell me the truth; he'll just tell me what he wants me to know, however much I plead with him.

Do you think you could go round to see her—preferably during the day, when Debbie's likely to be out. I don't want to bother you, but it would set my mind at rest to know for certain how she is.

I'm going to seal this now and get it off in the post straight away. I'll write properly very soon.

I hope you're all ready for your exams—I'm sure you'll be brilliant—I've got to prepare for one that's held at the start of August. & I look forward to seeing you in two months' time once they're all over with.

All my love,

June x

[Postmark Blundellsands Liverpool 9.30 A M 20 June 39]
Miss. V. J. Hepburn,
25, av d'Ouchy, 25,
Lausanne,
Switzerland.

22, COLLEGE ROAD NORTH.
BLUNDELLSANDS.
LIVERPOOL. 23.
17th June, 1939

Dear June,

I am sorry to hear your mother has been ill. I hope she will soon regain her health. I passed your stepfather just now as I was returning from the tennis club. He appeared to be about to add himself to the multitude, which throngs the shore and the Serpentine, waiting to see the new "Mauretania" set out on her maiden voyage. So, I nipped into "Alderley" to say hello to your mother. I'm not quite sure what I can tell you. She seemed genuinely pleased to see me, and if she was feeling blue, she didn't let on. But, her face seemed much puffier than I remembered it—and a bit red as if it were inflamed somehow. She was wearing a short-sleeved dress, and her arms looked quite red and irritated as well. She said she'd caught the sun while she was gardening. I didn't know whether to believe her, or if she was just pretending she was Okay. I'm sorry I can't tell you anything more definite than that.

I don't suppose it is a new thought which has not occupied you, but would it not be possible for you to come home for the holidays and return to Lausanne in time for the examination you mention? I should not let pleasure prevent progress. But here is yet another example of a doctor who will not take his own medicine. I am letting pleasure prevent progress. For I speak knowing full well that the Higher Certificate Examination begins in a week's time, and that I have neither done any work worthy of the name yet, nor feel any eagerness whatever to do any in the immediate future.

I sit here amid a wilderness of maps, hand-books, guide-books, itineraries and pamphlets sent by the French Railways, which are eager to serve us, though we propose to travel by bicycle. I am considering the respective virtues of various routes. We expect to pass through Lausanne on the 24th or 25th August; we shall probably cross the lake from Ouchy to Evian, where we hope to spend a day or two. But to say nothing of the chances of the way, the dictators may well seriously interfere with our plans. For they have not stolen anything for almost two months, and there is still no-one who is likely to prevent their indulging in further robbery if they so desire. The Nazis will certainly seize Slovakia—it is already theirs for practical purposes—and moves against Poland, especially in Danzig, may be expected. But we shall see.

The weather broke just over a week ago, and until yesterday evening we did not see the sun. We have been rained on by every variety of rain. But after more than three weeks of sun, drought and dirt, no-one can rightly grumble. I am sorry only that the rain has made the grass, scorched into yellow submission, start to grow again.

Last Monday morning was delightful. I went to Formby to swim. We had bathed often during the hot weather, but this morning a cool, wet wind was blowing. I had my first bathe in the rain as I cycled out. Julian Vaillant met me on the shore, which was quite deserted. Fortunately the rain stopped just before we arrived—our attempts to dress in pouring rain as well as wind would have been most diverting (for onlookers). Big waves were rolling up the shore, and a strong west wind was blowing the foam across the sand; the sky was a symphony in grey save where the end of the rainbow stood on the horizon. We could not swim very much, but it is always great fun to dash about in the surf. Upon us thus engaged, a beam of sunlight suddenly shone out of a rent in the clouds and brightened the foam into a dazzling whiteness. I can well understand why to the Greeks Venus was Aphrodite, "born of sea foam." It was wild and beautiful beyond words.

At the moment, as you may well perceive, I am in a lotus-eating mood.

> We only toil, who are the first of things,
> Nor harken what the inner spirit sings,

For a time I harken, but I must be doing something, though rarely what I am supposed to be doing. I shall harken on Saturday next, for it is Midsummer; I shall go and sit in a field and read Shakespeare. The fields are very pleasant now. It is the time of haymaking, but the rain hinders it; and so the grass still stands, full of poppies, and campion, and blue rocket and lots of other flowers. But now I must stop.

18th June

This morning I went swimming again, and after lunch I listened, as is my wont, to Orchestral Hour; and now I return to finish this letter. But I fear I shall have to interrupt the good (?) work again very soon in order to listen to Sibelius' Second Symphony. I have been hearing a great deal of music during the last fortnight, hugely to my delight, for it is a talisman that can turn even my leaden moments to gold. I have heard three of my favourite symphonies at the house of my friend Chadwick, who is to be my companion in France. (The fourth member of the party, by the way, is Arnold Tulloch.) Chadwick has complete recordings of nearly all the great symphonies. I have heard the last act of "Il Travatore" and the second of "Siegfried" and several of my favourite pieces, including Debussy's "L'Après-midi d'une Faune," Delius' "On hearing the first Cuckoo in Spring," the Prize Song from "Die Meistersinger," and Saint-Saens' "Le Rouet d'Omphale," with whom, as Alec thinks, you have qualities in common, and twice I have heard the music to my favourite ballet "Sylvia." If I have a daughter, I shall call her, among other things, Sylvia.

Last Sunday I heard an excellent rendering of Anton Chekhov's "The Seagull." It is a remarkably moving play, a sympathetic study of the emotions of various characters. It is the best play I have heard or seen since "Hassan." I am sure you would appreciate and enjoy it, though it is really a tragedy.

I am at present reading a book of essays and sketches by Axel Munthe, who, as you probably know, wrote "The Story of San Michele." He tells of Paris, and Mont Blanc and Capri. All these and the maps before me, and the postcard from my parents at San Remo, make me look forward more and more to my holiday in France.

As you say, the world is surely big enough to hold us all. But the world is in a state of economic chaos, which is the product of short-sighted individualism running riot, of what is euphemistically called "the liberty of the subject," which is really the liberty of a few unscrupulous individuals to exploit the rest of the world, whereby they hope, I suppose, to win power and wealth whence shall come happiness for themselves. I do not say that the rich are always unhappy. That is the "sour grapes" of the not-so-rich. But a man who is hungry or tired or workless or ill or oppressed cannot be happy. All morality has gone from the world. It lies on the edge of Catastrophe.

But to hell with economics. I must not preach; but let me just mention one other thing. You say that perfection is not your mark. I do not quarrel with this statement in its immediate context. I would not suggest that you should write all your numerous letters in rough and correct them with blue pencil before sending off a fair copy. My own letters would have to be almost completely ~~obliterated~~ (sic). I intend letters, but they often turn out more like essays. I forget the receiver, and delight in setting down thoughts and scenes and events. But to resume, one should surely always strive after perfection, remembering the while that that which is unnatural and laboured can never be perfect. Life is an everlasting search for something— if it were not so it would be unbearable.

And now I must close and dart off to the C. S. to hear about Spiritualism. I cannot prevent myself from thinking of you, though I do not look upon your face,

Michael

<table>
<tr><td>

Mlle. J. Hepburn
25 Av. D'Ouchy 25
Lausanne
La Suisse

</td><td>

Stranraer, Monday June 26ᵗʰ

My dear June,

I'm so sorry I can't come to stay. I've tried over & over to persuade Daddy it would be Okay, but he's adamant. He says it's far too dangerous for me to travel across Europe on my own, given the current political climate.

I'll write a proper letter and bring you up to date on all the news—Margaret says her big brother John's been poorly. They suspect the T.B. I'll try to find out more before I write.

Your best friend,
Betty xxx

</td></tr>
</table>

Miss Betty Gibson
Encliffe
Encliffe Lane,
Stranraer.

25, av. d'Ouchy 25
Lausanne
Monday July 3rd

My Dear Betty,

I got your card. I have to admit it knocked me back a bit. Especially since Oncle Jean says that Switzerland is the safest place in the whole of Europe in times of political conflict. Everyone respects its neutrality. But I'm sure we'll meet again soon, even if we don't yet know how or when.

To cheer myself up, let me tell you what my friends Michael and Alec have been up to. They've been listening to lots of modern music since I left in the spring, including Saint-Saens' "Le Rouet d'Omphale." (I don't know if that's a gramophone record that your father owns?) Anyway, Michael told me about it and said that Alec thinks I'm like Omphale. You remember her story from the twelve labours of Hercules, don't you? I can still hear Mamie Niven's voice telling it to us on a Friday afternoon.

I have to admit, I didn't make the connection to begin with, so I asked Tante Léonie. She jumped up from the piano stool, briskly crossed the room, took a 78 from her shelves and placed it lovingly on the gramophone. "Écoutez!" was all she said. I closed my eyes and listened. Pictures crowded my mind: beautifully dressed men and women at a ball. The women moved daintily; the men were jaunty. Weaving in and out, they danced an intricate dance; there was frenetic energy that made me want to nod my head and tap my feet, yet all felt measured and polite. Suddenly the mood changed. The ballroom disappeared. I thought of the sea; of my friends Michael and Julian battling with the waves when they went swimming during a storm at Formby—they really did, I'm not making that bit up. Now, in my mind's eye, the waves were huge, surging towards the shore, never quite breaking onto the sand, constantly held in check till it became unbearable. Somehow the music conveyed powerful Hercules held under the sway of the sorceress, Omphale.

And then, we were returned to the jaunty politesse of the ballroom. Yet those dark energies had seeped into the dance; the strings plucked raw passion, while men barely sustained the social niceties. Oh Betty! Do you understand what I'm getting at? Jove might chase Europa, but Omphale can subdue a passionate hero—that's what the music was telling me. And I am Omphale! You are Omphale! We are Omphale!

When it ended, Tante Léonie looked at me strangely. She didn't say anything, but I think she knew what I was thinking. I said, "C'est magnifique," and she smiled and nodded. She's quite special; we have an understanding even though we don't say much to each other. We just communicate through the music.

Changing the subject completely, I think Mummy's not well. She won't say straight out; just drops lots of aggravating hints. I should feel sympathy for her, but the effect is that I start to lose patience instead.

I told you we usually go walking up in the mountains at the weekends, didn't I? Well, last Saturday was our most adventurous walk yet. It was nothing like our strolls around the Loch at Stranraer. We walked so high that we were far above the snow-line, yet it was sweltering. We followed quite narrow paths—you have to be careful not to wander off them, it can be very dangerous. The scariest of all was on our way back. It was the middle of the afternoon, I was exhilarated but exhausted. You remember how breathless I used to get? Well, if that happens up in the Alps, Oncle Jean just gives me the bottle of red wine and tells me to take a gulp. And it works! He'd already done this a couple of times when the path gave out; there was nothing but loose scree and a huge drop beneath us. Oncle Jean didn't seem at all fazed, he just marched onto it and Mai Mai skipped along behind him. I lost my breath. I think I must have turned white as a sheet—or the snow at my feet! Oncle Jean turned back, handed me the bottle and insisted I drink. I was already thirsty and I glugged it down! Don't ask how I got across! It was like being in a waking dream, slithering and sliding to the other side, where the footpath picked up again. Anyway, I survived.

Afterwards, it made me think. My whole life these past few months has been like crossing that scree: past the point of no return, avoiding looking into the abyss, just getting through it in the hope that eventually I'll be back on firm ground. But will my life ever be the same? Will I ever be the same again? When I finally come back to Britain in two years' time, you'll have to be the judge of that.

But rest assured, one thing never changes; I'll always be your own best friend,

June xxx

M. H. M. K. Howson
22, College Road North.
Blundellsands.
Liverpool. 23.

Monday, 19th June

Dear Michael,

It's Monday afternoon. School finished at midday as usual. We've eaten "le déjeuner," and I've had my piano lesson with Tante Léonie. I can't go for my usual long walk by the lake because it's raining hard outside. I've already got drenched twice today, once on the way to school and once returning. If you'd seen me arriving back at the flat, you'd have mistaken me for a drowned rat!

So, I thought I'd sit down and have an afternoon catching up on letter writing. I wanted to tell you about our weekend. It was quite dramatic. And exciting. Especially for someone like me. Remember I told you how much I used to enjoy taking part in our operatic performances at the Stranraer Academy? But I'm running ahead of myself. First things first.

I'm sorry to hear about your friend John McCulloch. I remember him well. I couldn't quite understand why he joined the Volunteer Navy. When he came to the Curious Society that one time, I liked his manner. He would pause to reflect on what we were all saying before he said anything himself. I remember I said something rash about Rupert Brooke's "The Life Beyond." He considered it carefully and then said, "Surely you're too young to have suffered so much pain?" That made me stop and think. And now he's dead.

Anyway, the weekend's adventure. Instead of taking the "funiculaire" for our usual Alpine walk, Oncle Jean took us on the train all the way up to a small town on the edge of Lake Neuchâtel. And instead of the usual baguette and cheese, we went to a restaurant and ate fondue. It was delicious; lots of melted cheese in a big pan. We all had loads of bread cut into squares, which we stuck on the ends of long forks then dipped in the fondue and mopped up as much of the cheese as we could. Pure heaven!

Then we went to see a performance of "Les Contes d'Hoffmann." It took place in a castle. Apparently, it belongs to a famous fashion designer from Paris. It was all very chic and sophisticated. Oncle said it was a special treat for all his girls! I'm not sure if you know the plot; it's all a bit far-fetched. It's based on three stories by the writer, Hoffmann. Anyway, it's in three acts. At some point during the second act, it started to rain outside. And when I say rain: not like the kind of rain you get in Crosby, drifting in off the sea. In the mountains, when it rains it pours! I was hoping it would stop before we had to walk back to the station. But by the third act, it was tipping down louder than ever.

The opera is about a poet who's unlucky in love, because of an evil character. He has a different name in each act, but it's always the same singer who plays him. In the final story, it gets very complicated. The poet falls in love with a Venetian courtesan; then he fights a duel with another of her lovers—I'm not entirely sure why. He kills his adversary and his friend goes off stage—I think to fetch the horses, to aid their escape. So, the evil sorcerer decides to poison the poet. He puts a fatal concoction in his wine. Then somehow the courtesan drinks it instead. Just as she was putting the goblet to her lips, there was an almighty crack of thunder, and all the lights went out. I was quite terrified!

I've just reread what I've written so far. I wish I could write as vividly as you do. I don't feel as if I've managed to convey the excitement and terror of that evening. Living in Lausanne, getting up to go the French school ridiculously early every day, spending loads of time by myself—all this has started to seem "normal," but somehow, that clap of thunder, just as the beautiful soprano was about to die, made me feel—all over again—what a strange turn my life has taken.

I wish I could be back in Crosby and offering to lead a C. S. discussion on "The Tales of Hoffmann." I don't think I shall really understand why the opera and the thunder were so disquieting, until I'm back in our room above Frank's Café, debating its meaning with all you brainboxes!

That's enough for now. I shall get maudlin and weep buckets in competition with the rain if I carry on writing. Suffice it to say, I don't think I would ever tire of your company, if I were lucky enough to be back home in Crosby; but there's not much chance of that happening for at least another twelve months.

"Alone, most strangely, I live on."
Your affectionate,
June x

P.S. I nearly forgot:—thanks for going to see Mummy. From what you say she can't be that poorly after all. That's reassuring. All the same, she's so exasperating!

25, Av. d'Ouchy 25
Lausanne
Switzerland

Thursday 6ᵗʰ July

Dear Lionel:

Thank you for your letter and all the interesting gossip. I knew I could rely on you to bring me up to date. I hope this wasn't too big a distraction from your exam preparation! Although, the way things are developing in Europe, I worry there might be much bigger distractions and disruptions to come. It's so difficult to get any reliable assessment of how serious it all is and of what's likely to happen next.

Last weekend, Oncle Jean took Mai Mai and me on a longer excursion than usual. We caught the train and then a bus to Evolène. (I don't know if you can find this on the Atlas—it's just a small Alpine village.) The walking was harder than any we've done before, at times thrilling, at times terrifying. We've already past the longest day, yet we walked through crisp snow that dazzled my eyes and magnified the sun's rays on my legs and ankles. At one stage we slithered across scree. It's difficult to describe, but I felt exhilarated—and at the same time afraid.

Have you ever experienced "déjà-vu?" Well I did that day. And I still don't know what that precarious walk across scree was a repeat of, but I was sure I'd been there and walked across the selfsame scree before, when I couldn't possibly have done. Perhaps this was what prompted me to ask Oncle Jean about the rumours of conflict and war.

So yes, I said it out loud. I pronounced the unspeakable word, "la guerre."

Oncle Jean's brow furrowed and he glanced at Mai Mai, but his stride never faltered. "Il n'y aurait pas de guerre. Tu verras. Mais, même s'il y en aurait, tu serais protégée en Suisse. La Suisse est un pays neutre. Elle serait le meilleur endroit d'être pendant une guerre. Tu seras en lieu sûr ici."

I translate that as: "Switzerland shall be my safe haven." But I hardly needed my recent intensive French lessons to notice his deft switch from the conditional to the future tense. Mai Mai skipped on regardless.

Oh! Lionel! At times I'm really afraid for the future. And now you say that Mummy's looking quite puffy and ill. And that she didn't deny it when you spoke to her about it. She managed to pull the wool over Michael's eyes when he went to see her, but I knew you'd wheedle the truth out of her—you've got a conversational knack somehow. Even though it's not what I wanted to hear, I won't blame the messenger! I'm so grateful to you for finding out and telling me the truth. But now that I know, there's still nothing I can do about it.

Some days it feels so frustrating to be stuck here. And other days it feels like the greatest adventure a girl my age could possibly have. I'm sorry I wrote you on one of the former. Next time I'll write on one of the latter. But in any case, I remain,

Yours gratefully,
June x

Mr Alec Reid,
8 Park View,
Waterloo,
Liverpool 22,
L'Angleterre

Monday 10th July
Dear Alec,

I write in haste. I've received a telephone call from Mummy and I'm coming home right away.

I should be back a week today. I'll ring and explain all then.

Your ever-loving,
June x

M. H. M. K. Howson,
22, College Road North.
Blundellsands.
Liverpool. 23.

Monday 10th July

Dear Michael,

Mummy rang yesterday. She says I'm to come home immediately. For the first time, she's admitted she's ill and needs me back in Crosby. She can't stand to worry about me any longer. Debbie's agreed—or capitulated. I spoke to him briefly before I passed the receiver to Oncle Jean for them to make the arrangements.

It's all happening in such a rush. Everything's changed overnight—my sense of my future. Everything. I'm spending this week saying my goodbyes to everyone. And of course there's all the official stuff to do about getting the right travel documents. Oncle will help me with that.

But I'm coming home. I'm really coming home! Please can you tell all the others. I haven't got time to write to them all. I'm sending Alec a postcard and that's it. I need the time to get some sort of certificate or report out of the school here. And there's all the packing to do; I really didn't expect to come home for a couple of years—maybe more—and now I've got to bundle my life back into a suitcase that I can carry all by myself. I'll keep your letters, of course—but I can't keep all the correspondence I've received in the last few months. It would weigh a ton! So feel suitably honoured it's yours that I choose to keep!

In haste—I'll put a girdle round the earth and see you very soon. Then we'll have all summer to catch up with one another.

All my love,
June x

I remember scuttling across Paris, changing stations. A business acquaintance of Debby's met me at the station in London and put me up overnight.

These were times she didn't care to remember. She was used to seeing Debby's passport left on the table, because he had to report regularly to the local police station in Crosby. Now it was her turn. On 19th May, she'd had two Ville de Lausanne stamps placed in her passport and permission from the Polices des Etrangers to stay as a foreigner until 3rd August, 1940. Sixteen months of her life away from home.

Then on Saturday 15th July, 1939, June entered France at Vallorbe-Fraisnes (Doubs) and had her passport stamped by the Commissariat Spéciale d'Entrée. If she had caught the Direct-Orient Express from Lausanne at 22.57, she would have arrived in Paris, Gare du Lyon at 6.29, and been shunted around the banlieues for an hour before arriving at Paris, Gard du Nord at 7.25, with just time to hop off and buy fresh croissants from the platform vendor before departing at 8.10. She would have stayed on all the way from Lausanne to Calais, alighting to walk onto the ferry, boarding a train at the port of Dover and arriving in London Victoria at 14.50. Alternatively, if she had caught the Simplon-Orient Express, she would have left Lausanne at 0.58, arrived at Paris (Lyons) at 8.40, departed Paris (Lyons) at 9.46 (even more time for station platform café et croissants) arrived at Boulogne at 13.05 and London at 17.30. Or she could have caught the Night Ferry from Paris and stayed safely in her sleeping car all the way to Dover.

What went wrong?

July 14th, Bastille Day. The French commemorated the one hundred and fiftieth anniversary of the storming of the Bastille with a huge military parade. It was a deliberate show of force. A contingent of Scots Guards took part in the march past and RAF Wellington bombers flew over Paris. British war minister Leslie Hore-Belisha was a guest of honour, seated next to Premier Daladier. The Entente Cordiale was stronger than ever. The message was clear to the French people: and to Herr Hitler.

It was past midnight. A tearful goodbye on Lausanne station's platform number one. She was leaving. She felt sad. She would miss Lausanne. She promised she would return as soon as she could to visit them all. She meant it. She got into her compartment, politely greeted her travelling companion who requested that she take the top bunk, since she was so much younger.

'*Je n'ai plus vingt-et-un ans, moi.*'

June agreed. She was relieved to be travelling with a respectable middle-aged French woman. She flopped onto her bunk and fell into uneasy sleep. The events of the past week played over and over in her mind. The hurried travel arrangements. The packing. The goodbyes. The promises to stay in touch. She cried quietly into her pillow.

Just after 1.30, she was woken up. They had reached the border and had to go through passport control. Her travelling companion assisted her. When they returned to the compartment, June slept *comme une souche*.

Around eight, she was woken by her companion bustling around the compartment, smoothing her clothes, washing her face, applying rouge, and lipstick and fixing her hair.

'*Bonjour, Mademoiselle. Tu vais à Londres?*'

'*Bonjour, madame. Oui.*'

'*Tu sais le date aujourd'hui?*'

'*le quinze.*'

'*Eh bien?*'

June looked confused; she was still half asleep.

Yesterday was *Bastille Day*. There had been a huge parade. Paris was in defiant mood. Friday the fourteenth of July had spilled into Saturday the fifteenth. She should be prepared for some disruption.

'*Même à mon train?*'

'*Oui, même à l'Express d'Orient.*'

She was fully awake now. She jumped down and hurriedly got dressed, splashed some water on her face and ran a comb through her hair. Then she went in search of a guard.

Yes, she would have to walk across Paris *au Gard du Nord*, if she wanted to be sure to catch the connection. The carriages wouldn't be shunted up there today. The driver was going to celebrate Bastille Day. And so was *he.* They had missed the grand parade, but the revels would continue through the weekend. He wasn't certain whether the usual timetables would be adhered to on the Metro and the trams. It was unlikely; between Bastille Day and Sunday, *les cheminots* had declared an unofficial holiday. *Néanmoins*, she had a good hour to get between stations. *Pas de soucis!*

June knew Paris better than she knew London. She had been there on school trips. Once in 1937, when they'd stayed at *Hôtel St. Jacques* and again—only last year—when they'd travelled through Paris to the *Chateaux du Loire*. She remembered those trips. How carefree they seemed to her now. They had helped her to make friends: Audrey Sharples, Micky Minshull, Esme Peet, Renee Sythes and Joan Mason.

And Georges Lubrino. If only he should happen to be wandering around le Cours in front of the station, he could escort her all the way.

This was no time to fantasise. She recalled the quickest route was by *Place de la Bastille*. From what the guard had told her that might still be peopled by carousers from the night before. She tried to remember the route they'd taken when they'd crossed the Seine from *Hôtel St. Jacques* and walked north up to *le Musée d'Arts et Métiers*. She would find *le Rue de Rivoli*, follow it and then turn onto *le Boulevard de Strasbourg*. Then it would be straightforward. There was no time for breakfast in the sumptuous surroundings *du Buffet de la Gare de Lyon*. She promised herself that one day she would return and eat there, with time to sit beneath the chandeliers and stare at the Belle Époque décor. For now she must hurry.

But look calm. She was seventeen. She must pass for older and avoid attracting attention. Despite lugging her heavy suitcase—she hadn't expected to have to carry it any distance by herself—she must hold herself erect. She straightened her spine, pushed her shoulders back, balanced an imaginary book on her head and assumed her most nonchalant, disdainful look. She must look confident—*bien sûr*, she knew where she was heading. No eye contact. No smiling. She must pass for a *Parisienne*. Not a frightened British traveller, retreating from mainland Europe, not trusting *la Ligne Maginot*. She silently rehearsed phrases of street slang she hadn't known she knew. If any early morning *flâneur* accosted her, she would be ready for him.

At Boulogne, they must alight and pass through border checks. By now she was famished. She'd had nothing since *Tante Clara's* soup the previous evening. She was light-headed. The sea looked relatively calm beyond the harbour; she could risk having a bite to eat. There was a small bar at the port. She entered it. *She would ask for a coffee and a croissant.*

'*Deux œufs durs et un vin rouge, s'il te plaît!*'

Le patron didn't question her age. She passed for an adult.

Despite everything, the train arrived on time at London. At precisely half past five, June stepped onto the platform at Victoria Station. Charlotte was waiting for her just beyond the ticket barrier. June fell into her arms and the two women kissed—*bise, bise, bise*—first the right cheek then the left cheek and then the right again. June's eyes watered, but she kept on balancing that imaginary book and kept her chin up high.